VEILED DESIRE

"Cursed veil," he muttered. "How can a man kiss you when you are covered like that?"

"Kisses are precisely what veils are meant to prevent," she said. "How can you want to kiss me, Warrick? You don't like me."

"I never said so."

They stood wrapped in each other's arms, cheek to cheek with only the sheer purple veil between their faces, and Sophia feared she would die if Warrick did not snatch the veil away and kiss her. He pressed his mouth to her ear and she felt his warm breath through the veil. There was something incredibly alluring about that fragile obstacle to what she desired. Warrick's moist lips touched her chin, and Sophia knew that next he was going to kiss her mouth, kiss her through the veil....

The Magician's Lover

Flora Speer

LOVE SPELL BOOKS NEW YORK CITY

LOVE SPELL®

June 1998

Published by

Dorchester Publishing Co., Inc.
276 Fifth Avenue
New York, NY 10001

Cover Art by John Ennis

ISBN 0-505-52263-2

Printed in the United States of America.

Chapter One

Baghdad, A.D. 1138

"Remember everything that I have taught you about magic," Hua Te cautioned.

He was a man of slender build and quiet movement, whose features showed the unmistakable characteristics of his native Cathay. Never in all of Warrick's experience of him had Hua Te raised his voice, and he did not do so now. He spoke as if he wanted only to encourage the younger man. Still, Warrick was aware of the firm resolve that lay beneath his teacher's words.

"Now, Warrick, gather all of your strength and concentrate it," Hua Te instructed. "Focus your mind on the task. Do not allow your thoughts to wander. The spell requires your complete concentration, and your wholehearted belief that you will succeed. Never forget that it is belief that makes magic work."

"I understand," Warrick said on a sigh. Seldom had Hua Te been so insistent, and his intensity was beginning to irritate Warrick. The irritation created a pang of guilt. At once Warrick quashed the unpleasant emotion, sending it to oblivion as he had learned to do with most feelings that disturbed him. Serenity of the practitioner's mind and complete belief in what he was doing were vital ingredients in the success of a magical spell. "You have taught me well," he said, to ease any concern that Hua Te might secretly harbor about his abilities.

Warrick was twenty-nine years old and had been Hua Te's student since he was thirteen. He had grown into a tall man, with dark brown hair and eyes like smoky topaz that gazed out at the world with wary, guarded intelligence. He was firmly muscled, though not in the heavy, bulky way of men who practiced every day with sword and lance. Rather, Warrick moved with the steely, carefully controlled strength of a man who knew how to fight to win—to the death, if need be—yet who would avoid fighting until there was nothing else left to do. Hua Te had shown him effective methods of fighting that did not require chainmail armor or heavy weapons, though Warrick was well trained in the use of those, too.

Long ago, before they had left his boyhood home, Wroxley Castle in England, Warrick had sworn to Hua Te and to himself that he would learn to control the inborn magical powers that had tormented him throughout his youth, and that he would also control his guilt and anger at possessing those same powers. At his beloved teacher's urging he set aside his dislike of knightly weapons and began to train with them until he was as expert as any man in Christendom, or any man in the Islamic lands where he had lived for more than a decade.

He had learned much from Hua Te during their years together, and at every step along the path to knowledge it had become clearer and clearer to Warrick that his learning would never cease. He would continue to be a student and, very likely, a wanderer, for the rest of his life. He would never enjoy the pleasures of a settled home, a wife, or children. Warrick accepted that fact and did not allow himself to dwell overmuch upon the losses involved in the way of life he had chosen. For every loss there were compensations, among them Hua Te's friendship and the opportunity to see more of the world than most men ever did.

A cry from the street below disturbed his attempt at total concentration. Even at the third level of the house, and even so late at night, the sounds of the city intruded. Baghdad was never silent. Telling himself to ignore all distractions, to do as he was bidden, and, above all, to *believe*, Warrick began to work the magical spell.

He concentrated so hard that his head started to ache. He was used to the discomfort; he expected it. The conjuring art took a toll upon its practitioners. Warrick was willing to pay the price, but the pain that beset him on this night was well-nigh intolerable. He found it increasingly difficult to block out the headache while still concentrating on the spell. Nor could he shut out awareness of his surroundings.

He and Hua Te were in the dimly lit upper room of a three-story house that Hua Te rented from an astronomer friend. There were several unglassed windows set into the thick walls. Each window was covered with an intricately carved wooden lattice that did nothing to obstruct the street noises or the pleasant rustling of the fronds of a date palm that grew in the garden.

An open door beckoned occupants of the room to step outside onto the flat roof of the building. The roof was furnished in a manner similar to the room, with richly patterned carpets, divans covered with pillows, and several delicately carved and inlaid tables. It was the custom of the inhabitants of Baghdad to take to the rooftops after sunset, there to find relief from the summer heat that became oppressive at street level and that tended to seep through the walls and into the rooms on lower floors, making them uncomfortable.

A few streets away from the house the Tigris River glinted in the light of the setting half moon, and if one were to lean over the whitewashed parapet and try very hard to see through the darkness, it was possible to catch a glimpse of the smaller Diyala River just before it reached the point where it poured its waters into the Tigris. Hua Te's house was located in a prosperous section of the city, between the Tigris and its tributary.

The blue-black sky arched overhead, its cloudless depths studded with thousands of stars. The clarity of the heavens was a great blessing to the astronomers who spent their nights studying the movements of the planets and the positions of the constellations.

A faint breeze stirred, wafting through the open latticework at the window and touching Warrick's cheek in a gentle caress. It was a night made for lovers.

For Warrick, however, it was a night devoted to magic, to the performance of the latest test in the long series of tasks that Hua Te had set for him during their years of traveling and studying together.

Hua Te was watching him closely. He always did when Warrick was working a spell. Not wanting to disappoint his friend and teacher, Warrick forced himself to concentrate harder. Certain at last that he had properly focused all of his attention, he began to speak the words of the conjuration.

There was a low table sitting before one of the divans. The surface of the table was cluttered with books and scrolls, the untidy piles topped with a remarkable chart depicting the heavens as seen from Cairo. Hua Te had purchased the chart only the day before, intending it as a gift for his friend and landlord, John of Cornwall, who lived a short distance away. Suddenly the air above the table began to shimmer, as if tiny particles of gold were caught in a miniature whirlwind.

Warrick saw the movement out of the corner of his eye. Not willing to be distracted, he redoubled his efforts to keep his thoughts focused, to think of nothing but the magic he was working.

The golden particles settled onto the only bare spot on the tabletop, where they slowly ceased to rotate and began instead to coalesce into an egg shape. The brass oil lamp that hung from the ceiling illuminated a clear, aquamarine-colored egg, with the bits of gold suspended within it.

Hua Te had also noticed the strange apparition. Uttering a soft exclamation of surprise, he reached toward the egg. He plucked it from the table and then, holding it between his thumb and forefinger, he lifted it toward the lamp, as if he was trying to see the golden flecks inside the object more clearly.

A beam of moonlight that shone through the open door touched the largest of the golden particles within the egg. There was a soft clicking sound and the egg began to glow. Hua Te did not move, nor did he speak. He stood as if paralyzed, staring at the object he held, while the mysterious egg glowed ever brighter.

Warrick's concentration was lost. As intrigued by the shining egg as Hua Te appeared to be, he tried to move closer, to discover exactly what the thing was and what kind of mechanism was causing it to glow. He found that he could not move. Nor could he speak, though he made a valiant attempt.

Hua Te vanished. So did the egg and the light it produced.

An instant later, Warrick found that he was able to move and speak again. His head was throbbing with the painful aftermath of working a spell, even though he had not completed the conjuration.

"Hua Te, where are you?" he called. "Can you hear me? Is this a game intended to teach me some new lesson? Hua Te!"

There was no answer. The room was silent and no one was in it except for Warrick.

"Hua Te? This isn't amusing." Quickly Warrick went to the door and then onto the roof. Hua Te wasn't there either. The diamond-studded vault of the heavens rose above the city, the palm tree in the garden swayed in the breeze, the sounds and smells of the street in front of the house rose to touch Warrick's senses.

Astonishment began to give way to alarm. He was alone. Warrick knew it with absolute certainty. And he thought he knew why. It was his doing, all his fault.

Hua Te would never play a cruel trick on him, never pretend to disappear, unless he planned to return within a moment or two. That he had not reappeared was proof his absence was not voluntary. Hua Te had vanished because Warrick had done something wrong while attempting to work the new spell. He had not studied thoroughly enough the readings that Hua Te had assigned to him. He had not concentrated as he should have done. As a result of his laxity and error, Hua Te was gone, reduced to invisibility.

"There must be a way to bring him back," Warrick muttered. "Every spell has its antispell. Magic worked can be unworked. Inattentive fool that I am, I do know that much."

He hurried back into the room. Pushing aside the sky chart, he reached under it to seize a scroll from the piles of parchment and vellum littering the table. Willing himself to a calmer state, he unrolled the scroll and began to read.

"Here is the spell I was trying to work," he said, and moved to stand beneath the ceiling lamp so he could see the writing more clearly. He read carefully. After years of study it still took some time for him to decipher the old Arabic script. Warrick read the lines twice before he attempted to reverse the spell he had woven. He concentrated, said each word exactly as it ought to be spoken, made the correct gestures at the right times, and when he was finished he held his breath and waited.

Nothing happened.

There was not the faintest stirring of the warm air in the room, no particles of gold whirling about, no aquamarine-colored egg materializing upon the table. No Hua Te. Nothing.

"Dear God in Heaven, what have I done?" Warrick dropped the scroll on the table. He sank onto the divan and put his aching head into his hands. He could not think what to do next. His mind was blank with horror.

"Ho, Warrick!" The cheerful cry came from the room below. Footsteps sounded on the stairs and a moment later the speaker appeared. He was a man of Warrick's age, though there was a lighthearted, youthful air about him, in contrast to Warrick's dark seriousness. The newcomer's curly, reddish brown hair hung almost to his shoulders and his gray-green eyes danced with good humor. In one hand he carried a pomegranate that he broke open as he mounted the last few steps. The red juice from the seeds ran over his fingers and down his wrist.

To Warrick, just raising his face from his hands, the juice looked like blood. He stared at it, feeling sick. Then he met the gaze of his childhood friend, who had refused to stay behind in England while Warrick ventured abroad. Robin had insisted on joining Warrick and Hua Te on their journey, and he had been the best of companions, offering humorous relief from Warrick's continual studies.

"Have you finished work for this evening? What wonderful magic have you wrought this time?" Robin asked. He looked around the room in some curiosity, his playful expression gradually altering to questioning seriousness. "Where is Hua Te?"

"He is gone." Warrick found it difficult to speak,

for he had reached a terrible conclusion. "I have killed him."

"Never!" Robin exclaimed. "You would not harm him. What has happened?"

"As you know, Hua Te wanted me to try a new spell. I was in the midst of the conjuration when he disappeared."

"You had better tell me everything," Robin said. "But first let me clean my hands." He glanced around, seeking a place to put the pomegranate. Finding no suitable spot, he went to the stairway.

"Daoud," he called, "bring a pitcher of water, a towel, and a plate."

Almost immediately a short, plump man in a white robe appeared, bearing the requested items on a tray. While the servant waited patiently, holding the tray, Robin set the pomegranate on the plate and washed the juice from his hands.

"Where is Master Hua Te?" Daoud asked of Warrick.

"Have you seen him recently?" Warrick responded, not wanting to answer the query.

"No, master, I have not," Daoud said. "Not since the two of you told me you would be in this room and you did not want to be interrupted. Hua Te has not left the house by either the front door or the garden door. If he had gone out, I would have seen him."

"That will be all, Daoud." Rubbing at his still-aching forehead, Warrick rose from the divan.

"Let him stay," Robin advised. "He is devoted to Hua Te. He may be able to help us."

"Has something happened to the master sage?" Daoud asked, looking from Warrick to Robin.

Flora Speer

"Speak now, Warrick," Robin ordered, "and leave nothing out, not the smallest detail, for who knows what seemingly unimportant fact will help us to find our friend?"

Chapter Two

"Good morning, Father." Doing her best to conceal the anxiety that caught at her heart each time she saw him, Sophia watched her parent come down the steps from the roof. He looked even paler and more rumpled than usual and his hand trembled when he placed it on the wall to steady himself.

"It is barely sunrise," John of Cornwall said, scowling at her. "Why have you risen so early?"

"For the same reason that you stay awake night after night," Sophia answered him. "Because I have work to do."

"Ah." John took his hand from the wall and began to make his slow way across the hall toward the door of his private room.

"I will need money for the market," Sophia said.

"What, again?" John's scowl deepened. "You asked me for money not ten days ago."

"We must eat, and the larder is almost bare."

19

John had reached his chamber door and he paused to look back at his only child. Indicating the sheaf of parchment slips he held, on which rows of numbers were scrawled, he said, "See that you do not disturb me while I complete my calculations."

"The money, Father," Sophia reminded him. "Please, I do need it."

"Wait here." John went into his room and shut the door. A few minutes later he reappeared, to drop a few copper coins into Sophia's hand.

"This is hardly enough," she said.

"It's not my fault if you are extravagant. Now leave me alone. I have important work to do."

"Father, I am seriously worried about you," Sophia said.

"Don't bother me with your foolish concerns. I know what I am doing."

"I am not talking about your work, except as it impinges on your health," Sophia cried in frustration.

"My health is my own business. You must excuse me, Sophia. A brilliant idea occurred to me last night regarding the motions of the planets. I want to write my thoughts down at once, before they slip from my mind." John's voice took on a distant tone, as if he were already lost among the numbers he had jotted down during his astronomical observations. "You cannot appreciate how important my work is, Sophia. Your mind is too feeble to comprehend my theories."

"Forget your theories for a moment," Sophia exclaimed. "Why won't you listen to me? Are you deliberately trying to kill yourself? You spend your nights on the roof observing the stars, and your days in your study making arithmetical calculations. You seldom sleep, and you don't eat, so you lose weight."

"Enough!" John shouted at her. "I will not be subjected to yet another of your tongue-lashings. My time is short and I have more important things to do with it than listen to you."

"Father—"

"I will see no one today," John said, speaking right over Sophia's protest. "Unless Hua Te comes to call. Him you may admit and send to my room."

"Father!" Sophia cried, in near despair at his indifference to her worries. Then, in a louder voice, "Men!"

Hearing slow footsteps coming from the back of the house toward the hall, Sophia whirled, ready to continue her quarrel. Hanna, who had once been her nurse and now claimed to be their housekeeper, though Sophia did most of the work, approached Sophia slowly. The wrinkles in Hanna's aged face creased into an expression of grim satisfaction.

"You know nothing of men," she said to Sophia, "and if you do not moderate your tongue, you will never have the chance to learn. I warned you that Master John would not listen to you. The only one he listens to is Hua Te."

"True enough," Sophia snapped, "but where is Hua Te? He promised to bring more medicine for Father last night, and he never did. I was hoping to enlist him in my effort to convince Father to rest more often and to eat more. Why are men so undependable?"

"Oh, they are dependable enough," Hanna said, "so long as you are saying something a man wants to hear. If he thinks that what a woman has to say will make him at all uncomfortable, a man will take himself off to his work, as your father just did. Ah, well, perhaps Hua Te will come tonight instead. And perhaps he'll bring with him that handsome young pupil of his. You'd like that, wouldn't you, Mistress Sophia?"

"I most certainly would not like it!" Sophia responded with considerable heat. "I cannot abide that arrogant, self-absorbed—"

"Aye," said Hanna, snickering. "You're two of a kind, each pretending not to see the other. Well, now that you've driven your father into his private rooms for the rest of the day, you ought to go to the marketplace at once. It's almost full daylight, the market has been open for at least an hour, and you know how quickly the best foodstuffs are sold. If you were able to squeeze a few coins out of your tightfisted father, there are some items I need." She held out a list, for Hanna could write, though not very clearly. John refused to tolerate unlettered servants and had taught both Hanna and her son, Daoud, to read and write and, in Daoud's case, to count and tally lists of numbers.

"I really ought to beat you for your insolence," Sophia said, snatching the list out of Hanna's gnarled hand. "I am sure no other woman in Baghdad permits her servants so much freedom to speak."

"You won't beat me," Hanna said with great assurance. "Not your old nurse, the one who held you in her arms and let you weep after your poor mother died. Ah, Sophia, you are not a woman yet, for all your twenty years of existence."

"Be silent!" Sophia ordered. "While I am gone, brew a pot of coffee and take it and some fruit to my father."

"What a mood you're in," Hanna said with an offended sniff. "I pity the merchants in the marketplace this morning."

Sophia reached for the dark garment that hung on a peg near the door, the long veil that would cover her so completely from head to foot that no man would guess whether there was a comely maiden concealed beneath it, or an aged crone. With the veil in place, Sophia could move about Baghdad freely and never be accosted. She took the basket Hanna held out for her and left the house, slamming the door behind her.

Sophia was in a worse mood than Hanna guessed. Once again, she had allowed her father's indifference to drive her to anger. She paused in the street just outside the house to look at the coins in her hand.

"How am I supposed to buy everything we need with so little money? Oh, Father, you could have given me more; I know you have money hidden away." Sophia shook her veiled head in sorrow. "I know I am not beautiful like Mother, and I lack her sweet nature, but I am your child. How I wish you loved me. Perhaps if Mother were still alive you would love me."

She was well aware that all her father cared about was his work. Night after night John climbed to the roof of his house to gaze at the stars. His days were filled with work on mathematical calculations based upon the notes he made at night.

In addition to being a serious student of the heavens, John, like most astronomers, was also an astrologer. The horoscopes he cast were remarkably accurate and it was from the making of such prognostications that he earned his living. Even the sultan consulted him as to the most propitious or difficult days of the calendar. John was proud of his position as one of the court astrologers, despite the fact that the sultan was known to be a greedy and treacherous man, who too often dealt unfairly with those who served him.

Baghdad was a haven for astronomers, magicians, geographers, and physicists, for students of Islamic law, and for a wide assortment of other sages of many faiths and from countries all over the world. Foreigners were welcome to live in Baghdad, so long as they paid their taxes and obeyed the laws.

While John knew most of the foreigners living in the city, he called few of them his friends. One of the few was Hua Te, who was both healer and magician. Hua Te also had an interest in astronomy and often joined John on his rooftop late at night.

Alarmed by the signs of failing health that she had noticed in her father, Sophia decided she would insist upon speaking with Hua Te the next time he came to the house. Whether John objected or not, she would demand to know exactly what was wrong with her parent. She told herself she had a right to know; she had been distressed for some time by her father's refusal to speak about his illness. And she was afraid, because if he died she would have no one.

Chapter Three

"That is what happened," Warrick said, looking from Robin to Daoud. "I have told you every detail, twice over. Hua Te is gone, and I have no idea how to bring him back again."

"Do you really believe you made a mistake?" Robin asked. "I know how careful you are, and how well you study every lesson Hua Te assigns to you. Warrick, you commit to memory every word he speaks! How then could you be at fault when conjuring a spell?"

"I thought I had the words in order and that I pronounced them correctly," Warrick responded with open frustration. "Clearly I did something wrong, for Hua Te is no longer with us."

"You spoke of a mysterious, egg-shaped object that appeared out of nowhere," Daoud said. "Do you think that object might have something to do with Master Hua Te's disappearance?"

"I wish I could say yes," Warrick told him. "If it were so, then I could stop blaming myself."

"May I make a suggestion?" asked the servant.

"Daoud, you may say anything you like, if only it will help us to find Hua Te," Warrick responded.

"You know that Master Hua Te is a close friend to John of Cornwall," Daoud said. "So close, in fact, that Master John agreed to rent this house to Hua Te for the duration of his stay in Baghdad, and he also sent me from his own household to this one, to be Hua Te's servant. It is a position that honors me for, truly, Master Hua Te is a great scholar."

"Yes, I know all of that," Warrick said with a touch of impatience. "What of it?"

"My suggestion," said Daoud, "is that you ask Master John what he thinks you ought to do. While it is true that his most important area of study is astronomy, he is also interested in magic. It is the subject that first brought him to Hua Te, and their mutual interest in both astronomy and magic formed the original basis for their friendship. I am certain he will be as eager as you are to see Hua Te safely returned to us. At the very least, Master John can cast a horoscope for Hua Te, which may tell you where he is, or when we may expect his return."

"*If* he will return," Warrick corrected with a grim downturn to his mouth.

"I think we should take Daoud's suggestion," Robin said. "Let us ask Master John's opinion. And we may as well take along Hua Te's gift for him. From what I know of John, this will be a powerful incentive." Grabbing the sky chart from the table, Robin rose from the divan where he had been sitting and headed for the stairs, as if he were eager to be on his way to John's house.

"You cannot go to him just yet," Daoud cautioned with a glance toward the door and the lightening sky outside. "Master John spends his nights searching the skies."

"I don't care if he is searching the cave of Ali Baba," Warrick said. "I need to speak to him at once. Besides, he can't watch the stars during the daytime."

"No," Daoud agreed. "He sleeps during the daylight hours."

"Good," said Warrick, looking hopeful for the first time since Hua Te had vanished. With eager steps he followed Robin toward the stairway that led to the lower levels of the house. "If we hurry he will still be awake. But let us hope that John's irritating daughter is still fast asleep!"

"Daoud, my son," said Hanna, "what are you doing here so early in the day? Have you no duties in the house of Master Hua Te?"

"It is my responsibility to my master that brings me here," Daoud answered her. "Mother, we have a need to speak to Master John." With a wave of one hand Daoud indicated Warrick and Robin, who entered the hall behind him.

Warrick directed a furtive glance around the hall, seeking a sign of John's daughter. To his relief, Sophia was not present. Warrick had no desire to answer the probing questions she would inevitably ask once she had learned what his errand was. And yet he could not deny the small prickle of disappointment that teased at the back of his mind as he accepted her absence.

"Master John cannot be disturbed," Hanna said to the three men who confronted her. "As you would know if you paused to think before acting, he spends the mornings in his study. Then he will be sleeping during the heat of the day. If you wish to speak with him, return at nightfall, just before he begins his observations on the roof."

"We cannot wait that long," Warrick said.

"Why not?" Hanna demanded. "Why must young men always be so impatient? Ah, I could tell you tales—"

"Mother, it is urgent that we speak with Master John at once," Daoud insisted.

"I will not have you upsetting him," Hanna said. "Sophia would tell you the same thing if she had not gone out to the market. I know she is worried about his health."

"All the more reason for us to see him at once." Warrick brushed past the elderly servant. Since he and Hua Te were frequent visitors to the house, he knew where John's study was and he did not expect John to be angry once he heard the explanation of why Warrick and Robin were intruding upon him. Reaching the closed study door, Warrick rapped hard on it. After a few moments an irritated response from within bade him enter.

"Where is Hua Te?" John asked as soon as Warrick stepped into the cluttered room. "Isn't he with you?"

"Hua Te has disappeared and I cannot find him," Warrick responded. "Daoud suggested that I apply to you for help, since you are also interested in magic."

"I see. I think you had better come in and sit down." John looked from Warrick to Robin and Daoud, who were crowding into the doorway, and his eyebrows rose. "All of you come in. Hanna will bring us juices and pastry," he added with a nod to the servant.

It was difficult to find a place to sit in the study. Every available flat surface was piled with books or scrolls or charts of the heavens. Shelves built into the walls held still more scrolls. Slips of parchment on which numbers and algebraic formulas had been written were scattered about. Brushes, pens, and supplies for making ink were jumbled together on a table, along with two different sizes of armillary spheres, a crystal ball on a wooden stand, and the jawbone of some unidentifiable but assuredly long-dead animal. An astrolabe lay upon a stool, its brass tarnished by John's fingerprints. John always insisted that he knew exactly where to find anything he required for his work. Warrick, who possessed a more orderly mind, found the chaos confusing.

Robin and Daoud solved the problem of seating space by pushing aside several scrolls and books so they could drop down cross-legged on the rug. Warrick felt a need to be closer to eye level with John and so, after surveying several possible sites, he lifted three rolled-up scrolls and a large book from a divan and placed them on the floor. Having thus cleared a section of the divan, he sat there, being careful not to disturb any other materials that lay on the cushions.

Hanna reappeared bearing a tray with two pitchers of fruit juices, small cups for the juice, and a plate of honey-drenched pastries. These she served to John and his visitors. Warrick was used to the custom of seeing to a guest's refreshment before discussing business, so he repressed his sense of urgency while he nibbled on a pastry filled with dates and honey and washed the sweet down with a gulp of orange juice.

The sun was well up by now and the heat was increasing. The windows in the study that faced onto the street were tightly shuttered, only those opening on the garden being left open. There was no breeze. The study was uncomfortably warm and it smelled of old books and dust, of the freshly baked pastry, and of the remnants of a partly eaten orange that sat on the table John used as a desk. With an exclamation of annoyance at the untidy habits of her master, Hanna scooped the bits of orange into her hand and left the men alone.

"We have brought you this," Robin said, reaching from his seat on the rug to hand the sky chart to John. "Hua Te intended it as a gift to you, and we thought you should have it at once."

"Beautiful," John said, unrolling the square papyrus chart. He examined it with an expression on his face that was close to reverence. "Exquisitely made. Highly accurate. A treasure, a joy to own. I would be willing to wager that this chart is almost as valuable as—" He looked up from the chart to meet Warrick's eyes.

"About Hua Te," Warrick said.

"Yes, what is this about Hua Te vanishing?" John asked. He sat back in his chair, a tall, thin, gray-haired man, with lines of pain etching his once-handsome face. His blue eyes, usually focused on far-distant planets and stars and therefore vague when he regarded nearer objects, assumed a surprising sharpness when he looked directly at Warrick. "I know you too well to think you would interrupt me for any frivolous reason. All the same, are you absolutely certain that Hua Te has disappeared?"

"I am positive," Warrick said, "though I don't know how it happened." Once more he recounted the story he had already told to Robin and Daoud. This time he left out his feelings about what had occurred. If John knew him well, Warrick also knew John and knew how he detested emotional outbursts. Even so, he was startled by John's lack of distress at the disappearance of a man he had for many years called a friend. John just looked intensely interested in what he was hearing.

"I think it was the fault of the mysterious egg," Daoud said into the silence that fell when Warrick was finished.

"No," Warrick insisted. "It was my fault. I did it."

"And you, Robin," said John, turning his blue gaze upon Warrick's friend. "What is your opinion of this peculiar disappearance?"

"I'm not sure," Robin said. "I do think Warrick takes the blame upon himself much too easily. I am no magician; I know nothing of spells, but it seems to me there could be another explanation. Daoud may be right about the egg—or whatever that strange object was."

"There are legendary tales of magical eggs," John said. "Then there is the famous Philosopher's Stone, which some men believe is shaped like an egg. It is possible that the mysterious object you saw did have something to do with Hua Te's disappearance."

"Have you any idea how we can bring him back?" Warrick asked.

"I am not sure," John said with a perplexed frown. "I will have to do some reading on the subject of magical disappearances. I had planned to spend this day making calculations. And now I have this lovely chart to peruse." John touched the sky chart as if he deeply regretted the need to lay it aside in order to contemplate the absence of Hua Te.

"Surely," Warrick said, "Hua Te's welfare is far more important than your astronomical work. If there is anything I can do to assist you, just tell me what it is. I am at your service."

"So am I," Robin said.

"And I." Daoud leaned forward, elbows on his knees. "Master John, let us help you."

"Help me?" John's blue eyes assumed a vague, distant expression, as if he had retreated into the deep recesses of his busy mind.

"We must make haste," Warrick said. "Hua Te may be in danger, or he may be suffering. John, he needs our best efforts. Let us begin work at once!"

"So," John said, looking at Warrick with a shrewd gleam in his eyes, "you misworked the spell, did you?"

"It appears that I did," Warrick responded, striving to hold on to his temper at being made to admit it once again.

"And now you are feeling guilty, I suppose?" John said.

"Of course I feel guilty!" Warrick exploded. "How in the name of heaven do you expect me to feel? Damnation, John, why do you continue to ask questions that I have already answered? I came here hoping you would know how to find Hua Te. After all, he is your friend, too."

"I have every intention of helping you to resolve this mystery," John said. "In return, you will help me with a problem that has been nagging at me for too long. Come to see me again at noon tomorrow."

"Tomorrow?" Warrick exclaimed. "Not until then? But why?"

"It takes time to cast an accurate horoscope," John said. "Fortunately I have the necessary information about Hua Te's place of birth and the date. His previous horoscope suggested that a most unusual event would occur before the summer solstice, precipitating an adventure that would occupy him for some time. The solstice will occur tomorrow, so perhaps Hua Te has embarked upon that adventure. If so, a new horoscope for the coming year may offer some clues.

"I also intend to consult with fellow scholars," John added, seeing Warrick's hesitation at leaving. "Believe me when I say that I am not unduly worried about my missing friend."

"I wish I could be so sure," Warrick responded. It was all he could do to be polite as he said his farewell to John.

Chapter Four

"What do you mean, my father is still working?" Sophia cried. "He should have been in his bed hours ago."

"It's because of those men," Hanna responded. "I warned Daoud not to interrupt Master John, but he wouldn't listen to me, and neither would the other two."

"What men?" Sophia demanded. Then, "If Daoud was here, did he come with Hua Te? I hope so, because I want to talk to him about the state of Father's health." She bit her lip, not daring to speak aloud the name of the other man who might have come to the house with Daoud. Sophia took a deep breath, trying to calm her racing heartbeat at the thought of Warrick. "Hanna, are the men still with my father?"

"They left," Hanna said. "The tall one looked annoyed. And Hua Te wasn't with them."

"Perhaps I should see if Father is all right." Sophia brushed aside the irrational disappointment she felt at learning that Warrick was not in her father's private room. Before she could cross the hall, John appeared in the doorway to his study. There were dark circles under his eyes and his gray hair looked as if he had run his hands through it many times.

"Are you feeling unwell?" Sophia asked, concern for her parent pushing all other thoughts from her mind. "Father, you should be in bed."

"There is so much still to do," John said, ignoring her question about his health. "My time is growing short. I'll not waste any more of it. Come into the study."

"Hanna said you had visitors. Did they tire you?" Sophia went past her father and into his room. As always, it took her a while to decide where it was safe to sit. The study was in even greater disarray than usual, with books propped open upon other books, and scrolls carelessly tossed on tables and stools. Sophia noticed that several of the books were about the subject of magic, and two of the scrolls contained astrological information. It looked as if her father was launched upon a new project. She chose to remain standing, so as not to disturb anything.

"Visitors?" John repeated. "Oh, yes, Warrick and Robin were here. They had a question about Hua Te. I believe I have resolved that problem. When they return tomorrow I will explain to them as much as they need to know. Tell Hanna to admit them at once when they come to the door."

"Very well," Sophia said. "Father, I wish you would rest."

"Not yet," John said. He stood before one of the windows that looked out on the garden. Positioned as he was, John's face was in shadow. Sophia could not see his expression. She wondered if he had deliberately chosen that spot.

"Before your mother died I promised her that I would see to your welfare," John said.

"And so you have," Sophia responded with false cheerfulness. "I have not lacked for anything." In truth, there were things she wanted, but she knew better than to ask for them. John earned a handsome income from the horoscopes he drew up, and Sophia was aware that he owned several houses in addition to the one in which they lived. Still, most of John's money went for books or astronomical instruments, very little to household expenses, and there was none at all for feminine frivolities.

"You are deliberately misunderstanding me," John said in his irritable way. "I am not speaking of the present, but of the time when I will no longer be with you. Since you constantly subject me to interrogation about my physical condition, I assume that somewhere in your foolish, overemotional mind you are aware that the day of my departure is drawing near."

"No," Sophia declared, "I do not believe that. You have always said that Hua Te's medicines are of the best quality, but if they are no longer helping you, then we will appeal to the sultan and ask for his physican to see you."

"The sultan is exactly the person I want to prevent from knowing how ill I am," John said. "Soon enough he will learn the truth; I can only hope and trust it will not be until after all of my arrangements have been made."

"I have noticed that you are not as lively as usual, but it is only a temporary indisposition." Sophia spoke quickly so that she would not have to think about what her father was saying. "You must rest more than you have been doing. Soon you will be well again."

"I will never be well again, and you would be wise to accept that fact and pay attention to what I am telling you," John said. "While casting a new horoscope for Hua Te, I realized that several of the planets are in unusual alignment. Since those same planets have a strong effect on my own chart, I also cast a horoscope for myself. What I discovered is only what I have been expecting, based on other evidence I have noticed lately. I am going to die soon."

"Father," Sophia said in a voice choked with fear, "please stop talking this way. I cannot bear it."

"Soon you will have to bear more than unpleasant conversation," John said. "If your mother's wishes for you are to be fulfilled—and I intend that they shall be—you will need a female companion. Hanna is much too old for the task. I have made adequate provision for her. She will end her days in comfort, living in this house with Daoud. At the moment, your future concerns me most."

"Surely you haven't arranged a marriage for me?" Sophia cried, horrified by the idea. At the same time, she was touched to hear that her father did care what happened to her.

"Your mother did not want you to wed anyone who belongs to this foreign place," her father said.

"It isn't foreign," Sophia protested. "Baghdad is my home. It always has been."

"Helena believed that your true home lies elsewhere," John told her. "I am making arrangements for you to travel there after I am gone. In the meantime, I will provide the chaperone and companion that you will require for your journey."

"What companion? Father, what are you saying?"

"I am forced to confess that I will never become the great mage that Hua Te is. I no longer have enough time in which to acquire his incredible degree of learning. Still, he has taught me much. I believe what I have learned will be sufficient for the magic I intend to work this day." John plucked a cracked, ancient scroll from the floor. He began to unroll it with his right hand, while with his left hand he rerolled the yellowed parchment, working his way along the scroll until he reached the place in the writing that he wanted. "Here it is," he said.

"Here is what?" Sophia asked. She was thoroughly alarmed by now, not wanting to accept her father's prediction of his imminent death and bewildered by his talk of working magic and of giving her a companion. She was beginning to wonder if he was losing his wits.

"If you will just remain silent and pay attention instead of repeating everything I say, you will soon understand," John said to her. "The spell is simple enough to conjure. My skills ought to be adequate to the task."

"Conjure?" Sophia said. "Father, what are you going to do?"

"I told you to be quiet." John sent a quelling look in her direction. He read again the portion of the scroll that he held open. Then he took a preparatory breath.

"Father, I implore you, attempt to do no magic," Sophia cried. Fearing that her pleading would have no influence on him, she invoked the one person to whom John had occasionally paid heed. "Mother always deplored your forays into the magical sciences. She worried when you would not listen to her cautions."

John did not listen to his daughter's cautions either. As if Sophia had not spoken, he drew himself up and, reading from the scroll, began to recite in a loud, commanding voice.

"I conjure thee, oh jinni, instantly and without delay to appear unto me in comely feminine shape, without noise or hurt done to me or to my daughter, and to reply to all that I shall command thee, and to be subject to me and to my daughter, Sophia."

"Father, stop this at once! I beg you, stop!"

"Tetragrammaton . . . ischeros athanatos . . ." John continued to cast the spell, speaking words that Sophia had never heard before and could not understand. When he had finished he leaned, pale and sweating, against his desk, looking as if the very life were drained out of him.

There was an awful silence in the study. Sophia held her breath, not knowing what her father would do next, or what she ought to do in response. When she made a move toward him, he held up his hand to stop her.

And then, between one heartbeat and the next, without thunder or lightning, with neither smoke nor flame, nor the hellish stench of sulfur that was supposed to accompany magical manifestations, a third person appeared in John's study.

It was a female form, as John had commanded, and the shape was that of a young person, perhaps Sophia's age. The creature was comely, with a pert nose, pointed chin, clear gray eyes sparkling with mischief, and a mass of red, waving hair that tumbled to below her waist.

She was completely naked.

"Master," the creature said, placing her dainty hands together and making a deep bow to John, "I am here at your command. Ask of me what you will."

"This is outrageous!" Sophia sputtered, too amazed by the apparition to be afraid any longer. "What are you?"

"I am a jinni," the creature responded, bestowing a lovely smile upon Sophia.

"I thought the jinn lived in bottles or lamps," Sophia muttered. It was all she could do to avoid smiling back at the creature. She told herself a smile was not a natural impulse in such a situation; her urge to smile was a magical reaction caused by the creature, and she refused to give in to the enchantment.

Furthermore, the jinni smiling at her wasn't a real woman; it was a demon. Sophia knew she ought to be terrified and angry at its presence. Certainly she ought not to be experiencing a desire to welcome the dreadful thing—except that this particular jinni did not appear to be at all dreadful. It looked almost pleasant, almost friendly. Something in Sophia's lonely heart reacted with yearning warmth toward the jinni. She fought the impulse, telling herself that what she thought she saw in the jinni was an illusion created by magic.

"You have been listening to the tale of Aladdin, which is only partially true," the jinni said to her. "Bottles and lamps are not our only homes. We jinn are beings of flame or air, and we dwell in many places."

"Then I implore you, return to your true dwelling place, whatever it is," Sophia said.

"I cannot," the jinni told her. "I have been called into visible existence in this world by my new master and only he, or a magician greater than he, can speak the magical words that will return me to the Land of the Jinn."

"Father, send her back!" Sophia cried. "What were you thinking of when you spoke the spell that brought her here? We don't need a jinni in this house and I don't want one here." Of course she didn't. No sensible person would want a magical creature for a companion. Would she?

John wasn't listening to Sophia's pleas. He was regarding the jinni with a dark scowl.

"You are not at all the sort of creature I intended to invoke," he said to the jinni. "I wanted someone older, plainer, and more sternly serious, who is capable of acting as a strict chaperone to my daughter."

"Master, you did command me to appear in comely form," the jinni responded with a sweet smile.

"Only because I was attempting to avoid the presence of some hideous, demonic manifestation," John said.

"Father, this *is* a demon!" Sophia cried.

"Be silent, girl, or I will send you from the room," John told her. When Sophia subsided and stood chewing on her lower lip, John returned his attention to the jinni. "You do not appear to me to be demure enough, nor of a suitably mature and sober

41

nature for the task I plan to set you. I wish I had the strength to send you back."

"So do I," Sophia muttered, earning herself another frown from her father.

"Master," the jinni said to John, "when a person weaves a magical spell, sometimes he conjures not only what he thinks he wants, but also what he needs. And sometimes the magician does not understand what it is that he truly needs. I assure you, master, I have the ability to fulfill all of your daughter's requirements."

"Sophia's needs are irrelevant. You are here to fulfill my requirements for her," John said.

"I have no needs," Sophia cried, stung by the way her father was arranging her life without discussing her preferences with her. "I can take care of myself."

"You have lived in Baghdad for all of your life," John said to her. "You leave this house only for short periods, to do the marketing or, occasionally, to visit a friend with me. You know little of the world beyond these walls."

"I am well read, and thus I am aware of what the world contains," Sophia said.

"You know nothing, you foolish child," John told her severely.

"Nor do you understand how to deal with people," said the jinni.

"I deal very well with my father, thank you," Sophia snapped at her. "And with Hanna, complainer that she is, and with Daoud when he is here. I am usually polite to my father's visitors."

"Only usually?" said the jinni. "I think you have a lot to learn, Sophia."

"I will not be mocked by a nonhuman creature!"

"Sophia, I will not tell you again to be silent!" John shouted at her. "Why do you persist in trying my patience? There is an unfinished astronomical treatise sitting on my desk that will very likely still be incomplete at my death because I have taken valuable time away from my work in order to do what is best for you. If you cannot appreciate my efforts on your behalf, at least do not hinder them."

"I am sorry, Father," Sophia whispered, stricken by guilt at his words.

"Now, jinni," John said, turning his back to his daughter, "since you are here to stay, you must have a name. What shall I call you?"

"Whatever you wish, master," the jinni said. "Your slightest wish is my command."

"In that case, I will name you simply Genie. I don't have time to waste thinking of a name and that seems suitable enough," John said. To Sophia, he added, "From this day on, Genie is to be your companion and chaperone."

"I have no need and no desire for a chaperone," Sophia said, speaking very distinctly in the hope that her father would pay attention to what she wanted.

"I am sure you will find her useful," John said.

Sophia glared at her father in frustration. Then she glared at the jinni. She was so angry that several minutes passed before she remembered the most noticeable defect in her unwanted companion.

"Do you think you could put on some clothes?" Sophia said in an irritated voice.

"Clothing?" said the jinni, looking puzzled.

"It is the custom among civilized humans to cover the naked body," Sophia said. "If you are go-

43

ing to pretend to be a human, you will have to wear clothes."

"Oh, master," said the jinni, turning to John, "must I?"

"For once Sophia is right. Clothing is essential," John said. "Perhaps Sophia has something you can wear."

"I don't think so." Genie eyed Sophia's drab gray robe and the plain linen scarf covering her hair, and shook her head until the glorious red waves of her own hair shimmered. "Do you always dress like that?" she asked.

"I beg your pardon?" Sophia responded stiffly.

"I can see that this isn't a poor household." Genie made an expressive gesture, indicating the entire study. "Not with all these valuable books and scrolls lying in heaps and piles, and the glorious rug that is hidden beneath them, and the lovely garden outside. It's obvious that your father is a man of some substance. Sophia, you will never get a husband if you wear dull colors and cover your hair like a servant."

"I don't want a husband," Sophia said.

"You don't want a companion, and you reject the idea of a chaperone," Genie said with a mischievous grin. "You don't want a husband. You dress like a servant. I can see I will have to take you in hand as soon as possible. Tell me, Sophia, what do you want?"

"You are the most impudent, insolent, disrespectful—Oh!" Sophia cried, too furious to go on. After a moment she regained some control over her temper and asked, "What kind of jinni are you, to be so rude?"

"While we jinn are compelled to obey the masters

who call us into corporeal life, nowhere is it written that we have to be respectful. Besides," Genie continued, "you aren't my master. Your father is. I obey him, not you."

"Genie," said John, "I do hereby formally bind you to serve not only me and my wishes, but also my daughter, Sophia. I command you to obey her faithfully in all things, for the rest of her life, or until she or I release you from your present Calling."

"Oh, master, no," Genie cried. "I would far rather serve you alone. Your daughter does not want me. We have both heard her say so repeatedly."

"Nevertheless, Sophia is your mistress," John said. "I called you to this time and place to fulfill a specific purpose. Sophia is going to need you. She is such a foolish, witless girl that I seriously doubt her ability to carry out my plans for her without your help."

"Yes, master. I can only obey." With a resigned sigh that she made no effort to hide, Genie faced Sophia, placed her hands together, and made a formal obeisance. "Mistress, behold your humble servant and true friend. Ask whatever you will of me and, if it is within my power to do so, I will obey."

"I order you to go back where you came from." Refusing to let her father or Genie see how John's cruel words had hurt her, Sophia spoke as coldly as she possibly could. Nor was she going to pay heed to the small voice within her heart that told her she ought to be glad to have a friend who would not leave her. Instead she fought to convince herself that she did not want a companion created by magic.

"Mistress, I regret to say I cannot obey that particular order. I am here on Earth until the end of your life, or until the words of the spell that will return me to my former abode are spoken," Genie said, adding with a naughty twinkle in her eyes, "I do not think you know what that spell is."

"And I won't tell you what it is," John said to his daughter. "Knowing your overly affectionate heart, I am certain you will soon grow to be as fond of Genie as you would be of a sister."

"Fond of a demon?" Sophia cried. "I would as soon admit to a fondness for—" She stopped short, before Warrick's name could pass her lips. She did not want to think about Warrick.

"I am not a demon," Genie stated with an affronted air. "We jinn are spirits created only a little lower than the angels. It is true that some of us are wicked, just as certain angels have been wicked from time to heavenly time, but I am not one of those jinn. I do believe I can be of help to you."

"I don't care what kind of jinni you are," Sophia responded. She was feeling thoroughly exasperated with both her father and the jinni, so she snapped out her next remark in a cold voice. "I don't need your help and I don't want you here."

"Mistress, I do most humbly apologize for any offense I may have caused." Genie bowed low before her.

"If you are going to live in this house, we will have to find some clothing for you," Sophia said, reverting to the one problem she could remedy. Surely even a jinni could understand the need to cover her nakedness. Sophia headed for the study door, intending to find some of her own clothes for Genie to wear.

Hearing her father gasp, Sophia turned back into

the room, fearing he was ill. After the last hour, she wouldn't be surprised if he was sick. Conjuring up a demon must be exhausting work. Sophia wished he had spared himself the effort, and herself the result of that effort.

John wasn't sick. He was merely surprised, and he was gaping in bemused appreciation at Genie, who was clothed, after a fashion. A tiny, sleeveless, gold-encrusted bodice with a plunging neckline almost covered her breasts. Her midriff was bare to just below her navel. The lower half of her figure was enhanced by a wide golden band that matched the bodice. From the lower edge of the band sheer fabric ballooned into long trousers that were caught at her ankles with more gold. Genie's hair was dressed high on her head and fastened with golden ribbons. Her earrings were so long that they brushed against her shoulders, and her arms were covered from wrists to elbows in gold bracelets set with stones of many colors. She was even wearing rings on her toes.

"No," Sophia said as firmly as she could manage, given her outrage at Genie's appearance. "You may not dress like that. Not if you are to be my companion."

"I was afraid you wouldn't approve, but I thought I'd try anyway." Genie grinned and spun around once. When she faced Sophia again she was wearing a long, turquoise blue silk robe that flowed gracefully over her shapely form, covering but not concealing it. Her hair was still held by golden ribbons in a high, elegant style, and golden sandals were visible at the hem of her robe. Dangling gold earrings completed the new costume.

"I hope you find this raiment more suitable," Genie said to Sophia. "Left to my own taste, I prefer my previous outfit. Did you know that is the kind of costume the dancing girls in harems wear?"

"I have no idea what sort of costume is considered suitable for the women who live in harems, nor do I care to speculate about the possibilities," Sophia said in a quelling manner. Catching her father's stern glance, she decided to be more polite to her unwelcome visitor. Apparently she was going to have to deal with Genie for some time to come, and Sophia had sense enough to see that her life would be far more pleasant if she and Genie were on agreeable terms. "So long as you remain inside this house, the clothing you are now wearing will be acceptable. If for any reason you go outside, you must wear a long veil."

"Of course." Genie's smile was almost blinding in its innocent sweetness. "I wouldn't dream of being the least bit improper. The last thing I want to do is embarrass my mistress."

Realizing that she had just accepted a demon into her household, Sophia sent an accusing look in her father's direction. He merely nodded his head, then gave a longing glance at the open sky chart and the piles of papers on his desk.

"What am I to do with her?" Sophia asked.

"She could help with the housework," John responded, his eyes still on the materials spread across his desk.

"I will not have the housework done by magic!" Sophia snapped.

"That's a relief," Genie said. "I don't know how to do that kind of thing."

"I thought the jinn had all sorts of magical abilities," Sophia said.

"It depends upon how we are brought into this world," Genie said. "I was conjured to be a companion and a faithful friend. So I shall be, but my magical abilities are strictly limited by the spell that brought me here—an arrangement established for your safety as well as my own."

"Then what *can* you do?" Sophia asked, intrigued at the thought of limits being set upon a supernatural being.

"As you have seen, I know how to produce clothing and jewelry," Genie answered with considerable enthusiasm. She spread her arms to display her turquoise robe. Her golden earrings sparkled and shimmered.

"How very useful." Sophia looked at her with undisguised scorn. It was on the tip of her tongue to tell her father that, if he was determined to inflict an unwanted companion on her, the least he could have done was take greater care to give her someone whose mind was compatible with her own. From what she had seen and heard so far, Sophia was convinced that Genie was much too frivolous a creature.

"It seems to me that your wardrobe could use a bit of refurbishment," Genie said. "Unless you are wearing those unattractive clothes because you have some unpleasant household task to do today."

"These are the clothes I always wear." Sophia spoke as firmly and as discouragingly as she could. "What else can you do that might be useful?"

"Well," Genie said as if she were thinking through a difficult problem, "I believe I might be able to manage camels."

"Camels," Sophia said, staring at the pretty creature in her silk robe and dangling earrings. *"Camels? Are you joking?"*

"No, mistress. I do not know why I think I possess such an ability, but if ever you need to travel by camel, I am sure I will be of considerable help to you."

"I have no intention of traveling anywhere," Sophia said. "My home is here, in Baghdad. Tell me, Genie, do you sleep?"

"Yes, mistress, I do. When we jinn are in human form, we possess all the physical needs of humans. Not only do I require sleep, I must also eat and drink as humans do."

"In that case, I will prepare a room for you," Sophia said. There was nothing else to be done. The creature had been inflicted upon her and Sophia knew she was going to have to deal with her unwanted guest until such time as she could convince her father to send Genie back to the Land of the Jinn. However, there was one problem that called for an immediate solution. "Father, how do you want me to explain Genie's presence in your house?"

"When Hanna takes her nap after the midday meal," John said, "Genie will unexpectedly arrive for a visit. We will say she is your cousin, the daughter of your mother's sister."

"Did my mother have a sister?" Sophia asked, surprised by her father's inventiveness. "And if she did, will Hanna know of it?"

"To my knowledge, you have three aunts," John said.

"I have?" Sophia was stunned by this information. "Where do they live?"

"As I recall, all of them were distinctly unpleasant

women," John said. "You need not think of them. We will tell Hanna that your mother's eldest sister married a Greek trader who lives in Mosul, and Genie is their daughter, come to visit for a time. That ought to satisfy her curiosity."

"Is it the truth?" Sophia asked. If so, it was the first indication her father had ever given that she did have other family. Moreover, the remark about a Greek trader was intriguing.

"What?" John looked distracted. "No, of course there is no truth in the story. My only intention is to prevent Hanna from asking questions. Fortunately she is not a gossip. Now I must ask you to excuse me. Suddenly I am very tired."

"Master, where do you sleep?" Genie asked.

"In the little room behind this study," John said. "I prefer to sleep there so that, if I waken with an important insight into my astronomical calculations, I can come right back to this room and get to work without being distracted from my thoughts by having to speak to anyone else."

"I will sleep here with you," Genie said.

"You certainly will not!" Sophia declared. If she were not so disturbed by her father's pale face and shaking hands, she might have found the suggestion humorous. She knew how her father hated anyone to speak to him when he was in deep thought about astronomical complexities. And she was certain that John of Cornwall had not consorted with any woman since his wife's death.

"Since I am your mistress," Sophia said to Genie, "I order you to sleep in the room next to mine, and to make no complaint about the accommodations. Nor will you disturb my father when he is working."

"I knew I could make you declare aloud that you

51

are my mistress," Genie said with a mischievous grin. "Now that you have said so, I am truly your servant. Mistress Sophia, I am happy to do your bidding."

Chapter Five

Sophia slept badly on the night after Genie's arrival. She rose from her bed several times and crept up the stairs almost to the rooftop. Each time she paused on the topmost step and peered through the doorway, just to assure herself that her father was well enough to continue working.

She did not actually step onto the roof. No matter how warm the night or how hot the interior of the house, she never disobeyed her father's edict that the roof was his private domain and that no one was to intrude upon him while he was there. Sophia did not mind the prohibition. It provided the perfect excuse for her to avoid the fear and the sudden, absurd dizziness that plagued her whenever she stepped onto a high, open place.

Sophia much preferred to be at ground level, either inside the house or in the narrow, familiar streets that led from the house to the marketplace.

While others complained of the impinging walls of tall houses that kept many streets in shadow all day, and of the press of men and women who filled the alleys and markets of Baghdad from early morning until late at night, Sophia liked the close confines of the city and always felt safe there.

In addition to her concern for her father, the knowledge that Genie was sleeping in the room next to hers kept Sophia awake. Her feelings about Genie were confused. The creature was beguiling, apparently friendly and obedient, yet Sophia could not bring herself to trust anyone whose origins were magical.

She wished she dared to speak to her father about her reservations over his choice of companion for her, and implore him to reverse his spell and send Genie back to the Land of the Jinn. She knew very well that she would not speak to him. She feared his anger too much, and feared even more what might happen to his fragile health if he exerted himself to work another magical spell.

It was shortly after dawn when she descended the stairs to the hall and went in search of Hanna and a cup of strong coffee. She was just passing the front door when someone pounded on it. Sophia opened the door in haste, so her father would not be disturbed by the noise. When she saw who had been knocking, she was the one who was disturbed.

"Warrick. How nice of you to visit so early in the day," she muttered sarcastically.

The man who brushed past Sophia and stepped into the hall was at least a foot taller than she, broad-shouldered, and almost terrifyingly handsome. Flustered by his unexpected appearance, and with her heart suddenly beating more rapidly than normal, Sophia stepped away from the door.

Warrick always made her feel as if she were beneath his arrogant notice, and on this particular morning, after a nearly sleepless night, she knew she did not look her best. Her old gray woolen gown had a spot on the bodice, and her too-curly black hair was barely tamed into a knot at the back of her head. She knew she looked drab and colorless, and when Genie suddenly appeared on the stairs, Sophia could feel herself fading into the background like the nondescript servant Genie had termed her only the day before.

In vibrant contrast to Sophia, Genie glided down the steps wearing a flowing rose silk caftan. The luxuriant red waves of her hair were bound into a single long braid decorated with silver and rose ribbons. Her dangling silver earrings were set with moonstones that perfectly matched her silver-gray eyes. The faint scent of roses surrounded her.

Warrick wrinkled his nose and turned suddenly to stare at Genie. Then he looked back at Sophia. His frown was severe and his eyes were hard as glittering topaz jewels. Sophia could not imagine what she had done to offend him, but his apparent censure had the effect of stiffening both her pride and her spine. She lifted her chin and moved toward him.

"I was unaware that you had company," Warrick said to her. In a tone that belied his polite words, he continued, "My apologies for calling at so early an hour, but your father said I might come today to ask him about Hua Te. I hoped to time my visit between the end of his observing period and the beginning of his morning's calculations."

"Then you are probably here at the correct hour,"

Sophia said. For a moment she wished she had put on her second-best gown of deep blue silk, a shade that her mother had once told her made her eyes look bluer. Then she realized it would have made no difference what she wore. With Genie in the house, no man would look at any other female. Warrick was staring at Genie again, and Robin, coming through the front door close on his friend's heels, was gaping at the beautiful creature in open-mouthed wonder.

Sophia might have been invisible for all the attention the two men gave her. For the first time in her life she acknowledged a tremor of feminine jealousy. It was not a comfortable feeling.

"Mistress Sophia," said Robin, never removing his eyes from Genie, who gazed back at him with a sweet smile, "will you introduce us?"

"This is my cousin, come to visit from Mosul," Sophia said, remembering the deception her father had suggested.

Robin grinned as if he were struck completely witless and took Genie's hand to bow over it. Warrick merely inclined his head and gave Genie another dark and frowning glance.

"May I see your father now?" Warrick said to Sophia.

"He did tell me to expect you today," Sophia said. She headed for the closed study door and knocked on it. There was no answer.

"Could he be asleep?" Warrick asked.

"If he is, we ought to leave him to his rest," Sophia said.

"I need to speak with him," Warrick insisted. "It is an important matter."

"Not as important as his rest!" Sophia snapped

56

in response to Warrick's imperious tone.

"Perhaps he is only involved in some complex mathematical calculation and did not hear you," Warrick said. "Knock again."

"I most certainly will not," Sophia told him. "You may not order me about, Warrick. If my father is resting, it is because he is weary. Come back later, when he is awake."

"You don't understand. This matter cannot wait." Reaching over Sophia's shoulder, Warrick rapped hard on the study door. When there was no response from within, he pounded again. And then again.

"I cannot allow this," Sophia said, thoroughly annoyed by Warrick's actions. "Obviously Father is asleep in the inner room and we must leave him alone."

"No," said Genie, crossing the hall to join them. "Something is wrong. I can sense it. Open the door at once, Warrick."

"What are you saying?" Sophia cried. "Has something happened to my father? Genie, you wicked creature, what have you done?" She was aware of the startled looks that Warrick and Robin exchanged upon hearing her sharp words, and she flinched at the disapproving gaze both men turned upon her for the way she spoke to her supposed cousin.

Sophia decided she did not care what they thought of her. It seemed to her that every person she knew was bent on making her life more difficult and complicated, or on circumventing her expressed preferences. She wished she could have just a short time with her father, alone and uninterrupted, during which he would pay full attention to her. She was in sore need of someone who would listen to her point of view about recent events and give credence to her fears and doubts.

"I have done nothing to harm Master John," Genie said to her. "I am incapable of harming him, as you very well know. Sophia, if only you could be honest with yourself, perhaps you would admit that your father's recent warnings are true. His time with you grows ever shorter. He accepts that fact, even if you will not."

Sophia's eyes filled with tears that blurred her sight of Genie's lovely features. She was terrified for her father's sake, and angry with Genie for speaking a truth she would rather have left unsaid.

She saw Warrick watching her with an expression that was definitely sympathetic. She did not want sympathy from him of all people, and she feared that if he offered any kindness, she would burst into tears and not be able to stop crying. She refused to weep where Warrick could see her. Instead she exerted her will to pull herself together so she could speak.

"Open the door," she said to Warrick. "Genie, wait here. Do not enter my father's room unless I call you."

"I hear and obey," Genie said.

Warrick looked at Genie with raised brows, as if he were intrigued by her words. Then he pulled open the door and went into the study with Sophia right behind him. The untidy room was empty. They found John in the bedchamber beyond the study. He was lying on his bed. His face was chalk white and his eyes were sunken, with deep shadows under them. His breathing was shallow and clearly painful.

"Father!" Sophia rushed to him to clasp his hand. "Why didn't you call me? Can you tell us what is wrong?"

"Warrick." John's gaze moved from his daughter to the man who stood at her shoulder. "If you have some of Hua Te's medicine, the herbal mixture he makes for me, it will do much to ease the pain in my chest."

"There should be a new batch of it in the still-room at our house. I know he was working on it before he disappeared. I should have brought it with me this morning. I'll get it now, and I'll be back directly." Warrick stopped at the doorway to look at John. "What news have you of Hua Te?"

"I will live for a while yet," John replied, "and I will speak more easily after I have taken the medicine."

"Of course. I won't be long." Warrick left.

"Oh, Father." Overcome with fear for him, Sophia knelt beside his bed, but when she would have put her head on his shoulder, he pushed her away with surprising strength.

"Stop your foolish crying and listen to me," John said. "Sophia, I require a promise from you."

"I will promise anything," Sophia said. She was desperate to please him and to alleviate the suffering that turned his skin an unnatural, clammy white. "Only tell me what you want of me." In her mind she prepared herself to agree to any medical treatment her father desired, however expensive or bizarre it might be. She was not expecting his next words.

"I want you to swear that you will obey the arrangements I am making for your future."

"My future?" Once again Sophia fought back

tears as it became plain to her that her father was fully aware of the severity of his ailment, and had gone beyond thought of treatment or recovery. Instead he was thinking of her, of what would happen to her after he was gone. If her promise would comfort him, then she would give it gladly.

"Oh, Father, of course I will follow whatever arrangements you make for me," Sophia said. "I swear it."

"Yes, I was sure you would," John said. "You always were tenderhearted to the point of stupidity. Now listen to me carefully, Sophia. As soon as I am buried, you must take action. Do not procrastinate, as I have too often done. Simply obey your promise to me."

"Father, I don't understand."

"You will soon enough," John said. "Perhaps, if I am stronger after I take the medicine Warrick is bringing, I will decide to tell you more. For now I want to rest."

"Yes, Father, I think you should."

Sophia was uncomfortable not knowing exactly what it was she had promised her father she would do. But she could see that he was growing weaker, so she did not press the issue. She found a pitcher of cool water in the study and fetched a linen towel from the kitchen. She dipped the towel into the water and used it to bathe her father's face. She was just finishing when Warrick reappeared with a small wooden casket tucked under his arm.

"As I expected, I found a fresh supply of your medicine in Hua Te's stillroom," he said to John. "He was planning to bring it to you when he joined you on your roof to look at the stars, but he never got here, and I was too disturbed to think of it."

"Mars," said John, his thoughts apparently wandering. "For the past month we have been observing the motions of Mars."

"Mistress Sophia, if I might have a clean cup, I will administer the medicine," Warrick said. Opening the wooden box he was carrying, he took out a vial.

"Are you sure you know the correct dose?" Sophia asked. When Warrick turned a cold eye on her, she said, "Hanna told me why you came here yesterday. She had the story from Daoud. By your own admission, you made a mistake with a magical spell. I am not convinced that you are well informed about medicine either. My father's life is at risk. I want to be certain you will not poison him by another mistake."

"Sophia, do not be any more foolish than you can help," John said, struggling to sit up. "I have taken this same medicine many times before today, and I know how much to swallow. I want you to leave me now. Go and walk in the garden with Genie and Robin. I need to be alone with Warrick."

"I don't want to leave you." Sophia slid an arm beneath his shoulders and helped him to sit while he swallowed the medicine.

"Go away," John said to her. "Stop peering at me as if you expect me to die at any moment, when you know very well this medicine will strengthen me for hours to come, just as it always does. Get out! Leave me in peace."

"I will call you at once if there is any change in your father's condition," Warrick said.

With that, Sophia had to be content. Her father was so eager to speak in private with Warrick that she assumed their discussion would be about Hua

Te. Therefore what they said did not concern her. With a glance at Warrick that plainly beseeched him to take great care with her parent, Sophia did as her father had ordered and left his room.

Noting the look that Sophia cast in his direction, Warrick felt a twinge of sympathy for her and a surge of exasperation toward John. He closed the door firmly after her before he expressed his emotions to John.

"Sir, you are all Sophia has in this world. Without you she will be completely alone. It is only natural for her to be anxious."

"Before I die I intend to see to it that Sophia's life is properly organized. In the meantime, she is little more than a daily irritation, like desert sand constantly rubbed against my skin. I would wash her away if I could."

"She is your daughter," Warrick protested.

"You needn't remind me," John said dryly. "Sophia is the reason why I wanted to talk to you in private. I originally planned to speak to Hua Te, but now that he is gone, I have chosen you."

"Chosen me?" Warrick said. "For what?"

"Find a place to sit and hear me out," John ordered. He waited while Warrick removed a scroll and a pair of measuring rods from a pile of cushions and sat down. "I will be as brief as I can. I don't want to waste any more of my limited time than is necessary on that tiresome girl."

Warrick opened his mouth to point out that Sophia was no longer a child; she was an intelligent woman. Furthermore, Warrick had not come to the house to discuss Sophia, but the whereabouts of Hua Te. But seeing how pale his host was, and how his hands trembled as they rested on the bedcovers, he thought better of the scathing comments he wanted to make and instead remarked, "I am listening, sir."

"Sophia has been a burden to me since the day she was born," John said. "Nay, even before she was born she created problems. Her mother was the only woman I ever cared for, the only female who could distract me from my work. Before Sophia was born my poor Helena suffered through a perilous few months. I will not bore you with the details of that period of our lives. I will say only that the end of Helena's pregnancy was truly terrifying. Her hands and feet swelled so badly that she could not walk or dress herself. She endured blinding headaches."

"There are treatments for those afflictions," Warrick said. "I learned some of them from Hua Te."

"Yes, yes." John made an impatient motion with one hand. "Tea and certain herbs and restriction of salt. The physicians I called in tried all of them. Nothing altered Helena's condition. While she was in labor with Sophia, she was stricken with violent convulsions and came close to dying. After two days of torment she produced, not the son I had hoped for, but a mewling, squalling female."

"It was not Sophia's fault she was a girl," Warrick said, "or that her mother was so ill."

"I know that," John snapped, his tone and manner remarkably similar to Sophia's own way of talking when she was irritated. "Still, the fact is that after Sophia was born, her mother was an invalid for the rest of her days. The physicians warned me that if Helena ever conceived another child, she would surely die. Thanks to Sophia, I was denied the embraces of the one woman I wanted."

"There are ways for a man to love a woman and yet avoid conception," Warrick said.

"Don't you understand?" John snarled at him. "Helena was too weak after her long ordeal, too fragile to endure my lustful advances. Nor was I willing to risk what could happen were my passion for her to overcome me. If I made a mistake, if I laid aside caution for an instant, Helena would die. I could not risk it. For the remaining thirteen years of her life, we lived together as brother and sister."

"Now I begin to understand why you have been so devoted to your work," Warrick said. "The years of Sophia's childhood were the period when you first became famous for your discoveries in the heavens, and for your brilliantly accurate astrological charts."

"It was also the time when the sultan first took notice of my work," John said. "His patronage has made me wealthy. It has also placed my estate in danger. The sultan is a peculiar man. At the same time that he lavished gifts and attention on me, he nourished a growing jealousy of me. Perhaps he fears my astrological predictions, or possibly he envies me my library, or my collection of astronomical instruments or my sky charts. In recent years he has summoned me to the palace less often, and I have recently heard rumors that he has hopes of obtaining all of my belongings once I am dead."

"What do you think will happen to Sophia then?" Warrick asked, guessing the answer, but wanting to hear what John would say.

"The simplest way for the sultan to lay claim to my treasures is by taking Sophia into his harem and declaring that my estate is her dowry. The possibility of such an arrangement brings me to the crux of my present problem. So far as I am concerned, the sultan is welcome to Sophia. I doubt he'll find any pleasure in her. My library and my instruments are far more valuable. Above all I do not want that Seljuk barbarian to get his hands on the greatest treasure in my possession."

Warrick was too experienced to be shocked by John's attitude toward Sophia. He had known a few other men who resented the existence of a child whose birth had killed a beloved wife, and a great many men held daughters in low regard. In John's case his wife's death had been a slow and lingering one, and John had had years in which to nourish his bitterness over what he had lost.

"If your wife was an invalid, and you were consumed by your studies," Warrick said, "who raised Sophia?"

"Hanna was already in our employ, and she had almost finished nursing Daoud, who is two years older than Sophia," John explained. "She became Sophia's nurse, and Helena's nurse, too. For reasons I do not comprehend, considering the devastation Sophia's birth wrought upon our lives, Helena was fond of her daughter. She occupied her days in teaching Sophia to read and write, to count, and the rudiments of astronomy. Thanks to my tutelage during her own youth, Helena was remarkably well educated for a woman. I suppose Sophia learned from Helena and Hanna together how to keep my household."

"It was very convenient for you," Warrick remarked. "Sophia has taken all of the domestic management on her own shoulders."

"I suppose so. I never bother with such trivial matters. I prefer to concern myself with more important occupations. Let me speak plainly," John said, as if he had not been employing the bluntest language during the last half hour. "I will live only a few days more. Do not protest, or try to tell me I will recover my health."

"I wasn't going to claim any such thing," Warrick said.

"I wouldn't believe you if you did," John told him, "and I would think far less of you if you attempted to convince me that you could cure my fatal illness. What I admired most in Hua Te was his unflinching honesty. He has told me that you are equally honest. Therefore, Warrick, you will have to undertake the duty I was planning to require of him."

"Duty," Warrick repeated. "Friends ask; they do not impose tasks on each other."

"You will understand when I have finished explaining," John said. "Before my Helena died, she begged me to promise that I would see to Sophia's welfare. She had a specific wish for her daughter's future."

"Your daughter, too," Warrick said, unable to conceal any longer his disapproval of John's lack of affection for Sophia.

"After your visit yesterday morning, it occurred to me that there is a way in which I can fulfill my promise to Helena, while at the same time keeping my library and equipment out of the sultan's hands," John said. "You are to be the instrument of my plan."

"I have no intention of being your instrument." Too disgusted with John to remain in his presence any longer, Warrick rose and headed for the door.

"You will change your mind when I tell you that

I have discovered what happened to Hua Te," John said.

Warrick stopped with his hand on the door latch and slowly turned to face John again.

"Yes," John said, a knowing smile curving his thin lips, "I thought that would catch your interest."

"Where is Hua Te?" Warrick demanded. "Is he alive and well? How can I reach him and bring him back?"

"You cannot expect me to reveal all that I know," John said, "until you have sworn on your word of honor to do what I require of you."

"Let me dispense with courtesy and be as blunt as you have been," Warrick said. "You are offering to provide the information I seek about Hua Te, in return for my promise to carry out your late wife's wishes in regard to Sophia."

"That is essentially correct," John said, "with one minor but very important addition."

"I believe there is an impolite name for what you are proposing."

"Call it what you will," John said with another thin-lipped smile. "I prefer to think of it as a bargain between two honest men."

"Honest you may be," Warrick said, "but you are definitely not likable."

"I care not a fig or a date whether you like me," John told him. "I care only that you do what I want."

"You are no true friend to Hua Te," Warrick said. "If you were, you would do everything in your power to see him safely returned, and you would demand no bargain of me."

"Again, I care not what you think about that, or about anything else," John said. "By the time you see Hua Te again, I will be dead, and what will your opinion of me matter then?"

Since entering John's private rooms, Warrick had learned more about Sophia than he had ever expected to know, and from the direction of John's conversation, he feared he was soon going to learn more. He did not see that he had any choice. Finding Hua Te was far more important to Warrick than having to deal with Sophia. He spared a single, sympathetic thought for her, before he spoke again to her coldhearted father.

"I have never known anyone like you," Warrick said.

"I am sure you have not. What is your answer, Warrick?"

"I want Hua Te back, well and alive, and you are my best hope of locating him," Warrick said.

"Your only hope," John corrected him.

"I have no choice but to agree to your proposal," Warrick said. "Tell me what you expect of me in return for the information you have about Hua Te."

"First you must swear to me that you will do what I want," John insisted. "Swear on your mother's grave."

"If you had known my mother," Warrick responded with a dark and dangerous laugh, "you'd know what a foolish requirement that is. I have said that I will do what you want. More than that I cannot and will not swear." He held John's eyes until the other man looked away.

"Very well. I will trust you," John said.

Chapter Six

John heaved himself up in bed until he was sitting against the pillows. Thanks to the action of the herbal medicine he had swallowed, his color was more natural and his voice was stronger. Nor did his hand shake when he lifted it to point to the opposite side of the room.

"Warrick, I want you to open the cabinet in the corner."

Warrick went to the cabinet and pulled the double doors wide, so John could see the clothing folded on the shelves inside. Every shelf was also jammed with books and scrolls, with piles of parchment or papers inscribed with numbers and sketches of the heavens.

"Take out the clothing on the third shelf," John directed. "The shelf is removable. Take it out, too."

"All right." Warrick did as he was told. "There is

a long metal piece behind the shelf," he said as he slid the shelf off its supports.

"Press on the metal," John ordered. Warrick did so, and one of the boards in the back of the cabinet slid down to reveal a niche. In the niche sat several leather bags crammed full of coins.

"Leave the coins alone," John said. "It's the bundle wrapped in red silk that I want. Be careful; don't drop it."

The bundle, tucked behind the leather bags so it was not obvious immediately upon opening the niche, proved to be irregular in shape and as high as Warrick's hand was long. It was heavy when Warrick picked it up, and he could tell there were two pieces inside the silk.

"Bring it to me, Warrick." John took the object, cradling it against his thin chest as if it were a baby he held. "This is what the sultan will want most after I am dead. He is not certain I have it; he only suspects I do. I know him well enough to be convinced that he will order his men to search for it, and he may seize the rest of my possessions in hope of finding it hidden among them."

"What is inside that silk?" Warrick asked, his curiosity aroused.

"A crystal ball."

"There must be hundreds of crystal balls in Baghdad," Warrick said, "including one in your own study. I am sure the sultan has a room full of them. Why should he want this one?"

"This one is perfect," John said. He unwrapped the object slowly, his hands caressing the silk. When he held the globe on his fingertips, lifting it up to the light so Warrick could see it, the expression on his face was that of a man gazing upon his beloved.

"Most crystals have inclusions, or other imperfections," John said. "This is the only crystal ball I have ever seen that does not. It is so clear, so pure, that when I look into it, the crystal itself is almost invisible. And, in addition, there is the remarkable stand." He fumbled in the folds of silk and drew forth an exquisitely worked circle of gold that was set with sapphires, emeralds, and turquoises. The workmanship and the priceless jewels of blue and green paled into insignificance when John fitted the crystal ball into its three-legged stand and the crystal fairly shone with limpid purity.

"This is what you are to keep safe from the sultan's covetous grasp, what you are to give to Hua Te when next you meet him," John said. "I want the crystal carried to Cathay, so the sultan will never find it.

"My library and my instruments, my notebooks, and the astronomical treatise I now know I will never complete, I also leave to your care," John continued, his eyes still on the crystal ball. "If you must use the rest of my belongings as a diversion to keep this supreme treasure safe, then do so. This beautiful, irreplaceable jewel of all jewels, I entrust to you, Warrick, with the admonition that, no matter what happens to the rest of my estate, this must be preserved at all costs."

Warrick stared at the artifact that John held so lovingly, and then he looked at John's enraptured face, and he felt like strangling the man. How could John care more about a cold piece of crystal than he did about his own daughter? Or about a dear friend of many years?

"Tell me about Hua Te and where I am to find him," Warrick demanded. No longer caring whether or not he was unfeeling toward a dying man, he added, "Then tell me what I am to do with Sophia once you are dead. I warn you, John, I am growing impatient and you, by your own admission, do not have much time left."

"As to exactly where Hua Te is, of that I am not certain," John said. "Still, I can show him to you, as I saw him yesterday after you left me."

"You had information about Hua Te yesterday, and you did not send word to me?" Warrick exclaimed.

"I thought it best not to disclose what I had seen until after I considered all aspects of my plan," John answered.

"I was worried and bedeviled by guilt and you were well aware of it. Have you no heart?"

"In your own way, you are every bit as over-emotional as Sophia," John said.

"I care about my friends. It is plain to me that you do not."

"Look into the crystal ball." John held it out toward Warrick, while still keeping it balanced on his fingertips. "Look deep into it at the same time that I do. Clear your mind of all distractions and direct your thoughts to Hua Te."

Warrick did not waste time telling John that he knew how to use a crystal ball, or that he held serious doubts whether the visions conjured in crystal were accurate ones. It was always possible that the user could project his own hopes or fears into the crystal. Still, the crystal ball John was holding was so exceptionally clear that, as he had remarked, it approached invisibility. Perhaps, Warrick thought, he could learn something from it. He stared into its perfect depths and brought into his mind the image of Hua Te, as he had last seen his friend.

A faint trace of cloudiness appeared at the center of the crystal ball. Slowly the cloudiness spread outward and thinned, until Warrick perceived a scene. He saw a green lawn sloping down to a white stone seawall. Beyond the wall deep blue water sparkled in sunlight. Hua Te, clad in a robe Warrick had never seen before, sat on the wall with a woman—a remarkably lovely woman, whose red-gold hair was strewn with tiny blue flowers to match the blue of the sheer gown that was draped from twin brooches at her shoulders. The woman's arms and her throat were bare.

With the single exception of Hua Te's figure, nothing in the landscape was familiar to Warrick. In fact he had the impression that everything he saw in the vision was completely alien. Slowly the vision faded.

"Was that Cathay I saw?" Warrick asked when the crystal ball was completely clear once more.

"I do not know," John said. "Perhaps it was. Your duty will be to take the crystal ball to Hua Te, wherever he is, for the vision has shown us that he is alive."

"But where is he?" Warrick asked. He raised a hand to rub his forehead, and then realized that his head was not aching the way it usually did after working magic. Of course not. It was John who had used magic, and by the look of him, it was John who was suffering for it. The hand that held the crystal ball was shaking so badly that Warrick feared John would drop it.

"I told you, I do not know." John responded to Warrick's question in a weak voice, but with no faltering in his determination to hold Warrick to his word. "You will have to search for Hua Te—*after* you have fulfilled your sworn obligation to me, and to Sophia's future. Cease your continual questioning and listen to me, for I will not explain my wishes a second time."

Warrick made himself stay quiet while John described exactly what he wanted Warrick to do. When he was finished it was plain to Warrick that the older man had depleted what little strength he had left. Still, Warrick felt compelled to ask again about Hua Te.

"I have shown you what I could," John responded irritably. "You will have to find your own answers. Now let me rest."

Having left Warrick and her father to their private conversation, Sophia found Genie and Robin in the garden, where they were sitting in the shade on a stone bench. Not only were they talking together, they were laughing as if they had no cares and as if John of Cornwall were not desperately ill.

Observing the two of them, Sophia was stricken by a terrible longing for kindly affection, for someone to care about her and her feelings, someone to talk and laugh with her in a similar, easy manner. The pain of knowing she would never enjoy such a simple pleasure turned her face to stone and made her glare at the pair on the bench. Seeing her approach them, they fell silent.

Robin rose politely as she drew near. "I am sorry about your father's illness," he said. "I don't know him as well as Warrick does, but I admire him enormously. He is a great scholar."

"Thank you, Robin."

"Perhaps," said Genie, "if Master John were not so intent upon scholarly pursuits, if he had devoted a bit more time to his daughter, Sophia would not find herself desolate when this final illness is over."

"How dare you?" Sophia exclaimed, her loneliness and her fear for her father erupting into furious words. "Miserable, wretched creature, never speak that way again! You will show proper respect to my father. Do you understand?"

"Mistress Sophia, you ought not to speak so harshly to your cousin," Robin admonished.

"This creature is not—" Sophia stopped just in time. And oddly it was Genie, whom Sophia considered to be an unfeeling, inhuman creation, who saved her from embarrassment in front of a young man she scarcely knew.

"Sophia is understandably upset," Genie said to Robin, "and it is I who just spoke in an unkind way, because I am concerned for Sophia's well-being."

"You needn't be concerned for me," Sophia snapped at her. "No matter what you or my father may think, I do not require your help, Genie."

"No, you don't," Genie said. "But without me you will continue as you have been doing, living a restricted and lonely life. Is that truly what you want?"

"Indeed it is," Sophia said. After a few moments of tense silence she added, "I must ask you to excuse me, Robin. There are household chores to be done." She left the garden as quickly as she could without actually running away.

Sophia always found refuge from the worry and

loneliness that too often beset her by immersing herself in household tasks. On this day, of all days, she needed the solace afforded by her usual routines. She found Hanna in the hall, just beginning the day's work. As soon as she spotted Sophia, the old woman began to recite a long list of purchases that needed to be made at the marketplace.

"Hanna, could you go to the market this morning?" Sophia asked. "I would rather not leave the house when Father is so ill."

"What, with my old knees aching the way they are?" Hanna complained. "I doubt if I can walk as far as the next house, much less to the market and back."

"Let me go, Sophia." Genie had followed her into the house and had overheard the conversation with Hanna.

"No!" Sophia exclaimed. Seeing Robin emerge from the garden she added in a more pleasant tone, "Genie, you don't know your way around Baghdad. You will get lost."

"Robin can go with me, to act as my guide and to carry the purchases," Genie said with a gentle smile. "Please let me do this one small thing for you, Sophia. You take too much upon your shoulders, and I don't want to be a burden to you. I did not come here for you to treat me like a favored guest."

Sophia stared at her, disbelief in Genie's good intentions warring with her desire to be immediately available should her father want to speak with her again. Concern for her father won over her distrust of Genie.

"Very well," Sophia said, "if you are sure you don't mind."

"I am happy to do it." A mischievous twinkle appeared in Genie's eyes. "Hanna, tell me what you want me to buy. I am certain I will enjoy bargaining with the merchants. Sophia, may I borrow your veil?"

"Yes, of course." Sophia watched as Genie cloaked her glowing loveliness in the dark folds of cloth. Then, with a few coins tucked into a pocket in the ankle-length veil and with the basket Hanna gave her slung over one arm, Genie left the house with Robin in attendance.

Hanna returned to the kitchen, grumbling about the bread she was in the process of making.

The house fell silent. Sophia closed her eyes and took a long breath, relieved to know Genie would be gone for some time. Then she experienced a strange sensation of loss. She told herself it was ridiculous; she could not miss a creature she did not want in her house and whom she had known for less than a day.

"Sophia."

She whirled at the sound of Warrick's deep voice. In the poorly lit hall his face was in shadow, making him appear darker and more mysterious than she had ever seen him before. She sensed an odd menace in him, as if he were straining to keep some strong negative emotion in check.

"My father?" Sophia's voice faltered despite her attempt to keep it steady.

"We talked for some time and now he is sleeping."

"I hope you did not overtire him." Why did she always sound like a shrew when she spoke to Warrick? She did not mean it so, and especially not after he had done everything that Hua Te himself might have done for her father. Above all she did not want to anger him, did not want to unleash the tension she perceived in him.

"In fact, I think he did talk for too long," Warrick said, seemingly unoffended by the way she snapped at him, "but he made some interesting suggestions about Hua Te. He also had a few things to say that he insisted were vitally important to your future."

"My future has nothing to do with you," Sophia said.

"You must be aware that John's condition has been worsening for some time," Warrick said. "Hua Te was so concerned about him that he created two new medicines in the hope of alleviating John's pain."

"Well, I do trust the untried medicine you gave him has caused no harm." Horrified at her own sharp words, Sophia bit down on her lower lip and turned away so she would not have to see Warrick's angry reaction.

"These remarks about my incompetence are merely your fears for your father speaking," Warrick said in a milder tone than Sophia expected to hear from him. "I have done all that I can for John, and I think he is at peace after our conversation. He is sleeping now."

"I am not afraid," Sophia said, lifting her chin. "However I do thank you for bringing his medicine. I will sit with him now." She went to the study door, but stopped when she realized that Warrick had stepped to her side.

"You need not stay," she said, regarding him coldly. "I am sure you have other things to do."

"I will not leave you, Sophia." Warrick went into John's bedroom with her.

John appeared pathetically frail, his hands bony

on the coverlet, his face drawn. His breathing was slow, with long pauses between each breath. Sophia sat on a stool that Warrick placed for her beside the bed and took her father's hand in hers. He gave no sign that he knew she was there.

Warrick sat down on a pile of cushions, leaned his head back against the wall, and closed his eyes. He took a few long, slow breaths and as he did, the menace and the tension in him seemed to drain away. He said nothing to Sophia, but his presence was comforting to her. She had not expected that. She had thought she would be irritated to have him there, when his medicines were doing so little to improve her father's condition.

She began to wonder if she had only imagined the dark emotion in Warrick. Perhaps her own fears had made her see something in him that was not really there.

Sophia did not know how long she sat with her father until he stirred. As soon as he opened his eyes Warrick was at the bedside, ready with the next dose of medicine. Sophia lifted her father so he could swallow more easily. When he had taken the medicine he lay back against the pillows, his eyes closed again, as if accepting the treatment required great effort on his part.

"Warrick, I am capable of giving him his doses at the correct time," Sophia said.

"I know you are," he replied. "You are almost too capable. But you should not be alone."

"I am used to being alone."

"I know." His hand rested on her shoulder and she did not protest the touch.

"This is what Hua Te would have done," she said. "He would have stayed for as long as my father needed him." At once she regretted her thoughtless words, for at the mention of Hua Te, she felt the swift return of Warrick's tension. He withdrew his hand from her shoulder and went to sit against the wall again.

The day wore slowly on. John wakened briefly, then slept, wakened, and slept again, and periodically Warrick administered the medicine. When he was awake John did not speak, and Sophia assumed he was conserving his strength.

Sophia heard Genie's voice coming from the direction of the hall, and she heard Hanna's routine complaints in response. Robin appeared, to announce that he and Genie had completed their errands and to suggest that he stay with John so Sophia and Warrick could leave the sickroom long enough to eat. Both refused his offer.

A short time later Hanna brought them a tray of fruit and juices, saying Genie had told her to do so. When neither Sophia nor Warrick showed any interest in the refreshments, Hanna left, grumbling as she went that no one appreciated her culinary skills or the effort she had put into meals that were going uneaten. At last, as the muezzin sounded, calling the faithful to their sunset prayers, Sophia swayed on her stool, her head drooping.

Immediately Warrick was at her side. He lifted her in his arms and, ignoring her feeble protests, carried her out of John's rooms, across the hall, and up the stairs. To her chagrin, Sophia found herself relaxing into his strength and almost enjoying the sensation of being held and cared for. She could not recall the last time anyone had embraced her.

There were only three rooms on the second level of the house. Warrick made a quick survey and chose the one most likely to be Sophia's bedchamber. He kicked the door open and carried her inside. From the room's sparse furnishings and ascetic neatness, he knew he had chosen correctly.

"Please," Sophia said with her head upon his shoulder, "I cannot leave my father."

"You will be no use at all to him if you are ill, too," Warrick said. "I promise that either Robin or I will be with him all night long. If you sleep now, then you will be able to sit with him in the morning, while I return to my own house to prepare more of his medicine. Do not argue with me, Sophia. I can see how weary you are."

"Very well," she agreed. "I will rest, but only for a short time."

Warrick laid her gently on the bed and slipped off her shoes. Sophia's feet were small and narrow. Her stockings were made of cheap material and one was mended at the toe.

It seemed to Warrick typical of John that he would own a rare and perfect crystal ball with a magnificent, jewel-encrusted stand, that he would hoard bags of coins in a secret niche in his room, at the same time that he kept his only child so short of money that she could not even buy decent stockings for herself. But then John had plainly stated that he valued the crystal ball and his books and instruments far more than Sophia. Warrick touched her foot, running a finger along the dainty bones. His throat tightened with an emotion he did not care to examine too closely.

With a soft murmur Sophia turned on her side, tucked one hand beneath her chin, and closed her eyes. Noting the shadows on her lids and the dark rings beneath her eyes, Warrick had no doubt that she would sleep the night through.

He found a shawl neatly folded on top of the plain clothing chest that sat beside the bed and used it to cover Sophia. As he tucked the shawl around her shoulders, he allowed his hand to brush against her thick black curls. Her hair was crisp beneath his fingers, crackling with a life and energy that the fully awake Sophia did not often display. Sophia when wide-awake was almost always thin-lipped with tight self-control, entirely cold, sometimes deliberately nasty.

At the moment, curled up as she was, she looked soft and innocent as a child. Seeing her like that he found it hard to believe how disagreeable she could be when she was awake. She was a small woman and, except for her startlingly blue eyes, not especially pretty. Her features were too strong for mere prettiness, with her firm, square chin and her high-bridged nose that, like her curling hair, hinted at Greek ancestry. And her clothing was always dark and unattractive.

Even so, Sophia was the most disturbing woman Warrick had ever known. Perhaps it was her intelligence that caught his interest, for John's daughter was better educated than most women. Or possibly it was her total lack of interest in him that intrigued him. Warrick was not accustomed to being alternately ignored and insulted by any woman.

He tugged the shawl a little higher around Sophia's shoulders and let his fingers make brief contact with her hair again before he left her and returned to her dying father.

Chapter Seven

"Ah, Master Warrick, I am glad to see you return," Daoud exclaimed, opening the door of Hua Te's house just wide enough to let Warrick and Robin enter. "What news have you of Master John's health this morning?"

"Nothing good, I'm afraid," Warrick responded. Seeing how nervous the servant looked, he asked, "What is wrong?"

"A messenger of the sultan has been here," Daoud said. "He desired to speak with Hua Te. I told him my master was away from home. I think he believed me, but he will surely return later. What shall I tell him?"

"That Hua Te is still away and you don't know where he is," Warrick responded. "Did the messenger happen to mention what the sultan wanted from Hua Te?"

"No, Master Warrick, but his reticence with a

mere servant means nothing. He could have been sent with a request for an urgent medical consultation, or merely with an invitation to dine with the sultan."

"Well, there is nothing that Robin or I can do for the sultan and I doubt if he wants to see either of us in Hua Te's place," Warrick said. "Daoud, I would like a bath. Then I am going to compound a fresh batch of medicine for John."

"I will order the kitchen boy to prepare hot water. In the meantime you will want to break your night's fast."

Daoud paused, looking a bit fearful before he said, "Please, Master Warrick, provide me with a very good reason for Hua Te's absence that I can offer the sultan's man when next he comes here."

"I will think of something," Warrick promised. "Come to my room with the boy who brings the bathwater. I want to talk to you in private and that will be a good time for it. There are some important preparations that you are to begin making at the order of Master John."

"As you wish." Daoud left to see to the bathwater and the morning meal.

An hour later Daoud had been dispatched with a list of errands and arrangements to see to and Warrick and Robin, bathed and clad in cool caftans, sat in a shadowy inner room of the house eating fruit and flat Arab bread and drinking strong coffee.

"I ought to go to the stillroom," Warrick said. "It requires some time to make the medicine John needs." But he did not move from the divan where he sat. Suddenly he felt too fatigued to rise, too laden with responsibilities that he wished had not been heaped upon him.

If he was going to do his best work in the still-room, it was imperative that he clear his mind of all distractions so he could concentrate on preparing, in precisely correct combinations and proportions, the herbal medicines that would alleviate John's persistent pain and his difficulty in breathing. Instead Warrick's thoughts were crowded with the details of his previous day's conversation with the sick man, with the memory of the vision he had seen in the crystal ball, and with a belated realization of exactly how his bargain with John was going to alter his life.

And what that bargain would mean to Sophia. Into Warrick's mind flashed the image of Sophia lying asleep on her bed, hand beneath her chin, with all of her irritating sharpness of word and manner banished by sheer weariness. He remembered the sweet weight of her in his arms as he carried her up the stairs, he felt the crisp texture of her thick, curling hair against his palm, and the energy and life in it. He saw again her slender foot in its darned stocking, and felt a pang at his heart. For a fleeting instant he allowed himself to consider what Sophia would be like if she ever gave herself up to passion. He wondered if it was possible for desire and unstinting affection to soften her sharp-edged character. And in that wondering, he understood that he wanted her.

He put the thought away as unworthy. He had duties to fulfill, responsibilities to discharge. First among those duties was the overriding question of how to locate Hua Te. When Robin spoke, his words echoed one of Warrick's most serious concerns.

"You know as well as I do," Robin said, "that if

the sultan's messenger does not speak with Hua Te within a day or two, the authorities will begin to ask where he is. Hua Te is too well known in Baghdad for his absence to go unnoticed."

"I would give my very soul if he were here now," Warrick said. "I am in sore need of his advice, and not just about John's illness. We must get Hua Te back! Unfortunately I don't know how to do that."

"Did John have any thoughts about where he might be?" Robin asked.

"He is convinced that Hua Te is alive and that I was not at fault in Hua Te's disappearance. I found the proof John offered encouraging. Perhaps that is because I am so eager to believe him," Warrick answered. "John won't live much longer, Robin. The medicine I give him has little effect on his sickness. It only takes away the pain so that he is comfortable and able to sleep. When John dies I will be forced to undertake obligations I wish I had not felt I must accept," he ended on an unhappy sigh.

"If you want my advice, it's this," Robin said. "Since it appears unlikely that we will find Hua Te here in Baghdad, I think we ought to plan on leaving the city as soon as possible, preferably before the sultan decides that you and I ought to be taken in for questioning."

Warrick nodded his agreement. The Seljuks controlled a vast area ranging from the shores of the Mediterranean to the Indus River in the east, and from the Arabian Sea northward, beyond the high mountain passes and the stony deserts to the open steppes, where untamed tribesmen roamed on horseback. All of the varied races and religions of people who lived under Seljuk rule were wary of the army on which the sultan's power was based.

In every city the Seljuks had conquered, a garrison of the army known as the *shinha* served as the local police force. The *shinha* in Baghdad was particularly feared. It had a reputation for unflinching brutality. There were rumors that the present sultan, who was of a weaker character than previous Seljuk rulers, was little more than a puppet of the *shinha* commanders.

"With the *shinha*," Robin went on, "questioning is a euphemism for torture. Since we don't really know anything of Hua Te's whereabouts, we won't be able to provide the *shinha* with the information they will want, so they will continue to torture us until we die protesting our ignorance. From what I've heard of them, they are experts at their business. It will take a long, painful time for us to die. I would prefer to avoid that kind of unpleasantness if I possibly can.

"On the other hand," Robin continued when Warrick still remained silent, "if we leave Baghdad immediately, say within the next day, Hua Te's disappearance may not arouse suspicion. If we tell Daoud exactly how to answer the sultan's messenger, it may be assumed that the three of us have gone on a journey together. It is what we had planned to do within a month or so anyway, and quite a few of Hua Te's friends know of his intention to see Cathay again before he dies.

"It is also possible that we could discover in Cathay some clue that will enable us to find him," Robin said. "My suggestion is that we board one of the boats tied up at the docks down on the Tigris, and sail to Cathay—or to the Land of Hind, if there are no boats bound directly for Cathay. We can always take passage on another ship once we are safely in Bombay."

"That would be the sensible thing to do," Warrick said. "I am sure Hua Te would agree with your reasoning. However I cannot go. I must remain in Baghdad as long as John of Cornwall lives. I cannot leave a sick man who depends on me for the medicine that gives him comfort in his last days. And when John is dead there is a venture I have promised to undertake for him, for who can deny the request of a dying man?"

"In that case," Robin said with a wide grin, "I will stay in Baghdad, too. I wouldn't want to miss any excitement."

"You may change your mind after you hear about the bargain I have made with John," Warrick said, dragging himself to his feet. "Come with me to the stillroom while I prepare his medicine. It's only fair for you to know all the details of my conversation with him before you make your final decision."

That afternoon the *shamal* began to blow. The wind from the northwest brought no relief from the heat; rather, the *shamal* stirred up a sandstorm that bathed Baghdad in a dusty mist. At the house belonging to John of Cornwall the outer shutters and all of the doors were closed against the sand, but still it sifted through cracks and crevices until the floors and tables were gritty with it. The interior of the house was dark, lit only by oil lamps, and it was silent except for the howl of the wind and the sound of sand particles scouring the exterior walls. The heat was close to intolerable. Sophia remained in her father's room, wiping his face, his arms and hands, and even his chest with water in an attempt to cool him. But the water was tepid and she feared it did little good.

"This much at least I can do for you, and for him," Genie said, coming into the room with a large pitcher and a clean basin in her arms. These she set on the table near John's bed.

There were beads of moisture on the surface of the earthenware pitcher. When Sophia poured water from it into the basin, and dipped into the basin the cloth she had been using, she exclaimed in surprise.

"Genie, where did you find ice-cold water?"

"I made it," Genie answered. "That is, I cannot make water, but if I have water at hand, I can change the temperature of it. I thought Master John would find the cold refreshing."

"I am sure he will." Sophia looked hard at Genie, attempting to discern whether there was some trickery in the jinni's action. Seeing nothing except concern for John in Genie's beautiful face, Sophia gave voice to a sentiment that was difficult for her to acknowledge. "I thank you for your thoughtful kindness, Genie."

Having said as much, Sophia then could not bring herself to order Genie to leave her father alone when the creature bent forward and placed her dainty hand on John's forehead.

"What are you doing?" Sophia asked.

"I am not sure. Is he feverish? His flesh does not seem overwarm to me." Genie removed her hand. "If I could take away his pain I would. Unfortunately I am not versed in healing."

At any other time Sophia would have demanded in an angry way to know what Genie *could* do, since over the last two days she had heard mostly a listing of all the things Genie could not do. But she thought she saw genuine sorrow in Genie's eyes, and she did appreciate Genie's attempt to help by supplying the cold water, so she spoke more gently than she usually did.

"I fear there is nothing anyone can do for my father. If Hua Te were here, perhaps Father would get well again. I am not convinced that Warrick knows everything that ought to be done. I wanted to send for the sultan's physician, but Father absolutely forbade me. He said he did not want the sultan to know that Hua Te is not available, nor did he want the sultan to take an interest in me."

"Your father is a wise man. We ought to accept his decision," Genie said. "Once, in another Calling, when I assumed a different shape, I was a servant in a harem. I do not think you would be happy to be immured in such a place, either as a concubine or as a servant. I know I would prefer never again to live in any harem."

Sophia thought Genie's words over, and shivered. Like Genie, she had no desire to become a member of a harem, in any capacity. From time to time Hanna had told her stories of girls whom the sultan had taken into his household, supposedly under his protection, who were never seen or heard of again. Often the family property of those girls also disappeared, vanishing into the governmental coffers.

Sophia could not imagine that any man would find her attractive enough, or young enough, to arouse lust, but her father did own several houses, and he had valuable personal property in the form of books, scrolls, and his astronomical instruments. It was possible that the sultan would consider it well worth his time to take an interest in John's daughter once she became an orphan.

As for the usual duties of the female inhabitants of a harem, Sophia knew what happened between men and women. Her mother had explained about such things when Sophia had first begun to blossom into a woman. But then her mother had died, leaving Sophia to complete her maturing with only the advice of Hanna, for the subject was not one Sophia cared to raise with her abstracted father. Nor had she ever had a female friend of an age similar to hers, with whom she could exchange confidences. Not until the arrival of Genie.

"Genie, how many Callings have you had?" Sophia asked.

"Not many. As the jinn reckon time, I am still quite young," Genie answered.

"Were you ever married?" Sophia asked, curiosity overcoming good manners.

"Never," Genie said very firmly. "The jinn do not marry, and it is dangerous for someone like me to love a human in that way."

John moved restlessly and groaned, and Sophia let the subject drop. She was a little shocked at herself for asking intimate questions of Genie while her father lay so ill in the same room. Her conversation was unseemly, to say the least.

Dismissing all improper thoughts from her mind, Sophia again dipped the cloth she was holding into the cold water Genie had brought and used it to wipe John's face. He gave no indication that he was aware of what she was doing, and he did not move or open his eyes until Warrick returned with a new supply of medicine. At the sound of Warrick's voice John opened his eyes. He was unable to sit up without assistance, but his mind was clear.

"It is scarcely worth your time to make more of this each day," John said to Warrick as Sophia lifted him so he could swallow from the cup the younger man was holding out to him. "We both know it will not cure me."

"Father, do not say so," Sophia cried.

"Whatever else the medicine does or does not do for you, John," Warrick said in a carefully neutral voice, "it will ease your discomfort. Seeing that your pain is gone will give Sophia comfort, too. You ought to think about that."

"I suppose you are right," John said reluctantly. He took the cup of medicine in shaking fingers, drank from it slowly, and then handed the cup back to Warrick.

Sophia helped her father to resettle himself against the pillows. When she touched his hand it was icy cold. She waited until his eyes were closed before she turned away to wipe the tears off her cheeks.

"Sophia, go and rest now," Warrick said. One of his hands brushed across her shoulders in a gesture of reassurance that turned into a gentle push toward the door. "I will stay with your father again this evening, and Robin will come later for the remainder of the night."

"Come with me, Sophia," Genie said, adding her voice to Warrick's urging. "I will see that you have a cool bath and something to eat before you sleep." She put her arm around Sophia's waist to draw her out of the room. Sophia stopped at the doorway to look at the man who was seated on the stool she had vacated.

"Warrick, you have been kind to my father, and

to me," she said. "I am sorry if I misjudged you at first."

Warrick smiled at her and might have spoken, but John murmured something and Warrick bent low to hear him. Sophia was about to return to the room, not wanting to miss any word her father said, but Genie tugged at her waist and, being too tired to resist the pressure, Sophia allowed herself to be removed from the sickroom.

At midnight the *shamal* stopped blowing for a time. In the sudden silence John's breath was short and tortured. Warrick raised his head to look at his patient. John's eyes were open and in their blue depths lay the knowledge of his imminent death.

"Warrick," he whispered to the younger man, "remember your solemn oath. Do not fail me."

"You have my word," Warrick said, laying his hand over John's and pressing the cold flesh firmly. "I have given it to you before, and I give it again now. All that you have demanded of me, I will do."

"You will see Hua Te again in this life," John said. "I know it."

He lay quietly for a time and Warrick began to think he had fallen asleep, until suddenly John sat up in bed. An expression of surpassing happiness appeared on his pale face and his eyes sparkled as they must have done long ago, when he was young, before grief and the joyless passing of years had embittered him.

"Helena," he cried, holding out his arms. "My love! Here I am."

John remained as he was for a moment or two, with his arms outstretched and a happy smile on his face. When his arms dropped Warrick understood that the breath of life was gone from him. He gently laid John down on the bed, folded his hands across his chest, and closed John's sightless eyes.

He turned to leave the room, to wake Sophia and tell her what had happened, only to discover that she was standing by the door. Her eyes were huge and her face was almost as pale as her father's, but she seemed calm enough. Warrick could only admire her self-control on this occasion, for he had a fair idea of what her emotions must be upon losing the father around whom she had built her life.

"He spoke to my mother," she said, advancing into the room with her gaze fixed on her father's face. "Do you believe she was there to greet him when he left this life?" She brushed her fingertips along John's cheek and bent to kiss his cold brow.

"I hope she was," Warrick said.

Sophia turned away from the bed, trembling and blinded by tears she no longer felt obliged to conceal. She did not know what to do next. She felt like a lost child, wandering in an unknown land. Then Warrick opened his arms to her, and she walked into his embrace and permitted him to hold her while she wept against his chest. She did not consider in those first moments that he was a man she sometimes feared and did not particularly like. She knew only that he offered the comfort she so sorely needed, and that she was glad to have him there.

Warrick tightened his arms, feeling how small Sophia was, how delicately formed in spite of her lushly rounded figure. He found her disturbing in ways he would prefer not to think about, certainly not at the moment, when she was at her most vulnerable. Vulnerable or not, he knew she was a strong woman at heart, undoubtedly strong enough to fight him at every step along their future path.

In the next half hour, while he held Sophia and let her weep as much as she wanted, Warrick began to suspect that thinking about Sophia's safety and welfare would require his constant attention and all of his wits and humor and courage, until he had completed his unwelcome assignment. With Sophia nestled in his arms, Warrick could not decide whether to bless or to curse John of Cornwall for the cold-blooded bargain he had made.

Sophia felt as if she were encased in the sand that had blanketed the city for the past day and a half. The world around her seemed far away. If anyone were to touch her, she was sure she would shatter, would disintegrate into millions of grains of sand, to be swept away by Hanna's coarse broom, never to be seen again.

Her father's funeral had been held on the afternoon of the day of his death. In the midsummer heat burials were often performed swiftly. Sophia understood why it was necessary, but with her emotions raw the haste seemed cruel and undignified. The return of the *shamal*, which rose again during the midday heat, only increased the speed with which the funeral was conducted. Cloaked in her protective veil Sophia stood beside Warrick in the blowing, swirling sand while her father was interred beside her mother in the small Christian cemetery just outside the walls of Baghdad.

Now it was late evening and the prayers and condolences were over. The scholars who were her father's colleagues, and the nobleman who was the sultan's representative at the funeral, were finally departing, leaving the house strangely quiet after a day of continual conversation. Even the *shamal* blew less fiercely.

Sophia had not been so distracted by grief that she failed to notice how Warrick and Robin made certain that everyone attending the funeral understood that the two men were staying at John's house for an indefinite period of time. Sophia knew it was done for her protection; still she was annoyed that she had not been consulted before the decision was made and announced. If either man had bothered to ask her, she would have said that after the stress of the last few days, all she wanted was for everyone to go away and leave her to mourn for her father in peace. She did not think she could bear for much longer the presence of anyone except familiar, complaining Hanna.

And, perhaps, the presence of Genie, who had been all that one could expect of a close and loving relative. When Hanna, upon learning of her master's death, had dissolved into loud wails of sorrow and had begun tearing at her clothes in accordance with ancient custom, it was Genie who had seen to the many details of the funeral feast, which had to be prepared within a matter of a few hours. It was Genie who had produced proper mourning clothes for herself, Sophia, and Hanna. Genie was the only person who, in that entire sad day, had not once said a single word or taken any action that in any way further distressed Sophia.

"Well, that's the last of them." Genie closed the door on the departing mourners. "They certainly ate enough. But you, Sophia, have eaten nothing at all. I will prepare a tray and take it to your bedroom, so you can eat there and then go right to sleep. Some of the lamb kabobs and bread, then fruit and juice, I think. Or would you rather just have a bowl of hot lentil soup?" She broke off when Warrick stepped out of John's study.

"Will you come in here, please?" Warrick asked them. "I have something to say to both of you. I know you are tired, Sophia, but this cannot wait. It has to do with your father's last wishes, and with the requests he made of me."

That intriguing statement was enough to make Sophia forget her weariness and to propel her across the hall and into the study with no argument.

"I want to see you, too, Genie," Warrick said when she hung back. "You have an important part in the plans we must make."

John's study was slightly less cluttered without its inhabitant of many years. Sophia saw that books formerly left open had been closed and shelved, and that all of the scrolls were rolled up and put away. As a result, there was space on the divan where Sophia and Genie could sit, and John's desk was relatively bare. Even the crystal ball that he kept in the study was gone. Sophia could not see it anywhere. Perhaps Warrick had moved it to her father's bedchamber.

Sophia knew she should have been grateful that some of the work of sorting through John's possessions had already been done, but she was far from appreciative of Warrick's industry. She should have been the one to put away her father's belongings and to decide what ought to be done with them. She tightened her lips and bit her tongue on angry words, and waited to hear what Warrick had to say.

"I understand from your father that he extracted a solemn promise from you, that you would obey the arrangements he made for your future," Warrick began, looking at Sophia.

"So he did, but he never revealed to me what those arrangements entailed," Sophia said. "Whatever he was planning for me, I fear he did not have time before he died to make the provisions he intended." She was about to say that it did not matter, that she was perfectly content to continue to live in the same house, with Hanna as her only servant and Genie for a companion, since she had also agreed to her father's insistence that she accept Genie. Before she could say anything, Warrick spoke again.

"John told me what he wanted you to do," Warrick said. "And he made me swear to see to it that his plan would be carried through to its completion."

"You?" Sophia gasped. "What plan? Why would Father tell you about his intentions for me?"

"Actually, John at first wanted Hua Te to take charge of you," Warrick said. "After Hua Te disappeared and your father's illness worsened, he turned to me. Your future is what we discussed while we were alone in his bedchamber."

"I see." Sophia did not see at all; she was aware only that a knot of apprehension was forming somewhere in the vicinity of her stomach. Her father had said that he had not arranged any marriage for her, so she could be sure matrimony was not part of his plan. But she recalled the rest of that particular conversation, and how he had said that Baghdad was not her true home. Remembering her father's words, she was afraid. Nor was Warrick's remark about taking charge of her at all reassuring.

"Are you going to reveal this secret plan?" she asked him in her most shrewish voice.

"Your father wanted you to depart from Baghdad as soon as possible after his death," Warrick said.

"Depart?" Sophia cried. "I have no desire to leave my home. Why should I go?"

"Because without your father's protection you are not safe here," Warrick answered.

"That is ridiculous. This is my father's house. He owned it, along with several others, including the house you rent from him. I am sure I will have sufficient income. I can manage very well."

"Perhaps you could," said Warrick. "However at noon tomorrow this house will become Daoud's property, and you may no longer live here."

"No!" Sophia leaped to her feet. "It cannot be! My father would never be so unjust to me."

"It is what he wanted," Warrick said, calm in the face of her rising anger. "John decided to leave this house to Daoud in return for his years of faithful service, on the sole condition that Daoud keep his mother, Hanna, here at the house and that he care for her until the end of her days. Daoud is delighted to agree to the arrangement."

"How dared you discuss this with Daoud before you spoke to me?" Sophia demanded. She did not know whether she was more enraged with her father, with Warrick, or with Daoud, who would live in her home while she must depart from it forever.

"What your father wanted done needed to be done quickly," Warrick said. "You were in tears, and I thought it better to do as John wanted and tell you about it later."

"Well, then," Sophia said, "I will simply move into one of my father's other houses."

"That you cannot do. They are in the process of being sold," Warrick told her. "The day before his death, your father ordered Daoud to act as his agent and see to the sales as promptly as possible, while still getting a good price for the houses. Do not worry, Sophia; the money will be transferred to you. Minus Daoud's commission, of course."

"Transferred to Sophia—where?" Genie asked, when Sophia was struck dumb with shock at what her father had done.

"To Byzantium," Warrick said.

"Ah, the lady Helena," Genie said, nodding.

"Of course you would know about that," Warrick said to her. "Though I don't understand why the funds aren't to be sent to Mosul and from there on to Byzantium. Your father could serve as the middleman and keep the business, and the commissions, in the family. But then, John understood better than I how such transactions work; I have never owned a house. There may be some advantage to a direct transfer that I have overlooked."

"In this case there is," said Genie, "and I very much fear that Sophia and I are going to have to explain it all to you before any more time has passed."

"In the name of heaven, what are the two of you talking about?" Sophia exclaimed. "I am completely bewildered. What is all this talk of Byzantium?"

"It is where you are to go when you leave Baghdad," Warrick said.

"Why should I want to do that?" she snapped at him.

"Because you have family there, as well as in Mosul," Warrick said in a patient voice that set Sophia's teeth on edge. He sounded as if he thought she was an ignorant fool, who knew nothing of her own family.

"I have no family except my father," Sophia cried, determined to enlighten him at once and put a stop to the talk of Byzantium.

"According to John," Warrick said, "in addition to your aunt and uncle in Mosul, and your cousin, Genie, who is their child, you also have two aunts, an uncle, and several cousins in Byzantium."

"It can't be." Sophia put both hands to her head, feeling as if it would burst from the pressure of grief, astonishment, and a steadily mounting terror of what was still to be revealed.

"Why don't you sit down, Sophia?" Warrick suggested. "I know this is all a great surprise to you." He stretched out his hand, as if to help her back to the divan. Sophia lurched away, moving out of his reach.

"Don't touch me," she warned, "or I shall begin to scream and I do not think you will like that. Just tell me everything that my father told you, and be quick about it, for I am about to lose my patience."

"Your mother was the daughter of a noble Byzantine family," Warrick said. "Your father was a poor scholar who was hired as a tutor for your mother's brother. Because John had come from a land far away and, moreover, a land once conquered by Rome, your grandfather believed he was qualified to teach his son about distant places."

Warrick fell silent. Sophia believed he was giving her time to digest the incredible information he had just divulged. There was much more to the story, of that she was sure. It was possible that Warrick knew why neither of her parents had ever discussed their past lives.

"My father's learning must have been immediately apparent to his employer," Sophia said, trying to picture her parent as a young man.

"I am sure of it," Warrick said. "And I think your grandfather must have been an interesting man. The Byzantines I have known have cared little for anything, or anyone, beyond their own territories. From what John told me, your grandfather's tolerant attitude resulted in a household far more relaxed than most Byzantine homes. The womenfolk were not cloistered, as many Greek noblewomen are, and so your parents were able to meet frequently and to fall in love."

Warrick paused again. He watched Sophia as if he expected some wild reaction to what he had said. She refused to give it to him. She kept her face blank and her voice icy.

"Go on," she said. "Since you know so much that I was never told, perhaps you will also explain how my parents got from Byzantium to Baghdad."

"When your mother discovered there was a consequence to her love for your father, a consequence that could be hidden for only a few months, John asked for the lady Helena's hand in marriage. Your grandfather's tolerance did not extend to the seduction of his daughter. John fled for his life, and Helena went with him. John insisted to me that if she had remained with her family, Helena would have been imprisoned for the rest of her days in a strict convent, where silence was the rule, so that her wrongdoing could never become a public scandal. The child she carried would have been taken from her at the moment of birth, never to be seen or heard of again. From my personal observations of the Byzantines, I believe John's story and his assessment of what awaited his lover. There was nothing he or Helena could do except run away."

"And that is the family to which my father has commended me?" Sophia cried.

"Your parents' love affair happened more than twenty years ago," Warrick said. "Your grandfather was an old man at the time; he must be long dead by now. John's hope was that his former pupil, your uncle who still lives in Byzantium, would accept you into the family. Or, if he would not, then possibly one of your aunts or one of your cousins would have you."

"I cannot believe my father wanted such a future for me," Sophia cried. "I am to be sent to live with relatives who would have imprisoned my mother because she loved my father and wanted to marry him? The same people who would have taken me from her at the instant I was born—and done what to me, Warrick? Exposed me on a hillside to die? Dashed out my infant brains against a stone lest scandal touch their precious family name? Or would they have tossed me into the Bosporus when I was only just learning to breathe?

"How could my father expect me to go willingly to live with those monsters? I should have known better than to hope he might care about my feelings, and I cannot believe my mother wanted me sent to so unloving a family." Remembering her gentle mother, who had never hurt another living person, Sophia could barely breathe for the rage that engulfed her.

"It was the ancient Greeks, not the Byzantines, who made a practice of exposing unwanted children on open hillsides," Warrick said, as if he thought that historical fact would calm her. "Sophia, I am bound to tell you that in every country I know of, fathers look askance at men who seduce their daughters. To your father's credit, he did marry Helena as soon as he possibly could, and well before you were born. John told me that their union was blessed by an Armenian priest who was kind to them. How they reached Armenia from Byzantium I do not know, nor do I know the details of how they finally reached Baghdad. John preferred to expend his failing strength on the important issue of what was to become of you after his death."

"I will not go to Byzantium," Sophia said. "I will not leave Baghdad. You cannot force me to go. You have no authority over me."

"But I have," Warrick said. "Your father entrusted your safety to me. You may be certain that I will not fail in my responsibility to you, Sophia."

Chapter Eight

"Your responsibility to me?" Sophia was going to argue further. She intended to release Warrick from all obligation to see to her welfare, to tell him she was perfectly capable of conducting her own life, that she had been making important household decisions ever since her mother's death and she could continue to make similar decisions now that she was alone.

That was exactly how she felt—alone and betrayed by the one person in all the world who ought to have cared about her. If only her father had spared an hour or two from his nightly observations or his daily mathematical computations to tell her what he wanted her to do after his death, and to reveal the truth of his past and her mother's, then Sophia would not feel so lost and unloved now. She and her father might have reached an agreement that allowed her some degree of happiness while at the same time satisfying John's belated fatherly concerns. Instead, her grief was compounded with angry frustration that left her helpless in its grip.

"We will leave for Mosul as soon as we can secure places in a caravan," Warrick said.

"Mosul?" Sophia repeated with a glance in Genie's direction. "No, we cannot go there."

"Your father said something similar, but I disagree. It is the best place for us to go," Warrick told her in the tone of a man who has made up his mind and will not change it. "First, because I have a duty to return Genie safely to her parents who live in Mosul. Second, I want Genie to introduce us to her parents, since from what your father said to me, you have never met them. Sophia, after you spend a few days with your aunt and uncle in Mosul, if you make a favorable impression on them, perhaps they will consent to write a letter for you to take to your family in Byzantium, recommending you to their care. Such a letter will make your entry into your mother's family easier for you. And lastly, since your uncle in Mosul is a trader and Mosul is on the direct northern route, he ought to be able to help us reach Byzantium by caravan. What is your uncle's name?"

The imperious way in which Warrick was attempting to take control of Sophia's life struck her as both inappropriate and utterly senseless. Warrick's well-laid plans were impossible, given the truth of Genie's origin, and Sophia was going to have the pleasure of telling him so. She could not help herself; she began to laugh and, once started, she could not stop. She sank down on the divan, held her sides, and howled with laughter until her eyes were streaming and hysterical mirth degenerated into tears. Warrick watched her, unmoved, his expression disapproving and a bit impatient. Each time she glanced at his serious face she laughed harder.

"I can't"—she gasped, doubling over, trying to catch her breath—"can't go to Mosul—no relatives there. Oh, oh, Genie, tell him. Please, you tell him why."

"Are you sure?" Genie asked, putting an arm across Sophia's heaving shoulders. "Master John did say not to tell anyone."

"Warrick won't care that you are a jinni," Sophia said with a fresh burst of laughter. "He's a magician. Not a very good one, though. Be careful of him, Genie. He loses people."

The look on Warrick's face sobered her, stopping both mirth and weeping in an instant. Sophia had not thought it was possible to cut a man to the heart with mere words, but she could see that she had just done so to Warrick. She was so angry with him—and with all other unreliable, thoughtless men who imagined they could direct women's lives as they wished—that she was not going to apologize. She stared into his topaz eyes, where a flame burned that frightened her. She caught her breath when he took his gaze from her to look at Genie. As if in response to his probing stare, Genie tightened her arm around Sophia's shoulders.

"Yes," Warrick said to Genie, "I am a magician. Whether I am a good one or not remains to be seen. So you are one of the jinn. I suspected as much the first time I saw you. Aside from your unnatural beauty, there is the scent of roses about you. My mother was a sorceress. Wherever she went her rose fragrance followed her. She conjured it to conceal the stench of evil."

"There is no stench to me. I wear this perfume because I love roses," Genie said quietly. "If the scent offends you, I will choose another perfume."

"Your perfume does not matter," Warrick said. "What does matter is that neither of you has relatives in Mosul. John did not tell me about Genie's magical origin. I find myself wondering what else he neglected to tell me."

"So far as I am concerned," Sophia said, unrepentant of her verbal cruelty toward Warrick, "I have no relatives at all, anywhere at all. I reject every one of them, and my father, too. Cease your attempt to force me to leave Baghdad, Warrick. I don't want to go anywhere with you."

Warrick was saved from having to make a response to her defiant statement by a knock on the study door. At Warrick's call Robin came into the room. There was sand embedded in his red-brown curls and grains of sand clung to the shoulders and sleeves of his tunic. He carried a cloth sack slung over one shoulder by a long strap. Robin removed the sack, brushed off the sand that had collected on it, and handed it to Warrick.

"What news?" Warrick asked his friend. He put the sack down on John's desk.

"Daoud and I have sold most of our belongings, so we will have enough money to begin the trip," Robin said. "We have brought our few remaining possessions here. There is nothing left at our house to give the lie to the story that Hua Te has departed on a journey and that you and I have delayed only long enough to see John into his grave and to clean out our house. We have told several people that we plan to join Hua Te along his way. The tale will likely circulate as quickly as that kind of information always does in Baghdad. We can only hope the *shinha* will believe the story. Warrick, we ought to leave Baghdad at once. Tonight if possible, tomorrow at the latest."

"I agree with Robin," Genie said. "Sophia will be safer out of the city. The sultan's representative who attended the funeral will report to his master before the sun sets tomorrow. I noticed how carefully he examined the contents of each room he entered, and especially this study. I am sure he carried away in his mind a listing of John's books and scrolls and of all the instruments."

"What do I have to say to convince you that I am not going anywhere?" Sophia spoke slowly and loudly. "This is my home and I will not leave it."

"Sophia, your stubbornness is only making what I am sworn to do a more difficult task," Warrick told her. "There is no way for you to convince me to give up. You promised your father on his deathbed that you would accept the arrangements he made for you, and I gave him my solemn oath that I would see you safely to Byzantium before I continue my search for Hua Te. You may break your promise if you wish, but do not expect me to forswear my word of honor, for I will not. You are going to Byzantium."

"You are doing this because you failed Hua Te, because you made him disappear!" Sophia shouted at him. "You imagine you can redeem yourself for that colossal mistake by insisting that I must leave the only home I have ever known on a day's notice, to go to live with relatives who do not want me. I am sorry I ever said you were kind. You are the most wretched, cruel, unfeeling man I have ever known!"

"Leave me," Warrick said in a voice so cold and devoid of emotion that Sophia, were she in normal possession of her wits, would have run from him. But she was not in possession of her wits; she was beside herself with rage and loss and fear of an unknown future, and she believed the only person she could rely on was herself.

"This is my father's study!" she shouted at Warrick. "I will stay in it as long as I please."

"Your father is dead," Warrick said, his icy manner unchanged by her emotional outburst. "I am merely carrying out his wishes. Genie, take Sophia to her room. Help her to pack what she will require for the journey. We cannot take much with us, but I am sure Daoud will be happy to send the rest of her belongings to Byzantium."

"I will not be treated this way," Sophia said, attempting to match his coldness with her own.

"You will do as I tell you." Warrick's eyes blazed with golden light and his face appeared to be set in stone.

Sophia did not know whether he was using magic to control her, or whether it was the force of his will. Whatever it was, she discovered that she could no longer fight Warrick. She did as he wanted. With Genie's arm around her, she left the study.

When the door shut behind the women, Warrick relaxed. He sat down hard on the divan and put his head in his hands.

"If I am to protect her from harm," he muttered, "who is to protect me from her?"

"She is terrified," Robin said.

"I know." Warrick raised his head to look at his

friend. "She is also used to having her own way. John's neglect of her allowed Sophia a remarkable degree of freedom, far more than most women in this land enjoy. I do not think she will easily relinquish that freedom.

"The last thing I want is to travel anywhere with Sophia," Warrick went on, "particularly when she is in her present mood. But she cannot make the trip to Byzantium alone. I must say that I am forced to agree with her on one point. John was incredibly unfair to her when he decided to send her to live with relatives who coldheartedly rejected her mother. I cannot deny that I harbor a certain sympathy with Sophia's plight."

"Well, then it's on to Mosul for us," Robin said with every appearance of cheerfulness, as if a greedy sultan were not waiting to pounce on Sophia and all she was due to inherit, and as if no questions were being asked about Hua Te's unexplained absence.

"We aren't going by way of Mosul. Our plans have changed," Warrick told him. "We will go the way John originally suggested, and take the road to Tabriz."

"It's the busiest route out of Baghdad," Robin said thoughtfully. "That will be helpful to us. Because that road is so heavily used, the *shinha* will find it difficult to check on every single person who joins a caravan heading for Tabriz. They won't expect us to go by caravan anyway. Hua Te made no secret of his plan to travel by ship and Daoud and I have done our best to foster that notion as we dealt with the local merchants. We can hope the *shinha* will be misled for at least a day."

"Good," Warrick said. "There ought to be a caravan leaving tomorrow morning."

"We will want four places," Robin said. "I will secure them tonight. We'll need food for the trip. And water. And camels. How I hate camels. The beasts know it, too."

"Take Genie with you," Warrick said.

"A woman? I admit she knows how to bargain for foodstuffs, but dealing with a camel trader is another matter. What could a gently bred girl know about choosing camels?"

"Genie may surprise you," Warrick said. "I am sure she has lured Sophia into bed and a deep sleep, so she will be free to go with you right now. While you make our travel arrangements, I have some special packing to do."

After removing John's crystal ball and its jeweled stand from the secret niche, Warrick rewrapped the priceless object in plain linen and hid it in the sack Robin had brought from Hua Te's stillroom. He added the bags of coins from the niche. The heavy cloth sack contained herbs and salves and linen for bandages, all of which would be needed during the journey to Byzantium. The pots and jars of various sizes ought to provide adequate concealment for John's treasure, and Warrick's claim to healing skills would be reason enough for him to keep the sack close at hand.

Having seen to the valuable crystal ball, Warrick used the red silk covering to wrap up the ordinary ball and stand that John had kept in his study. He put the decoy into the niche, closed the wooden board that covered the niche, and replaced the shelf in front of the metal bar.

His next task was to attempt to create some order out of John's haphazard collection of books, scrolls, and astronomical instruments so that he could tell Daoud what to sell and what was valuable enough to justify the expense of shipping it to Sophia in her new home. He spent an hour or two working steadily. Daoud stopped by to report on his activities of the day and Warrick gave him a few more instructions.

After Daoud left, several nights of little sleep caught up with Warrick. Unwilling to lie down on John's bed in the adjoining room, he cleared the divan by dumping a last, untidy pile of books onto the floor. He was asleep as soon as he stretched out on the soft cushions.

The study was in complete darkness when the door to the hall opened. Warrick heard the whisper of the hinges moving and immediately came wide-awake, alert for trouble. He did not know what time it was; he knew only that it was still deep night and that the *shamal* had become a fitful breeze that occasionally rattled the wooden shutters.

He stayed quiet on the divan, his eyes closed to mere slits, watching beneath his lids as the door swung inward. He relaxed his guard when Sophia entered, carrying a small oil lamp in one hand. Her thick hair was bound into a single braid that lay across one shoulder and hung to just below her nicely rounded breast. She wore a plain linen night-dress with a rounded neck and loose sleeves and her gray shawl was draped over her shoulders. Her feet were bare.

Sophia set the oil lamp on John's desk, and then moved to the doorway of his bedchamber. She reached within, caught the edge of the bedroom door, and closed it. Moving silently, she returned to the desk. After picking up the lamp she began to search the shelves behind the desk, peering intently at the contents of each shelf.

The shawl slipped from her shoulders, allowing Warrick an alluring glimpse of the nape of her neck. A few dark tendrils had escaped from her braid to curl along her hairline. Warrick experienced a sudden, irrational impulse to touch those curls and to place his lips on her soft skin.

From the care she took not to make any noise, Warrick received the impression that Sophia thought someone was sleeping in John's bedroom, so she had closed the door and now was trying to be as quiet as possible so as not to wake the sleeper. He guessed that she thought he was the one in her father's bed. After a few minutes Warrick heard a whispered oath, words a sheltered young woman ought not to know. Sophia had reached a series of empty shelves from which Warrick had earlier removed books and papers.

He swung his feet to the floor and stood. Sophia must have heard the faint rustle of fabric on the divan cushions, for she went perfectly still.

"If you will tell me what you are looking for," Warrick said, "I will be happy to help you search."

Sophia spun around so fast that she nearly dropped the oil lamp. Warrick grabbed it before the oil could spill, and set the lamp in the center of the desk.

"It will be safer there," he said. "Sophia, what are you doing out of bed in the middle of the night?"

"This is my home," she declared, lifting her chin and regarding him with undisguised distaste. "You have no right to question me about anything I choose to do within these walls."

"I have every right, as you would admit if only you would give up your stubborn resistance to your father's wishes," Warrick said. "Did you want a particular book? Perhaps I can find it for you."

"I do not think anyone can find a single book amid this disorder." Sophia glanced around the dim room until her challenging blue gaze reconnected with Warrick's. "I can see that you have been dismantling my father's library. I suppose I ought to thank you for waiting until after he was buried," she said with haughty sarcasm.

"I have been attempting to make Daoud's job a little easier," he said. "By John's own order, his belongings are to be packed up and removed from the house by morning. I had stopped for a short rest when you appeared. You still haven't told me why you are here, undressed, at such an hour."

Sophia did not flinch at the reminder that she was in her nightdress. "I wanted to see this room one more time," she said. Her voice was wistful, her face sad. "I am trying to understand why my father treated me as he did, why there is so much that he deliberately neglected to tell me. I had a foolish notion that if I were to spend half an hour in here, in his private rooms, I might discover some meaning to his decisions concerning me. It is horribly unsettling to be so angry with one's own parent."

"Yes, it is," Warrick said, recalling his own youthful rage at his wicked mother. Sophia gave him a cold look that suggested she did not believe he understood her distress. Or perhaps she was regretting that she had revealed her innermost thoughts to him.

"Genie says I have no choice in the matter, that I must go with you whether I want to or not."

"I am sorry you find leaving so painful," he said.

"But not sorry enough to alter your plans."

"Shall I tell you again what my reasons are?" he asked. "First, because your father insisted that as soon as he was buried, I must get you away from Baghdad without delay—"

"I know," she interrupted, making an impatient gesture. "I have heard the explanations over and over. During this evening you, Genie, and even Daoud have all impressed on me how dangerous my position will be when the sultan realizes that I am living alone, unprotected by any man, and with a handsome estate at my command. All three of you have warned me that if I remain in Baghdad, I will probably end my days in the sultan's harem with all of my inheritance confiscated to be used as my dowry. But I tell you, Warrick, I cannot believe the sultan will find me the least bit attractive."

"No?" Warrick murmured, moving a step nearer to her.

"Not when he has a harem filled with women of far greater beauty, who are likely to be more kindly disposed toward him than I will be."

"Now there you may have a point," Warrick said. "I cannot predict the sultan's exact reaction should you use your sharp tongue on him, except that the outcome will not be pleasant for you. In fact, I prefer not to think about what will happen to you if you provoke the sultan."

"It is true that I am not accustomed to moderating my speech in order to please any man," she said.

"Not even your father?" Warrick was finding it remarkably difficult to keep his hands out of her hair. The tight braid had loosened as she slept, producing a dark halo of tiny curls all around her face. Warrick's fingertips itched to smooth the wisps of curly black off her forehead and cheeks.

"My father paid little heed to what I said or did," she said. "He cared only that his work should go on undisturbed." There was a lifetime of painful resentment in her tone.

"A great mistake on his part." Unable to restrain himself any longer, Warrick laid his large hands on her delicate shoulders. The fragile bones beneath his fingers had borne too much responsibility for one so young. After his conversations with John, Warrick was aware that Sophia had known little joy in her life, certainly not in the years since her mother's death. He could no longer see her eyes; she had lowered her lids as if she were embarrassed at having allowed him access to her private sorrow. "John was a blind fool to neglect you."

"I am not without flaws myself," she said, "and I know I was a great disappointment to him." Tears seeped beneath her eyelids and ran down her cheeks.

"Ah, Sophia, I did not mean to make you cry." He took one hand from her shoulder, to wipe the tears off her cheeks. Her skin was as smooth as the finest silk.

Warrick pushed a few damp curls back into the thickness of her hair. Sophia turned her face into his palm as if she found comfort in his touch. Warrick's heart gave a great leap and something cold and hard inside him began to unknot. Her cheek rested against his hand as if she trusted him, as if they were friends—or lovers. There was pleasure and a certain masculine satisfaction in discovering that he could provide the comfort she needed.

Sophia's lips were trembling, softly parted, like velvety pink flower petals. Warrick lowered his head and put his lips on hers. She gave a faint gasp of surprise but did not pull away. Warrick gathered her closer and deepened the kiss.

Desire slashed through him, white-hot and well-nigh uncontrollable. Sophia's body was warm under her linen gown, and richly curved and inviting. Warrick let his mouth stray along her throat to the wide neckline of her gown. His hand cradled the rounded fullness of her breast. He felt her nipple harden at his touch, in the same way that his own body was hardening. Warrick yearned to push her onto the desk and bury himself in her warmth. He pulled her up against him, letting her feel his arousal.

Sophia's choked moan of surprise brought Warrick back to reality. He knew better than to do what he was doing; he had spent a decade and a half learning to control his thoughts and his physical responses. If he were to take advantage of Sophia's emotional distress and her inexperience, the act would dishonor him as well as her.

Nor could he deny his own emotional distress in recent days. Sophia had lost her father, and her trust in her parent had been destroyed; Warrick had lost his teacher and dear friend. It was only natural for them to seek comfort in each other. There was nothing wrong in their mutual need for solace.

But it would be wrong for him to act on his body's urgings. He was stronger than Sophia in many ways, and he was far more experienced. He was reasonably certain that no one had kissed Sophia before this night and her startled reaction to his body's hardness told him she was a virgin and unfamiliar with a man's responses.

There was only one honorable thing for him to do. He must place his hands on her shoulders again and kindly but firmly set her apart from him. He would do so . . . after one more kiss, one more caress. Ah, but her mouth was moist and her breath was sweet. Her buttocks were rounded and firm beneath his caressing hands and she came to him so willingly, so eagerly. . . .

It took every drop of courage and every bit of moral strength Warrick possessed to make himself take his hands from Sophia and step back from her. She looked at him with wide blue eyes. Looking into Sophia's eyes was like gazing deep into heaven.

Never had Warrick wanted a woman as he wanted Sophia. He did not know why it should be so, when she had made a habit of being unpleasant to him. He did know that she was the one woman he could not have. He was honor-bound to deliver her safely to her relatives in Byzantium, even if it cost him his life to do so. Or his sanity.

Deliberately he turned his back on her and walked to the window that overlooked the garden. He threw open the shutters. Sand sifted from the windowsill onto the floor. Warrick scarcely noticed. He did note that the *shamal* had stopped. He drew in a breath of hot, dry air and looked up at the stars glittering in a sky swept clean of dust and clouds. When morning dawned caravan traffic would begin to move again.

"Warrick?" Sophia came to stand beside him. She placed one hand on his arm, and Warrick had the impression that she intended to say something that would change the cool distance he was attempting to put between them.

He could not allow his desire for her to dictate his actions. Even less could he afford to express the tenderness he felt, not if he was going to maintain an appearance of honor and decency over the next few months. He was confident of his ability to control desire; he had done it often enough since reaching maturity. But tenderness could undo all of his good intentions.

"We will begin a long and arduous journey tomorrow," he said. "It will be best if we take care not to repeat that embrace. We will need to be on guard at all times, and an intense emotional involvement can become a dangerous distraction."

"I understand," she said in a tight little voice. "Truly I do. Having embraced me once, you do not wish to embrace me again."

"That is not what I said, Sophia."

"It is what I heard," she told him. "My father did not care about me, and neither do you."

Warrick started to explain his actions more fully, but then thought better of it. If Sophia believed he did not want her, perhaps she would keep her distance from him. If she thought he had rejected her, she would very likely make bitter use of her sharp tongue whenever she spoke to him. And then he, in turn, might find it a little easier to keep his distance from her.

Chapter Nine

Sophia left her father's study at a near run. She did not want Warrick to see how hurt she was by his rejection. She was horrified to discover that he had the power to hurt her. She had always believed she was immune to feelings of passionate affection for any man and, therefore, safe from the kind of pain she was experiencing.

The prospect of spending months in close company with Warrick was unbearable. Her life would be made even more intolerable if Warrick learned that she entertained strong emotions regarding him. Let Warrick begin to treat her as if he pitied her and Sophia knew she would snap and snarl at him, and at everyone else in her vicinity, until before long she would become in truth the hateful person Warrick thought she was.

She wished she dared to slip away from the house and hide, so she could remain in Baghdad when

Warrick left. She knew it was a foolish idea. Warrick would use his magical skills to find her, not because he cared about her, but because he had made a promise concerning her. And she did possess more good sense than either he or Genie gave her credit for having. She understood the perils involved in staying where she was and she knew in her heart that the house where she had lived all of her life was no longer her home. It was just that the events of the last two days were so difficult to accept, and now she had to consider her peculiar reaction to Warrick's embrace as well.

She had never thought of herself as a sensual person. It seemed she had been wrong about that, for she had enjoyed Warrick's kisses and the way he touched her. If she were completely honest with herself, she must admit that she wanted him to repeat everything he had done, and then to continue on to more profound intimacies. But Warrick had found her lacking in some important feminine quality, or he would not have stopped so abruptly and would not have told her he could not embrace her again.

It was painfully clear to Sophia that the journey to Byzantium was going to be extremely difficult.

Just as she reached the stairs in her rush from the study to the safety of her bedroom, the front door blew open.

"I thought the door was latched for the night," Sophia muttered. She changed direction, intending to shut the door. A swirling column of sand blew into the hall and the door closed before Sophia reached it. The column of sand began to disintegrate. Sophia blinked in surprise and a veiled figure stood in the hall. Sophia recognized the veil as her own.

"Genie, is that you?" Sophia whispered.

"It is, though it would have been Robin, if he'd had his way," Genie said, pulling off the veil. "He begged me to stay with the camels and let him return to give you the information we have gathered. He reluctantly agreed to take the camels to the caravansary and keep them there after I pointed out that I am capable of disguising myself so that I can pass completely unnoticed."

"Why should you need to pass unnoticed?" asked Warrick, coming into the hall.

Sophia kept her back to him, painfully aware of his presence and willing herself not to let him see how he affected her.

"There is a man watching the front door of this house," Genie said, "and another man guarding the back door. Robin and I went to the house where you have been living and men from the *shinha* are watching there, too. Robin said to warn you that we must leave the house at once, that it will be safer for us to don disguises and wait at the caravansary. We have places in the caravan that is to leave at dawn."

"No. I won't go." Unreasoning panic flared in Sophia's mind. She planted both her feet firmly on the familiar tile floor and prepared to stand her ground. She had never lived anywhere except in her father's house, had never slept a night in any bed but her own. She would not be rushed into leaving her home. "The *shinha* want you, Warrick, not me."

"Don't be a fool," he said. "I will not repeat again all of the reasons why you must leave. If you continue to refuse, I will use magic to ensure your compliance."

While Sophia stared at him, trying to decide whether or not he would actually do as he threatened, Daoud appeared from an inner room to join the group by the door.

"Master Warrick, I heard alarmed voices. What has happened?" Daoud asked. "Is something wrong?"

"The house is being watched by the *shinha*," Warrick said. "For your safety as well as our own, we will leave at once."

"Warrick, you have forgotten something in your haste to force me out of my home," Sophia said, grasping at the excuse offered by Daoud's appearance. "If we go, Daoud and Hanna will be left behind to deal with the *shinha*. What will happen to them?"

"Why, nothing," Warrick said. "Neither Daoud nor his mother has broken the law. They are no more than two faithful servants whose late master left to Daoud a rather small house in recompense for his years of work. This house is not remarkable in any way, so no one will covet it, not even the avaricious sultan."

"That is not true," Sophia said, delighted at catching Warrick in an error. "You know very well that it is my father's books and his astronomical instruments the sultan wants."

"By your father's orders, all of them will be gone from the house by morning," Daoud reminded her. "I will see to it. Do not ask how, simply know that it will be done. The sultan's men may search every room of this building if they wish. They will discover nothing to interest them, or their master. I am in no danger, mistress, nor is my mother, though I do thank you for your concern.

"However, I fear that you are in danger," Daoud continued, "and so is Master Warrick. Questions have been asked about Hua Te's absence from Master John's funeral. All of Baghdad knows the two were the best of friends and that Hua Te would have been present if he could. In the name of Allah, mistress, leave now, at once."

"This is not the first time that I have wished my father were not so famous an astrologer," Sophia said bitterly. "If he had been a simpler, unknown scholar, like so many other men who live in Baghdad, I would not have to flee. And if Hua Te were not famous and Warrick were a better magician, perhaps he would not have to run away either," she added with malicious pleasure.

"But run away we must, and as soon as possible," Warrick said, his face turning grim at the insult. He took a step in Sophia's direction. "I will listen to no more arguments from you. Genie, take Sophia to her room and see that she dresses promptly, in clothing that is unremarkable in any way and suitable for travel. Dress yourself in the same manner. Get back down here to the hall as soon as you can."

"Strictly speaking," Genie said to him with a wry smile, "I am not supposed to act on orders from anyone except my mistress. On this occasion I do not think she will issue the necessary command, and I do honestly believe her life may be threatened. Under these special conditions, I am permitted to circumvent the rules under which I function in this Calling. Therefore I obey your wish, Master Warrick. Will this raiment be adequate?"

Genie caught Sophia by one hand and spun her

around twice. Genie spun with her and when both women faced Warrick again they wore dark gowns covered by the long veils that respectable ladies wore when venturing out-of-doors. Both of them were wearing soft leather boots.

Sophia looked in surprise at her new clothes and patted the garments she could not see because of the veil. The clothing was perfectly fitted and remarkably comfortable.

"Excellent," Warrick said in approval. "Genie, you have met all of my specifications for clothing. I can see that you will be a useful addition to our traveling group."

"We will need food," Sophia said, glaring at Warrick through the eye opening of her veil. "And water. I have no intention of starving or dying of thirst before I reach Byzantium."

"Do those words mean you are reconciled to leaving Baghdad?" Warrick asked.

"They mean only that I prefer your protection over that of the sultan," Sophia snapped. "At least I can comfort myself with the certain knowledge that your protection will eventually end."

"I am honored by your high regard," Warrick responded with a glint of amusement in his eyes. "I will not fail the trust you place in me."

"See that you do not," said Sophia.

Warrick grinned at her as if he understood her need to have the last word with him. She was glad of the veil, which hid all of her except her eyes; if she kept her lids lowered, he could not even see them. Thus Warrick would not be able to read the fear that must be plain to see on her face. Nor did she think the sudden tremors shaking her body were noticeable while she was heavily covered by her woolen gown and the veil.

Sophia took a bold step toward the front door, preparing to leave behind all that she had known and cherished. The only thing left to her was her pride. It was pride that would save her. Pride would prevent her from showing her fear, from pleading with Warrick to hold her in his arms and keep her safe. With her first step outside her childhood home she would begin to conceal all of her feelings from Warrick, for she did not believe he was any more dependable than her father. And, like her father, he would leave her in the end. When they reached Byzantium, Warrick would be gone from her life as surely as her father was.

"Stop," Warrick said, catching her wrist as she lifted a hand to the latch. "You cannot walk out the front door. Weren't you listening to Genie? The *shinha* have the house under observation."

"Genie came in through the front door," Sophia said, wrenching her wrist out of his grasp.

"I blew in as if the wind blew the door open," Genie said. "I cannot perform the same magic for all three of us without rousing the spy's suspicions. Doors do not routinely blow open twice in just a short time."

"Then how are we to leave the house?" Sophia demanded.

"We go over the rooftops," Warrick said.

"The roofs?" Sophia said in a weak voice.

"It's the only way," Warrick said. "If there is anything you feel you must take with you, that you can carry easily or slip into a pocket, get it now. I have a sack filled with medical supplies that Robin brought to me. It's in the study. I'll get it and join you on the roof. Go now, Sophia."

There was no arguing with his command, or with the need for haste. With Genie urging her along, Sophia lifted her skirts and hurried up the steps. She was so distracted by the manner of their leaving that she did not dally in her bedchamber. She took only a small wooden box that held her mother's jewelry.

"There is nothing else here that I could possibly carry, except for clothing," she said, looking around the room.

"I can supply all of the clothing we will need," Genie said, "and in prettier colors, too. Leave these boring gray and black gowns behind."

"I want to say good-bye to Hanna."

"No, Sophia," Genie protested. "I know you are unhappy about leaving, but do try to be sensible. Hanna is asleep, and if you wake her she will weep and wail and make so much noise that the men watching the house will know something unusual is happening."

"I suppose you're right," Sophia said. "It's just that Hanna has been with me since I was a child." She clenched her teeth on a sob, believing in her heart that Genie could not possibly know how painful it was to leave one's home. But she realized it was useless to make any more excuses, and dangerous to cause further delay. In silence she followed Genie up the last flight of stairs to the roof.

Warrick was just a few steps ahead of them. He pulled open the door and stepped onto the roof. It was completely bare, the rugs and furnishings having been removed as soon as the *shamal* began to blow. A fine layer of sand covered the rooftop and made a gritty sound beneath their feet. The moon had set, so the only light came from the stars and from the few city lights still burning, their glow reflecting off the whitewashed walls of nearby houses. A faint hint of pink in the eastern sky warned that sunrise was near. Soon the muezzin's call would waken the faithful to a new day.

"What now?" Sophia asked, hoping her voice did not betray her terror. She was not going to tell Warrick how afraid of heights she was. He would think she was foolish to be frightened when he was not. She could not even bring herself to look over the edge of the roof to the garden below.

"The house next door is vacant," Warrick said. "All we have to do is step over the space from one rooftop to the next. There is an outside staircase leading from the neighboring roof down to the garden, and there's a door in the far side of the garden wall that we can use to get onto the street. Genie, did you notice anyone watching the houses in this block from that side?"

"I didn't," Genie said, "though that is no guarantee there won't be someone waiting for us. Still, it's our best chance to get away unnoticed. You can use magic if necessary, and so can I, but it will be less tiring if we proceed without magic."

"I agree with you. I'll save my magical efforts until they are absolutely necessary." Warrick slung the sack of medical supplies over one shoulder. Then he stepped onto the parapet surrounding John's roof and jumped to the neighboring parapet. Balancing there with apparent ease, he set down his bundle before he turned and held out a hand. "You are next, Sophia."

To Sophia's eyes the parapet of her own house

was too high for her to climb onto it. The parapet next door was even higher. And the space between them was an unbridgeable void. Despite his statement that he would not, she was sure Warrick had used magic to cross that terrible space so easily.

"Come on, Sophia," Warrick said. "Take my hand and step across."

She wasn't going to ask him to use his magic to make this easier for her. She certainly didn't intend to tell him how frightened she was. There was nothing for her to do except follow his directions.

Sophia tucked her mother's jewelry box into a pocket she discovered inside her veil, then gathered her long, heavy skirts into one hand. She wanted to close her eyes, but she knew she couldn't do that. She had to be able to see where she was going. Ignoring Warrick's proffered hand, she put one foot on top of the parapet and levered herself upward.

She had never noticed before how narrow the parapet was. On the rare occasions when she could not avoid going onto the roof, she had always stayed well away from the parapet. Now she stood with both feet on the smooth, whitewashed surface, balanced precariously as she prepared to step to the house next door, where Warrick awaited her.

She made the mistake of looking down. Below her stretched a bottomless chasm, black and endless. Her foot slipped on the edge and she teetered there on the brink of emptiness, too horrified to cry out, too terrified to take the step that would save her.

"Stop dawdling, Sophia," Warrick said somewhat impatiently. "Give me your hand."

His voice steadied her. She put out her hand and Warrick grasped it. He tugged hard and Sophia had no choice but to take a wide step into empty air. She fully expected that both she and Warrick would plummet to the ground below. Instead she landed on the neighboring roof. Warrick let her go at once and turned to assist Genie.

With his female companions safe on the roof, Warrick picked up his sack and headed for the narrow stairway that ended in the garden three floors below. Sophia and Genie followed him, Sophia biting her lip and keeping one hand on the wall as she went down, staying close to the inner side, though she was not as terrified by the height of the steps as she had been by the roof.

Actually Sophia was rather pleased with herself. She had succeeded in concealing her fear from Warrick, and she had done something she thought she could not do. Perhaps the next time she was called upon to perform an extraordinary act, it wouldn't be so difficult for her.

Her spirits rose as she followed Warrick and Genie through the overgrown garden. She had to stop to untangle her veil from the thorns of a rose-bush, and when she reached the door in the garden wall, she found Warrick and Genie discussing the fact that the door was locked and there was no key.

"Only magic will work here," Genie said. "Shall I open it, or will you?"

"Go ahead," Warrick responded in a whisper. "But be quiet about it." He took Sophia's arm and pulled her close to him.

Sophia was going to protest and attempt to put more distance between them, until she looked in Genie's direction. Then she was glad she wasn't standing next to Genie. At the place on the garden door where the rusted lock was, a pale green glow appeared. Sophia could see Genie's raised left hand colored green by the reflection of the light. Genie moved her hand and the light vanished into the keyhole, as if it had been sucked inside. Sophia held her breath, and in the silence she heard a faint clicking sound.

"It's open," Genie said, and pulled the door back far enough for the three of them to pass through.

"Thank you, Genie," Warrick said. "Be sure to close and lock it after us, and restore any rust you had to remove to make the lock work. We want the door to look as if it hasn't been used."

With his hand still tight on Sophia's arm, Warrick guided her out of the garden to the street. Sophia heard the door creaking shut and looked back. She saw a momentary green glow around the lock. Then all was dark again and Genie was at her side.

"This way," Genie said, her voice soft. "I can see in the dark. I will take you to the caravansary."

Sophia regularly used the streets that led from her father's house to the large market square where she bought food and household supplies. She knew the *souks* where the rug merchants traded in carpets from distant lands, and she knew where the silk merchant's shop was. She had even, on a few occasions, explored a few odd little alleys where open-front shops offered unusual wares. She had always thought the section of Baghdad where she lived was familiar to her. But following Genie in the dark, she was lost within a few moments. It was like walking through a foreign country, and it was frightening to realize that she was unable to find her way back to her old home.

And then she reminded herself that she had stepped from one rooftop to another without falling and without giving in to her fears or pleading for help, and she pulled away from Warrick's guiding hand and lifted her head and walked proudly between him and Genie.

Baghdad was wakening from the night's half-resting state. Carts filled with fresh produce brought to the city from nearby farms, or with wares unloaded from the ships tied up at the wharves along the Tigris River, trundled through the streets to the marketplace, where the goods were to be spread out for the inspection of early-rising customers. Camels and donkeys bearing heavy loads, the occasional packhorse, and even a few human bearers with merchandise strapped to their backs, all hurried toward their destinations at shops, bazaars, and the big open market. With the animals came their drivers, who made no attempt to be quiet. The orders they shouted to their animals and their calls of greeting to each other echoed off the high walls of the surrounding buildings.

Meanwhile, merchants went by on their way to open their shops. Here and there the fragrance of coffee overcame less agreeable odors. Sophia had never realized how busy the city was in the hours just before dawn.

The streets became ever busier as Warrick and his companions approached the caravansary. This building was the place where arriving caravans halted, to be met by traders expecting to unload the merchandise they had ordered, by merchants prepared to haggle over the price of goods brought to the city on speculation that whatever arrived there would sell for a handsome profit, and by people who were meeting travelers. It was also the departure point for caravans leaving Baghdad. The caravansary was a large, square edifice with a single entrance. Inside there was an open arcade built around all four sides of a central court, with rooms behind the arcade.

Because of the sandstorm caused by the *shamal*, no caravan had left the city for two days. As a result the rooms were more crowded than usual and the court was overflowing with people, animals, and baggage. Torches stuck into sconces along the arcade illuminated the chaotic scene. A few members of the *shinha* were present to try to introduce a bit of order into the confusion, though their attempts were futile. Everyone in the courtyard seemed to be shouting. So far as Sophia could tell, no one was listening. The smells of animals and humans packed into too small a space were distinctly unpleasant. Sophia's first instinct was to turn and run.

Seemingly oblivious to noise or odors, Genie moved through the mob with ease and quickly located Robin. He was at one side of the courtyard, standing guard over five camels, several baskets, and a number of cloth-wrapped bundles. He was garbed in a long black wool robe and his hair was covered by an undyed woolen scarf secured with a cord in the Arab style. With his suntanned skin and gray-green eyes, Robin did not look much different from many of the other men in the caravansary.

"I am glad to see you," Robin greeted them with unconcealed relief. "Genie, these camels you chose are the meanest-tempered, most obstreperous animals I have ever had the misfortune to deal with. How you expect us to reach Tabriz with our bones and our lives intact if we ride these beasts, I do not know. Here, you take them. I need a rest." Robin thrust all five of the camels' reins into Genie's hands.

"They are not ill-tempered," Genie said. "If you know how to treat them they are sweet, affectionate animals. Aren't you, my dears?" She began to rub the nose of the nearest camel. It pushed its head closer to Genie, as if asking for more stroking. The other camels moved nearer, awaiting their turns.

"I don't know how she does it," Robin muttered to Warrick. "The one she's petting now, that mangy-looking, dark brown beast, spit at me a little while ago. Just look at it with Genie. You'd think it was an overgrown kitten."

To Sophia, the camels looked every bit as vicious as Robin claimed they were, and she wished she did not have to go near them. Then her trepidation about the camels was forgotten as she realized what Robin had said in addition to his complaints.

"What did Robin mean when he spoke of Tabriz?" she asked Warrick.

"It is where we are going," he said in a casual way that suggested their destination was of no importance to him. "Sophia, take care to stay near me. There will be several caravans departing between now and sunrise and you don't want to get lost in the confusion."

"Don't I?" she asked with a deliberate sneer. Then, as all of her concerns about undependable men rose to torment her, she demanded, "Why wasn't I told that we are going to Tabriz?"

"I didn't think it was necessary," Warrick said. He wasn't paying much attention to Sophia. He was looking about the courtyard as if he was checking each face he saw.

"Not necessary!" Sophia cried, her voice rising.

135

"Not necessary to tell me where you are taking me? Let me tell you, Warrick, that you are as poor a geographer as you are a magician. Tabriz lies in the wrong direction."

"Bridle your tongue, Sophia," he said, still not deigning to look directly at her. "One of the *shinha* has heard you and is looking this way."

"I do not want to go to Tabriz!" she exclaimed. "Nor to Byzantium, nor anywhere else with you. You are just like my father. Like him, you say you care about my welfare and you make promises, and then you become involved with your own concerns and you forget that I even exist. When we reach Tabriz, you will send me on to Byzantium alone, while you go off to Cathay to search for Hua Te. That is your secret plan, isn't it?"

"I said, be quiet!" Warrick seized her arm and dragged her behind the camels. He was not gentle about it.

Sophia stumbled over a basket and would have fallen if Warrick had not jerked her upright. She opened her mouth to say something scathing to him. Then she clamped her jaw shut when Warrick spoke again in a voice no less furious for being low enough that only she could hear him.

"Thanks to your lack of caution, we are now under surveillance by a *shinha* guard. Sophia, I have tried to be patient with you because of your sorrow over losing your father and then your lifelong home. But I will not permit you to jeopardize my life, or Robin's, or your own. I have told you that you may trust me, and I expect you to do so without constant criticism of my capabilities. That includes my magical abilities."

"I am sorry," she said, managing to sound not the least bit sorry.

"Repentance will do you no good if you are caught," he said. "I grow weary of your lack of consideration for the feelings or the safety of anyone except yourself."

"That's not true," she cried.

"If you ever again act in a manner as blatantly stupid as you just did, I promise I will tie you up and gag you and carry you along on this cursed journey as if you were a piece of inanimate baggage. Do you hear me, Sophia?"

"I hear you," she said in a sulky voice. She tried to pull away from him. Warrick tightened his grip on her arm.

"As for why we are joining the caravan that ends at Tabriz," he said, "we are taking the route suggested by your father. He believed it would be the safest way for us to go, precisely because it is the wrong direction. At Tabriz we will join another caravan, one bound for Trebizond, and from Trebizond we will take passage on a ship to Byzantium. There are other details still to be worked out as we travel, but that is the general plan. Do you care to quarrel with your father's reasoning?"

"No," Sophia said, and this time she kept her voice low. "But if you had taken a few moments to tell me what you were doing and why, then I would not have been angry. I am used to ordering my own days, Warrick, and to following a routine that seems logical to me. You cannot expect me to give up control over every aspect of my life to you, especially when you don't explain your intentions. You may be able to read other peoples' minds, but

I cannot. I never know what you want of me, or why."

"My magic does not extend to mind reading," Warrick said. He glanced over Sophia's shoulder, his attention caught by something behind her in the courtyard. His fingers were like iron bands on her arm. "However, I can make both of us temporarily invisible, and I am going to have to do so now."

"Why?" Sophia asked. She tried to turn to see what he was looking at. Warrick would not allow her to move. He kept her facing him.

"The *shinha* guard whose interest you roused is coming this way," he said. "I suspect he wants to know why we have been hiding behind the camels for so long. I want to avoid having to answer any questions he may ask of us."

"This is my fault," Sophia said, chilled by the prospect of interrogation by the *shinha*. "Warrick, tell me what you want me to do."

"Say and do nothing," Warrick said. "Simply stand close to me."

She took a step nearer and as she did, she felt a queer tingling sensation, completely unlike anything she had ever experienced before. The tingling started at her scalp and quickly surrounded her so that her nose and chin prickled with it, and her fingertips and toes tingled. It was not a painful sensation, just an unfamiliar one, as if a crackling, sparkling net had been tossed over her from head to foot, enclosing her in the same space with Warrick.

She felt completely safe there with him, with their bodies just lightly touching. She was close enough to feel his warmth and to smell the clean scent of the soap he used. When she leaned a little closer, Warrick did not object. Sophia thought that she was still capable of speech, though she did not say anything, for Warrick placed a finger on the veil at the place where her lips were and she nodded to let him know she understood the need for silence.

The sky was rapidly lightening and the net of invisibility that Warrick had cast over them did not prevent Sophia from seeing what was happening beyond the place where they were standing. It was fascinating, and not at all frightening to realize that, while her view was unobstructed, no one could see her.

She watched the *shinha* guard approach the five camels. He paused before reaching the animals, and kicked at one of the baskets waiting to be loaded, knocking it over so the foodstuffs inside went tumbling onto the ground. A packet of raisins, a larger pack of dried dates, and a clay jar full of lentils spilled out of the basket. The lid of the lentil jar rolled across the court and disappeared. The guard shrugged, scuffing the lentils into the dirt. Then he walked around the camels, keeping his distance from them but peering intently between them, as if he expected to find Sophia or Warrick hiding there.

"Where are the two who were with you?" the guard said to Robin.

"*Salaam alaykum.* Peace be upon you," Robin responded in Arabic as if he did not understand the question.

"*Wa alaykum as-salaam.* And upon you be peace," the guard responded in a gruff way that suggested peace was not on his mind. His cold expression and the curl of his lips expressed his lordly disdain for an uneducated man who spoke only Arabic.

"The man and the woman," the guard said in Farsi, the language of all educated men who lived under Seljuk rule. "They were here a moment ago. The woman was making a great deal of noise."

"Ah, that would be Ibrahim and Fatima," Robin said, still speaking Arabic. "She is his second wife, and Ibrahim dotes on her. She was noisy because she feels ill, and he is overly solicitous because he hopes she is with child. Ibrahim longs for a healthy son. He took Fatima inside to find a quieter place for her to rest until the caravan starts to move. Shall I try to find them for you? It will be difficult, I think," Robin said, looking over the crowd as if he were searching for the pair the guard wanted.

"I'll find them myself." The guard looked down his nose at Robin for a moment before stalking off toward the arcade at one side of the caravansary.

"Robin, how clever you are to make up such a detailed story so quickly, and to pretend you speak only Arabic," Genie said with a giggle. "I think that guard believed it was beneath his dignity to question a lowly person like you."

"That's what I wanted him to believe," Robin said. "Warrick, it's safe to reveal yourself now. Just remember the names I gave you, in case the guard returns."

Warrick grabbed Sophia's hand and pulled her between the camels, making his way toward Robin and Genie. The tingling sensation that Sophia had been experiencing ceased abruptly. At once the nearest camel cast a malevolent eye on her and let loose a horrific braying sound. Sophia yelped in surprise and jumped to one side, bumping into Warrick. He yanked her out of the way just in time, as the camel turned its head and spat a stream of vile-smelling brown fluid in her direction.

"Master Warrick," Genie chided, laughing at him, "you ought to know better than to drop your guise of invisibility in a place where you can startle people and animals. The poor camel was frightened half to death to see you and Sophia appear out of the air."

"Frightened indeed," Robin scoffed. "That disagreeable beast was just waiting for an excuse to spit at someone."

"Warrick, are we really visible now?" Sophia asked.

"We are," he said. He touched the veil over her cheek with a gentle hand, as if to assure her that she could be both seen and felt. This touch was quite unlike the hard way he had held her in place when the guard was searching for them.

"There are no lasting effects," Warrick said. He took his hand from her cheek and turned away, rubbing at his forehead.

There was a lasting effect, though it was one Sophia hoped he would not recognize. Her heartbeat and her breathing were more rapid than normal, and she longed to go into Warrick's arms, to feel safe and protected by him. Knowing her reactions were irrational, Sophia looked around in search of a subject she could raise that would not remind her of Warrick and herself bound together by invisibility, alone in the midst of a crowded courtyard. She discovered that the subject she sought was conveniently near at hand.

"Why do we have five camels, when there are only four of us?" she asked.

"The extra beast will carry our baggage," Robin explained. "We do have a few things to take along, in spite of the hasty way we are leaving. We have to supply our own food and water, so Genie and I bought what we'll need for the first leg of the trip at the same time that we bought the camels. Warrick and I have clothing, but I notice that you and Genie aren't carrying any baggage. Where are your clothes?"

"We are wearing them," Sophia said, adding in a sarcastic tone, "Unlike Genie, I care little for fanciful adornment."

"Perhaps you should care." Genie spoke in a voice that, by its very lack of response to Sophia's sarcasm, was a rebuke to her.

"Speaking of baggage," Warrick said into the uncomfortable silence, "I think we ought to load the pack camel at once. It looks to me as if the caravan leader is almost ready to start." He put his hands to his head again, rubbing his temples as he had done before.

"How long will the pain last?" Genie asked him.

"It depends upon the spell," Warrick answered. "Sophia and I were invisible for only a short time, so the headache ought to be gone before I have to mount one of those charming camels," he said with a rueful smile.

"Do you mean that working magic causes you pain?" Sophia asked in surprise. "I know that his rare attempts at conjuring wearied my father, but I never heard him complain about pain."

"I always develop a headache," Warrick said, "because of the intense concentration required to work a spell."

Sharp words hovered on the tip of Sophia's tongue. She longed to remark that obviously Warrick hadn't been concentrating very hard when he lost Hua Te. Then she intercepted a hard look from Genie, and saw the slight shake of Genie's head beneath the veil, and Sophia remembered that Warrick's present headache was the result of his attempt to protect her from a guard whose attention Sophia had drawn upon herself. By her earlier loud, sharp words, she had put all of them in danger, and Warrick had rescued her. Thus the headache he was suffering was her fault.

"Is there something that I or Genie could do to ease your discomfort?" Sophia asked Warrick.

"No, but I thank you for the offer," he said.

"And I ought to thank you for saving me from the guard," Sophia responded.

Warrick's gaze held hers for a long time. There was a warm light flickering in his brown eyes, as if he saw something in her that he found likable, though she did not think he had liked her at all until that moment. She did not think he liked her even when he kissed her.

Then Warrick smiled at her, and Sophia smiled back at him. She was sorry he could not see the curve of her lips beneath her veil, but perhaps he could see the smile in her eyes.

Chapter Ten

"You two men will have to load the camels," Genie said. "It would look most peculiar for a woman to do it."

"Can you at least make this loathsome beast stand still while I fasten the girths?" Robin asked. "And then convince it to kneel while Warrick and I pack the saddle?"

"If you would only think more kindly of Salima, she would sense your affection and not dislike you so much," Genie said. "Then she would do as you want."

"How anyone can like a camel is beyond me," Robin grumbled, "much less give it a name like Salima." He pulled the saddle girth hard. With a loud groan Salima shied away and the saddle fell to the ground. Salima swung her head around to look at Robin. Her lips began to work in obvious preparation for spitting. Robin jumped back and the foul-smelling mess just missed him.

Genie began to giggle.

"Damnation," Robin muttered. "Genie, will you kindly make this unnatural creature behave so we can get ready to leave? It is growing lighter by the minute, and the caravan will soon begin to move. We don't want to be left behind just because a cursed camel is misbehaving."

"You don't understand," Genie said, still giggling. "Misbehavior is perfectly natural for a camel. In that trait, camels are not unlike some humans." She was holding Salima's reins and she gave them a tug, pulling the animal's head down to shoulder level. She began to stroke the camel's nose, murmuring words in a language that Sophia did not understand. Apparently entranced by Genie's attentions, the camel knelt while Robin replaced the pack saddle, then rose and stood still while Robin fastened the two girths, one in front of Salima's single hump and the other behind. Again Salima knelt at Genie's soft command, so Warrick and Robin could pack their baggage onto the saddle. When they were finished, Genie spoke to Salima and the camel stood up. The two men moved on to saddle the remaining camels for riding.

Sophia was standing next to Genie, watching the procedure with interest. As Salima rose to her feet, Sophia stared up at her. The camel was extremely tall, at least half again as tall as Sophia was. The animal's hump towered above even Warrick's head. Sophia had known that she was going to have to mount one of the animals, but until that minute she had not realized how high she would be sitting.

During her excursions into the streets of Baghdad, Sophia had seen camels many times and had often observed people riding them. Never had she imagined that she would have to ride one. As she stared up—and up—at Salima's hump, she considered Robin's disparaging remarks about camels in a new light. She was not prepared to deal with a cantankerous, vile-tempered animal.

As she took a long look at Salima, the last of Sophia's residual exultation over her successful leap across the rooftops vanished and all of her fear of heights returned in a rush of horror. Every day for days on end she was going to have to climb onto a camel and stay there all day long, under the broiling sun. She would fall off and be crushed beneath the camel's feet. She would die of thirst and too much sun. She could not do it, could not join the caravan.

Sophia longed to return to the cool, shadowy rooms of her father's house and to stay there, far from the noise and confusion around her, and safe from the need to get up on a camel's back. She made herself put aside her longings. The past was gone and nothing she could do would bring it back. She had to deal with the present, and with the future, as bravely as she could.

"Time to mount," Warrick said, coming to her with the reins of the smallest camel in his hand. "Have you ever done this before?"

"No." Sophia's mouth was dry. She had never ridden on any animal in her life, but she was not going to tell Warrick that. If she began to complain, the fragile new peace between herself and Warrick would be disturbed. He would begin to dislike her again, and see her as a nuisance.

"I will help you," he said, "but once you are mounted, it will be up to you to stay on the camel. It's not the most comfortable ride, but you will get used to it after a while."

She did not ask how long a while. She was too afraid to say anything. When the camel gave her a baleful look, Sophia thought she was going to faint.

"This is Nura," Genie said, patting the camel affectionately. "Be nice to her, Sophia."

"You ought to be telling Nura to be nice to Sophia," Robin said with an encouraging smile for Sophia.

At Genie's bidding, Nura went to her knees. Warrick helped Sophia to mount, showed her where to put her feet, and gave her the reins. Sophia had never before been so close to a camel. Nura smelled dreadful, and she appeared to suffer from a skin disease. Furthermore, sitting in the saddle was most uncomfortable.

Sophia wished with all her heart that she dared to dismount and refuse to ride Nura, but she knew she could not make a fuss. If she did there would be another argument with Warrick that would surely draw renewed attention from the *shinha* guards, and that could easily result in arrest for all of them. Worst of all, if she refused to stay on the camel, Warrick would learn how afraid she was.

Thankful that the heavy veil she wore would hide her facial expressions, Sophia gritted her teeth, closed her eyes, and thought of leaping blithely from one roof to another. She told herself if she could do that and survive her terror, then she could learn to ride a camel, which was nowhere near as tall as her father's house.

Genie spoke and Nura began to stand. Sophia

was rocked sharply forward and then backward just as hard. She almost screamed. She bit off the sound because she opened her eyes and the first person she saw was the guard who had gone into the arcade looking for her and Warrick. She would not attract his attention to herself. She clutched the reins until her knuckles turned white. Still she rocked with dangerous instability each time Nura took a step. Sophia wound the reins around her hands and held on for her life. Slowly Nura paced toward the tall gate of the caravansary. As Sophia began to adjust to Nura's gait she started to believe she wouldn't fall off after all.

Feeling a little more secure on her high perch, Sophia risked a quick look around. She half expected to see a band of *shinha* coming after her, but the man who had been interested in her and Warrick was nowhere to be seen. There was only a single, bored-looking guard at the gate.

As her concerns about staying on Nura's back and about arrest receded, Sophia began to pay more attention to the makeup of the caravan. There were several men whose skin tones and almond eyes marked them as natives of Cathay. Another group of about a dozen wearing tunics, trousers, and wide-brimmed fur hats were clearly tribesmen from the far northern steppe lands. They rode small, shaggy ponies instead of camels, and their packhorses were overloaded with water skins, which Sophia guessed were intended for the horses.

Also included in the caravan were dusky-skinned, dark-eyed men from the Land of Hind and a few Greek traders. The largest contingent of travelers was made up of Arabs in flowing robes and headscarves. There were even a few other women traveling with the caravan. Not many, only half a dozen or so, but there were enough females riding on camels that Sophia and Genie were not particularly noticeable.

The caravansary was located just inside the city, so it took less than an hour for the entire, slow-moving caravan to pass through the al-Muazza gate in the northern wall and out onto the fertile, grassy plain that surrounded Baghdad. The guards at the gate waved them through. No one stopped them or even asked a question; no member of the *shinha* came after them, and Sophia began to breathe a little easier.

She was still watching the other travelers and wondering about their lives, when she heard a baby cry. A woman riding ahead and to one side of Sophia's group moved about on her camel as if she had been born riding it. Sophia decided the woman was adjusting her clothing in preparation for nursing, for her left arm lifted, her veiled head bent forward, and the baby's crying suddenly stopped.

Sophia imagined the woman was the wife or concubine of the man who rode near her at the head of several heavily loaded camels. Sophia thought the man was a trader setting out from Baghdad with his wares, who did not want to leave his woman or his child behind. He also brought with him a slender youth who was helping with the camels and who, by the similarity of their faces, was the trader's older son.

"How are you?" Warrick asked, guiding his camel close enough to speak with her. Before mounting he had donned a robe and headscarf similar to Robin's costume. He looked disconcertingly like one of the Arabs. It was a simple and effective disguise.

"It's not difficult to ride a camel," Sophia said. That was a lie. The constant rocking motion was having a most unsettling effect on her empty stomach.

"I'm happy to know you are enjoying yourself," Warrick said with a grin.

"Do we ride all day?" Sophia asked. "Or do we stop now and then to eat or to stretch?"

"Since the weather is not overly hot at present, we will travel without stopping until sunset," he said.

"Not overly hot? It's midsummer," Sophia exclaimed. She felt as if she were inside an oven, covered as she was in the veil and heavy woolen dress.

"The *shamal* cooled the air, and the caravan leader told Robin that he intends to take advantage of the change," Warrick said. "The sooner we reach Hamadan, the more profit he will earn, since he can then immediately lead another caravan back to Baghdad. If the days turn hot, we will have to travel at night and that will mean the caravan will move more slowly in the dark and take longer to reach Hamadan."

"Hamadan," Sophia repeated. "You said we were going to Tabriz."

"So we are," Warrick responded mildly. "The route goes first to Hamadan, then on to Rayy, to Qasvin, and finally to Tabriz. At each stop we will have to arrange to join a new caravan. It is certainly not a direct road to Byzantium, but I think your father was right that it will be the safest way."

"Once again you failed to disclose your plans to me," Sophia said in an injured tone.

"I thought you knew all about the caravan routes," he said, sending an amused look in her direction.

"How should I know about such things?" she snapped at him. "I am not a merchant. You should have told me, Warrick."

"Since you insist upon knowing all of my plans," he said, "perhaps it will please you to learn that we won't be riding camels all the way to Tabriz."

"We won't?" She sounded absurdly hopeful, and Warrick grinned at her again.

"At some point we will switch to horses or donkeys," he said. "I will take care to let you know beforehand."

"Thank you," she responded coldly. She heard him chuckle as he dropped back to talk with Robin.

Sophia thought about getting down and walking. The camels moved so slowly that she was sure she would have no difficulty in keeping up with the rest of the caravan. Her own camel kept stopping along the way to eat the leaves of the few unappetizing-looking bushes that grew beside the gravel road. Sophia could see that other people were walking. The problem was that if she got off Nura, she would eventually have to remount. She had been so frightened by the way Nura lurched to her feet back at the caravansary, pitching her passenger forward and back again, that she did not care to go through the process a second time in one day. She stayed on the camel.

By the time the caravan leader called a halt at sundown, Sophia was light-headed from lack of food and so stiff from riding all day that she could hardly stand.

The caravansary where they were to stay for the

night was far smaller than the building in Baghdad, and the caravan was so large that there was not enough room inside it for everyone.

"I don't want to sleep here," said Sophia, lifting her skirts above her ankles and holding the fabric close to her sides so it would not touch the dusty-looking wall. "I am sure there are a great many nasty bugs crawling on the walls and floors." She was too tired and much too hungry to care that she sounded overly squeamish and critical, or to worry about what Warrick thought of her opinions. All the same, she was grateful when Robin suggested an alternative to the caravansary.

"Some of the other travelers are planning to sleep outside the caravansary," Robin said. "For example, the northern tribesmen, who are Kumans, are concerned that bandits will sneak down from the hills in the dark and steal their horses. Their leader, Gafar, has decided they will spend the night sleeping next to their mounts. And the man who was traveling just ahead of us intends to set up a tent because he thinks it will be quieter for the baby."

"How do you know all of this?" Sophia asked.

"I overheard them talking," Robin responded with no hint of embarrassment at eavesdropping.

"But they speak several different languages."

"True enough." Robin grinned at her. "During my travels with Warrick and Hua Te and the years I've lived in Baghdad, I have learned bits and pieces of a dozen languages. I am not fluent in any of them, you understand. Languages are Warrick's skill, not mine. But I do know enough to make sense of what most people I meet are saying, and I can speak enough to assure me of food, water, and lodging wherever I go.

"It's too bad we don't have a tent," Robin continued with a displeased glance at the building. "If we did we could avoid this decrepit caravansary."

"There I can help you," Genie told him. "Master Warrick, what say you? Shall we sleep in cleanliness and comfort out on the plain?"

"I think it would be a very good idea," Warrick said, "so long as we can arrange to locate our tent between the camps of those fierce tribesmen with their valuable horses to guard, and the fellow who will have an interest in protecting his child. Robin and I can offer our services as sentries, and the three parties can take turns protecting each other through the night."

"I like the sound of that," Robin said, "but where is our tent? We did not pack one onto Salima's back, and Sophia and Genie brought no baggage at all."

"You underestimate me, Robin," Genie said. "Only choose a site and I will erect a tent on it."

"First we ought to introduce ourselves and make a few polite inquiries," Warrick said. "Sophia, Genie, wait here with the camels. Robin, come with me."

The two men struck out from the caravansary entrance, heading for a slight rise in the ground a short distance away, where the tribesmen were building campfires. They had staked out a small corral for their horses and had apparently agreed to camp in close proximity to the man who was traveling with his family. The camels were tethered a short distance from the horses, and the unloaded goods were stacked beside a small tent.

Warrick and Robin were both tall and muscular, and they had brought along several weapons apiece. It did not take them long to work out an agreement for mutual defense among temporary neighbors. Robin raised a hand and beckoned to Sophia and to Genie, who was holding the camels.

"We are to pitch our camp just up the slope from the tribesmen," Robin said when the women joined him. "Warrick is still talking, settling the details of who is to take which watch tonight. Genie, if you will keep Salima under control, I will unload our belongings and then help you with the tent."

When they reached their designated campsite, they discovered there was a tiny stream winding around the bottom of the grassy slope.

"It's the water supply for the caravansary," Robin explained. "It runs down from the mountains. In this season it's more of a trickle than a real stream. It will probably dry up completely before summer is over, and the people who manage the caravansary will have to resort to well water. We are fortunate to be upstream from everyone else; there will be more than enough clean water in the stream for all of us as well as for the animals."

"We trade the security of caravansary walls for open air and water," said a deep voice. "Not a bad bargain. I am Sadiq, your neighbor on this hillside."

Sadiq was the man with the baby and the heavily laden camels. He was a tall, heavyset man with a loud voice that carried across the camp, and he had a habit of interrupting when others were speaking. As he talked to Robin, Sophia learned that he was a merchant, as she had guessed, but he was not on a business trip. He was moving his family from Baghdad to Qasvin and the baggage the camels carried represented all of his worldly goods. He did not disclose the reason for the move.

When Sadiq departed to return to his tent, Genie made Salima kneel so Robin could retrieve his and Warrick's belongings. Then, with the five camels tethered nearby, Genie turned to Sophia.

"Where shall our tent be?" she asked.

"There." Sophia pointed to a level area where a fold of the hillside would protect the tent from gusty winds. She could not think of any other qualifications for a campsite, though she did think of a limitation she ought to place on Genie. "You have a predilection for gaudy colors. Our tent should be a simple structure that will not draw attention to us."

"I, gaudy?" Genie exclaimed. "Well, perhaps a little. Very well, then, Sophia, you shall have your plain and simple tent. However, for my own sake, and for the sake of our two charming male companions, it will also be comfortable on the inside."

Genie turned around once, pausing to look in the direction of the tribesmen's encampment, and then to gaze toward Sadiq's tent.

"No one is watching," Genie said. "Now, then." She lifted both arms in a high, swooping gesture and when she lowered her arms, a tent stood in the spot Sophia had selected. It was made of dull brown felt and it was a simple structure when seen from outside, though it did seem to be larger than was strictly necessary for four people.

"Aha!" said Robin, nodding his head sagely. "I thought you must be something other than a mere human. No mortal could handle camels the way you do. Genie, are you a magician, or are you a supernatural being?"

"Do you mean she hasn't told you?" Sophia cried.

"She is a jinni. My father conjured her into existence shortly before he died."

"How fortunate you are, Sophia, to have such a companion," Robin said.

Sophia considered his words for a little while before she responded. "Do you know, Robin, I believe you are right! At first I was so appalled by the sudden appearance of a jinni, and by my father's insistence that I accept her into my life, that I stubbornly refused to think about the positive aspects of Genie's presence. She has been consistently cheerful and useful. She was kind and supportive of me when my father died. Even when she irritates me, she is acting in my best interests. She cannot do otherwise, of course, but if she were to disappear, I confess I would miss her."

"Thank you, mistress," Genie said in a demure way that was totally at odds with her usual independent and humorous manner.

"How long is she to stay with you?" Robin asked.

"Indefinitely," Sophia said. "My father died before revealing to me the words of the spell that will send her back to the Land of the Jinn, so I do not know how to get rid of her. I am no longer sure I want to get rid of her."

"If you ever do learn the words of the spell," Robin said, "speak to me before you utter them."

"Well," said Genie, "I am sure Sophia would like a warm bath, and I expect Robin and Warrick would, too. I believe there is a pitcher in the tent."

Sophia's back and thigh muscles were aching after a long day of sitting on a camel saddle, and she was thirsty. Thinking that movement would alleviate her muscular discomfort and also prevent stiffness when morning came, she decided to walk to the stream to drink there. She had little concern about safety. She remained veiled and she would be in full view of the camp on the hillside.

She had almost reached the stream when she heard a footstep behind her. She looked over her shoulder, expecting to see Genie. It was Sadiq's veiled wife who followed her. The woman held a large copper jug in her right hand and Sophia recognized her by the way she held her left arm, where she carried her baby under the veil.

"Are you going to the stream, too?" Sophia asked. She used Farsi, so she would not insult the woman if that was her preferred language. She could switch to Arabic if the woman did not understand Farsi. They were the two languages Sophia knew best, though her mother had instructed her in Greek and Latin. She also had a smattering of a tongue that Helena had referred to as Norman French.

"I will wait until you have finished," the woman answered in Farsi.

"I'm sure there is room for both of us to drink at the same time," Sophia responded politely. Then, noticing a movement on the left side of the woman's veil, she said, "I see that you have your baby with you."

"Yes. Musa is so warm that I thought a bath would cool him."

"It must be awfully hot for him under that veil."

"My husband says Musa must be shielded from the burning sun. I am Alya," the woman said shyly.

"I am Sophia. Would you like me to hold Musa while you wash and—er—attend to personal matters? I noticed some bushes on the other side of the stream that will provide shelter for you. I wouldn't mind holding him. I'm sure I won't drop him," Sophia promised, though she had never actually held a baby before.

The offer was an impulsive one, made out of sympathy for another woman who had also endured a day under the hot sun while wearing a heavy veil. Sophia could not help feeling a bit sorry for Alya. Sadiq had impressed her as a pompous type who was probably an overbearing husband. She could not imagine how tiring it must be to have to carry a child all day, while at the same time trying to keep one's balance on a camel. She rather thought Sadiq should have taken the child for part of the time. She knew how unlikely that was. Having listened to Hanna's complaints all of her life, Sophia was well aware that in Baghdad, and very likely elsewhere, too, women did most of the world's work.

"I would so much like to remove my veil and feel the cool air on my face," Alya whispered.

"Then do so," Sophia said. "I will keep watch and warn you if anyone approaches, so no strange man will see your face or the back of your head. Besides, you can't possibly bathe your son while you are wearing that heavy shroud."

"Shroud," Alya repeated with a sigh. "Yes, that is how it feels to me." She set the copper jug down by the stream and used her right hand to lift the veil so she could give the baby to Sophia. He was very small, with a red face, bright dark eyes, and a damp fuzz of black hair. His tiny body was tightly swaddled in wet, smelly cloth.

"I was not able to change his cloths during the day," Alya said. "As a result, I fear, he has developed a rash."

"Would it help if I removed the cloth?" Sophia

asked, hiking up her own veil so she could take the small bundle into her arms.

"Yes, it would. You are so kind." Alya pulled off her veil to reveal the flushed face of a girl at least five years younger than Sophia. Her dark hair was drawn into a single braid that was damp with perspiration. Her earrings were gold hoops set with turquoise, and her plain dark gown was of the finest wool. Alya knelt at the edge of the stream to splash water onto her face. "Oh, that feels wonderful. Do you mind watching Musa while I go behind that bush?"

"Of course not. I said I would watch him."

"I shouldn't ask so much of a stranger," Alya whispered. "Still, my need is urgent."

"While you are gone I shall undress Musa and splash cool water on him," Sophia said. She looked down into the baby's face. He stared back at her with wide, shining eyes and Sophia experienced an odd, sweet tenderness. Almost without thought she cuddled the baby closer.

Alya disappeared behind the bushes and Sophia began to unwrap Musa. He was not only wet, he was dirty. Sophia wrinkled her nose in distaste and laid him down on a clean patch of sand at the edge of the stream. She held him in place with one hand while with the other hand she used Alya's jug to dip water out of the stream. Not knowing how else to get him clean, she simply poured the water over Musa's lower body. In response Musa turned bright red and shrieked with rage, his little fists and feet flailing wildly.

"Oh, hush, hush." Sophia picked him up to hold him close to her in the hope he would stop crying. The sensation of Musa's small, warm body in her arms touched a chord in Sophia's heart that had never been stroked until that moment. She was pierced by a bittersweet longing. Before she had a chance to consider the unusual feeling, Musa went rigid against her shoulder and began to scream in her ear.

"Sophia, what are you doing with a baby?" Genie asked, coming down the slope to the stream.

"I am trying to help Sadiq's wife," Sophia said. "Genie, I don't know anything about babies!"

"I can see that." Genie put out a finger to stroke Musa's blue-veined little head. Instantly he stopped crying and stared at the figure in the dark veil, who crooned to him in a soft voice. "There, there, my little man. If I can gentle recalcitrant camels, I ought to be able to quiet you. Sophia, what did you do to him?"

"He was overheated and very dirty," Sophia said, "so I poured cool water over him. I haven't harmed him, have I?"

"No. He's just angry." Genie put her finger beneath Musa's tiny chin. "If you were hot and tired and hungry and someone suddenly poured cold water on your belly, you would scream, too."

"I suppose I would," Sophia said. "I was only thinking of getting him clean and cool as soon as possible."

"May I hold him?" Genie put out her arms to take Musa. "Oh, he's beautiful. What bright eyes. You can see that he's very intelligent. I do so like babies."

"That's a strange thing for a jinni to say. Although, now that he's not screaming anymore, I must admit that he is a handsome boy," Sophia said. Seeing Alya reappear, she introduced Genie as her cousin from Mosul.

"May we help you to bathe him?" Genie asked.

"Oh, I don't want to give him up. What a sweet little thing he is."

"Thank you. I am very proud of him, and so is Sadiq." Alya took Musa from Genie. Kneeling on the thin strip of sand she slowly immersed the baby in the stream, splashing water onto his feet and legs, making a game of it and talking to him until he was submerged to his armpits and apparently enjoying the experience. Genie produced a bowl of soap from under her veil and the two began to wash the baby, with Sophia looking on in fascination.

"Alya, you were right. He does have a rash," Sophia observed.

"I am sure Warrick will have a salve that will help," Genie said.

"He will?" Sophia asked in surprise.

"The sack Warrick carries is full of bandages and medicines," Genie said. "Alya, I will ask him for a pot of salve and bring it to you shortly."

With Musa clean and wrapped in fresh cloths, and the old cloths laundered in the stream using more of Genie's soap, Alya expressed profuse thanks and then took her leave.

Sophia watched her climbing the slope with the baby slung on one hip, carrying Musa's wet cloths and the copper jug full of water, cloaked in her dark veil and, somehow, in spite of all the encumbrances, managing to keep her balance.

"I wonder if she's happy," Sophia murmured.

"Alya is surely content with her baby, if not with her husband," Genie said.

As Sophia turned her eyes away from the young

mother and her burdens, her attention was caught
by the tall, broad-shouldered figure standing atop
the little hill. He appeared to be scanning the horizon and the mountains through which the caravan must soon travel. Then Warrick looked down
at her and their gazes locked and held. A slight
tremor went through Sophia and for just a moment, in her memory, she was back in her father's
cluttered study, with Warrick's arms around her
and his mouth warm and searching on hers.

Sophia did not understand how it happened or
what it meant, but the memory of Warrick's embrace was suddenly interwoven with the longing
she had felt while holding Musa. She became aware
of a stirring deep within her body, of an aching
emptiness in her heart and her mind. And she
wished that Warrick would stroll down the hillside
and put his arms around her.

Chapter Eleven

"I cannot create water," Genie explained to Sophia, "but if I have a supply of water at hand, I am able to increase it, and to change its temperature."

"You mentioned that once before, in Baghdad. Why is that so?" Sophia asked. She was pleased to discover a subject that would take her mind off Warrick and distract her from desires she knew she ought not to have. She wasn't quite sure exactly where those desires might lead her; she only knew that Warrick aroused them and that they, and he, frightened her. She did know that it was wrong of her to yearn for Warrick's arms around her when he cared nothing for her. She was an obligation to him, nothing more. Eager to turn her thoughts away from dangerous wishes, she pursued the issue Genie had just raised. "I have seen you create objects out of the air. Our clothes, for example. And the tent. Why can't you make water, too?"

"It's because water is a basic element," Genie said. "Earth, air, fire, and water are the four primary substances. They can be created only by the One who is greater than I."

"The One?" Sophia repeated. "Are you saying that the jinn have religious beliefs?"

"The One," Genie said, "is the ultimate creator. More than that I cannot tell you, for I do not think you would believe me, or comprehend the subtleties of the principles involved. That is not intended to be a criticism of your intellect, Sophia. Most humans cannot understand cosmic complexities."

"I suppose that means I am not to ask any more questions," Sophia said with a little laugh. "Don't worry, Genie; I'm not offended. I am used to being put off with excuses about my inability to understand complicated theories. My father did it all the time."

The two women were on their way from the stream to the tent. Robin met them on his way to join Warrick at his lookout spot.

"Are you going to allow Warrick and me to use the tub, too?" Robin asked Genie.

"What tub?" Sophia said.

"Do you mean you haven't looked inside the tent yet?" Robin asked.

"No," Sophia said. "I've been busy."

"Prepare yourself for a grand surprise." Robin smiled his boyish grin at Sophia. "If Genie's cooking skills match her homemaking ability, we are going to have a very pleasant journey." With that Robin walked on to meet Warrick.

Sophia and Genie approached the tent that Genie had produced by magic. Like most tents in that part of the world, it was constructed of felt made from camel hair. Seen from the outside it boasted no decoration; it was simply a round dwelling about ten feet in diameter and ten feet high at its center post. The flap over the entrance was closed. Sophia lifted the flap and stood back to allow Genie, who was carrying a pitcher filled with water from the stream, to enter first. Sophia followed Genie inside—and gasped in amazement.

The interior walls and the ceiling of the tent were hung with panels of silk in several shades of blue. Lush carpets patterned in red, blue, and gold covered the dirt floor. A copper bathtub was placed on the carpets. Two pierced brass lanterns attached to the center pole shed a soft light on large, square silk cushions of blue and gold. A blue silk curtain was drawn back to the tent wall. Sophia could see how the curtain could be pulled across the interior of the tent to make a small inner room. The only objects in the tent that were familiar to Sophia were the baskets and bundles belonging to Warrick and Robin, which were stacked to one side of the entrance.

"Genie, what have you done?" Sophia exclaimed, looking around. "If any other travelers come in here, what will they think? This cannot be the same kind of tent they are using. Not even Sadiq will have a place like this to sleep in."

"It is highly unlikely that anyone will intrude on us," Genie said. "Caravan travelers tend to be weary at day's end and are not much given to visiting their temporary neighbors. If any guests should come, I will make certain that they see only a plain, ordinary tent."

"You shouldn't have done this," Sophia cried. "It is far too luxurious. In fact this tent looks much as

I imagine the sultan's harem must look and I do not care to be reminded of him."

"You have lived a sadly deprived life if you think this is luxury," Genie said with a wave of her hand toward the silk walls and the cushions. "I assure you, sultans live in a degree of splendor that would dazzle your eyes.

"Mistress, I was only trying to make you comfortable. The rest of us, too. We have all endured a long and tiring day after a night of little sleep. Let me prepare a bath for you, and conjure clean clothing. I must admit that I would enjoy a hot bath, too."

"Can't you just clean all of us by magic?" Sophia asked.

"I could, but a relaxing soak in hot water is so much more pleasant," Genie said. "Come now, before the men return, remove your clothes and I will heat your bathwater."

Sophia wanted to protest. To her mind there was something decadent in the silk-walled tent and in Genie's blandishments. She did not want to undress when Warrick might stride into the tent at any moment. On the other hand, her muscles were still aching, she was hot and tired, and the front of her veil was damp and soiled from holding Musa. The thought of washing in plenty of warm water and of rising clean from the bath to put on fresh clothing was too alluring to resist.

Sophia yanked the hated veil away and let it drop to the carpet. Then she quickly stripped off the rest of her garments and tossed them on top of the veil. The interior of the tent was comfortably warm; still, Sophia shivered when she was naked. No one except her mother and Hanna had ever seen her without clothes. Somehow she did not mind if Genie was with her when she undressed. It was the thought of Warrick that made her tremble. Sophia wished she could stop thinking about Warrick and stop wondering if he would find her attractive, should he step into the tent at that moment. She told herself she ought to be ashamed of such thoughts.

"Come, Sophia." Having poured into the copper tub some of the water from the pitcher she carried, Genie beckoned her to the bath.

The tub was larger than Sophia had realized, and it was filled with hot water topped by pale blue bubbles. The scent of hyacinth wafted through the air.

"You did this by magic," Sophia exclaimed, drawing back from the tub.

"It is easy enough to do, and only takes an instant." Genie showed her the pitcher, which still contained a good portion of water. "I have saved enough for myself and for the men, too. Go on, Sophia. A little indulgence will do you a world of good."

When Sophia stepped into the tub she discovered that she could stretch out in it to her full length. She leaned back, resting her head against the curved rim.

"Give yourself up to the pleasure," Genie crooned in the same voice she had used with Musa. "Let every aching muscle and joint relax, breathe in the fragrance, and think only of happy scenes and joyful experiences."

"I haven't had many happy experiences," Sophia murmured with her eyes closed.

"I know," Genie said, her voice like a gentle

breeze. "Soon enough joy will overcome sadness, if only you will let it."

Sophia wriggled her fingers and toes in delight and stretched her legs out until her feet reached the end of the tub. The water was a perfect temperature, neither too hot nor too cool. Allowing her thoughts to drift aimlessly, Sophia gradually slipped into a state of peaceful contentment. How long she soaked in the warm, flower-scented water she did not know or care. Time did not matter. She did not rouse herself from the sweet lethargy until she heard Warrick's voice outside the tent. Then she sat up abruptly, sloshing soapsuds onto the carpet.

"Here." Genie handed her a sponge and a bowl of hyacinth-scented soap. "You will want this. There is no need to rush, Sophia. I will tell Warrick we are bathing and that he is not to enter the tent until his own bath is ready."

Left alone, Sophia used the soap and the sponge, and she washed her hair, too. She remained in a relaxed, dreamlike state until Genie returned carrying a large towel. Sophia left the tub and allowed Genie to dry her.

"I have never had a maidservant," Sophia said. "I am used to caring for myself."

"You haven't done a very good job of it," Genie told her, holding up Sophia's hands to examine her work-roughened skin and untended nails. "Never mind, I will see to what needs to be done." She slipped a loose silk robe over Sophia's head, and then led her to the pillows that were piled against the back wall of the tent.

"Lie down," Genie said. "Rest for a while." She

pulled the blue silk curtain across the tent, enclosing Sophia in a private space.

The pillows were wonderfully soft. Lulled by the warmth and perfume of her bath, and by Genie's hypnotic voice, Sophia fell into a light sleep. She was dimly aware of the sound of splashing water and of voices at some distance. And she smelled wonderful fragrances. First there was a spicy scent that somehow reminded Sophia of Genie. Recalling Warrick's objection to Genie's rose perfume, Sophia wondered if the creature had changed her fragrance.

"But she's not a creature," Sophia murmured to herself. "She's a person. A friend. I have never had a friend until now."

Next came a whiff of clean lemon scent that Sophia, even half-asleep as she was, instinctively knew was intended for Robin. It was like him, straightforward, uncomplicated, and pleasant.

And then, finally, Sophia smelled green leaves caught in the windblown mist from a fountain's jet. Once, her father had taken her to the home of a fellow scholar so she could visit with the daughters of the house while John discussed astrological projections with the girls' father. Sophia had not cared much for the simpering, uneducated girls, but she had never forgotten the marvelous garden of their house, with its fountains and moisture-splashed leaves. The fragrance she was presently breathing was very like the air in that garden.

"Sophia?" Genie pulled the curtain aside. "Are you ready to eat?"

"I am hungry." Sophia sat up and stretched, running her hands through her hair. Her fingers brushed against earrings. There were amethyst-studded, golden bracelets on both of her wrists. The skin of her hands was smooth and her fingernails were shaped into neat ovals and buffed until they gleamed. Looking down, she saw that her toenails were also buffed, and they peeked through the dainty straps of gilded leather sandals. Sophia noted that the silk robe in which Genie had earlier dressed her was deep violet in color, with gold trim at neck and wrists. When she rose to her feet, the silk flowed against her body in a disturbingly sensual way.

There was a tiny mirror on the tent wall. In it Sophia saw that her earrings were large gold hoops with amethysts dangling from them. The purple shades of jewels and robe combined to make her eyes appear more violet than blue, a dusky, mysterious shade. When she moved, a faint trace of hyacinth reached her nose.

Genie had seen to her own wardrobe, too. She was clad in a pair of ballooning trousers and a tight bodice that left her midriff bare. Both garments were made of silk in a wild shade of pink that should have clashed with Genie's bright red hair, yet did not, perhaps because of the distraction created by the gold necklaces, bracelets, earrings, and rings, all set with multicolored gems, in which Genie was draped. She even had a gem-encrusted gold chain wound into her hair. She saw Sophia's stare and grinned.

"I restrained myself somewhat when I dressed you," Genie said.

"If you did this to us," Sophia asked, "what have you done to the men?"

"Come and see." Genie pulled the dividing curtain back the rest of the way, allowing Sophia to look around the remainder of the tent. The bathtub was gone. In its place was a low table set for a meal, with cushions placed around it on the carpet for seating.

The men wore caftans. Robin was in blue. Warrick wore a shade of smoky topaz that matched his eyes. The robes were so plain that Sophia suspected Warrick and Robin of joining forces to override Genie's tendency toward excessive decoration.

Warrick needed no decoration. His tall, broad-shouldered figure made the most of the silk caftan. His smoldering gaze caught and held Sophia's attention. She saw his amusement at her unusual costume, so unlike the plain, dark clothing she normally wore. And she saw something more in the topaz depths of Warrick's eyes. A flame burned there, warm and inviting, drawing her to him. She took a step in his direction.

"Can we eat now?" Robin asked in a plaintive voice. "I have been smelling that roasting bird for much too long. Genie, if you don't feed me soon, I will faint and you will have to use your magic to carry me to my bedroll."

"If you faint," Genie said, "I will let you lie where you fall."

"Cruel wench." Robin grinned and helped Genie to sit on one of the cushions.

Sophia did not think Genie needed assistance in order to sit. Sophia certainly did not need help, and she was going to say so until she looked into Warrick's eyes again. He smiled and put out his hand. Sophia stared at his long, tapering fingers and thought of midnight and a leap from one rooftop to another. It occurred to her that placing her hand in Warrick's tonight would be more dangerous than on that other occasion. But Robin and Genie were waiting and Robin was sniffing at the roasted bird on the table as if he would inhale the meal, rather than waiting to eat it properly. Sophia gave her hand to Warrick and felt his strong fingers close around it. With Warrick to balance her, she folded her legs and lowered herself to the cushion.

Not having eaten since the previous day, Sophia was every bit as hungry as Robin claimed to be. She devoured a lentil and vegetable stew that she scooped up from the serving pan with flatbread. She accepted from Warrick a large chunk of breast meat from the roasted bird, ate it with great pleasure, and then licked her fingers. She washed down the meal with hot mint tea, and still found room for one of the oranges that Genie produced at the end of the dinner.

"What a feast," Robin said, smacking his lips. "Genie, you are a wonder."

"Yes," Genie said, "I am. Sophia, why don't you and Warrick take a nice walk while Robin and I clean up the dishes and leftover food and prepare the tent for sleeping?"

Sophia was about to point out that Genie could easily use her magic to clear away the remains of the dinner, but again Warrick held out his hand to her and smiled, and the sarcastic comments died on her lips. The warmth in Warrick's eyes compelled her to go with him. If she were to tell the truth, she would be forced to admit that she did not struggle very hard against his wish, or her own desire to be with him.

"I will need my veil," Sophia said. "Genie, where did you put it?"

"This will be adequate for a night when the moon

is waning," Genie said, waving a hand.

Instantly a sheer cloud of purple fabric floated over Sophia's head and shoulders. Unlike the heavy veil she had worn all day, this veil was almost weightless, and she could see through it.

Outside the tent the other travelers were settling down for the night. The caravansary building was dark except for the gleam of an oil lamp here and there, and the fires of those who had chosen to sleep outside the caravansary were burning low.

Warrick led the way around the side of the hill to a spot where the land lay stretched flat before them for long miles, until it began to rise toward the mountains in the far distance. Sophia saw the mountain peaks black against the star-spangled sky. Above the mountains hung the curve of the waning moon.

"How open it is," Sophia said. "How empty. And we must cross all of the land we see, and the mountains, and beyond. I did not realize until now just how far our journey will take us."

"Tomorrow will be easier," Warrick said.

"Will it?"

"I have always found the first day of a journey to be the most difficult," he said. "Thoughts of the place I have just left are still with me and I have not yet fallen into the rhythm of travel."

"I do not think I will ever stop thinking of Baghdad, or of my father," Sophia told him. "Still, I have found some of our fellow travelers interesting."

"I saw you holding the baby," Warrick said with an odd note in his voice.

"I told his mother I would not drop him, and she believed me, but I wasn't so sure of myself as I pretended to be," Sophia confessed. "I have never held a baby until today. Warrick, did Genie ask you for a salve for Musa's rash?"

"Yes. I took a pot of it to Sadiq's tent earlier. He was profoundly grateful. Or so he claimed."

"Genie claims that the sack you keep with you all of the time is filled with herbs and medicines," she said.

"Herbal medicines, bandages, and gold," he answered. "And one or two other things besides."

"Gold?" Sophia whispered.

"We can't travel without money."

"Of course not. I should have thought of that." Sophia fell silent, pondering her next words as they walked along the hillside. "Recently I have been unforgivably thoughtless in many ways. I have been rude to you and to Genie."

"You are hurt and angry because of the changes in your life," Warrick said. "I can understand that. I have experienced similar emotions from time to time."

"Have you?" She paused to look at him and saw only shadows. "I can never be certain what your feelings are."

"In some ways you and I are similar," Warrick said. "We have both made a habit of concealing our deepest emotions, sometimes even from ourselves. It's as good a method as any to avoid heartache."

Sophia stumbled on a tuft of rough grass and Warrick's hand was at her elbow to steady her. Then his arm was around her waist. She quivered in his grasp.

They were very much alone on the hillside, out of sight of the tents, though not of the Kuman sentries. But Gafar's men, who paced at the bottom of the hill, were looking outward in the direction of the plain or back along the road they had traveled that day. So far as Sophia could tell, the sentries did not even glance at the couple on the hill.

"Are you afraid of the emptiness out there?" Warrick asked softly. It was as though he could read Sophia's thoughts. "So much space can be daunting to one who has spent her life in a small house, or in enclosed and crowded streets."

"Today I have discovered a remarkable sense of freedom," she said. "I no longer have any daily chores, and no duty except to sit upon Nura's back and let her carry me into the future."

Warrick's arm tightened a little. Sophia looked up at him and saw his hard features slightly blurred by her veil. She noticed the gleam of starlight in his eyes as he bent his face to hers.

"Cursed veil," he muttered. "How can a man kiss you when you are covered like that?"

"Kisses are precisely what veils are meant to prevent," she said. "How can you want to kiss me, Warrick? You don't like me."

"I never said so."

Warrick drew her closer and placed his free hand on her shoulder. Sophia went completely still, holding herself stiff. It was the only way she could control the shudders that rippled inside her, and keep Warrick from sensing her reaction to him, the only way to protect herself from him. The veil and her silk gown offered little protection. The texture of the silk only made her skin more exquisitely sensitive where Warrick was touching her, and the heat of his hands easily penetrated the fabric.

She should have protested when his hand moved from her shoulder to her breast and stayed there. She could have told him to stop, ought to have claimed that she did not like or want what he was doing. Instead she let him caress her until her nipples were hard and tight. She permitted the long stroke of his palm from breast to thigh and back again. Nor did she object when his large hand splayed across her hips to press her female warmth against himself. Far from complaining of his actions, she put her arms around his waist and strained against his hot manhood. By then she was sure he knew how she trembled in his embrace, how she ached for a completion beyond her experience. If she could not bring herself to say so in words, surely Warrick could hear her confused longing in the soft, gasping sounds she made.

They stood wrapped in each other's arms, cheek to cheek with only the sheer purple veil between their faces, and Sophia feared she would die if Warrick did not snatch the veil away and kiss her. He pressed his mouth to her ear and she felt his warm breath through the veil. There was something incredibly alluring about that fragile obstacle to what she desired. Warrick's moist lips touched her chin, and Sophia knew that next he was going to kiss her mouth, kiss her through the veil.

She held her breath, waiting for Warrick's kiss and for the strange experience it would bring. Warrick's breath stirred the fabric between them. The lingering scent of green leaves from his bathwater mingled with her hyacinth fragrance—as their lips and tongues would mingle in another heartbeat or two.

Suddenly Sophia heard heavy footsteps approaching, crunching on sand and pebbles, stepping carefully where unexpected patches of grass grew. Warrick drew away from her and turned toward the sound, pushing Sophia behind him as he moved. From the weight of the footsteps, Sophia guessed who the intruder was before the man spoke.

"Do you make a habit of embracing your woman where others can see you?" Sadiq asked, his voice hard with disapproval. "For shame, Warrick."

"I do not suppose you are wandering around the hillside at night for pleasure," Warrick said. "You were searching for me, Sadiq. What was it you wanted of me?"

"To ask that you take my watch, and I will take yours," Sadiq replied. "My older son, Farouk, will stand guard with you. Alya has finally gotten Musa to sleep, and I have in mind the same sort of entertainment that you were just enjoying."

"I have no objection to switching our watches," Warrick said. "Tell Farouk to meet me at the bottom of the hill. It won't take long for me to conduct my lady to our tent and to change my clothes. I will join Farouk shortly."

"You are most generously agreeable, Master Warrick," Sadiq said. "Allow me to express my most sincere and profound thanks. I shall convey your kind message to Farouk, who will be honored to stand guard with you."

When Warrick made no response to Sadiq's elaborate speech, which was in keeping with the Arabic custom of exaggerated thanks, Sadiq took his leave. Warrick stood looking after him in silence for so long that Sophia began to fear he had forgotten she was there.

"Warrick." She touched his arm to remind him of her presence.

"I need to change my clothes," Warrick said. "We'd better get back to the tent."

"You don't like Sadiq," Sophia said, walking beside Warrick.

"There is something about the man, a slippery quality that I don't trust," Warrick said. "I have lived in Baghdad long enough to see past the effusive language that well-bred men use with each other. I am able to discern whether or not a man is honest. I do not think Sadiq is honest."

"Does that matter to us?" Sophia asked. "Once we reach Qasvin we won't see Sadiq again. He and his family will be staying there."

"Sadiq's lack of honesty concerns me only if it puts us in danger," Warrick said.

"I don't like Sadiq either," Sophia told him. "My dislike is based on purely feminine reasons. I do like Alya, and I feel sorry for her. Genie doesn't think Sadiq is a very satisfactory husband. I'm not sure what she means by that. I suppose you know better than I what Genie was talking about."

"What I know," Warrick said, "is that Sadiq was right when he said that I shouldn't have been embracing you on a hillside for all to see."

"I could have objected," Sophia said, "but I didn't. So I am as much to blame as you are."

Warrick stopped walking and turned to her. His big hand gently touched her face. He sighed and started to walk again.

"Thank you," he said.

The fierce heat that Warrick had roused in Sophia was gone, vanquished by Sadiq's interruption and his coarse words. A gentler warmth remained, a banked ember that Sophia feared Warrick could coax into flame again anytime he cared to do so.

Sophia thought about Alya, and about Sadiq touching her, and she decided she did not envy Alya at all. She did not even envy Alya her beautiful baby. There were interactions that occurred between men and women that Sophia did not understand. After listening to Sadiq's suggestive, oily tones when he spoke of Alya, she was not sure that she ever wanted to understand such transactions.

Unless the transactions involved Warrick, whose touch was so bewitching, so conducive to delicious, heated fantasies. Sophia had to warn herself very firmly that Warrick was a magician and that he was, as he himself admitted, adept at concealing his deepest emotions. She wished that she were able to hide her own feelings as easily.

She was very glad to return to the tent. There all traces of the evening meal had disappeared, including the table. Where the table had been, cushions were laid out for sleeping, with blankets folded on top of them.

On two separate cushions placed near the tent wall, Genie and Robin were sitting, their heads close together, talking in quiet voices. Genie looked up when Sophia entered. Her silver-gray eyes searched Sophia's face. Her brow creased into a puzzled frown that cleared when Warrick described Sadiq's request for a change in guard duty.

Sophia did not want to talk to anyone. With a rough gesture she hauled the dividing curtain across the tent and retired behind it. She did not sleep well, and when she did doze, she dreamed of Warrick stalking her across a wide and barren landscape, where a chill wind blew and there was no shelter and no protection.

Chapter Twelve

In midafternoon of the third day out from Baghdad, a troop of *shinha* attacked the caravan. They came from the direction of Baghdad and they rode horses, not camels, a fact that indicated they had brought supplies of food and water with them, or else they had ready access to the water and food that horses required. This, in turn, implied that they were on official business and not just raiding for the pleasure of it.

Warrick spotted the horsemen first. He and his party were riding toward the end of the long caravan, with Sadiq and his family just behind. The outriders, the men hired by the caravan leader to protect the travelers and their merchandise from plundering bandits, were some distance ahead. They were more concerned with a large shipment of aromatic woods and resins that had come from far across the Arabian desert than they were with stragglers. Upon sighting the cloud of dust that signaled the approaching band of riders, Warrick moved his camel nearer to Sophia and her mount.

"Robin," he called, "ride ahead. Find Gafar and tell him to be on guard until we discover exactly who is following us and what they want. And warn Hamid, the caravan leader, in case he hasn't yet noticed that we are pursued."

"My goods! My spices!" Sadiq cried. He had overheard Warrick's instructions to Robin and, following the direction of Warrick's pointing hand, he had also seen the approaching horsemen. "My possessions! My sons! Allah save us!" he wailed.

"And not a word about Alya," Sophia muttered to Warrick. "It's easy to tell what Sadiq loves best. Who are the riders, Warrick? Bandits? Assassins?" She shivered at that thought. Horrible tales were told of the cult of assassins who lived in the high mountains several days' journey north of Baghdad and who carried out cold-blooded murders.

"Neither," Warrick said, squinting to see better. "Those are *shinha*. From the way they are riding, I do not think their mission is a peaceful one."

Warrick's words struck terror into Sophia's heart. Again Sadiq had heard what Warrick said and his renewed cries assaulted Sophia's ears.

"*Shinha!*" Sadiq screamed. "We are doomed! Oh, that I should die like this, beneath the desert sun. Oh, Allah, have mercy! Save me!"

"Father," Farouk said to him, "if we are to die, let us do so bravely. I am willing to fight to my last breath to protect you and my little brother."

"Give up my son, my heir?" Sadiq exclaimed. "No, we cannot fight. We must flee." He continued to make so much noise that his camels became upset and began braying. Their sound drowned out even Sadiq's fearful cries. Farouk was holding the reins of the pack camels belonging to his father and he was hard put to keep them from breaking away.

Through all the uproar Sadiq was causing, Alya sat alone and ignored on the camel she was riding. Her shoulders were hunched and her head was bent forward, as if she was prepared to offer as much protection as she could to her infant son.

"Sophia." Warrick's commanding voice brought Sophia's attention back to him. He pulled a long-bladed knife from his saddlebag and held it out to her, hilt first. "Take this. You will need it."

"No, I can't." Sophia turned away and her hands on the reins directed her camel to step to one side.

"I said, take it." Warrick's camel moved close again. "There is no time for you to provoke an argument on this subject, or for me to answer your complaints. I will defend you as best I can, but you must have your own weapon."

Warrick reached across from his camel to put the knife into Sophia's hand and wrap her fingers around the hilt. For a moment his hand communicated strength and a remarkable sense of calmness to her. Then Warrick's hand was gone from hers and Sophia was left holding the cold, dangerous weapon.

She stared at it, at the polished metal hilt inlaid with brass and the silver-blue blade that gleamed in the sunlight. She had been afraid many times in recent days. But the terror she felt with a sharp knife in her hand, a restless camel beneath her, and the *shinha* fast gaining on them was enough to drive her to near madness. She decided that she was going to open her fingers and allow the ugly knife to drop to the ground.

Then she looked from the weapon to Warrick's intense, smoky eyes. The expression she saw there convinced her to obey him and not her fear. Warrick was genuinely worried about her safety.

"Do not hesitate to cut anyone," Warrick told her. "If it comes to self-defense, protect yourself however you can. And try to stay on your camel; it's your best hope of escape if that becomes necessary. Where is Genie?"

"Here I am." Genie guided her camel through milling animals and shouting, frightened people to Warrick's side. "I regret that I cannot make Sophia invisible. Only you can do that, and I think you ought to."

"Not in this instance," Warrick said. "If I make Sophia invisible, then I must make both of us invisible, and there will be too many distractions to my concentration. Nor can I justify protecting only the two of us when others are in danger." He paused to look around. "I see Robin riding this way with Gafar and his men. They will fight with us. Genie, stay close to Sophia. I will return to you as soon as I can." As he spoke Warrick drew the sword he kept attached to his saddle, and then a second wicked-looking knife.

There was no time for further discussion. There wasn't time to mount an organized defense, or to speculate on the actual intentions of the oncoming band of riders. The *shinha* troop put a hasty end to any doubts about what they planned. They attacked the straggling end of the caravan like a fierce desert storm, stirring up clouds of sand and howling their battle cries like the keening northern wind. Swords slashed, knives rose and struck downward, then rose to strike again. Blood spurted and men and women screamed in pain and fear. Genie's camel went down and Genie rolled onto the ground and lay still.

Sophia saw Warrick on his camel, fighting his way through the chaos of rearing horses and battling men, and her instinct told her he was trying to reach her. Nura balked, snapping her sharp teeth at an oncoming warrior. Sophia nearly fell from the saddle, then regained her seat when Warrick arrived to engage the warrior and force him away from her. Warrick moved on, keeping the *shinha* at a distance from Sophia, keeping her safe from them.

All around Sophia the battle raged, swift and brutal, yet for a few moments she was caught in the eye of the storm. Perched high on Nura's back, she was in a good position to see how Gafar and his fellow Kumans fought at close quarters with their curved swords until they could draw their opponents away from the caravan by pretending to flee.

Once at a safe distance from the travelers of the caravan, Gafar's men sheathed their swords and plucked their short bows from the saddle horns where they were kept in readiness. Arrows were also near at hand in quivers attached to their saddles. The tribesmen turned around in their saddles and proceeded to loose arrows over their horses' backs and into the bodies of the pursuing *shinha*. During this maneuver they guided their horses with their knees, so that their hands were free to use their deadly weapons. And all of it was accomplished at a full gallop.

Sophia caught her breath and stared wide-eyed

at the remarkable display of horsemanship and weaponry. Her fascination with the way the Kumans were fighting almost cost her her life, for not all of the *shinha* were foolish enough to leave the battle and chase after the wild tribesmen. A good number of them remained with the caravan, inflicting considerable damage on humans and animals alike.

While Sophia's attention was directed toward Gafar and his men, a dark-cloaked *shinha* raced toward her camel, his long, curved blade raised for attack. Sophia did not notice him until he was almost upon her. She had scarcely the blink of an eye in which to question whether he intended to kill her or Nura; she knew only that the moment had come to use the knife she still clutched, for Warrick was nowhere to be seen.

She pointed the knife straight at the man, braced herself, and jabbed outward just as he began to swing his own blade in a downward arc. She saw a flash of surprise in the man's eyes when he realized she held a weapon and would use it, and she knew his swift-stroking sword was meant for her and not the camel.

The knife was wrenched from her fingers. She heard a loud scream at the same time that she felt a searing pain along her upper left arm. Then she was flying through the air.

She landed so hard that the breath was knocked from her lungs, but her heavy woolen garments provided enough padding to save her from serious injury. She lay where she had fallen, dazed and unable to move, while the fighting continued. Miraculously, no one else attacked her.

After a while she was able to breathe again and

she tried to sit up. The veil and her long gown were tangled around her legs and arms, hampering her movements. When she finally got to her knees and looked about, she saw that the fighting had moved away from the immediate vicinity of the caravan. In the continual motion of men and animals she could see neither Warrick nor Robin.

Her left arm throbbed. Sophia rubbed at the sore spot and her hand came away bloody. She stared at her hand, then wiped it on her slashed and dusty veil. She could still move her arm and wriggle the fingers of her left hand, so she decided the wound was not serious. She would worry about it later.

"Genie?" Sophia called, staggering to her feet. "Genie, where are you?"

"Ohhh." A short distance away, a rolled-up bundle of dark cloth stirred and began to unwind itself. "Oh, my head. There are days when I do not like my human form."

"Genie, is that you?" Sophia stumbled along the rough pebbles of the caravan road until she reached the figure that was now on its knees, trying to rise. "Are you hurt? I saw you fall."

"I landed on my head," Genie said. "I think I was unconscious for a while. What about you, Sophia? What happened?"

"I lost my seat on Nura," Sophia said. She was unwilling to discuss the way she had lost Warrick's knife, or the wound in her arm. For the moment she preferred not to examine too closely her first experience of battle. Like the wound in her arm, she would think about it later. "Fortunately I am not badly injured."

"I'm glad to hear it. I wasn't much help to you, was I? Not a very useful jinni." Genie sank back to the ground. "Let me sit here for a little. I can't work any magic until my thoughts are clearer. Where is Robin?"

"I don't know," Sophia said. She looked across the plain to where the men appeared to be rounding up those who were defeated. She was greatly relieved to see Gafar's sturdy figure atop his horse, directing the operation. "I think the battle is over, and I believe our people have won, but I can't find Warrick or Robin. Genie, please, try to think clearly. I need your help."

"That's nice to hear," Genie said. "I will do what I can. Just understand that at the moment, my magical abilities are somewhat limited."

"We cannot go on without Warrick and Robin," Sophia said, a note of desperation in her voice. "Genie, where are they?"

"I have no idea where our menfolk are," Genie replied, "though I do hear a baby crying. I assume that means Musa is alive and well."

Sophia looked around, searching for Alya, as well as for Warrick and Robin. The road on which the caravan had been traveling was littered with broken baskets and bundles torn open with their contents spilled out. Wounded men sat or lay on the ground while their servants or traveling companions bound their wounds. The camels continued to bray their noisy dislike of battle.

"Sophia!" Alya called, lifting her skirt with one hand so she could move more quickly around the obstacles in her path. She was limping badly. "Have you seen Sadiq? Or Farouk? My camel was killed. I had such difficulty freeing my leg and my veil from under its body. And now I cannot find my husband or my stepson, or any of our other camels.

187

What shall I do? Sophia, help me, please." Alya ended her speech with a sob and her shoulders began to shake.

Sophia looked from the weeping Alya with Musa crying loudly beneath her veil, to Genie, who was still sitting on the gravel caravan road rubbing her head with a hand that was surprisingly pale and fragile when seen against her dark veil. Sophia had never thought of Genie as vulnerable to injury or pain. And suddenly Sophia understood that it was going to be up to her to care for both the distraught young mother and the stunned jinni.

"Genie, do you think you can stand up?" Sophia asked. "I see a large rock just off the side of the road a short distance ahead, and I think we will be safer and more comfortable in the shadow it casts than we will be out here on the open land."

"I will try," Genie said.

Sophia had to help her get to her feet, and she kept her arm around Genie as they stumbled toward the rock. Alya trailed after them, limping and weeping softly. Musa continued to cry vigorously. The rock was twice as tall as a man and wide enough to offer generous protection from the sun. Sophia got her charges into the shade and made them sit down. Genie leaned her head against the rock.

"There is nothing very wrong with me except a few bruises and a bad headache," she said. "I will be completely recovered soon. Alya, in the name of the Prophet's blessed daughter, will you *please* put Musa to your breast so he will stop screaming?"

"I am sorry." Alya moaned. "He isn't hurt. I checked him carefully as soon as I got out from under that poor dead camel. But I didn't think about feeding him."

"Think about it now," Genie said in a tone that strongly suggested she was gritting her teeth against all the noise Musa was making.

Alya adjusted her torn veil and moved around under it until Musa ceased his howling and began to make contented sucking sounds. Genie emitted a long sigh and closed her eyes.

"Now," Sophia said, aware that she was going to have to take command, "since Genie claims to have no severe injuries, I think the first thing I should do is look at Alya's leg. Genie, if you are recovered enough perhaps you can locate Warrick's camel and find the bandages he keeps in his basket of medicinal supplies."

She lifted Alya's skirt to reveal a large bruise and a long area below her knee that was bloody. Sophia sat back on her heels, considering the wound and trying not to shriek or faint at the sight. Not for the first time, she was grateful that her veil concealed her facial expressions. The inconvenient garment did have its uses.

"That's just a scrape," Genie said, opening her eyes to look at Alya's leg. "It will be easily tended with some herbal salve and a bandage. I see Warrick's camel. Perhaps I can coax it to us without having to get up. I am still dizzy when I move my head quickly."

Genie began to call to the camel in the unknown language she used with animals. The grazing camel lifted its head from the prickly bushes it was chewing and walked slowly to the rock. Sophia glanced at Alya, concerned about her reaction to Genie's ability to control the animal. Alya wasn't paying attention to Genie or to the camel. Her head was lowered and she was alternately weeping and talking to Musa in a broken voice.

Sophia felt like crying, herself. If Warrick's camel was there, but Warrick was not, did that mean he was lying dead or seriously wounded out on the hard, stony ground of the plain? She wanted to run away from the rock and the tearful Alya, to drag Genie with her and insist that Genie use her magical powers to locate Warrick. And Robin, who was also missing.

Duty kept her where she was. She scrambled to her feet and approached Warrick's camel. At Genie's order the beast went to its knees and stayed there while Sophia found Warrick's sack and the supplies it contained. She rummaged though jars, packets of herbs, and a few bulkier, heavier items she did not stop to identify before she located and pulled out a clean bandage and a pot of salve.

She tended to Alya's injured leg, cleaning it as best she could, covering it with salve, and binding it tightly to stop the bleeding. When she was finished she leaned back against the rock, shaking in reaction to all that had happened. Weariness was seeping into her limbs. She yearned to lie down and sleep. But first she had to find Warrick. She forced herself to stand up again.

"Please, Sophia," Alya begged, "take the baby. I think I am going to be sick."

Sophia reached beneath Alya's veil and lifted Musa out of its protective folds. The baby smacked his little pink lips together and frowned, as if perplexed at being so rudely removed from his meal. He gave a large, milky belch. Smiling at him though he could not see her for the veil she wore, Sophia placed him against her shoulder and he snuggled there, content. Alya groaned.

"Put your head down," Genie advised. "Stretch out flat. That will help."

Alya did as she was told.

"It's so quiet," Sophia said. "Where is everyone?"

"Here they come now." Genie stood up very slowly, hanging on to the rock until she was fully upright. She pointed to a group of men who were still some distance away.

"I see Warrick," Sophia said, fighting back tears of relief. She held Musa a little tighter and cleared her throat before she spoke again. "And there is Robin. Thank heaven they are safe. Alya, I think Sadiq is with them."

Alya only groaned again. She made no attempt to rise to greet her husband.

Warrick and Robin were in the forefront, both of them walking so easily that Sophia was at once re-assured that neither of them was hurt. Sadiq was still mounted on his camel and also appeared to be uninjured. They were followed by other men of the caravan who had helped to defend it, and by Gafar and his tribesmen on horseback. Gafar's men led the survivors of the *shinha* troop, captives all, on foot and with leather ropes tied about their necks. At the end of the procession was Sadiq's son, Fa-rouk, riding a horse and holding the reins of the *shinha* horses.

Warrick was dusty and bloodstained. When he saw Sophia standing by the rock with Musa in her arms and the wind whipping her veil and her skirts, he stopped abruptly to stare at her. Then he walked on, coming directly to her, while Gafar directed his men and the captives to one side.

191

For just a moment Sophia thought Warrick was going to put his arms around her. She wanted him to hold her and assure her that they were safe. Her shoulders and hips were beginning to ache from the fall off Nura, her upper left arm continued to throb, and she was unbelievably tired. If Warrick held her, she knew her aches and pains would vanish, and she would no longer want to cry.

"Sophia." Warrick's smoky topaz eyes glistened in his dirty, sweat-streaked face. "You are safe. Thank God for that. I have been so worried. I tried to protect you, but I lost sight of you during the battle and I could not find you again."

"I lost your knife," she said. "It's stuck in someone's arm—or his throat. I'm not sure which. I am sorry, Warrick. I should have taken better care of your property."

"Dear Heaven." He swallowed hard and wiped a dusty hand across his face, leaving his cheeks even more badly dirt-streaked than before. "*I* should have taken better care of *you,* so you would not have had to use a knife."

"Well, as to that, I did see how busy you were with fighting that nasty *shinha* warrior for my sake. And I am skilled in the kitchen. It wasn't much different from cutting up a chicken." Her voice cracked and she stopped talking.

"Yes, it was different," he said. "I know it was."

"My son!" Sadiq dismounted from his camel and rushed to the group by the rock. He snatched Musa from Sophia's arms. "Allah be praised! Both of my sons have survived the dreadful battle. My Farouk is a hero, and Musa is safe."

"You might ask about your wife," Sophia said to

him. "Alya injured her leg protecting Musa. You could thank her for her brave deed."

"Warrick, I have warned you before about the freedom you permit to your woman," Sadiq said, scowling at Sophia. "She will bring you to shame. Far better to sell her than to keep a woman like that."

Warrick's face tightened as he regarded Sadiq. "Rather than sell her, I would die to keep a woman like this safe," he said.

Sophia blinked in surprise at his unexpected words and a new warmth crept into her heart with the knowledge that Warrick approved of her actions that day.

"It is Sadiq who ought to die," Gafar announced, joining them.

Seen on foot, the Kuman leader was short, the top of his head reaching only to Warrick's shoulder. His long, oiled mustache and the wide-brimmed, pointed felt hat he wore combined with his slightly bowed legs to produce a comical appearance. However, there was nothing amusing in the fierce black stare he bent upon Sadiq, and the larger man quailed at Gafar's frown.

Sophia had had ample time since leaving Baghdad to notice that Gafar mounted on his short-legged, precisely trained horse was an impressive figure, and that his men followed his orders with obvious respect and few questions. Something of that air of easy command surrounded Gafar as he and three of his lieutenants reached the group by the rock. With them was Hamid, the caravan leader, whose expression when he looked at Sadiq was equally as dark and dangerous as Gafar's.

"You, Sadiq," Gafar said, "are the cause of the

skirmish we just fought. You brought the *shinha* down on us. I lost one of my men in the fighting. You owe me, and Bortun's family, reparations for his death."

"I?" Sadiq cried, his round face turning red at Gafar's accusations, and redder still at Gafar's last words. "Why should I pay you? I am not at fault. I am only a simple merchant who is moving his family to a new city in hope that my business will prosper there."

"I have just finished speaking to the *shinha* we captured," Gafar said. "They tell me that in Baghdad you are charged with selling inferior spices, and that you are running away from the sultan's justice."

"I am running because no one will believe me," Sadiq shouted. "I have an enemy, a man who wanted Alya for himself. When Alya's father gave her to me, the man vowed revenge. Somehow he saw to it that the good spices I imported to sell in my shop were exchanged for adulterated spices. Then he informed the authorities that I was breaking the law, and no one would listen to my explanation. My business in Baghdad was ruined. When Farouk learned that he and I were to be arrested, and Alya handed over to my rival, we packed as much as we could onto my prized camels and joined the first caravan leaving Baghdad."

"In my homeland, Sadiq," Gafar said, showing sharp teeth below his black mustache, "you would not have lived long enough to travel so far from the place of your crime."

"There was no crime!" Sadiq cried, looking from face to face as if he hoped to find confirmation of his innocence among the onlookers.

"Perhaps not," Gafar said. "Or perhaps there was. It matters little to me one way or the other. You are fortunate in your son, Sadiq."

"I am?" Sadiq said in a quavering voice.

"Farouk fought bravely with us this day. He strove as boldly as any Kuman warrior to save my friend, Bortun, when Bortun was besieged by five of the *shinha* at one time. Therefore, for the sake of brave Farouk and for your second, infant son, and because I bear no love in my heart for the *shinha*, I will say no more of the accusations made against you.

"I have sons of my own and I would scourge the earth to keep them safe. But as I am an honest warrior," Gafar continued in tones of utter contempt for Sadiq, "I would not stoop to the degradation of flight to keep them safe. I would stand and fight with them by my side. Farouk must have inherited his courage from his mother, for his father displays little of it."

"I am no warrior," Sadiq cried. "I am only a merchant, unjustly accused."

"You have not seen the last of the *shinha*," Gafar warned. "As I wish to live until I greet my sons again, I will travel no farther with you, Sadiq."

"What do you mean?" Sadiq cried. Turning to the caravan leader, he said, "Hamid, you cannot plan to abandon me here on the road, with no protection for the goods I bear with me. Think of my defenseless wife and my infant son."

"You should have thought of your family before you committed an act that brought you to the notice of the *shinha*," Hamid said.

"I have told you, it was a plot devised by an enemy who wanted revenge on me."

"I care not what it was," the caravan leader told him. "Your presence endangers everyone who is in my charge."

At this, Sadiq drew himself up in anger, as if preparing to face down the caravan leader. "I have paid the full price for places in your caravan as far as Hamadan," Sadiq said.

"So you have," said Hamid, "and as I am an honest man, I will generously permit your family to travel at the end of the caravan. You must agree to leave a certain space between yourselves and the next group of travelers."

"That will leave me undefended," Sadiq protested.

"I will not allow you to put the other travelers, or the goods we transport, at risk for your misdeeds. Nor will I bargain with you any more. Take my offer, or reject it as you please," Hamid told Sadiq. Then, turning to the Kuman warrior, he said, "Gafar, I take regretful leave of you. Your aid, and that of your men, has been invaluable."

"How will you deal with the captured *shinha* we have turned over to you?" Gafar asked.

"I will speak to the captain of the guard at the caravansary where we stop tonight," Hamid responded, "and tell him what has happened. The *shinha* are supposed to protect caravans, not attack them, and their very purpose for existence is to maintain order, not to wound or kill honest men. I believe I can persuade the captain to allow my caravan to continue on its way, while he holds the renegades we have captured until someone can come from Baghdad to investigate the matter."

"It's an arrangement that will allow Sadiq to

reach Hamadan without being arrested," Gafar said, raising his eyebrows.

"And give you ample time to disappear into the mountains," Hamid said with a conspiratorial smile.

"I and my party will also bid you farewell," Warrick said, speaking to the caravan leader.

"What?" Sophia cried, and then fell silent at a stern look from Warrick.

"Robin and I are agreed that, like Gafar, we have no desire to continue traveling in Sadiq's company. Hamid, I have noticed that several camels were killed in today's skirmish, and that several more were wounded too severely for them to carry any load until they have recovered. Perhaps you, or some of the other travelers who have lost their camels, will be interested in purchasing ours," Warrick said to the caravan leader.

"I believe an arrangement can be reached that will prove satisfactory to all concerned," Hamid responded.

"A prompt arrangement, Warrick," Gafar said. "The day is fast ending. We do not have hours to stand here guarding your women while you and Hamid argue about the worth of a few camels."

"It will not take long," Warrick called over his shoulder as he and Hamid moved off to where a group of travelers stood scratching their heads over the problem of how to move their baggage without pack animals.

"Does Warrick intend to leave us stranded in the desert?" Sophia demanded of Robin.

"You know he never would," Robin answered.

"Then what does he have planned?" she asked. "What are we to do without our camels?"

"If you ask my opinion, we are well rid of those loathsome creatures," Robin said. "Sophia, I beg you to keep silent until after the caravan has gone."

"If he expects Genie to magically transport us to—"

"Silence!" Robin shouted at her. "Sadiq is right; you women talk too much. Not another word on this subject from either of you!"

Sophia's jaw dropped. Never had she heard Robin speak so firmly, nor had she ever seen his eyes flash with anger. Into her weary mind came the thought that there was more to Warrick's decision than she had been told, and that she would do well to obey Robin, at least until Warrick returned from selling the camels.

"Sophia, my friend." Alya touched her hand. "I must say farewell to you. Farouk is rounding up our surviving camels and the first section of the caravan is already beginning to move again. They will not wait for us."

"They want to reach the next caravansary before dusk," Genie said. She patted Alya on her shoulder. "Take good care of Musa."

"I hope you reach Hamadan safely," Sophia said, "and that the next leg of your journey to Qasvin is also safe."

"I am not supposed to tell anyone, but you are both friends and I trust you. We are not going to Qasvin. Sadiq has plans to travel on to Hind," Alya revealed. "He has business associates there, in Bombay, whom he believes will help him to begin again in the spice trade, far beyond Seljuk rule."

"Perhaps that is for the best," Sophia said. "You will be safe in Hind."

"Alya!" Sadiq yelled. "Come here at once!"

"Go safely," Sophia said, surprised to discover there was a lump in her throat at parting from the overly meek Alya, who was more child than woman. "Live as contentedly as you can."

With a last, whispered farewell to Sophia and Genie, Alya obeyed her husband's loud summons.

Chapter Thirteen

"Now that the caravan has left, may I speak?" Sophia asked Warrick.

"If you speak briefly," Warrick said, his lips curving into a quickly supressed smile. "Gafar is impatient to leave."

"Does that mean we are going with him?"

"We are," Warrick said.

"I want an explanation." Sophia was so tired that she feared she would faint from sheer weariness. Still, she stood her ground with Warrick, determined not to allow him to make decisions that affected her without consulting her. She planted her feet firmly on the gravel of the caravan road and rested her fists on her hips. Gafar was issuing orders to his men, but he paused long enough to grin at her as if he approved of her belligerent stance. Encouraged, Sophia put aside her fatigue and went on the attack.

"Warrick, I have a right to know why you have changed your plans," she said. "You told me we were going to Hamadan. After today's incident, I believe our best course is to continue under the protection of a large caravan."

"So far as we have been able to learn from the captured *shinha* officers that Gafar has questioned," Warrick said, "they were on official business. Their orders were to arrest Sadiq and his family and return them to Baghdad. Sadiq and Farouk were to be handed over for trial, and Alya and the baby taken to her father's house."

"Then it was a revenge plot, as Sadiq claimed?" Sophia asked.

"It is possible that he told us the truth, though I would not vouch for Sadiq's honesty. I do think that Farouk and Alya are innocent of his schemes, whatever those schemes may be. There are two points for you to keep in mind, Sophia. The first is that, while the *shinha* were sent with a warrant for Sadiq and his family, they overstepped their orders when they attacked members of a caravan. As Hamid said, the *shinha* are expected to protect honest folk. They are, without question, at fault for attacking Hamid's caravan."

"At least they weren't after us," Sophia said. "That is good news, Warrick. Perhaps you and I, and my father's possessions, are not as important as we imagined. I am happy to know that. Aren't you?"

"I would be happy, if I could believe as you do," Warrick said. "But I don't believe we are of no interest to the *shinha*. Which brings me to the second point I wanted to make. While the first band of *shinha* was sent after Sadiq and not us, the next band that rides out from Baghdad may have a warrant for you, or for me. That is why we have left the caravan. When the *shinha* return, we will have vanished."

"Vanished?" Sophia repeated. "Do you mean you are planning to work magic?"

"Not until it is absolutely necessary," Warrick said. "The cost to me is too great, and I am going to need all of my strength for what lies ahead of us."

"And exactly what is that?" Sophia asked. She faced him with her hands still on her hips, prepared to question any decision Warrick had made.

"We are going to ride into the mountains with Gafar and his men," Warrick said.

"I see no advantage to such a plan, with or without Gafar," Sophia said in an angry tone.

"There is another route to Tabriz that winds through the mountains. It is more difficult and dangerous than the main road, because the path is narrow and steep in places, so the caravans don't use it," Warrick explained with remarkable patience. "For that very reason it will be the safer route for us. Gafar has agreed to allow us to travel with his band until we reach Tabriz. He was favorably impressed with the way Robin and I fought today.

"Gafar is also grateful for the respect we have shown to him and his men," Warrick continued. "Most people in Baghdad regard all northern tribesmen as wild barbarians. This in spite of the fact that the Seljuk rulers of Baghdad were themselves once wild horsemen who roamed the steppe lands beyond the high mountains and the inland seas. In return for the protection of Gafar's band, Robin and I will be expected to fight with them again if the need arises," Warrick said.

"I see." Try as she might, Sophia could think of no arguments against Warrick's decision, and she guessed that he had not discussed it with her beforehand because he had been preoccupied with the aftermath of the fight with the *shinha*. There was only one complaint that Sophia could dredge up from the depths of her weary mind and, out of habit more than because it mattered very much, she voiced her reservation in a sarcastic tone. "After inflicting a camel on me, now you expect me to ride a horse?"

"Speaking for myself," Robin put in with a wide smile, "I am happy to be rid of those malodorous, cantankerous camels. I should think you would be glad to be through with them, too, Sophia."

"I shall miss the camels," said Genie. "Especially Salima. However, I think I can manage a horse."

Warrick was still looking at Sophia. His brows were raised, as if he was waiting for her to say something more.

"Hamid, Sadiq, Farouk, and even Alya, must all guess that we will travel with the Kumans," Sophia said. "Why else would you sell our camels? If the *shinha* come seeking us with arrest warrants in hand as you expect, I do not think any of them will hesitate long before revealing where we have gone."

"We should have a full day before anyone begins to search for us," Warrick said. "Enough time for us to ride well into the mountains, where it will be difficult to find us."

"We will ride hard," Gafar said, joining them. "I want to reach the foothills before dark. We will light no fires tonight. You will eat what food is in your baskets. Tomorrow we will rise before dawn and continue all day without stopping. Can you do

203

it?" he asked, looking directly at Sophia.

"I will, and I thank you for your protection on our way, Gafar," Sophia said. She could tell that he was eager to be moving northward. His impatience mirrored her own. Though she would far rather lie down next to the sheltering rock and sleep instead of mounting a horse, Warrick's remarks about the next band of *shinha* coming to arrest her, or him, had sown the seeds of renewed fear in her heart.

Gafar brought with him four of his spare ponies, which he was lending to them until they reached Tabriz. They were not the kind of horses Sophia was used to seeing. The sultan and the nobles of Baghdad all rode the famous "flying horses" that were first bred in Persia, tall, beautiful animals with heavy shoulder muscles, long, slender legs, and sleek coats. The Persian horses were capable of incredible speeds. They were also high-strung and could be difficult to control.

Gafar's mounts were milder in temperament. Originally from the steppes, they were short, shaggy-haired ponies, with sturdy legs and great endurance. They could withstand the bitter northern winters, and Sophia had seen for herself how swift and surefooted they were when taken through complicated maneuvers by skilled riders.

Sophia would have been terrified if she were expected to ride one of the tall Persian horses. But after sitting on Nura's back for three days and having grown accustomed to the camel's rolling gait, she was not at all afraid when Warrick selected one of Gafar's ponies for her and boosted her onto it. Her legs hung down on either side of the small leather saddle, and her skirt was hiked above her knees.

"You need trousers," Gafar said, giving her legs a disapproving glance. "At least your boots are suitable."

"We have trousers in our baskets," Genie told him. "Sophia and I can easily go behind the rock and change our clothes."

"Change when we stop for the night," Gafar said. "There is no time now. We leave at once."

Robin assisted Genie into the saddle of her horse, then helped Warrick divide their scanty baggage and attach the baskets and bundles to their horses' backs. Warrick and Robin swung onto their mounts and the four of them started off across the plain, hurrying to catch up with the Kumans.

Sophia quickly discovered that a horse's gait was very different from that of a camel. When her pony broke into a trot, she bounced in the saddle and her bare legs rubbed against the leather. Nor was it as easy to stay on the pony's back as it had been to stay on Nura's. Sophia gritted her teeth and held on tight, willing herself not to fall.

Gafar apparently did not spare a thought for the female riders in his party. Perhaps, Sophia thought, Kuman girls were taught at an early age to ride as well as the men. For the remainder of that day she thought a good deal about Kuman women, and how they traveled from place to place. After Nura's relaxed, ambling pace, Sophia found the speed of the Kuman horses terrifying. It was also uncomfortable. Before long her buttocks began to ache and her thighs were chafed and sore. Having given her word to Gafar that she would not slow his band, Sophia made no complaint.

They were well into the foothills and it was almost completely dark before Gafar called a halt.

His men roped their horses together and left them to feed on the sparse grass, with two of the Kumans to guard them. Each of the rest of Gafar's band pulled food from his saddlebag and ate it; then the men who were not on sentry duty stretched out on the ground to sleep. These activities were accomplished quickly and with a minimum of conversation.

In the meantime Sophia dismounted and handed the reins of the pony she had ridden to Robin. When he led it away, Sophia lowered herself slowly to the ground and sat there, holding her left arm close to her chest to ease the throbbing pain that had bothered her for hours. Not only her arm hurt. Her whole body was aching. She wished desperately for Genie's magical tent and bathtub, in which she longed to soak. Instead of sitting in a hot, fragrant tub, she sat on the hard earth and watched while Genie rifled through the contents of their baskets and bundles, searching for food.

"Without a fire we can't cook lentils," Genie said. "We do have some day-old bread and dried dates, and one orange for each of us."

"There is a spring nearby," Robin announced. After leaving the horses with the other ponies, he had done a bit of exploring on his way back to his friends. "We won't go thirsty, and we can wash, if you don't mind ice-cold water."

"Sophia, what is wrong with your arm?" Genie said. "I noticed earlier today that you were favoring it, but I haven't had a chance to ask about it."

"One of the *shinha* stabbed me," Sophia answered.

"What did you say?" Warrick exclaimed. He was also rummaging through their baggage, looking for more food to add to what Genie had found. He grabbed the sack of medical supplies and knelt beside Sophia. "Why didn't you tell me you were wounded?"

"Because I didn't think it was serious, and then I didn't want to cause a delay," she said. Warrick was so near to her. She yearned to put her head on his shoulder and rest for a while. That yearning told her how perilously close to tears she was.

"It's not every day that I kill a man," she said, hoping to divert Warrick's attention away from the moistness she could feel gathering in her eyes.

"You don't know that he's dead." Warrick gave her a look that penetrated to her heart. "Do not grieve for him, Sophia. If you had not stabbed him, he would most certainly have killed you."

"I know that, but all the same, I can't help feeling guilty." She was glad that her veil prevented him from seeing the single tear that rolled down her cheek. As if he sensed her complex emotions, Warrick let his hand brush against her veil and come to rest on her shoulder.

"I recall how I felt after my first battle," he said softly. "For a man—or a woman—of a thoughtful nature, it is not a pleasant experience. You have been remarkably brave, Sophia."

"I?" she said, surprised at the conclusion he had reached. "Oh, no, Warrick. The truth is, I was too frightened to be brave. I just did what I thought I ought to do at that particular moment."

"Don't you know that's what bravery is?" he said. "Courage is the ability to overcome fear, so you can do what must be done. Every fighting man knows that—and every woman who has borne a child or nursed someone who is deathly ill. Now," he said with a tender smile, "let me see your wound so I can decide whether it's serious or not." Warrick pulled at Sophia's veil to lift it away from her arm.

"Ouch!" Sophia clapped her hand over his to stop him. "So much for my bravery. That hurts, Warrick. The cloth has stuck to the wound." She was glad to hear that her voice barely trembled and she did not think he could guess how close to breaking down she was. She did not feel the least bit courageous. It was all she could do to keep from weeping with pain and exhaustion.

"Robin, bring me some of that cold spring water," Warrick ordered. "Genie, I have flint and a few candles among the supplies in my sack. Can you light one of the candles?"

"Yes, I can use flint," Genie responded. "I'll just gather some dried leaves and grass to make the first flame."

"I said, no fires!" Gafar loomed over them, a menacing shadow in the gathering darkness.

"Sophia was wounded in the battle with the *shinha*," Warrick told him. "She has ridden all this way leaving the sword cut on her arm untended because she did not want to delay you. If I do not treat the wound tonight, and she develops an infection and a fever, she will not be able to travel."

"If that happens we will leave her by the wayside, as we do with our own people," Gafar said. "If she dies of the wound, it is the will of Heaven. If she lives, she can follow us when she is able to ride again."

"I will not leave Sophia behind." Warrick stood to face Gafar. He towered over the Kuman leader, and he employed his most compelling voice. "You offered to escort the four of us to Tabriz in return for my sword arm, and Robin's, should we be attacked. You and I made an honest bargain, Gafar. Will you break your word at the first opportunity? I will require only a single candle for a brief time."

"I will shield the light," Genie said when Gafar did not respond immediately. "I will make certain the light does not extend any farther than the area Warrick needs to see, in order to tend Sophia's injuries."

"If any of your men have need of my healing skills, I will treat them as well as Sophia," Warrick said.

"My men will care for their own hurts, as is our custom. If we are discovered because of the light you require . . ." Gafar left the threat unfinished and switched to another subject. "Sophia left her blood on the saddle she used today. She must wear trousers if she is not to slow us down with another complaint."

"I have not complained!" Sophia cried, stung by the criticism, and by the truth of Gafar's words. She was not going to be able to keep up with the others unless she had protection for her sore thighs.

"As I told you before we began our ride," Genie said to Gafar, "we have trousers in our baggage. Sophia and I will put them on as soon as we wake in the morning."

"Put them on now," Gafar said in a kinder voice, "so you do not delay us in the morning while you dress." He made a movement in the darkness, as if he was leaving them. Then he paused and spoke again. "The women of my people do not veil themselves."

"Now there we are in agreement," Sophia said. "I would gladly fling my veil into the nearest gorge."

"Then do so," Gafar said. For the first time Sophia heard amusement in his heavily accented words. "Ride free of that insulting restriction to your sight and movement."

"Suppose we meet someone as we travel through the mountains," Genie said. "Won't two barefaced women cause hostile comment? I thought you wanted to escape notice, Gafar."

"So I do." Gafar's response to Genie's question was a practical one. "I have seen women who wear scarves on their heads to cover their hair and protect themselves from the sun. If such a scarf is arranged with one long end hanging loose, it can be pulled across the face in the event that we meet someone."

"I do like the idea of covering my hair," Genie said. "Thank you for the suggestion, Gafar."

With a grunt, the Kuman leader stalked off into the darkness. Genie removed her veil, then knelt to strike the flints together a few times, until a flame caught in the tiny pile of dry grass and leaves she had pushed together. She blew on the flame, and when it was large enough she lit the candle from it.

At that point Robin returned from the spring carrying a leather bucket full of water and Genie gave him the candle to hold. She passed her hand over the bucket, uttering a few unintelligible words. Then she took a clean cloth from Warrick's supply of bandages, dipped the cloth into the bucket, and placed it, dripping wet, over Sophia's wound. Sophia braced herself for the shock of ice water stinging the open cut, but she should have guessed what Genie was doing. The water was warm.

It took a while for Warrick and Genie, working together, to soak the gashed sleeve of Sophia's gown and the torn edges of her veil until they could gently ease the fabric away from the wound. Once the clothing was free, Genie removed Sophia's veil. She took a knife and cut away the sleeve of Sophia's dress at the shoulder. Sophia shivered as cool air touched her skin.

"It is a long cut," Warrick said, examining the wound, "but not deep. It has bled freely, which is a good sign. It is a clean cut. I will wash it and put on an herbal compound, then bind it with linen. It won't require sewing."

"I am glad of that," Sophia said through chattering teeth.

Warrick tended her arm with a rapid skill that bespoke long experience. When he was finished, Sophia shifted to a more comfortable position—and groaned with a different kind of pain. Warrick gave her a sharp glance.

"Let me see your legs," he said. He reached for the hem of her skirt, which was already bunched up around her calves. Sophia tried to push his hand away. Warrick caught her wrist.

"Don't give in to foolish modesty," he said. "The injury to your arm is a minor inconvenience so long as you keep it clean. But if you cannot sit a horse, Gafar really will leave you behind."

"I think," said Robin, "that this is a good time for me to fetch a pail of clean water. The first one I brought is dirty." He handed the candle to Genie, picked up the bucket, tossed away the water it held, and then disappeared into the darkness.

Without further discussion Warrick pulled Sophia's skirt up to her hips, revealing the chafed areas on the insides of her thighs.

211

Genie gasped. "Oh, dear. Sophia, why didn't you say something?"

"A complaint would have meant we would have to stop," Sophia said. "We were all eager to be as far away from the caravan route as we could get. And you heard Gafar's cruel threats."

"He isn't cruel," Warrick said, "and he has not threatened you. He simply told you how his people handle injuries or illnesses when they are traveling. Individuals may be forced to stop because they cannot go on; the group continues to move. It is the safest way for the greatest number of people."

"Well, we cannot leave Sophia behind," Genie said. "Warrick, have you an ointment that will work on this? It must be terribly painful and I think it could become serious if the chafed area festers."

"There is an herbal ointment that will take away the pain," Warrick said, searching among the stoppered jars and small clay pots in his sack. "As for healing those particular wounds, time is the best cure. Genie, can you conjure long underdrawers with some kind of padding that will offer protection for Sophia's thighs?"

"Of course I can." Genie smiled at Sophia and patted her hand. "I promise that your ride tomorrow will be far more comfortable than today's was. Now what is keeping Robin? We will want more water. Sophia, please hold the candle. I'll take another bucket and see if I can find him."

"Do we have a second bucket?" Sophia asked. "I didn't know we had the first bucket. Genie, do you create them by magic, like the tent and the tub and hot water? How I would like a hot bath."

"Not tonight," Genie said. She thrust the candle into Sophia's hand, took up a bucket that Sophia had not previously seen, and headed in the direction Robin had gone.

"Warrick, have you noticed how Genie gives me orders more often than she accepts commands from me?" Sophia said. "I always thought the jinn were compelled to be obedient to their masters. Genie is remarkably independent."

"I have been too busy recently to notice Genie's behavior," Warrick said. He pulled a jar from his basket and lifted the cork lid. Dipping his fingers into the jar, he brought forth a quantity of ointment. "This will sting at first, but soon the pain will stop and you will be aware only of a pleasant warmth," he said.

He knelt beside Sophia and stretched out his hand. His ointment-covered fingers touched her inner thigh. At the instant of contact Sophia's hand, which was holding the candle, shook violently, and a drop of hot wax splashed onto her wrist. She made a short, quickly muffled sound of pain. Warrick did not seem to be aware of her distress.

Warrick stroked up and down her thigh, spreading the ointment. An agreeable, minty odor reached Sophia's nose. The warmth that Warrick had promised began to spread and slowly the pain disappeared. The warm sensation grew, making Sophia more and more aware of the pressure of Warrick's fingers on her sensitive flesh.

By the candle's light she saw his rugged features thrown into harsh shadows and highlights. He was intent on what he was doing, his mouth tight with concentration, his expression absorbed, his lids half-closed over his smoky eyes. She thought he was no longer aware of her, so involved was he in his work.

Sophia sat on the ground with her legs spread and her skirts pulled high, exposed to Warrick's gaze and his hands as she had never before been exposed to any man. The ointment was slick and smooth, and when Warrick's hand slid beyond the chafed area the heat from his fingers followed a path upward. Sophia held her breath and bit down hard on her lower lip to keep herself from crying out. She was not sure whether it was pleasure or pain she felt. She knew only that it was like no sensation she had ever experienced before, and she wanted it to continue.

It did. Warrick's hand stroked from her knee almost to her groin, and it was as though a bolt of lightning shot through her, leaving a flaring heat in the most private places of her body. She barely managed to stifle a groan.

Warrick risked a quick glance at Sophia. She was chewing on her lower lip, and her blue eyes were misty and soft. He knew well enough what she was feeling. In order to rub the ointment into her delicate skin so the herbs would do the most good, he was forced to emulate a lover's caresses. Sophia had never known a lover's touch. Warrick was fully aware of the faint trembling of her limbs, which she tried to control, and he could too easily imagine the melting warmth that was flowing through her veins.

The two of them were completely alone, held together in the glow of one single candle and surrounded by the velvety night. Sophia's bare shoulder above the white linen bandage, and the delicate shape of her lower arm and wrist and hand, all shone in the candlelight as if they were illuminated from within. And the skin of her thighs was so transparent that Warrick could have traced each small blue vein. Only the angry red streaks of chafing marred the perfection of her thighs. And there, just above the red area and barely hidden by the hem of her dark gown, lay the place where her thighs joined.

"Now your other leg," Warrick said. His own voice sounded unnatural to him, husky and thrumming with desire. When he dipped his fingers into the warm, moist ointment, he shook with an almost uncontrollable emotion.

Warrick was torn by opposing desires. One part of him—the hard, masculine part that was about to burst asunder with male need—ached to push Sophia onto her back and plunge himself into her so he could ease the lust that was roaring through his blood and his brain with the mighty thunder of a river in full flood. The other part of him longed to kiss her trembling lips with tender care, to gather her close to his heart and swear to protect her from every danger. That gentler part of him wanted to hear her whisper that she cared about him and trusted him.

Sternly he reminded himself of the years of training in self-control he had undergone. He told himself that he was sworn to deliver Sophia safely to her uncle in Byzantium, and that *safe* meant in her present, virgin state and undefiled by any man, including Warrick of Wroxley.

He could not, in honor, indulge in any of the passionate fantasies that the sight and silken touch of her beautiful thighs engendered. It was entirely possible that he was going to suffer from unfulfilled male need until he reached the fabled fleshpots of Byzantium. Regarding Sophia's smooth, pale thighs by candlelight, Warrick doubted there was any other woman, in Byzantium or anywhere else, who could give him what he truly wanted.

"There, I've finished." Warrick removed his hands from her. He was nowhere near finished. He had not even begun. He could think of a hundred wonderful, erotic delights that his hands and his lips could work upon her, until she was eagerly pleading for him to administer the final, most intimate caress of all.

"Thank you," Sophia whispered. "The pain is completely gone. There is only a very pleasant warmth in my thighs—" She stopped suddenly, as if she had just realized what she was saying.

Warrick looked upward from Sophia's thighs, which were still gleaming with the ointment he had smoothed onto them, and met her eyes. He discovered that he could not look away. Innocent, questioning blue met smoky, troubled topaz. Warrick knew if he did not tear his eyes from hers, he would surely lean forward and kiss her. If he kissed her he would pull her to him, and then nothing would stop him. His years of ascetic self-denial for the sake of higher learning and his stern admonitions of the last hour would count for nothing.

Not only did he want Sophia, he wanted no other woman, nor ever would. The sudden knowledge of what lay hidden within his own heart came close to shattering him.

He almost wept from relief at the sound of Genie's voice.

"Here we are at last," Genie said, advancing into the circle of candlelight. "Robin neglected to mention how far away the spring is. Gafar ought to make his camp nearer to a water source."

"As you saw, Genie, there isn't much water trickling from the spring," Robin said. "Gafar's explanation was that he doesn't want the horses to befoul it, and he wants his men close enough to the horses to guard them. So he makes us all walk to the spring." Robin's voice was a bit strained. His cheeks were a little flushed and his eyes were overbright. He kept looking at Genie, who ignored him.

"Sophia, are you feeling better?" Genie asked.

"Better?" Sophia repeated, thinking about the question. "Oh, yes, the herbal ointment was helpful."

Again Genie used her magic to heat the water in both of the filled buckets that she and Robin had carried from the spring. She produced a bowl of soap from one of the bundles among their baggage, and all four of them used it to wash their faces and hands.

"With the beards the two of you have been growing since we left Baghdad," Genie said, looking from Robin to Warrick, "you will appear quite natural should we meet anyone along our way. I understand that there are people who live in these mountains, inhospitable as they seem."

They extinguished the candle, and ate their evening meal of flatbread, dates, and oranges in the dark. From the same bundle that she had taken the bowl of soap, Genie brought forth four cups, which she filled with water. Warrick added dried tea leaves from his herbal supplies, and Genie pronounced a few of her mysterious words. When she handed one of the cups to Sophia, the liquid in it was almost hot enough to burn Sophia's tongue.

"This is delicious," Sophia said, sipping the tea.

"With this in my stomach I won't mind the lack of a full meal."

"Genie, while you and Sophia change your clothing, Robin and I will prepare the bedrolls," Warrick said after they had finished the tea.

Sophia was not at all surprised to see that the men unrolled four pads for sleeping, instead of the two they had brought from Baghdad. Before she could comment on the magical additions, Genie took her by the arm and drew her aside.

"Gafar and his men are honest," Genie said, "and out of respect for the prowess that Warrick and Robin have displayed in battle, they will show respect to you and me, as warriors' women."

"We are no such thing!" Sophia protested, raising her voice to try to drown out the whisper in her mind that told her a warrior's woman was exactly what she wanted to be, so long as the warrior in question was Warrick.

"Hush, Sophia," Genie warned. "Do not draw attention to us. These are also superstitious tribesmen, who will be terrified if they learn what I am. Superstitious fear can lead to violence. Let us not make our situation any more complex or hazardous than it is already. Gafar has set sentries about the camp, and we may be questioned if any of them come upon us. I have brought you and one of our bundles away from the camp so that we can pretend to be seeking privacy while we change our clothes, and that is the excuse we will give if we are challenged.

"I don't have clothing in the bundle," Genie continued. "I will use magic to provide what we require, but I don't want Gafar and his men to know that."

"Genie, I am sorry I shouted," Sophia said. "I am so tired that I am not thinking very clearly."

"I understand," Genie said. "So am I weary. There was a moment by the spring with Robin when I was not thinking clearly either. Enough on that subject. As soon as we are wearing our new clothes, we can both sleep. Since we want our traveling companions to believe these garments have been carried from Baghdad in our baggage, they will have to be wrinkled, and Warrick has warned me to make them dark and plain. Oh dear, I much prefer silks in bright colors, and lots of jewelry."

"You did say we mustn't draw attention to ourselves," Sophia reminded her. Knowing Genie's predilection for gaudy costumes, she wondered with some amusement just what sort of clothing the two of them were going to be wearing.

"When I have finished with our costumes, I do not think the most observant soul will see anything in us to cause comment," Genie said with a sigh. "Turn around, Sophia."

Sophia did as instructed. She was unaware of her tattered gown vanishing, or of being dressed in new clothes, yet when she faced Genie again, both of them were clad in loose trousers and collarless shirts in the dark colors Warrick had wanted. The dull clothing was topped by coarsely woven woolen coats made with wide sleeves and no fastenings. The coats were held in place by cotton sashes that were wrapped around their waists several times. Sophia was still shod in the comfortable boots she had worn since leaving Baghdad and her new trousers were tucked into them. On her head was the scarf Gafar had suggested and she could see in the dim light that Genie's flamboyant tresses were also securely covered by a scarf.

Furthermore, Sophia was aware of an unfamiliar undergarment that reached to her knees. There was soft padding in the thighs of the garment. A few steps convinced her that her movements would be unrestricted. In fact the new clothing was surprisingly easy to move in, and the earlier discomfort where her thighs were chafed was gone.

There was yet another new experience awaiting her. Sophia had never slept outside a house or, lately, a tent. In spite of her exhaustion, she lay wide-awake on her bedroll. She was intensely aware of Warrick on one side of her and Genie on the other, of Gafar and his men and the horses. All of them made occasional soft noises when they changed position.

Above her spread the night sky and the stars, bounded to the north and east by the tall peaks of the mountains they had still to cross. The sky was without a cloud and the moon would not rise until much later, so it was possible to count the stars, if she wanted to.

After years of disliking the sight of the night sky, Sophia was not thinking about astronomical observations. Her thoughts were focused on the people around her, and on how amazingly content she was to be with them. Warrick, Genie, Robin, even Gafar in his gruff way, all had shown interest in her well-being. Sophia was not used to anyone taking care of her. She admitted to herself, privately, that she rather liked knowing she was the object of so much concern.

Images of the day passed through her mind, from its ordinary beginning to the sudden battle, the departure of the caravan, the wild and, for her, painful ride to the mountains, and the quiet evening that had followed. Foremost in her thoughts was the image of Warrick tending her wounds. The recollection of the way he had touched her blended with the memory of his kisses in her father's study back in Baghdad. Once again the warmth his hands had generated flowed into the secret places of her body. Sophia groaned and moved restlessly on her pallet.

"Are you in pain?" Warrick's voice was little more than a whisper, and surprisingly close to her ear.

"I am just a little stiff when I move," she responded, wishing she dared to ask him to hold her and stroke her thighs again, and kiss her.

She could not do that, of course. She was ignorant of much of what occurred in private between men and women, but she did know that if a man held and touched a woman for more than a few moments, he would want to perform the deed that Hanna always spoke of with digust. It was painful for women, Hanna had said, hot and messy and it carried serious consequences for any female. According to Hanna, Sophia would do well to avoid the act for as long as she could.

And yet Sophia could recall her mother speaking with tenderness about the love she bore for her husband, and of her deep regret that she was too ill to be a true wife to him any longer. Sophia had always found it difficult to reconcile the two opposing attitudes. She had assumed it was a subject on which she would never have to make a choice, since there was no man who was interested in marrying her.

"Your stiffness will wear away tomorrow, as you move around," Warrick said into the darkness.

"Your healing skills are remarkable," she murmured.

"I have known greater healers," he said. Silence stretched between them, and Sophia knew he was thinking of Hua Te, for whose disappearance Warrick blamed himself.

"All the same," she said, "it was good of you to be so kind to me, when I have too often been rude to you."

"Or angry with me," he added.

"I have been angry for most of my life," Sophia said with a sigh that came from deep within her soul, "and not just with you. For years I was angry with my mother for dying and leaving me, though I knew well enough it was not by her choosing that she died. I was angry with my father because he ignored me in favor of astronomy and mathematics and even for his occasional excursions into magic. It always seemed to me as if any subject that caught his interest was more important to him than I was."

"That much was true," Warrick said. He did not add that John had resented even having to think about his daughter, or about her future. "I respected your father as a scholar, but he did neglect you. It was clear to me why you were such a difficult girl."

"And what good has all my anger done?" she asked. "It has hardened my heart and turned people away from me. Only in the last few days have I cared about others and their problems, or felt that I am important to anyone. How odd that I should have to lose so much in order to gain a faint glimmer of comprehension about other people."

"I always found you fascinating," he said. "Troubling, disturbing—"

"And difficult," she finished for him.

Warrick chuckled and put out his hand to grasp hers. He heard Sophia catch her breath just before her fingers curved around his. He was painfully aware that he ought not touch her at all. The softness of her small hand reawakened his earlier hunger for her. He told himself again that she was not his to take, and never could be. She was a member of a noble Byzantine family, and he was a failed magician, landless by his own choice, a seeker of knowledge who was appallingly ignorant after decades of study, a man with few possessions to his name and no prospect of ever having land or home or wealth to offer her.

On the far side of Genie's bedroll, Robin stirred, turned over, and muttered a sleepy word or two. Warrick released Sophia's hand.

"We had best get to sleep," he said. "Morning will be here before you realize it."

Chapter Fourteen

Gafar had spoken no more than the truth when he warned Sophia that he and his men were moving on before daylight. The darkness of night had barely begun to soften into the first, faint hints of dawn when the Kuman leader wakened Warrick and Robin with the same kick to the shins that he administered to those of his own men who did not rise when they should have.

Warrick and Robin, in turn, wakened Sophia and Genie, though far more gently. Warrick laid a hand on Sophia's shoulder. Her blue eyes opened with a puzzled look in them, until she saw who was bending over her. She sat up so quickly that Warrick jumped back to avoid a collision with her head. Sophia glanced around the campsite.

"Gafar is leaving already," she said, and got to her feet.

"We won't have time to break our fast," Warrick

said. "Not if we want to keep up with our Kuman friends."

"I won't delay you." Shivering a little in the cool morning air, Sophia bent to fold her bedroll.

By the time Robin had their horses saddled and Warrick helped Sophia onto the pony she was to ride, the sky was turning pale, the last stars were fading, and Gafar and the other Kumans were some distance ahead.

It was almost an hour later before the sun rose above the eastern mountain peaks. Sophia lifted her face to it, welcoming its warmth. The ache in her wounded arm was minimal and the padded undergarment that Genie had created protected her thighs from any further abrasions. Feeling remarkably healthy and well rested, she smiled at the sun and the clear blue sky, and smiled again at Genie, who urged her horse forward so she could ride next to Sophia.

"Here," Genie said, holding out her closed fist. "Take these. You must be hungry. I know I was."

Sophia reached toward Genie and Genie opened her fingers, letting a fistful of dried dates fall into Sophia's hand.

"Thank you." Sophia began to munch on the dates.

"I am sorry there wasn't time to prepare coffee," Genie said, "or even cups of Warrick's tea. I hope Gafar will allow his men to hunt today, so we will have meat for the evening meal."

"Will he let us build a fire to cook it?" Sophia asked.

Warrick, who was riding ahead of her, heard the question and turned in his saddle to answer it.

"If we ride for a good distance today, Gafar may

decide we are far enough ahead of any pursuers that a campfire won't pose a risk. He has told me that on a previous trip through these mountains he had no difficulty bargaining for safe passage with the Kurds who live in the high valleys. We will be able to buy food from them. In the meantime I would relish the taste of a few of Genie's dates."

Genie reached into a pocket hidden in her coat. She pulled out a handful of dates and gave them to Warrick. Presumably she had already fed Robin from the same supply.

Sophia finished the last of her dates and licked her sticky fingers. Seldom had dates tasted so delicious to her. Perhaps it was the mountain air that sharpened all of her senses. Or possibly it was the unfamiliar feeling that she was among people who cared about her and who, she believed, would do the best they could to prevent harm from befalling her. Whatever the reasons, her contented mood of the previous night continued unchanged throughout the day. To her own astonishment she was enjoying herself. She took pleasure in Warrick's company, and in the friendship of both Genie and Robin, and even in Gafar's rough manners.

While they were still in Baghdad and, later, during the early days of their journey, Sophia had been alternately puzzled and then amused by Robin's boyish adoration of Genie. Now that Sophia knew Genie better, and had enjoyed some of the advantages of Genie's magical resourcefulness, she could understand why Robin was drawn to the jinni. It wasn't just Genie's unearthly beauty that made her so attractive. There was an openness of heart and a good-humored sweetness to Genie that encouraged both men and women to trust her. Even Sophia, who expected everyone she knew to prove undependable, relied upon Genie to do what she promised to do.

On the second evening of their passage through the mountains, Robin drew Sophia away from the camp on the pretext of gathering twigs and branches to keep their small campfire burning through the night. Gafar's men had not brought back any game from their brief attempt at hunting, but Gafar decided that fires could be lit.

"The next two days are the most difficult part of this route," Gafar told them. "Cook your lentils, bake your bread, eat well tonight, and prepare extra food to eat along the way. I want no one to slow us down because of weakness," he finished with a fierce look that included Genie as well as Sophia.

"I have not slowed you," Sophia declared.

"No, you have not." Gafar bestowed one of his ferocious grins on her. "I expected a gently raised woman of the city to cause trouble and frequent delays. You have kept up with the rest of us. You have been a pleasant surprise to me, Sophia."

"I intend to continue to surprise you, Gafar," she said.

He nodded and left her to rejoin his men.

"Now that was a fine compliment," Robin said as he and Sophia went off together in search of firewood. "And a rare one, too, I think. I hope you are properly appreciative of the honor Gafar has paid you."

"It's the greatest honor I have ever received," Sophia said with a grin to match her companion's. "I mean it, Robin. Gafar has just warmed my heart and inflated my pride. He doesn't trouble himself to praise many people."

"And you aren't used to being praised." Robin's smile faded and he changed the subject. "Sophia, how well do you know Genie?"

"Not as well as I like to think I do," Sophia said. "She appears to answer all of my questions honestly. She says that is because a jinni is incapable of lying to her mistress. If I ask she will explain why she is working a particular kind of magic, and she has given me some very good advice. However, knowing what she is, I am certain there are realms of experience and levels of existence that she has known, yet cannot describe to mere humans. She claims to be a very young jinni. I do not know what that means."

"Has she said anything about men?" Robin did not look at Sophia as he spoke. He had one foot on a long tree branch that had fallen to the ground. Grasping an end of the branch, Robin lifted it, rocking it back and forth against the weight of his foot, trying to break it into more manageable lengths.

"Men?" Sophia repeated. "Do you mean teachers or friends, or masters during her previous Callings into human form? I don't think she has male relatives, because the jinn aren't born as humans are. They are individually created."

"That is not what I meant," Robin said in a hard voice. He gave the branch he was working on a vicious jerk. With a loud crack the branch split into two shorter pieces. "I was asking about lovers. Previous lovers."

"Oh." Sophia thought about Genie's possible lovers. She was very glad that darkness was fast settling over the mountains. Her face was probably bright red and she did not want Robin to see how embarrassed she was by the direction the conversation was taking. Still, Robin had asked for her help and she had no intention of disappointing him. As dispassionately as she could, she considered the idea of Genie lying with a man, and of Robin wanting to caress her as Warrick had touched Sophia. She decided there was only one piece of information she could honestly supply. "Genie did speak once of having been a servant in a harem. She said it was not one of her more pleasant Callings, and that she had no desire to repeat the experience. She did not elaborate about what her duties in the harem entailed."

"That's all?" Robin asked. "She didn't say anything else?"

"It is not a subject that women discuss at any great length," Sophia said.

"You don't?" Robin chuckled. "I thought women talked about men all the time."

"Well, we don't. At least not the women I have known. Of course, I haven't known many women; just my mother and Hanna and some silly girls whose father was an astronomer like my father. And, recently, Genie and Alya." His comments had raised a question in Sophia's mind that she could not resist asking. "Robin, do men talk about women?"

"Some do, but only when they are successful."

"I see," she said in the same cold voice she had employed so often while still living in her father's house. It was entirely possible that Warrick had considered himself successful with Sophia and thus had talked to Robin about the embrace they had shared after her father's death, or about the evening when Warrick had caressed her while they stood on a hillside. Sophia lifted her chin, assuming an air of icy, injured dignity, which Robin probably could neither see nor interpret in the early evening darkness.

Almost as if he understood what was troubling Sophia, Robin added, "No well-bred man ever discusses his private moments with a lady. It is dishonorable to do so."

Silence enveloped them for a while after that, while Sophia thought over everything Robin had said. She set herself to collect as many small branches as she could discover. Robin broke up pieces of several saplings that had been uprooted in some violent mountain storm and added them to the branch he had found.

"Robin," Sophia said after a while, "why did you want to know about Genie's possible previous lovers? I cannot believe you would do anything dishonorable with her."

"I suppose what is dishonorable is a matter of opinion," Robin said. "I put my arm around Genie twice. Or rather, I tried to put my arm around her. Each time she suddenly wasn't there anymore."

"I have never known Genie to vanish," Sophia said.

"She didn't exactly vanish. When I touched her, she just wasn't where I thought she was. When I looked around she was standing a few feet away. She continued our conversation as if nothing had happened."

"Why did you put your arm around her?" Sophia asked.

"I didn't. As I just told you, I tried, but she wasn't there." Robin let out a long breath. "I wanted to kiss her."

"Why?" Sophia asked.

"Sophia," Robin said with a touch of impatience, "I hoped you would know whether Genie likes me."

"I have never considered her likes or dislikes," Sophia said. "She has told me that it is dangerous for a jinni to become overly fond of a human. I'm not sure whether she meant it's dangerous for the jinni or for the human, or for both of them."

"In that case I suppose there's little hope for me," Robin said.

"Hope for you to do what?" Sophia demanded, outraged by what she saw as Robin's dishonorable intentions toward Genie. She had misjudged Robin. She would never have guessed that such a nice young man could entertain wicked thoughts about any honorable female, especially one who would not even let a man put his arm around her, but there it was. Hanna was right to complain so often and issue so many warnings about the nefarious desires of wicked, lustful men.

"Hope for Genie to learn to love me," Robin said in response to her question. "Because I love her with all my heart."

"Love?" All of Sophia's anger at him disappeared as if by magic. "Oh, Robin, I did not know."

"I have been trying to hide it," Robin said. "But I am desperate to know what Genie's feelings toward me are, and I believed you were the one person who could tell me."

"Oh, Robin," Sophia said again. At that moment she could not think of any other words to speak, and only one thing to do occurred to her amazed mind. What she wanted to do was so surprising that she did not allow herself time to reconsider the impulse. She dropped the branches she was holding, ran the few steps to where he was standing, and put her arms around Robin's waist and hugged him tight. He stiffened at first; then his own arms came around her and he laid his curly head upon hers and let Sophia pat him on the back as if he were an unhappy child.

After a time Robin straightened and peered down at her through the evening gloom.

"You are very different from the woman I first thought you were," he said. "You are not at all a vinegary spinster. Under your cool exterior you possess a kind and caring heart."

"Vinegary?" She laughed up at him. "What a word."

"It's my mother's phrase," he said.

"Your mother is alive?"

"The last time I saw her she was very much alive, and healthy, and expecting a child with her new husband."

"Your mother married a second time?" Sophia could not comprehend why any woman would ever want a second husband. "Was it an arranged marriage that was forced on her?"

"Hardly." Robin laughed. "She and Captain Oliver are passionately in love."

"Oh. The affliction runs in your family, then." This remark elicited a full-bodied laugh from Robin.

"When love is returned, as it is between my mother and Captain Oliver, it is a joy, not a bane," he said. "Nor do I think of my feelings for Genie as an affliction. Sophia, we have been away from the campsite for some time. Warrick will begin to worry about us if we do not return soon."

Sophia said nothing. Her mind was too full of new ideas for her to speak. Quickly she regathered the firewood she had dropped. Robin picked up the larger pile of wood that he had collected, and the two of them hurried back to the camp.

They found Genie kneeling by the fire to stir the lentil stew that would be their dinner. She said something to Warrick, who was turning the flatbread that was baking on a stone, and Warrick laughed. Seeing the easy humor on his face, Sophia sighed. Warrick looked up and noticed Sophia. He stood and came to her, not taking his gaze off her.

"Let me." He reached for the firewood she was holding, to lift it out of her arms. His hands touched hers and lingered under the firewood, unseen by Robin or Genie. "You have brought enough for the whole camp. No wonder you were gone for so long."

The words were ordinary enough. Sophia imagined there was another meaning to them, that Warrick had missed her and had been waiting for her return.

Sophia did not speak much during that evening. In her thoughts she went over and over her conversation with Robin. Now that she knew of his love for Genie, she could see it in every gesture he made toward her, and hear it in each word he spoke. If love returned was a joy, as Robin claimed, then love that was not reciprocated must be a torment. Robin still held hope that Genie might learn to love him. Perhaps hope would forestall his torment for a time, until Robin finally understood that his hope was in vain.

And then there was the matter of Robin's mother, who had willingly married a second husband for love. From what Robin had said Sophia could only conclude that she had gone with joy to her new marriage bed. If a woman with previous experience of a man's lust could happily take a second husband, then perhaps Hanna was wrong after all, and the thing that men did to women was neither as painful nor as messy and unpleasant as Hanna had always claimed. Perhaps it was as wonderful, and as disturbing, as Warrick's hands on Sophia's thighs.

"Sophia, are you asleep and dreaming already?" Warrick lightly touched her cheek. He was smiling and holding out a cup of steaming tea to her. Their fingers touched as she accepted the cup, and he did not remove his hand, but let it stay where it was for a moment or two, as he had done earlier with the firewood.

Sophia's cheeks flamed. She was grateful that Warrick could not know what she had been thinking. And yet she feared he suspected something of her confused yearnings. The look he gave her was a searching one and there was a warm light in his eyes. Was it possible that he remembered, and wanted to repeat, his caresses?

Not for the first time, Sophia wished she knew more about men, and wished there were an experienced older woman who was willing to tell her what she wanted to know. She could talk to Genie, but Genie wasn't human, so her experiences were probably different from those of a normal woman. Besides, Genie was deep in conversation with Robin. Sophia looked across the campfire to where they sat. She saw Robin's face turned toward Genie, and noticed the shadow in his eyes, and her heart ached for his unreturned adoration.

"You are sad," Warrick said softly. "Or is it sympathy for Robin that I see in you?"

"He will be very unhappy when Genie finally returns to the Land of the Jinn," Sophia whispered.

"Perhaps he believes it's worth some grief later, if he can be with her now," Warrick said. "It is possible that he prefers not to think about the future."

Sophia came to the conclusion that she, too, would do well not to think about the future. If all went as they hoped, their journey through the mountains would not last long. When they reached Tabriz they would bid farewell to Gafar, and then the circumstances of her life would alter once again. With every plodding step her pony took along the mountain path they were following, she moved closer to Byzantium and to the unknown new life that awaited her there.

In the meantime she decided to take as much enjoyment as she could from each hour and every moment. She ate the lentil stew that Genie cooked, scooping it out of the common pot with the flatbread Warrick had prepared, and she wiped her mouth with the back of her hand and licked her fingers afterward. She drank cups of water heated by Genie's magic and flavored with Warrick's supply of tea leaves. She lay on her thin pallet on the rocky ground and gazed at the stars until she fell into the deep sleep of physical weariness, and she wakened refreshed and eager for what the day would bring.

She reveled in the sense of freedom that the mountains gave her, and she appraised the scenery they passed through with the fresh eye of one who had never been outside a city until recently. The mountains were taller than she had ever dreamed mountains could be and, even in the present summer season, the highest peaks were capped with snow. The air was clear and fresh, tiny flowers grew along the sides of their path, and rivulets or full-fledged streams provided all the clean water they needed.

"You would like my homeland," Gafar said to her one day, when she paused at a natural lookout point to survey a narrow green valley that sloped downward from the path they were using. They had been climbing steadily for days and the air Sophia breathed was thin and bracing. She turned in her saddle to look at Gafar with surprise, since he seldom spoke directly to her. He continued to talk in a soft voice, as if he could see in his thoughts the place of which he spoke. "The steppes roll on to the horizon, and the heavenly blue sky spreads above us. There a man can be free to gallop as far as a good steed can carry him, until man and horse become one and there is no obstacle to make them stop until both are tired and happy."

"You are homesick," Sophia said.

"I am not sick," Gafar responded with a scowl. "Illness is an unmanly weakness. But it is true that I long for my own land. My people were not born to dwell in cities.

"I and a few of my men are going there, to the tents you see below in the valley," Gafar said to Warrick, pointing to a tiny settlement. "Those people are Kurds. Have you coins, or gold, that we can use when bartering with them? If you have, I can make certain that your party is included with mine in the agreement we make for safe passage through the rest of these mountains."

"Why do you have to pay them? Are they robbers?" Sophia asked, her eyes on the distant tents, which were made of a dark material and blended into the shadow-dappled landscape. She could see the smoke from a few campfires and by squinting she was able to make out figures moving about the camp. "Will they expect us to join them in their tents?"

"They are not brigands," Gafar said, "just sharp-witted men who have few ways of earning enough goods or coins to keep themselves alive. They require a toll from travelers who use these paths, and most assuredly they know we are here. We will not join them in the valley. Rather, we will invite the men to partake of our hospitality."

"Why must we pay them? That small band cannot be strong enough to control these mountains." Sophia frowned to see Warrick open the sack he wore slung over one shoulder and begin to count out not only copper coins, but a few gold and silver pieces as well. "Warrick, do not hand over all of our money. How are we to live and continue to travel if you do not reserve some coins?"

"You will have nothing left at all, including your life, if you refuse to pay them," Gafar said. "There are more of them than you think, Sophia. You cannot see the men who have concealed themselves along our way to watch us go by. I do not blame them for protecting themselves and their families, and neither should you blame them. Warrick, give me what you have and I'll make the best bargain I can."

Warrick dropped a handful of coins into the leather purse that Gafar held out to him. The Kuman called an order to two of his men and the three of them set off on the rugged trail that led from the main path into the valley. The rest of Gafar's men and Warrick's group spread out, seeking vantage points from which to watch what happened below. No one dismounted. There was a possibility that they would have to move quickly, and they did not want to be unprepared.

"Gafar is the robber," Sophia muttered to Warrick. "He won't return any of the money you gave to him. We will find ourselves destitute in a strange land."

"Gafar is a shrewd man, but an honest one when judged by his own standards," Warrick said.

"We should have gone with him to make certain of that," Sophia grumbled.

"For days we have trusted Gafar with our lives in increasingly rugged territory," Warrick reminded her. "You have been on friendly terms with him. Why do you suddenly question his honesty now?"

"Because he is riding away with our money," Sophia said. "Why didn't you go with him?"

"Gafar has dealt with the Kurds in the past. They know and trust him."

"So he says."

"Ah, Sophia, is there no one you trust?" he asked, shaking his head.

She was about to tell him that she had never found men to be dependable, when he spoke again.

"I remained behind to keep you safe."

She looked into his eyes and saw humor and complete honesty. She also saw with sudden clarity that Warrick was one man who *was* dependable. He had not failed her yet.

He sat his stocky little pony as if it were a magnificent warhorse. His hands rested lightly on the pommel of his saddle, the reins caught loosely in his fingers. Sophia knew his ease was only on the surface, knew with no shred of doubt that, with no more than an instant of warning, Warrick was prepared to do as he had said. He would keep her safe.

She longed to reach across the space that separated them and place her hand on his. Instead she tore her gaze from his and looked toward the valley, where Gafar and his men were approaching the Kurdish encampment.

"Warrick," she said after a few moments, "are your parents alive?" She was so aware of him that she knew when he turned his head and sent a piercing look in her direction.

"Why do you ask, Sophia?"

"I know nothing about your family. Robin has told me of his mother's second marriage, and so I began to wonder about your mother."

There followed a long silence that was filled with a tension Sophia did not understand, until Warrick said, "My mother is dead."

"I know what a sorrow that loss is. I was inconsolable when my mother died," she said.

"My mother's death was no loss to me. It was a blessing."

"How can that be? Oh, Warrick, was she ill for a long time and in great pain? Was there nothing left that you could do for her? Is that why you call her death a blessing, because now she is at peace?"

"My mother was a sorceress," he said in a flat, cold voice. "She loved no one, least of all her children. Her life was entirely consumed by her wicked magic and by the power over others that magic gave to her. She used her power for evil purposes and, in the end, it destroyed her. I was not the only person who rejoiced when she was no more."

"I am sorry. That sounds trivial, doesn't it? But there is nothing else I can say." She paused until curiosity and her need to know more about him drove her to speak again. "Is that why you are so cautious about employing your own magical powers? In all the days we have traveled together, you have only used magic once, that I know of, in the caravansary before we left Baghdad. It seems impossible to me that you would do anything evil, but do you fear you will grow to be like your mother?"

"Once, many years ago, when I was young and my abilities were still untested, I did harbor a fear that my blood carried the taint of her evil, and I was terrified of the magic born in me," Warrick answered. "My youthful revulsion is gone now, thanks to the many years that Hua Te spent training me in the proper uses of magic, in ways to control it, but using magic is still painful to me."

"The headache," Sophia said.

"Not all magicians suffer as I do," Warrick said, "but, for reasons I do not understand, I am always left with a headache after working magic. Sometimes I am blinded by the pain, and I can hardly move. If I should need to defend myself or someone else while I remain in that state, I could not do it."

"How long does the painful paralysis last?" Sophia asked.

"It depends on the spell I've worked, and on how much of my life's energy I have sacrificed to the conjuration."

"Genie uses magic all the time, and she doesn't seem to suffer for it," Sophia remarked.

"Hers is a different kind of magic. It is an aberration for magical ability to be inborn in a human. That is why there are so few true magicians, and so many who only pretend."

"I apologize if my questions disturb you," she said.

"It's natural for you to be curious. We are together day and night, and you know very little about me. I can tell you something far more cheerful about my family, if you care to hear it."

"What is that?"

"After my mother's death, my father married again, and made a far better choice. When I left England he and Mirielle had an infant son and I rather suspect I have several more half siblings by now."

"Another happy second marriage," Sophia said. "Warrick, have you ever been married?"

"No," he responded with a laugh. "I fear wedlock as much as ever I feared magic."

Her feelings unaccountably hurt by his humorous words, Sophia nudged her horse, directing it away from the spot where she had been watching the valley with Warrick. She found Genie and Robin together, Genie having dismounted to drink from a spring that trickled out of a crack in the rock.

"This is the sweetest water," Genie said. "Sophia, shall I catch a cupful for you?"

"Yes, please. My throat is parched."

"Sophia," Warrick called from his vantage point, "cover your face. Genie, remount at once. Gafar is returning and he has several Kurdish men with him."

Sophia and Genie hastily drew the loose ends of their scarves across their faces so that only their eyes showed. Sophia did not know whether Kurdish women veiled themselves, but so many women did keep themselves covered from the eyes of men

241

who were not their husbands that she did not think the approaching Kurds would find the arrangement unusual. For that very reason the scarf made an excellent disguise. She resolved to take care to keep her eyes lowered, so no one would notice their color.

The dark-haired, sharp-featured Kurds were mounted on ponies similar to those used by Gafar's band. They were heavily armed, each man having a sword and several knives, but they seemed to be on friendly terms with Gafar. They wanted to meet the men who had ventured into the mountains with the tribesmen from the far north, and they brought along a handsome array of foodstuffs, for which they were willing to bargain. Sophia and Genie were ignored for the most part, and they were careful to remain in the background.

After assessing their toll and being paid, and having sold half a lamb, a sack of lentils, a large container of yogurt, and a basket of small, tart apples to the travelers, the Kurds sat down around the campfire Gafar's men had made and proceeded to help eat the food. Genie and Robin improvised a spit out of some green branches and saw to the roasting of the lamb, while Sophia prepared the lentils and made flatbread.

It was a merry evening despite the fact that the Kurds spoke mostly their own dialect and knew only a few words of Farsi. Gafar spoke some Kurdish and so did Warrick. Exaggerated gestures and much laughter filled in the gaps in language.

The Kurds ate most of the feast and then lay down on the ground to sleep. To Sophia's surprise Warrick made his bed much closer to hers than usual. When he stretched out on it, he turned on his side and put his arm across her waist.

"Our guests think you belong to me," he whispered. "It will be safer for you if they don't learn otherwise."

"What difference will it make?" Sophia whispered back. "They paid no attention to Genie or me."

"All the same, it's better to be cautious."

Sophia could not argue with that sentiment. She did not really want to argue. Lying safe beneath Warrick's strong arm, she could feel each breath he took and hear the beating of his heart. Warrick slid his other arm under her head and pulled her close. Sophia's head was tucked on his shoulder, with his lips against her forehead. Somehow her legs had become entangled with his.

A short distance away, one of their Kurdish guests snorted in his sleep and then began to snore. Loudly. Constantly. Producing an incredible variety of sounds.

Sophia giggled. Warrick chuckled. Sophia could not stop laughing and burrowed her face into Warrick's shoulder to smother the noise. Warrick's chest rumbled with silent laughter.

"I can't breathe." Sophia gasped. "My scarf is smothering me." It was still over her face and as a result of her moving around, it was blocking her nose.

Warrick caught the edge of the scarf and pulled it away from her face. His hands lingered at her chin.

Sophia could not help herself; she laughed harder with every snort or growl or cough that came from the nose or throat of the Kurdish snorer.

"Hush," Warrick whispered in her ear, "you will wake someone."

"I'll wake someone? He will have everyone in this camp wide awake, while he sleeps on. Warrick, what can we do to stop him?" Her last few words sounded loud and clear, for the snorer suddenly fell silent. There was peace for several heartbeats until the man gave a strangled gasp and began to snore again.

And Sophia began to laugh again. But this time Warrick put his mouth on hers to quiet her. His lips were firm and warm and Sophia was engulfed in a wave of pleasure. Warrick was almost on top of her, pressing her into the ground, and the fire of his kiss sent tremors from her toes to her hair. And, most especially, to the very center of her body.

They were both fully clothed, wearing layers of heavy woolen garments. Only their faces and hands were uncovered. Warrick made the most of what was available to him. He kissed Sophia's nose and eyelids, and as much of her throat as he could reach. He pushed back her scarf so he could nibble at her ears.

Sophia touched his cheeks, wove her fingers through his thick, dark hair, and returned his kisses with increasing fervor. She dipped her head to kiss his throat beneath his stubbly beard, and she moaned in longing for the touching they could not do.

"We must stop," Warrick said, very low.

"I don't want to stop," she whispered.

"Neither do I, but at this rate we will soon drive each other mad. Turn around, Sophia; put your back to me and lie still. Don't move or I won't answer for the consequences."

She did as he asked. She could feel him trembling, too. During the next few hours she became aware of the willpower he was exerting to force himself to lie with her, with his arm arranged across her hip in a possessive way, while he did nothing more. She knew the determination he required of himself, for she was fighting her own madness to keep herself from turning to face him so she could initiate a new embrace. The desire to feel Warrick's mouth on hers again spiraled into a longing that tore deep into her heart, keeping her awake for most of the night.

In the morning the Kurds woke with Gafar's first yawn. They saddled their horses and vanished down the track to their village before the travelers were mounted.

Chapter Fifteen

The party led by Gafar continued its northward trek through the mountains. As day followed cloudless day Sophia was invigorated by a new sense of freedom. Her fear of high places diminished until she seldom remembered to be afraid and only the most precipitous downward view from the edge of the narrow trail could produce the old stomach-churning, dizzying terror.

She did not know why it was so. Perhaps the constant need to conceal her fear from her companions had banished it; or perhaps being forced to face her fear repeatedly had made it seem less important. Whatever the reason, Sophia began to rejoice in the grandeur of the mountains and the high, open vistas. The rugged journey was doing wonders for her spirit. She was beginning to feel like a new and different person, a more cheerful, friendlier soul. She was almost sorry when Gafar began the descent toward a wide, bowl-shaped plateau, for she did not want to lose her newfound exuberance and she wasn't sure it was going to last at lower altitudes.

"That is Lake Urmia," Gafar told Warrick, pointing toward a glittering body of water in the distance. "It is well out of our way, so we won't go near it. Instead we'll strike out directly across the plateau until we meet the caravan road. The traveling will be easier from there into Tabriz, with only one more mountain pass before we reach the city."

All of the men's faces were sunburned, Gafar's most of all. To a man they had refused to use the ointment that Genie produced by magic and which she claimed she had been carrying in her bundle of belongings ever since leaving Baghdad. Sophia did not refuse; she and Genie used the ointment every day on their hands and faces to prevent burning.

Sophia rather liked Warrick's newly bronzed look. It went well with his smoky topaz eyes, and whenever his bright smile flashed in his tanned and bearded face her heart always skipped a beat or two.

There had been no repetition of the passionate kisses they had exchanged on the night of the Kurds' visit to their camp. Warrick kept scrupulously to himself, positioning his bedroll at a distance from Sophia each night and, though he treated her with gentle kindness, Sophia could see nothing of the lover in him. She could not understand Warrick's actions, or his behavior, yet in her present relaxed state of mind she trusted him to explain himself later. She knew how to be patient; she would wait.

They drew near the main road, which was no more than a path worn into the dry ground by centuries of frequent use. Just as they reached the road they met a caravan that was traveling to Tabriz from Isfahan. After paying its leader, they were allowed to follow the end of the caravan through the last ridge of mountains, thus making use of the safe passage insured by the caravan guards. The guards rode on a higher track, above the wider caravan road, so they were in a position to notice any sign of imminent attack.

"I am glad they are there," Gafar said to Warrick. He squinted against the noontime sun, looking up at the armed men. "This last bit of road before reaching Tabriz can be the most dangerous part of the trip. Folk tend to relax their guard as they approach their destination, and a narrow valley like this one is a perfect place for bandits to attack."

Sophia gazed up at the steep mountainsides. She could see no one lurking in the heights, only the guards who were supposed to be there and who appeared to be performing their duty with admirable alertness. All the same, she was glad when they rode out of the mountain defile and onto a wide gravel road. The walls of Tabriz were just a short distance away.

With mountains or high hills on three sides and a broad plain to the east, Tabriz was located at the junction of several caravan routes, those running from east to west, as well as the north and south roads.

"So much trade is carried on there," Gafar said, "that many of the citizens are wealthy. They are also said to be surly and inhospitable, but I have never found them so, as long as I do not haggle too vigorously over prices. With the large caravan ahead of us arriving at the same time we do, the caravansary will likely be overcrowded. I know of a decent inn where my men and I will sleep. You are welcome to join us there."

"We will, and I thank you for the suggestion," Warrick said. "If anyone is still searching for us, it will be a good idea to avoid the most obvious places. Nor do we need to stay in the caravansary to find a place in the next caravan that will be heading west."

"Do you really think the *shinha* will come so far to find us?" Sophia asked.

"It's possible." Warrick's response was so clipped that Sophia began to worry.

"Surely we are well ahead of anyone following us, since we came directly through the mountains," she said. "You told me before we left Hamid's caravan that it would be several days before anyone started looking for us."

"The *shinha* have use of the fastest horses bred today," Warrick said, "and all along the main roads there are posting stations that are set up to service the sultan's messengers. A man on urgent business for the sultan can stop and change horses at any of those stations. If he is too tired to continue, he can pass his orders on to a fresh rider. I would not be surprised if there are *shinha* in Hamadan, in Tabriz, even in Mosul and several other cities, all sent there to look for us."

"Why?" Sophia cried. "Why should they bother? The sultan has no reason to expend so many men or so much time and money on me, not when he can track my father's possessions and seize them as they are en route to Byzantium. We carry nothing of value with us, and I cannot believe that I am important enough for the determined search you describe. I have never believed the sultan desires my person."

"You may be right," Warrick said, adjusting the sack of medicines that he carried slung across his shoulder. "All the same, we will stay at Gafar's inn and be grateful for the protection offered by him and his men."

"I don't plan to stop in Tabriz for long," Gafar said, having listened to the discussion. "Most likely I'll stay for only two nights, so we can rest the horses and buy more supplies. Then we'll be on our way. I am eager to see the steppe lands again, and so are my men."

Still trailing the caravan, they entered a city built of mud bricks and stone. Having lived in Baghdad, Sophia did not find Tabriz overwhelmingly grand. At the city gate the sentries told them two caravans had arrived that day. As a result the streets were crowded with a wonderful mixture of races. Tall, blond, and blue-eyed men rubbed shoulders with dark-haired folk from Cathay and with turbaned men from the lands of central Asia. Bearded Arabs in flowing, corded headdresses, Ethiopians in brilliant colors, sober-looking Jewish merchants, and a fair number of tribesmen mounted on ponies similar to Gafar's all contributed to the noisy babel of many languages.

Then there were the animal sounds. Camels brayed, horses neighed in response to the camels and sometimes reared upward, endangering anyone caught near their hooves. A group of caged monkeys jabbered at each other and screamed at anyone who approached their cage. A herd of sheep being driven through the jammed streets bleated continuously, as if they understood that they had been brought to the city for sale to the butchers.

Gafar knew his way around Tabriz and quickly led his companions off the main streets and into a somewhat quieter district. The inn he chose presented a whitewashed front to the street, with one large door. Gafar leaned from his saddle to bang with his fist upon the door. A short, fat man appeared, his round face splitting into a wide smile when he saw who was waiting for him.

"Ah, Gafar, it's good to see you again, and especially to see you looking so prosperous," the little man said. "Welcome, welcome. How many guests? You will fill my humble establishment to overflowing. What a pleasure to house you once more, and all of your friends, too. A pleasure indeed. Come in, come in."

Gafar dispatched some of his men around the corner with the horses to the stable entrance at the back of the inn. The rest of the travelers were ushered into the common room with many effusive compliments from their host, whose name was Mosud. Trestle tables and benches filled most of the space in the common room, and the smells of roasting lamb and baking bread permeated the air. Two men sitting in a corner eating bowls of stew glanced up at the newcomers with idle curiosity, then returned to their meal. There were no other customers to be seen.

The inn was built around a center courtyard, with guest rooms above the common room and on one side of the courtyard. A door in the rear wall opened into the stable, and rooms along the fourth side of the courtyard provided living quarters for Mosud and his family.

"This looks reasonably secure," Warrick said to Gafar in a low voice.

"It's why I make a habit of sleeping here," Gafar responded. "Mosud is a scoundrel and he'll cheat you of as much money as he possibly can, but he has no taste for seeing his guests murdered in their beds or even in the public areas of his establishment. It would be bad for business."

"A sensible man, your friend Mosud," Warrick said with a grin.

"We will have water readily available," Genie said, eyeing the well at the center of the courtyard. "Just what we need. We can all have hot baths, and I will see to new clothes for each of us."

"Genie, I warn you," Warrick said, bending close to her and speaking quietly, "conjure nothing extravagant and leave no evidence. I will not reject a hot bath, but we must try to remain inconspicuous. Do nothing to raise any suspicion that might set someone on our trail."

"I am deeply offended to learn that you think I have no sense of caution," Genie said. "I will not put any of us in danger. Speaking for myself, after days of riding through the mountains with only an occasional opportunity to wash my face and hands, I think I deserve a bit of luxury."

"Sophia," Warrick said to her, "I want you and Genie to eat in your room, apart from the men and out of sight of customers who come into the common room. Genie can fetch the food, provided she covers her face. Please don't argue with me about this."

"I wasn't going to," Sophia replied. "I know we can't be as informal here in the city as we were while traveling. I didn't expect to be invited to eat with the men." The warm look Warrick gave her was all the reward Sophia needed for hiding her disappointment at being confined to her room. She had hoped to explore the city for an hour or two in Warrick's company, but she was willing to postpone that pleasure until the morrow.

It was settled that Sophia and Genie would share a chamber on the second level of the inn, with Warrick and Robin in a room on one side of them, and Gafar and two of his men on the other side. Warrick scarcely had time to declare his approval of the arrangement before Genie closed and bolted the door.

"Now," she said to Sophia, her eyes gleaming with mischief, "off with these worn and filthy clothes. In their place I decree perfume, hot water, and then fresh, silken robes. What pleasure! What comfort! Our room leaves much to be desired, but I can take care of that little problem in a trice."

"Warrick was correct to warn you," Sophia said. "We must take care not to raise Mosud's suspicions. Genie, I want you to provide for us exactly the same kind of clothes that we have been wearing. Clean, yes, but wrinkled as if they have been packed in our bundles for days on end. You may add a little perfume if you must. It's not unreasonable to expect a woman to carry some of her favorite fragrance with her when she travels. But do not supply us with anything that we could not have carried with us in our baggage. And don't change a thing about this room."

"What, no silk draperies for the walls, no soft cushions to recline on?" Genie cried. "I can produce them and then make them vanish in the morning."

"No," Sophia said. "Mosud, or one of the inn servants, may come in here at any time. You will have to restrain your desire for luxury until we are traveling in a caravan once more."

"You cannot want to sleep on this thin straw mattress!" Genie said, poking at the mattress on the single bed. Her lip curled disdainfully and her extended finger quivered with her revulsion. "I am sure there are bugs living in it. They will bite us when we are trying to sleep."

"Very well, you may remove the bugs," Sophia said. "And later you may add a blanket that is cleaner and warmer than the one Mosud has supplied. You may do nothing more to this room. Be very clear about my intentions, Genie. I will not permit you to disobey Warrick's stated wishes. If Mosud begins to regard us with more than normal curiosity, I will hold you responsible for his aroused interest."

"Yes, mistress." Genie's face and voice were demure, yet a hint of laughter lurked in her eyes, as if she did not quite believe in Sophia's acceptance of Warrick's commands.

After a refreshing bath and a meal of lamb, lentils, and flatbread, with tiny red apples from Astrakhan as dessert, Sophia fell into bed and into a deep sleep. She and Genie were sharing the bed, which Genie had made more comfortable with a thicker mattress and clean covers, and it was wonderful not to be sleeping on the hard ground. Genie was more restless than Sophia. Her repeated tossing woke Sophia in the middle of the night.

"No," Genie mumbled. "Do not ask me. I cannot. I dare not. Oh, Robin, if you knew what it will cost me, you would not insist."

"Genie." Sophia touched her companion lightly

on the shoulder, not wanting to startle her into sudden wakefulness.

"What?" Genie sat up in bed. "Sophia, do you need something?"

"You were thrashing about and talking in your sleep," Sophia answered.

"I woke you. I am sorry." Genie lay down again. Sophia could not see her in the darkness, but she heard a long sigh.

"If you have something on your mind," Sophia said, "something that is troubling you, I will listen and not repeat what you say."

"I cannot tell you," Genie said. "I ought not to admit it, not even to myself." Genie's voice broke off with what sounded suspiciously like a sob. Then a moment later, "Sophia, I am here to help you, to be obedient to your wishes, not the other way around. Do not concern yourself with my feelings. They are—they must be—ephemeral. It cannot be otherwise, for I am only a temporary visitor to this time and place."

"While you are in human form," Sophia said, "you have human needs for food and water and sleep, and you can be injured as if you were human, as we learned when you were thrown from your camel. Why shouldn't you experience human emotions, too?"

"I am not allowed the luxury of human emotion," Genie said. "It is forbidden to the jinn. I was brought into your life to act as your chaperone and to see to your safety and comfort during your journey to Byzantium. There can be nothing more for me in this Calling."

Not knowing what to say to that, Sophia kept silent. They lay quietly until Genie's regular breathing indicated she had fallen back to sleep. Sophia remained wide awake, considering the meaning of Genie's words, and recalling Robin's confession of love for Genie. How sad it was that Genie was not permitted to admit to feelings Sophia was certain she did have. Perhaps some dreadful punishment awaited Genie if she were to admit to love for a human.

As she thought about Genie's situation, the last barriers against the jinni vanished from Sophia's mind and heart. Genie was the loyal friend for whom Sophia had always yearned. And so long as no one spoke the magical spell that would return Genie to the Land of the Jinn, she would not leave Sophia.

"There will be no caravans departing for Erzurum and Trebizond for at least six days," Robin reported. "The most recent caravan left two days before we reached Tabriz. We are too far behind to catch up with them, so all we can do is wait for the next caravan."

They were gathered in the room shared by Sophia and Genie, both of whom had spent most of the previous day and half of the present day in their quarters. After the freedom she had enjoyed in the mountains, Sophia was growing restless.

"We can use the time to choose horses and to buy supplies for the next portion of our trip," Warrick said.

"Genie, are you as good a judge of horseflesh as you are of camels?" Robin asked.

"Why, Robin, are you finally admitting that the camels I selected in Baghdad were fine, lovable animals?" Genie said with a delighted grin. "If so, I will be happy to help you for a second time."

"I will never love a camel," Robin said. "Not any camel in this world. But I could use your help with the horses."

"There must be something I can do to contribute to the preparations for the trip," Sophia said, seeing her chance to leave the inn and taste just a bit of freedom.

"We will need more lentils and a sack of flour and dried fruit," Genie responded. "You are used to bargaining for foodstuffs, so we can leave that to you."

"We can buy everything we'll need and arrange for the animals in a day or two," Robin said. "What shall we do after that?"

"I'll think of something," Warrick said, his eyes on Sophia.

Gafar and his men departed from Tabriz on the third morning after their arrival. "We are bound for Derbent, for the shores of the Caspian Sea, and then northward between the sea and the eastern edge of the Caucasus Mountains, until we reach my homeland," he said. "Fare you well, my friends." Gafar lifted a hand in salute. Without any further good-bye he rode off to the city gate, his men following him, leading with them the extra ponies laden with all the goods he had purchased in Baghdad and Tabriz.

"I will miss him," Sophia said, looking after him with misty eyes. "I never dreamed I'd call a wild tribesman my friend, but that is what Gafar has been to me."

"To all of us," said Warrick, placing his hand on her shoulder for a moment.

"I have learned a great deal about honesty and courage while in his company," Sophia said. "And also that there are places where women are expected to be as resilient and intelligent as men. I will never be the same after knowing Gafar."

"He hasn't changed you that much," Robin told her. "And he would shudder to know you are sorrowing at his leaving. Gafar told me once that the women of his tribe send their menfolk off to war or on long journeys with laughter and loud cheers."

"How can the Kuman women be happy when someone they love leaves?" Sophia asked. "It's terrible to be left alone. Departures are like deaths."

"Well, now," Warrick said briskly into the silence that Sophia's sorrowful words had engendered, "it's time for us to begin making preparations for our journey. It will take a day or two to collect the supplies we will need. Robin, Genie, I entrust the selection of our riding horses and one packhorse to you. Sophia and I will see to the food. We can meet later at the saddlemaker's shop."

"You are trying to divert my thoughts from Gafar," Sophia said to him.

"And my own," Warrick murmured. "Honest men are rare. I will miss him, too. But it's more than the loss of a friend that troubles me. Since the first hour we arrived in Tabriz I have felt as if someone is watching me. I fear a time will come when I will wish I had Gafar and his men at my back, armed with their swords and bows and arrows."

The main marketplace was densely crowded and there were so many different kinds of people abroad that Sophia did not bother to cover her face. She saw other unveiled women at the market, so she did not think she would be singled out for notice. She was so fascinated by the exotic varieties of merchandise spread out for customers that she soon forgot the entire issue of veiling, and also forgot Warrick's remarks about feeling as if he were being watched.

Carts heaped with produce and tented booths offering meats, sacks of various grains, dried fruits, spices, or breads were jammed side by side across the open square, with customers four and five deep bargaining with every merchant. Long waits to make purchases were routine. It was midafternoon before Sophia finished haggling over the last packet of dried apricots. She waited a bit impatiently while Warrick completed arrangements to have all of their purchases delivered to the inn.

"I'm hungry," Sophia declared when Warrick rejoined her. "I see a vendor just ahead who is selling *shawarma.*"

"I can smell it." Warrick smiled at her. "I think the latest batch he's making is chicken. Will you haggle over the price, or shall I?"

"I am so famished I'll accept the vendor's price," she said with a laugh.

"Not likely," Warrick teased. "You enjoy bargaining too much to miss a chance to save a few coins."

Together they pushed their way through the throng to the booth Sophia had spotted. Warrick bought two large servings of *shawarma,* balls of chopped chicken meat fried and served several at a time wrapped in big rounds of flatbread.

"Wonderful." Sophia didn't care that the spicy meat was almost hot enough to burn her mouth. She took a second bite of chicken and bread, savoring the taste.

"It's a bit salty. We'll need something to drink with it," Warrick said. He held his bread folded around the *shawarma* in one hand, while with the other hand at Sophia's elbow, he guided her away from the stall. "If I could find a juice seller—ah, I see one at the side of the square. We'll have a choice of orange or pomegranate juice."

Warrick dropped his hand from Sophia's arm and took a step in the direction of the man who was selling juices. Apparently assuming that Sophia was directly behind him, he did not look back. Sophia paused for a moment, her attention on the food in her hand as she took another bite of the *shawarma*. When she looked up again there were at least a dozen people between herself and Warrick and all she could see of him was his head above the crowd.

She was not worried at being separated from him. He was so tall that he was easy to see and she had no trouble locating the juice vendor, who had set up his business in the rear of a small cart that had a tentlike bright orange sunshade erected over it. Let Warrick make the agreement on prices; by the time she reached him, he'd have a cup of cooling juice in hand, ready for her to drink. She was thirsty enough not to care whether it was orange or pomegranate juice.

A burly man in a dark robe was blocking her way. Sophia tried to push around him. He moved so that he was still in front of her. She attempted to step past him on the other side. The man moved again. Not wanting to call unnecessary attention to herself, Sophia struck out at an angle, intending to pursue an indirect path to the juice vendor.

A black-clad arm snaked around her from behind and a hand covered her mouth. She was pulled hard against an armored chest.

"If you make a sound," a harsh, masculine voice said, "I will slice your throat open from ear to ear."

She couldn't make a noise anyway; his hand was still over her mouth. But she could fight her assailant's attempt to drag her to the far side of the square, and she did. She kicked her heels into his shins, she struggled to get away from the hand that was smothering her, and when that failed, she opened her mouth as wide as she could and bit down hard on his hand.

The man cursed and removed his hand. It was for only a moment, but long enough for Sophia to draw a deep breath and let out her loudest scream.

"Warrick!"

She could see him looking over the crowd, searching for her. The man holding her cuffed her on the ear and clamped his hand over her mouth again. Sophia kept her eyes on Warrick, praying that he had heard her over all the noise in the square.

Warrick's gaze found hers and held. Then he surged forward, pushing his way through men and women, dodging around carts, slapping a donkey on its hindquarters to make it move aside. The big man who had first blocked Sophia's path stepped in front of Warrick in a deliberate act to stop his forward motion.

"Get her out of here at once," growled a new voice.

The man holding Sophia spun around at the order, dragging her with him, so that she could no longer see Warrick. But Warrick was coming for her; she knew he was and she fought harder to get free. A stinging blow to her cheek brought her struggles to an abrupt end. She stared into dark eyes set in a thin face, clean-shaven, ascetic, and utterly ruthless.

"Kalid, she's a demon," said the man holding her.

"She is only a female, and considerably smaller than you are," Kalid responded with icy hauteur. "Take her out of the marketplace and hold her until I join you. Beat her if you must, Jalun, but do it."

"I am trying." Jalun's grip on Sophia tightened.

She continued to fight as best she could. Warrick was coming. If she kept struggling, if she slowed the attempt to get her away from the market, then Warrick would have time to rescue her.

Kalid slapped her again, and this time Sophia's ears rang and her senses blurred from the force of the blow. She could feel herself sagging in Jalun's arms and she was suddenly too weak to fight any longer.

The next thing she knew, the loose end of her headscarf was wound about her lower face, effectively gagging her, and Jalun was lifting her onto a horse. The cold-faced Kalid, who was already mounted, took her from Jalun and set her in front of him.

"If you behave you may ride with me like this," Kalid said to her. "Make any attempt to escape, or to loosen your scarf and cry out, and I will toss you upside down over my horse's back and tie you there, to travel that way. Do you understand me?"

She nodded, but she wasn't looking at him. She was trying to find Warrick. She could not. They were at one side of the marketplace, near a street leading away from the open square. Sophia saw the milling crowd, noticed a few curious faces turned in her direction, and observed how swiftly all eyes were averted.

She knew why. The dark robes of Kalid and Jalun were all the proof she needed. She had been captured by the *shinha* and no one in the marketplace was brave enough to interfere with the fierce warriors who held her.

"What about Haroun?" asked Jalun, who was now mounted on his own horse.

"He knows where to find us," Kalid said. "If he survives his confrontation with the foreigner, he will follow us. If not—" Kalid's shoulders rose in an expressive shrug.

"If not," Jalun said with an evil grin, "we will share his portion of the reward between us."

To this comment Kalid did not respond. Instead he wheeled his horse about and set off along the street, racing for the city gate. People scattered before them; children were snatched out of the way. Sophia could hear the hoofbeats of Jalun's steed close behind them. Then they were through the open city gate, guards saluting as they passed, traffic on the road into Tabriz halting and drawing aside to let the *shinha* officers ride by without delay.

Kalid's thighs tightened and his horse leaped forward, no longer constrained by narrow city streets. Had Sophia not been gagged she would have screamed in terror. Kalid's left arm held her securely, but all the same she reached out and wound her fingers into the horse's flowing mane and clung as tightly as she could.

She was learning why the famous "flying horses" were so highly prized. So rapidly did they travel that Kalid's mount scarcely touched hoof to ground until they were well away from Tabriz and almost into the mountains.

Chapter Sixteen

One of the disadvantages of the flying horses was that they could not continue to run at top speed for very long. That detail did not matter to Sophia. By the time Kalid allowed his horse to settle into a slower pace, Tabriz was so far behind them that she was certain there was no hope of rescue. Warrick could never catch them; worse, he did not know where they were going, so he would not know in which direction to begin a search.

"We'll have to rest the horses soon," Jalun said. He and Kalid were riding abreast and Jalun turned in his saddle to look back toward Tabriz. "Haroun is following us. I can't see his face clearly for all the dust his horse is stirring up, but it is his horse."

"That's too bad," Kalid said, his face and voice completely without emotion. "If Haroun rejoins us, there will be less reward money for you and me."

"True." Jalun's face wrinkled with perplexity,

then cleared as if a new thought had come to him. "What a shame it would be if Haroun should meet with an accident just as he reaches the mountains. How terrible if he were ambushed by the bandits who lurk in the hills, waiting for hapless travelers who foolishly ride alone."

"A pity indeed," said Kalid.

"I will rejoin you shortly," Jalun said, "at the meeting spot we all agreed on, the camp where we stopped for a night on our way into the city."

"I'll be there," Kalid responded.

Jalun dropped back. Sophia was too frightened to look around to discover what happened when he met Haroun. She assumed that Haroun was the burly man who had blocked her path, and she cared not at all if Jalun killed him. In fact she hoped they killed each other.

That wish is the result of Gafar's fierce influence on me, she thought, fighting the urge to giggle hysterically. If she laughed, she would probably choke to death on her own scarf. The fabric was crammed into her mouth so tightly that she wanted to be sick. She decided to make herself think of something else, so she wouldn't think about gagging on the scarf. The reason why she had been abducted was the most obvious subject to consider.

Kalid had mentioned a reward. Offered by the sultan, no doubt. But why? As she had repeatedly said to Warrick, she was not important enough or beautiful enough for the sultan to pursue her, and if Daoud had shipped her father's belongings to Byzantium as promised, the sultan could order them confiscated along the way, while they were still in Seljuk-controlled territory. He didn't need Sophia in order to get his hands on her father's library or astronomical instruments. Valuable as those possessions were, they were not enough to justify sending *shinha* officers out to search for her.

Did they want Warrick, and believe he would try to rescue her, and they could capture him by using her as a hostage? No; in the marketplace they could have captured Warrick as easily as Sophia. They hadn't taken him, which meant it wasn't Warrick they wanted. It was Sophia.

Was her mother's family important enough in Byzantium that they could afford a huge ransom? No again, for if the sultan knew about Sophia's relatives in Byzantium, surely he also knew that the family had cast off Sophia's mother and, therefore, would never pay a ransom for Helena's daughter.

Why, then, did the sultan want her? What did she have that was worth so much trouble? And expense. The reward offered for apprehending her must be large if it could entice one *shinha* officer to kill another in order to gain part of the dead man's share.

So caught up in her thoughts was Sophia that for a long time she did not notice the route Kalid was taking. When she finally looked around she saw that they were not on the caravan route, but on another, narrower path that wound toward the foothills and then on into the mountains. The day was drawing to a close and shadows were lengthening across the plain where Tabriz lay.

Kalid made a sharp turn off the path and a little farther on he urged his horse between two massive boulders that were so close together Sophia marveled that horse and riders were able to squeeze through the passage. They rode into an open area about twenty feet across, walled in by solid, towering rock. A trickle of water ran down the rock face into a pool no larger than a kitchen basin, and a shallow cave at one side provided shelter. By the cold remains of an old fire and the stack of wood nearby, Sophia guessed that this was the place where Kalid and his companions had camped on their way to Tabriz.

Kalid seized her by her upper arms and tossed her roughly to the ground. Sophia fell on one knee, then scrambled to her feet in a hasty attempt to avoid the horse's hooves.

Kalid swung down from his saddle in a graceful motion and at once began to tend to his horse. The animal was flecked with foam and its sides were heaving. While Kalid removed the saddle and blanket and set them on the ground more gently than he had lowered Sophia, his prisoner unwound her scarf and pulled it out of her mouth.

"Scream as loud as you want," Kalid said with a glance at her. "No one will hear you."

At the moment, Sophia was incapable of making any sound. Her mouth was too dry. She went to the little pool and dipped water out of it with her cupped hands, drinking until her mouth and throat were moist again.

Kalid paid no attention to what she did. He was busy rubbing his horse down with a handful of dried grass. The animal's eyes were wild and it tossed its head and snorted. Sophia kept her distance from both man and horse. But she refused to keep silent.

"Ponies from the northland don't require so much care," she said, her voice dripping scorn, "and they can travel for greater distances."

"Northern ponies cannot run as fast as this horse can," Kalid said. "I suppose your comments are the result of observing the horses of your Kuman traveling companions."

"You've been spying on us," Sophia cried. "All this time, ever since we left Hamid's caravan, you've been watching us."

"Not I," said Kalid. "Men of lesser rank do the spying."

"The Kurds didn't tell you where to find us," she said. "They are too independent to tell the sultan's men anything, especially about travelers who paid them for safe passage and shared food with them. And I know it wasn't Gafar or any of his men either."

"The *shinha* do not stoop to depend on barbarians," Kalid said. "We have better and more accurate sources of information."

"I suppose Sadiq told what he knew about where we had gone. I cannot imagine him withstanding even the most gentle interrogation."

"Does it matter who provided the information, now that I have found you?" he asked.

"What do you want with me?"

"The sultan wants you," Kalid said.

"But why?" Sophia cried. "I don't understand."

"It's not for you to question the sultan's wishes. I expect he will let you know when he's ready." Kalid finished grooming his horse and tossed the dry grass he had been using onto the spot where the old fire had been. He picked up a few pieces of wood from the pile and laid them on top of the grass.

"There must be a reason why you were after me," Sophia persisted. "What did your orders from the sultan say?"

"I captured you solely for the reward you will bring." Kalid looked her up and down, from her damp face to the hands she was drying on the end of her scarf to her toes, and his piercing gaze seemed to see right through the layers of her clothing to the skin beneath. "However, there was nothing in the offer of a reward that indicated what your condition is to be when you are handed over to the sultan, so long as you are still alive and able to speak."

"What does that mean?"

"You are younger than I expected." Kalid's hand shot out to capture Sophia's chin in a grip she could not break. "I don't often see blue eyes."

"Let me go," Sophia whispered. She gasped when Kalid did as she demanded. But he released her chin only to snatch off her headscarf. Her hair was braided and fastened around her head. Kalid undid the braids, letting the pins scatter on the ground, his fingers digging into her scalp, pulling hard to loosen her hair.

"Stop it!" Sophia jerked away from him. "If you abuse me I will tell the sultan and you will be punished."

"I doubt it." Not by a twitch of his face or a glimmer in his eyes did Kalid give any indication of emotion. "The sultan has women far more beautiful than you, readily available to him. I do not think he has summoned you to his bed. Therefore he will not care if I use you before I give you up to him."

"You cannot be sure of that. He and my father were friends. It is possible that the sultan intends to protect me, or arrange a good marriage for me. You don't want to interfere with a plan like that, Kalid."

"You lie," he said. "Rulers have no friends, least of all our present sultan."

"All the same, I will accuse you." For a moment or two she imagined her threats had convinced him, for he changed the subject.

"Light the fire. You will find flints in the cave. Do not waste time searching among my belongings for a weapon. I wear my weapons on my person. After the fire is burning, you will cook my evening meal. And when I have eaten, I will make what use I want of you." With his hands still in her hair, he pulled her against himself and stared down at her from cold eyes. "While you are preparing my food, imagine what I will do to you. I warn you, Sophia, I am not a gentle man when I am consumed by a fit of lust. I will hurt you badly. Think of the coming pain as you cook, and let your fear of me build until you can taste it. I will taste it, too, as I anticipate the sweet ending your terror will provide to the meal you make for me."

"I am not afraid of you," she said, pushing against his chest with both hands.

"You are. I can see it in your eyes. Your fear excites me." Kalid's eyes bored into Sophia's until she was convinced he did, indeed, see the fear and revulsion she was trying to hide. Then Kalid thrust her away so sharply that Sophia stumbled and almost fell.

"You will find rice and herbs in the cave, near the flint," he said.

"Aren't you going to hunt?" she asked. "Will there be no meat for the pot?"

"Rice will be adequate. I will not leave you. There is no chance that you can escape, but I do not choose to waste my time chasing after you, should you decide to attempt flight."

Sophia could think of no way to avoid obeying

Kalid. She would have to cook his dinner. She knew she was not going to eat a bite. Fear knotted her stomach, and all of the warnings about coldhearted men that Hanna had issued during Sophia's girlhood returned to haunt her.

If only Kalid had been willing to hunt and had brought back meat, she could have asked for a knife with which to prepare it, and then she'd have a weapon to use against him. The rice and herbs she did prepare could be eaten with the flatbread she baked on a smooth stone pushed into the edge of the fire. No utensils were required save for the battered wooden spoon she found in the cave, which she used to stir and serve the rice.

"You are no cook," Kalid said. "The rice needs more dried mint, and the bread is singed black on one side and barely baked on the other side."

Sophia longed to tell him to cook his own food, if the meal she had made did not please him, but she did not dare speak what was on her mind. She wasn't sure her tongue would work, for once again her mouth was as dry as the dusty plain outside Tabriz.

Kalid threw the uneaten portion of his rice and bread into the fire. Rising to his feet, he approached Sophia. His face was as cold and immobile as it had been all day, yet his eyes were burning with an unholy flame.

"Now it is time for you to feed the other hunger," Kalid told her. "Remove your clothing."

"No," Sophia said. "I won't. You can't make me."

"On the contrary," Kalid said, his voice soft and deadly, "I can make you do whatever I want, force you to any act I desire. I am larger and stronger than you. I am armed and you are not. There is no help for you, Sophia. If you have any intelligence at all, you will not make me angry."

"What difference will it make whether you are angry or not, if you are doing something I do not want?" She wished her voice did not tremble so badly, but at least she kept her chin high. She did not want Kalid to imagine that he could terrify her into willing submission. She wanted him to know that she was going to object vigorously to anything he did to her.

"You will discover that my anger, or lack of it, makes a great difference to you," Kalid said in an odd, purring voice. "Here in the wilderness no one will hear you scream. In fact I eagerly await your howls of pain. They will only increase my delight. Now take off your clothes."

"No." Sophia bit down hard on her lower lip and faced him as boldly as she could. She was not going to dissolve into tears, and she was going to fight Kalid to the end. If she saw the slightest chance of getting away from him she was going to take it. Better to face the night alone in the mountains, better to deal with the bandits who lived there, than let Kalid take her in cruel lust. "If you kill me, you will lose the reward you want so much, because if I am dead, you cannot turn me over to the sultan."

"You will be amazed to discover the things I can do that will not leave a mark on your body, that will leave you alive while you wish that you were dead," Kalid told her.

He grabbed her sash and tore it away, then pulled off her loose coat and flung it aside. His hands fastened on the neckline of her linen shirt. He ripped the shirt down the front, baring Sophia to the waist.

After his warning that no one was nearby to hear

her, and after her decision to defy him to the end, she did not know what made her scream. Perhaps it was the terrifying coldness of his face, where no emotion ever showed. It could have been the wicked light in his eyes. She knew without a doubt that Kalid was going to do horrible things to her that would scar her soul forever, while she wanted with a desperate urgency to keep inviolate the sweet and gentle part of herself that had begun to blossom and flourish since leaving Baghdad. She would rather die at Kalid's hands than let him destroy the flame of love and friendship she cherished within her newly tender heart.

And so she screamed at the top of her lungs.

In response Kalid struck her hard, nearly knocking her down.

She screamed again, knowing there was no one to hear her, knowing she wasn't going to win her fight with him, yet unable to give up the battle. Fury over all that he was carelessly going to crush, rend asunder, and obliterate, possessed her. Thrusting both hands out, she pushed her palms hard against his chest, and her angry strength forced him to take a step backward.

Kalid stared at her as if he could not believe that anyone would dare defy him. He said nothing, and his expressionless face did not change. Only his eyes changed, and in them Sophia read her doom. Kalid would surely deliver her up to the sultan so he could claim his reward for her, but she would not live long after that day, and the manner of her death would be horrible beyond imagining.

Into the silence that stretched between them came a whisper of sound, the soft slide of a sword being withdrawn from its scabbard.

And into the shadowy opening in the rocks stepped a tall figure clad in a dark robe and headdress, with a curved sword in one hand and a dagger in the other.

"Jalun?" Kalid barely glanced at the man. "Is that you?"

"No," said the dark-robed man.

"Haroun, then," said Kalid. "So you escaped from Tabriz and came safely to our meeting place. Did you meet Jalun along the way?"

"I saw him," the man said. "He is dead. So is Haroun. I killed both of them." He stepped closer to the fire and Sophia saw his face more clearly.

"Warrick," she whispered. "You came for me."

"Did you think I would desert you?" he asked, not taking his eyes from Kalid, who was standing perfectly still.

"I thought you could never catch up to us," she cried, "and you didn't know where we were going." When she tried to brush past Kalid to go to Warrick, Kalid caught her wrist and yanked her in front of him, holding her there as a shield.

"You will have to kill her in order to kill me," Kalid said to Warrick. "Put down your weapons."

"No, Warrick, don't listen to him!" Sophia twisted and struggled in Kalid's tight grasp until she managed to turn just enough to use her free hand against him. With no hesitation at all she stuck her fingers hard into his eye. Kalid let her go without a sound, and Sophia rushed to Warrick's side.

"Stay behind me," he said. "Keep out of the way. I don't want you hurt."

"Warrick—"

"There is blood to be spilled here," he said.

"Indeed." Kalid drew his sword. "Your blood,

Warrick. After you are dead, I shall take Sophia back to Baghdad. All of your efforts in her behalf have been for naught."

"We shall see." Warrick faced Kalid with a cold resolve that Sophia had never seen in him before.

"Warrick," she said, "he's wearing armor beneath his robe."

"Thank you, Sophia. That information will prove helpful, I am sure. Now kindly stand back."

The two men began to circle each other, and Sophia moved, too, staying behind Warrick, as he had told her to do. She wasn't going to offer Kalid a chance to snatch her away from Warrick's protection and use her against him.

Steel clashed on steel, blades sliding together in a deadly and strangely graceful dance. Sophia knew nothing of warfare, but it seemed to her that Warrick and Kalid were well matched. They circled each other as if they had mutually agreed on the size of their battlefield. Every few steps one of them moved forward to deliver a blow, parried his opponent's answering blow, then stepped back. The sounds of their panting breaths and the frequent clang of their weapons meeting echoed against the rock.

Suddenly Kalid's curved blade caught the edge of Warrick's sword and sent it flying to the cave entrance. Cool as ever, Kalid lifted his weapon for the death blow as Warrick drew his dagger. Sophia pressed her back against the rocks, both hands at her mouth to stifle the scream she dared not utter, lest her cry divert Warrick's attention.

Warrick darted forward, slipping under Kalid's downrushing arm to drive his dagger blade into Kalid's groin. Kalid let out a short, startled cry. His sword slipped from his fingers and Kalid sank to his knees. Warrick stepped away from him, leaving the dagger where it was.

"There are others hunting you," Kalid said. "You will not escape." He fell on his side and lay still.

"Is he dead?" Sophia asked.

"If not yet, he will be in a moment or two," Warrick said. "Thank you for telling me about his armor. Without that knowledge I'd have gone for his belly instead of the large blood vessel in his groin, and my dagger would have been useless against him."

"I am glad he's dead," Sophia said. "Kalid was the most evil man I have ever met. He had no feelings at all."

"He can't hurt you now." Warrick stared at her torn shirt and bare breasts and his jaw hardened. "Put on your coat, Sophia. We cannot stay here. There may be other *shinha* who know of this camp. With only the one entrance, we could easily be trapped."

She couldn't feel anything; her mind was a blank. She obeyed Warrick's instructions without question, pulling on the coat Kalid had taken from her and retrieving the sash to wrap around her waist so it held the coat closed over her breasts. When she was finished, she was surprised to see that Warrick had saddled Kalid's horse.

"We can't leave it here to starve," Warrick explained, "and the two horses I brought with me, which Kalid's men were riding, are so winded after my urgent run to reach you before Kalid could harm you that neither of them is fit to carry my weight."

"You arrived just in time." Her lips began to tremble and her throat tightened.

"I know," he said. "It's lucky that I heard your scream. Sophia, try not to collapse just yet. I will find a safe spot that is well away from here, and then you may cry all you want. Can your tears wait a little longer?"

He did not touch her and his gaze on her face was cool and assessing. It was better that he wasn't overly kind. In her present emotional state she couldn't have borne sympathy. One touch, one well-meant word from him, and she would have dissolved in the tears he did not want her to shed.

"I can wait," she told him. "I can go on. Only tell me what you want me to do."

"Put out the fire and follow me," he said, bending to pick up and sheathe his sword.

"What about Kalid? Shouldn't we bury him?"

"We can't dig a hole in these rocks. If we could, I'm not sure I'd want to spend the time. If any of his friends find him they will see to what needs to be done."

Sophia kicked at the fire, scattering the ashes, and then she went through the narrow opening in the rocks, hurrying after Warrick. He was waiting for her with Kalid's mount and the two additional horses.

"I'll give you the horse I've been riding," he said. "It ought to be tired enough to be gentle. Up you go."

He did not give her time to protest; he simply boosted her into the saddle as if he expected her to know what to do. Thanks to weeks of riding Gafar's ponies, she did know. She took the reins with a firm hand and her weary mount offered her no trouble. Warrick vaulted onto Kalid's more rested horse and then led them out of the rocky area to the plain.

"And now back to Tabriz," Sophia said.

"Not tonight. Not in the dark. We don't know if Kalid or another *shinha* officer has deployed men along the way to stop you if you escape, and the city gates will be closed before we reach them. We'll sleep beneath the stars tonight."

"I've done that often enough. Which way shall we go?"

"North," Warrick answered, "and we'll stay close to the foothills in case we have to find a hiding place on short notice."

With Warrick holding the reins of the extra horse, they set out, riding in silence at first. The moon was just past its full phase and provided adequate light. They met no one, and once they had crossed the caravan road and continued north of it, Sophia began to relax a little.

"The sultan has offered a large reward for me," she said. "That's why Kalid and his friends were following us."

"I am sure there are others with the same thought in mind," Warrick said.

"I can't understand it. Why does the sultan want me so badly?" When Warrick made no reply, she asked, "What are we going to do with the horses? If we ride them into Tabriz, they will be recognized as *shinha* mounts and we will be questioned."

"I plan to turn them loose in the morning," Warrick said. "In a place that will confuse searchers as to which direction Kalid has taken."

When they were several miles due north of Tabriz, Warrick turned eastward, leading them into the foothills. By moonlight he selected a sheltered spot with a stream, a few bushes, and a patch of dusty grass for the horses. He unsaddled the animals and tethered them so they could reach the water and graze on the grass as they wanted.

"They are used to more elegant fodder than this," Warrick said, "but they won't starve or lack for water. Nor will we starve tonight. I have a packet of dried apricots hidden away, beneath these cursed *shinha* robes."

He pulled off the robe and headdress and flung them aside with a gesture of disgust that Sophia could not mistake, even in the dark. Warrick removed the sack of herbs and medicines that he had worn slung across his shoulder and chest beneath the robe. They sat together on the ground with their backs against a boulder and Warrick drew a small, cloth-wrapped package from the sack. He opened the package and offered the dried fruit to Sophia.

She took an apricot and raised it to her lips, only to discover that she could not eat it. Without warning she was overcome by a storm of trembling and weeping. At her first sob Warrick's arm was around her, drawing her close to his side. She leaned against him, put her head on his shoulder, and let the tears flow.

"You came for me," she said between sobs. "You didn't desert me. I thought I'd never see you again and suddenly there you were to rescue me. How can I thank you for being so brave?"

"By rights you ought to scold me," he said. "I should never have left your side. What happened to you is in large part my fault."

"You blame yourself too easily." She sat up straight again and Warrick removed his sheltering arm. Sophia shivered a little at the loss. "Kalid and his men were determined to win the reward for capturing me. They were going to take me from the

279

marketplace even if you were at my side with an arm around me and your sword in your hand. They'd have killed you without thinking twice."

He was silent for a time, and she saw his strong profile silvered by the moonlight. Then he turned to look at her, his eyes dark, mysterious pools. His fingers were gentle, wiping the remaining tears off her cheeks.

"Have you finished weeping so soon?" he asked. "I thought you would want to cry longer than you did."

"You make me feel safe, so there's no more need for tears. Warrick, how did you know where to find me?"

"I saw you being dragged from the marketplace," he said. "And I saw how no one dared to interfere with what the *shinha* were doing. I went after you immediately, but there was a burly man in my way. He wore the black *shinha* robes, so I assumed he was one of the abductors."

"Haroun." Sophia supplied the man's name.

"Yes, Haroun. He prevented me from reaching you by dragging me into an alley just outside the market square. I had the impression that he planned to slit my throat. He seemed surprised when I drew my sword and ran him through."

Warrick paused and Sophia put a hand on his arm. Warrick had shown her a side of himself that she had not known existed. She still did not know how a man who devoted his life to scholarly pursuits could be so skilled with weapons that he could best three fearsome *shinha* warriors in one day. She was only grateful that it was so. Her life had depended on Warrick and he had not failed her. That was all that mattered to her.

"Haroun's companions had left his horse waiting in the street," Warrick continued. "I put on his robe and headdress, took his horse, and went after you."

"But how did you know which way to go?" Sophia asked.

"By following the cloud of dust that indicated horses galloping at top speed," he said. "Then Jalun dropped back to intercept me and I was forced to kill him, too. Afterward I collected Jalun's horse and took it along with me so you would have something to ride. If I found you alive," he finished, touching her cheek again.

"I am amazed that you did find me in that hidden camp among the rocks," she said.

"I wasn't sure where you were until I heard you scream. I am very glad you cried out, Sophia."

"Kalid was threatening to do terrible things to me. He was so cold, so unfeeling. I am not sure exactly what his plans for the night were, but what I did comprehend was enough to frighten me almost out of my wits."

"Frightened or not, you stood up to him, Sophia. That was courageous of you."

"I was determined to die fighting," she said. "I was absolutely certain I would never see you again. Or Genie or Robin either. And then, suddenly, there you were, like an avenging angel. Oh, Warrick—"

She was in his arms, he was holding her tight, and she knew she really was safe. Warrick had cared enough to do battle with the *shinha* in order to save her. It no longer mattered what she had been through during that long day. Forcible abduction, abuse, terror, and threat of worse to come, all faded to nothing in the face of one blinding truth:

Warrick cared about her. He had faced death to rescue her.

Sophia raised her lips to his. She felt Warrick begin to withdraw. She could not allow it. He deserved a reward and after her ordeal, she needed the closeness and comfort that only he could provide. She put her arms around his neck and drew his head down to hers.

With a low growl Warrick crushed her to him and gave her the kiss she wanted. His mouth was hard, forcing her lips apart. Sophia did not mind at all. She delighted in his urgency; she shuddered at the sensation of his hot, velvety tongue surging into her mouth. Her fingers curved through his thick, dark hair, holding him close, accepting everything he chose to offer.

She was not sure exactly how it happened, for she had only a fleeting impression of Warrick's hands working at her torn clothing, but she was lying on her coat, which was spread out upon the rocky ground, and Warrick was pushing her ripped shirt off her shoulders. Then his mouth and his hands were on her bare breasts and she cried out at the wonder of his touch and the mixture of sensations that assaulted her. Cool evening air, Warrick's heated flesh against hers, and the moist swirl of his tongue on her nipples combined to create a sweet languor that slowly spread throughout her body. Her skin tingled wherever he touched her, and burned in the places where he put his tongue.

She yearned to wrap herself around him, to bring him so close that he would dissolve into her, become one with her. And yet her very bones were melting; she could not initiate any action by her own strength or will. She simply accepted what

Warrick was giving, and let him know of the joy she was taking in him. It did not occur to her to moderate her cries of pleasure, or her moans, or the broken phrases by which she repeatedly begged him not to stop.

Again and again he returned to her mouth, to taste her gently or plunder with fierce passion. When Sophia, growing bold, caught his face between her hands and slid her tongue into his mouth, Warrick gave a great shudder and went still. And then, a moment later, he began to suck and stroke and tease her tongue until Sophia was whimpering with delight.

So entranced was she by the slow and sensual dance of their tongues that she did not at first realize he had untied the drawstring of her trousers and was pushing the fabric downward. She knew it only when his hand caressed the bare skin of her thigh and fastened around her knee.

"Warrick." She dragged her lips away from his. "Warrick, I want—I don't know what I want. Please help me!"

"I know, Sophia. I'm here. Trust me."

"I do. It's just that no one has ever—Oh, Warrick!"

His hand trailed along her inner thigh, higher and higher, until he reached the thatch of curly dark hair that guarded the entrance to the most intimate part of her body. Sophia was intensely aware of Warrick's finger stroking into her and she felt the slick, moist heat that spiraled inward from the place where he touched her, to coil tighter and tighter in the very core of her being.

Warrick's mouth caught hers once more, his tongue sliding into her as easily as his fingers were doing. Sophia stiffened, paralyzed for a long moment. Suddenly, far inside her, a beautiful flower unfurled, blossoming in a series of convulsions so delicate and lovely that she thought she was dying, then thought she was reborn to a different world, a new and shining place, where hearts were free and love was constant and eternal.

Warrick held her close, his hand stroking her steadily while the beautiful sensations spread outward and outward until, gradually, they ended.

A long time later Sophia came back to herself to discover Warrick's cheek pressed against hers and his hand still resting on the place between her thighs that was the origin of the remarkable transmutation that had taken place within her.

"Magician," she whispered. "Alchemist." She longed to say she loved him, but she wasn't sure enough of herself just yet. The emotions filling her heart and her mind were all too new to her. She contented herself with turning her face to kiss his cheek. A faint frown touched her brow as she became aware of the tension in him. Warrick was not as relaxed as she was.

"I am not experienced in these matters," she said. "I know only the barest facts. Still, I know enough to understand that you have not found the relief a man needs. After the pleasure you have given me, I am willing to allow you to do what is necessary for your comfort. I do not think I will mind very much."

"Dear saints in heaven." Warrick sat up abruptly, leaving Sophia feeling cold and lonely. "You don't understand at all."

"Why don't you explain?" She sat up, too, not caring that the remnants of her shirt slipped down her arms, or that her hair tumbled across her shoulders in a tangled mass of curls. "Don't you want me, Warrick?"

"Look at you," he said, "all but naked. And look at me, still fully clothed. Why do you think I have not undressed, Sophia?"

"I wish you would undress," she said. "I want very much to put my hands on your bare chest, to feel the muscles in your arms, and press my breasts against your chest."

"Stop it," he commanded, speaking through gritted teeth.

"I have only said what I feel," she told him. "I begin to think you don't care about me as much as I believed. But if you don't care, why did you do that lovely thing to me?"

"I want you so badly that my teeth ache from it," he said. "So badly that I think I may very well die if I don't take you right now. But I cannot have what I want. I swore to your father that I would conduct you safely to Byzantium. I took you from your father's house as a virgin, and you will be a virgin when you reach Byzantium. I have already done far more to you than true honor allows."

"You don't know that I'm a virgin," she cried. How glad she was that the darkness hid her flaming cheeks. Why was she still able to blush like a shocked maiden after what they had done? "For all you know, I've had dozens of lovers."

"Sophia," Warrick said, laughing softly, "I touched your maidenhead just now. It is intact, and I deliberately left it so."

"Oh," she said in a small voice, chagrined and more than a little ashamed. Then her old familiar anger flared and she realized that increased experience had not changed her as much as she hoped.

"If you are so determined to keep my virtue intact," she snapped at him, "why did you do what you did to me?"

"I saw and heard enough of Kalid before I revealed myself to know what his threats and his abuse against you meant," Warrick said. "You withstood him well, Sophia, but it seemed to me that you required a sweeter kind of knowledge to overlie the bitter memory of what Kalid did."

"And so in your great wisdom you decided to apply medicine to my wounds, like one of your herbal salves?" she jeered. "How good of you, Warrick. How kind and generous."

"What I did was done out of concern for you," he said, "to give you relief from terrible emotions."

"Oh, really?" she responded, all but snarling at him in outrage. "What a feeble excuse you offer for your wicked deed."

He drew a sharp breath and made a sudden motion. In the darkness Sophia could not tell if he was angry, until he spoke quietly and slowly.

"I will confess that I have wanted to touch you in that way for weeks," he said. "It is more than a little unnerving to lie down beside you every night and know that I must not embrace you."

Sophia thought about that, and about her own desire to have Warrick embrace her. He had restrained himself, while she had not. Moreover, he was right about affording her relief. The memory of Kalid and his vicious threats seemed remarkably unimportant when compared to what Warrick had just taught her about her body.

"I am sorry I called you wicked," she said. Then,

"Warrick, have you touched other women that way?"

"I am almost thirty years old," he said. "Of course I have touched other women. But you are the first woman for whom I have risked my life. You are also the only woman with whom I quarrel so frequently." He put out a finger, caught her chin, and lifted it. He planted a quick, light kiss on her lips, then took his hand away.

"What shall we do now?" she asked, and heard a soft expulsion of breath from him, a sound that could have been either a laugh or a low curse.

"You sleep," he said, "while I keep watch."

"I am sure I won't be able to sleep."

"I am sure you will. Wrap up in your coat and lie down and close your eyes. Stay a safe distance away from me. And stop talking."

"I am not a child, to be ordered about like that." But she did as he wanted, settling herself a few feet from him. She very quickly discovered that she was drowsy. She gave in willingly to the encroaching mists of sleep, letting the day's events slip from her mind, clinging only to the memory of Warrick's arms around her, his mouth on hers, and his hands working an indescribable magic on all her senses.

Chapter Seventeen

When daylight arrived Warrick wrapped the saddles and the horses' other trappings in the discarded *shinha* robe and headdress. With Sophia's help he hid the unwieldy bundle amongst the rocks, piling more rocks on top of the cloth until he was satisfied that it would not be easily found.

After a breakfast of dried apricots and stream water, Warrick picked up his sack of medicines, slinging it from his left shoulder to the right side of his waist, as he always carried it. They set out on foot for Tabriz, leaving the horses to wander as they wanted.

"Warrick, those animals were tenderly treated by their masters," Sophia said, looking over her shoulder at the horses. "Will they be able to survive on their own?"

"I don't think they will be on their own for very long," Warrick replied. "I am sure someone will find them, especially if they stray near the caravan route."

"Questions will be raised about them."

"I hope to be gone from Tabriz before this day ends," Warrick said, "so no one can ask questions of us."

"Do you think Genie and Robin will be waiting for us at the inn?"

"I wish we didn't have to return to the inn."

"Why not?" she asked.

"Because I learned from Jalun before I killed him that he paid Mosud for information about us. Did you recognize Jalun? He was one of the men eating in the common room the night we arrived at the inn, one of the spies set around Tabriz to watch for us."

"I can't say that I looked very closely at Jalun," Sophia said. "I was too frightened to notice anyone but Kalid. Warrick, what about Genie and Robin? Do you think they've been captured?"

"I pray not," Warrick said. "We will just have to try Mosud and see what we can learn from him."

When they reached the road to Tabriz they met a caravan plodding along toward the city. Sophia covered her face with her scarf and they fell into step at the end of the caravan, joining a few stragglers who had chosen to walk the last miles into Tabriz. They were soon joined by individuals going to the city for a day or two on business, and by farmers with cartloads of produce. By the time they approached the eastern gate there was a small crowd of people entering directly behind the caravan, and Warrick and Sophia slipped into Tabriz unnoticed among them.

"We must be careful, in case the *shinha* still have

spies watching the place," Warrick said as they neared Mosud's inn. "I suggest we enter through the stable."

There were only two horses in the stable at the back of the inn. Neither animal was familiar, and neither was of *shinha* quality. The courtyard was empty, and so was the common room.

"I'm not surprised," Warrick said. "It's midmorning. Lodgers will be out of the inn and going about their business in the market."

"If Robin and Genie are waiting for us, one of them ought to be here at the inn," Sophia said. "Shall I go upstairs and check in their rooms?"

"Do not leave my side," Warrick ordered.

Mosud, hearing voices in the common room, bustled in from the kitchen with a welcoming smile wreathing his plump face. When he saw who his guests were he stopped short, the smile disappearing and his jaw dropping open in amazement.

With a movement too rapid for Sophia's eyes to follow, Warrick seized the innkeeper by the front of his robe, lifted him off his feet, and slammed him against the common room wall so the shorter man was nose-to-nose with the grim and coldly angry Warrick.

"You betrayed us!" Warrick said in a ferocious growl. "You gave us up to the *shinha* for money."

"No, not for money," Mosud cried. "The big officer threw a coin or two on the floor as he left, but that wasn't why I told him what I knew."

"Oh, no?" Warrick pushed Mosud harder against the wall. "Why then? Did he threaten your greasy neck?"

"Not my neck," Mosud said. "He threatened my son. He and the man with him stretched my boy on the table and swore they would castrate him then and there if I did not tell them what they wanted to know. What was I to do? I was terrified for my son. How could a father refuse to answer questions when such a threat was hanging over his beloved child? I ask you, Master Warrick, what would you have done in my place when faced by *shinha* officers?"

"Those men have committed acts more worthy of outlaws than of true *shinha*," Warrick said. He set Mosud back on his feet, but the rotund little man still leaned against the wall, quivering in fear.

"Where are our companions, Mosud?" Warrick asked. When Mosud did not answer quickly enough, Warrick raised his voice. "The man and woman who were traveling with us—where are they?"

"I do not know, Master Warrick. I have not seen them since yesterday morning."

"Do you mean they haven't returned to the inn since then?" Sophia cried.

"I have not seen them," Mosud repeated, "and your rooms are empty. Whether your friends returned secretly and carried your possessions away, or whether the *shinha* took your belongings, I do not know."

"We are leaving." Warrick headed for the courtyard door. "Come, Sophia."

"Where will you go, Master Warrick?" Mosud asked.

"Do you really think I will tell you, so you can betray us again?" Warrick asked with a cold laugh.

"But if your friends should return and inquire after you, what shall I say to them?"

"You may tell them that we have continued our

journey along the path we agreed upon," Warrick answered. "They will know what that means."

"Please, Master Warrick, do not cross the courtyard. Go out by the front door," Mosud begged. "There are guests in the second-level rooms who might see you and remember you later. I am sure the street door will be safer for you—and for me."

"Allah forbid that we should place you in any danger," Warrick said dryly. "Come along, Sophia. Stay close to me." Warrick pulled the door wide, standing so that he and Sophia were hidden from Mosud by it, yet were still unseen by anyone watching from the street.

Sophia felt again the peculiar tingling sensation she had first experienced in Baghdad, of a sparkling net being thrown over her, and she understood that Warrick was making both of them invisible until they were away from Mosud's inn and from the chance that *shinha* spies watching the inn might see them.

They reached the end of the street and, still invisible, turned the corner onto the wider street that led to the marketplace. The city was crowded and Warrick took care that they did not bump into anyone.

"How long are we going to remain invisible?" Sophia asked as they entered the open square where the market was held. "We can't possibly cross this square without brushing against someone, or an animal, or a cart or tent. Won't a collision disturb the net?"

"We'll take the chance," Warrick said. "We have only a little farther to go. It's quicker to head straight for the opposite side of the square, rather than trying the narrow streets and alleys around the market."

" 'We,' " Sophia muttered. "Once again you are making decisions without consulting me." Raising her voice she asked, "Where are *we* going?"

"To the western gate," Warrick answered. "If we are separated, make your way there and leave the city. Take the caravan road that leads west, and look for Robin and Genie. I am almost certain you will find one or both of them along the way, and they will be looking for us."

"That's what you meant by the message you left with Mosud," she said. "You and Robin have agreed on a plan, in case of trouble." She was going to say more, to scold him for neglecting to inform her of the plan. She intended to give him a stern tongue-lashing just as soon as she got a firmer footing. Walking was suddenly very difficult. The ground beneath her feet seemed to be vibrating.

"Warrick, what is wrong with your magic?" she demanded. "Make the shaking stop at once, or else make us visible again. Please, I can't keep up with you." She halted where she was, unable to take another step for the violent trembling of the ground.

She noticed a few startled glances that told her she and Warrick were no longer invisible, but no one was paying serious attention to the two of them, because the earth kept moving. She wasn't the only one aware of the tremors. All around her people were clutching at each other or at tent poles or carts for balance. On the far side of the market square the front wall of a building cracked open and began to crumble.

Warrick was weaving on his feet, both hands at his head as if he was in terrible pain. His mouth opened in a grimace, but no sound emerged.

"Warrick!" She caught at his arm, hoping to regain her balance by holding on to him. "What is it? What's happening?"

"Earthquake." He spoke as if the very word pained him. "Augh, my head! Sophia, stay with me. Don't get lost."

She clung to his arm, her teeth chattering with fear. As the rumbling deep in the earth died away, the confusion surrounding them increased. Men and women screamed in terror and tried to flee from the square. All of the merchants' tents and stalls had collapsed. Produce, meat, and fish were scattered everywhere, along with trailing bolts of fabric, brass bowls, and copper cooking pans, so that movement was made almost impossible by the slippery food and other objects underfoot. Horses and donkeys and the few camels in the square sought in panic for a way out, racing through the crowd, scattering people right and left as they went. Near the broken building two dark-robed *shinha* officers appeared and began to give orders that few people bothered to obey.

"We can't stay here," Sophia said, her eyes on the *shinha*.

"Hold on to me, Sophia, and don't let go," Warrick commanded. He began to work his way across the square. His face was chalk white under his tan and his teeth were clenched together as if he wanted to be sick and was determined not to be.

Sophia kept both hands wrapped tightly around his left arm, certain that if she released him she would never find him again in the milling throng. Something struck her ankle and she looked down to see a melon rolling by. Warrick stepped on a fish and slipped, almost falling. Sophia steadied him, aware that the headache of which he always complained after working magic had in some way been made worse by the earthquake. Warrick had the look of a man who could think of only one thing at a time. For the present he was plowing his way through the crowd to the streets that led from the marketplace to the western gate.

Slowly they pushed and shoved and forced themselves across the square. Sophia did not see many seriously injured people. Most had suffered only cuts and bruises, but their fear was a tangible emotion. She could understand why. She had always thought of the ground as solid and immovable beneath her feet. When the earth itself began to move there was no place to run and nothing to trust.

Except for Warrick. Unlike the earth, Warrick did not fail her. In such pain that he was barely able to walk, still he pressed onward, and she knew he was going to see her to safety or die trying. In the face of his courage and endurance, Sophia could not allow herself to give way to the panic that threatened to stop her in her tracks.

At last they were out of the square and fleeing with others down a narrow street where masonry lay strewn around as if a giant child had been playing with blocks. And there the tremors in the earth began again.

Sophia heard a loud cracking sound above her. Before she could look up to see what the noise meant, Warrick caught her around the waist and threw her down, shielding her with his body. Then all was dark and silent for a time.

"Warrick?" Sophia touched his face, which was

jammed against her shoulder. "Warrick, speak to me. Are you all right?"

"Ohh, my head." He groaned, and she could tell by the way his muscles flexed that he was trying to sit up. Apparently he could not do so, for he sank back against her with another groan.

At any other time she would have taken delight in such close contact with him. Warrick lay on top of her, his right arm pillowing her head, and she could feel the strong length of him—except for his left arm, which was wrapped around his sack of medicines.

Her pleasurable reaction to his enforced nearness lasted for only a heartbeat or two. Both of her arms were free. Reaching around Warrick's shoulders she pushed hard against the broken stone that confined them.

"We're buried," she said, discovering that she could not budge the stone. "Buried beneath the rubble."

"I know," he said. "My right leg is caught by the stone and I can't move it." He groaned again.

"Oh, Warrick, are you badly hurt?"

"It's not my leg; it's this cursed headache. I can't think clearly because of the pain. I can scarcely see."

"I'm not surprised about your sight," she said. "It's so dark in here that I can't see well either. Warrick, I am going to try to wriggle out from under you, and then I'll try to move the stone that's holding your leg."

"It will be too heavy for you to move."

"Well, then, I will just have to shove a few lighter stones out of the way so I can crawl out of here and find someone stronger than I to lift that big stone off your leg."

She sounded so optimistic that Warrick didn't tell her he feared the bricks and stones that had tumbled onto them would shift if she began to move so that, if she did succeed in getting out from under him, the weight of the stones on his back would press him into the street and crush him to death. If Sophia had the slightest chance of getting out of the pile of rubble that imprisoned them both, he was not going to deter her by word or gesture.

Her fingers stroked his cheek in a gentle caress and Warrick was astonished to find his body reacting to her touch in a decidedly masculine way. Even in the midst of chaos, buried beneath earthquake rubble, he could not stop wanting Sophia.

"I'm going to try to move now," she said.

Warrick exerted all of his strength and lifted himself as far from Sophia as the encroaching stone permitted. Slowly and cautiously she began to slide out from under him.

"The space we are in isn't very high," she said when she could see better, "but it's wide enough for me to move about a little. I think I ought to take care not to push the stones around until I discover exactly how they are balanced."

"A good idea," he said dryly. "Thank you for thinking of it."

After a bit more wriggling, she was separate from him, lying beside him, and Warrick lowered himself to the ground. The stones above him did not move. He let out a long breath of relief. Without Sophia under him he had more space, but his leg was still trapped and held at an even more uncomfortable angle than before.

"I see daylight," she said. "Can you see it?"

"I can't turn my head far enough to look in that direction," he told her.

"Oh. Well, I think I can slide over there on my back and look out. I can call for help, or I can try to move the stones around the opening."

"Be careful," he warned.

"I will." Once again her fingertips brushed his cheek. Then she was wiggling and kicking her way toward the narrow crack of light that he could sense, but not see directly. At every move she made, mortar rained down on them. Warrick held his breath and tried to banish the frustration he was feeling at not being able to help her. He heard a scraping sound and a grunt from Sophia. The stone shifted a little, and more light entered the place where Warrick lay.

"I have moved one stone, so I can see out now," Sophia announced. "There is no one in the street."

"They've all run away," Warrick said with a sigh. "Who can blame them?"

"I think I can squeeze myself through the opening I've made," she told him. "I'll go for help."

"Wait, Sophia." Warrick tried to think through the fog of continuing pain. The thought of Sophia recaptured by the *shinha* while he lay helpless to aid her nearly drove him to madness. There was only one way to protect her. "Listen to me and don't argue. Just do as I say."

"I am sure that in the next block or so I will find someone who will be willing to help us," she said, as if he hadn't spoken.

"No!" He made a convulsive movement and mortar showered down again. "Will you kindly listen to me?"

"Very well." She sounded as if she were speaking to a small child or an invalid. "Tell me what you think I should do, and I will consider your suggestion."

"It is not a suggestion; it is an order," he said. "We are close to the western gate. Find your way to the end of the street and turn left. The gate will be a block or two away. Leave the city."

"I will not desert you," she cried over his words.

"I have no intention of arguing with you," he said as forcefully as he could, given his prone position and immobility. "I want you to leave the city, and be careful that you are not caught by the *shinha* on your way. Once you are outside the city wall, find Robin. More important, find Genie. She will know how to protect you, and she may know how to move these stones that entrap me."

"Of course. I should have thought of Genie."

"You should have done what I told you to do without arguing," he grumbled.

He was surprised when she slid back to lie beside him again. She kissed his cheek and put her lips near his ear.

"I don't want to leave you," she said.

"The sooner you leave me, the sooner I will be out of here." He didn't want her to go; he wanted to keep her with him and protect her, but he still had sense enough left to know he wasn't capable of helping her. His head felt as if it were going to split open at any moment, and he feared that the renewed pain meant there would be another earthquake. He knew they often occurred in a series of tremors, hours or days apart, and he wanted Sophia safely outside the walls of Tabriz before the next quake happened. He prayed the *shinha* were too busy dealing with the aftermath of the first and second quakes to spare a thought for a woman in dusty and tattered clothing, who was fleeing the city along with many others.

"Keep your face covered," he said, "and avoid any *shinha* you see."

"I will. I'll be back as quickly as I can."

"Go," he ground out, uncertain which hurt more, the headache or her leaving. "Go at once, Sophia."

Finally she did as he ordered. His little space was very quiet without her. The stones surrounding him blocked out much of the noise of men calling to lost friends or relatives, of frightened children and babies crying, of women wailing. None of the voices came close enough to Warrick for him to cry out for help. He rested his cheek on the ground where Sophia had lain, closed his eyes, and waited.

Sophia had no difficulty finding the western gate or leaving Tabriz. Townspeople who feared more earthquakes were heading for the open countryside, and the guards at the gate did not stop or question anyone. The caravan road was well marked and easy to follow, but there were so many groups encamped along the road that Sophia's progress was slowed by the need to check the groups frequently, lest she miss Robin or Genie. The day was almost over and she was beginning to despair when a dimunitive female shape flung itself into her arms.

"I have been so worried about you!" Genie exclaimed, hugging her tightly. "Where have you been for the last two days?"

"I was captured by the *shinha* and Warrick rescued me," Sophia said, fighting back tears of joy at finding Genie.

"What? Oh, if only your father had granted me more extensive powers when he conjured me into existence, then I could have discovered you and rescued you and saved Warrick the trouble. Where is he?"

"Still in Tabriz. We were caught by the earthquake. Warrick is trapped under a pile of fallen stones. Genie, do you know where Robin is? We are going to need his strength to move the stones and free Warrick."

"No, we won't," Genie said. "Robin is standing guard over our horses and supplies. If he leaves them everything we own will be stolen. There are hungry and desperate folk abroad today." Genie took Sophia by the elbow and began walking back toward Tabriz.

"The stones holding Warrick are too heavy for us to move by ourselves," Sophia protested. "We must have Robin with us."

"I had a major argument with Robin before I convinced him to let me set off alone to search for you," Genie said. "Can you imagine the quarrel we'll have if we tell him what has happened to Warrick? Trust me, Sophia; I will find a way to free Warrick without Robin's assistance."

"Trust you," Sophia repeated. She took a calming breath and made her decision. "All right, I will."

"We'll have to hurry," Genie said. "We want to be in and out of the city before the gates are closed for the night."

"I question whether the gates will be closed at all," Sophia said. "Just look at the people who are leaving. Half the population of Tabriz must be camping in these fields."

"There are bandits living in the mountains to the east who will be eager to take advantage of an opportunity like this," Genie said. "If the gates are left open, they will sweep into the city to loot and rape and kill while the authorities are trying to deal with fallen buildings and panicked citizens. The gates will be closed tonight, and you and I will have to get Warrick out of Tabriz before they are bolted shut."

Once again Sophia passed through the western gate unquestioned by the guards. Inside the city there was no change in the level of fear and confusion. No one paid any attention to the two women. Sophia remembered all too clearly the location of the street where Warrick lay. The pile of stones appeared to be undisturbed, but when she called to Warrick, there was no answer.

"I'm going in there," Sophia said, dropping to her knees to crawl through the hole she had made.

"No, you are not. I won't allow it." Genie caught the back of Sophia's coat and pulled her upright again. "I cannot believe you got out of that pile alive. I have seldom beheld a more unstable mess. If you disturb those stones, you may cause Warrick's death instead of helping him."

Having assured herself of Sophia's full attention, Genie released her coat and began to prowl around the edges of the pile of debris, examining each of the fallen stones.

"I marvel that you and Warrick were not killed instantly," she said.

"There seems to be a long, solid slab that is holding everything else up," Sophia said, pointing to the stone she meant. Hearing a heavy footstep she looked around eagerly, in hope of discovering someone who would offer a third pair of hands to lift the stone off Warrick. She froze when she saw the black-robed figure of a *shinha* officer.

"What are you women doing here?" the *shinha* demanded. "We just finished clearing this street. It's too dangerous for anyone to be here. Get into the market square. Move, now!"

"Oh, please, kind sir," Genie cried, holding both hands out to him in supplication. "My sister's husband is trapped beneath these stones. Will you help us to free him?"

"If he's under there," the *shinha* said, aiming a kick at the rubble, "he's dead. Come away."

Sophia watched in horror as the stones over Warrick began to shift and settle as a result of the kick. The *shinha* shrugged and began to walk away.

"Come back," said Genie in a soft, enticing voice. Her left hand was raised, one finger beckoning. "*Shinha* warrior, return to me."

The black-robed figure stopped, then slowly turned around to face Genie again. His face and eyes were blank, as if the man's will had retreated far inside himself, as if only his body was present to do Genie's magical bidding.

"Come and help me," Genie said in the same soft voice. She beckoned again and the *shinha* moved toward her.

"Genie, your spell on him may work for a little while," Sophia objected, "but when you release him he will kill you and me, and Warrick, too."

"No, he won't," Genie said, not changing her voice. "Stand back, Sophia, and let this man's shoulders and arms do the work."

"If he begins to move any of those stones, the rest of them will crash down and kill Warrick," Sophia cried.

"You said you would trust me," Genie reminded her. "I do not think we have a choice in this matter. No one else has appeared to assist us. Let us make use of the one servant we have discovered. We are pressed for time, Sophia. The gates will soon be closed for the night and I, for one, do not intend to stay inside Tabriz until morning. It will be too dangerous."

Sophia stepped out of the way. The *shinha* came forward to follow Genie's precise commands as if he were the servant she had termed him. In a remarkably short time he had moved aside all of the smaller stones, leaving only the long, heavy slab of stone that was keeping Warrick trapped, and the single block on which the long stone rested over Warrick's head.

With so much of the debris shoved out of the way, Sophia could see Warrick's motionless, dust-covered figure. He was lying facedown beneath the precariously balanced slab. Sophia wasn't sure if he was aware of what was happening, or even if he was still alive.

"Warrick, don't move," Genie said to him. "Movement could be dangerous for you. Just tell me if you are awake."

"I'm awake," Warrick said. "My eyes are closed because of all the dust you've stirred up, and I'm not moving because I don't want to unbalance the stones."

At the sound of his voice, Sophia clamped her lips shut on a cry of joy. She did not want to make any noise that would disturb Warrick, or interrupt the spell by which Genie was holding her *shinha* helper.

"Keep your eyes closed, Warrick," Genie said. "There will be more dust. I have a kind gentleman with me who is going to lift the stone off your leg. Don't try to move until I give the word. When I tell you to, roll toward the sound of my voice. Can you do that?"

"Yes," Warrick said.

"Very well, then. Lift the stone," Genie said to the man helping her. "That's right; put your hands on either side and lift it slowly."

The stone was massive. Sophia watched as the *shinha*'s face grew red with the strain of raising it.

"Just a little higher," Genie said to him. "Now, Warrick, roll away!"

Warrick rolled over twice and stopped at Sophia's feet. She went to her knees to embrace him.

"You may let the stone fall now," Genie said to her helper. Still under Genie's spell, he took his hands from the stone and stepped back. The stone crashed down flat on the street, sending up a new cloud of dust.

"Warrick, can you walk?" Genie asked.

"I will most certainly try," he answered. He looked around the darkening street. "Where is my sack of medicines?"

"Here it is." Genie plucked it from the rubble. "The strap is broken, but otherwise it seems to be undamaged. I will carry it for you."

"No, I'll take it." Warrick put out his hand and Genie gave him the sack.

"You need a new sack," Sophia remarked, helping Warrick to his feet, "and probably fresh herbs and new bandages, too."

"That's not all I have in the sack," Warrick said, laying an arm across her shoulders. "When we are all together again, I will show you why I am so careful of this bundle, and why I keep it always near me.

"What about him?" Warrick asked, observing the *shinha*, who was sitting against the largest stone, his eyes closed and a dreamy expression on his face.

"He's asleep," Genie explained. "He will wake when morning comes, with a hazy memory of having exhausted himself to rescue earthquake victims. Since he did help us, I can't bring myself to harm him."

"Fair enough," Warrick agreed, "but let us depart from here before any of his friends come looking for him."

Chapter Eighteen

They were among the last people out of Tabriz before the gates were closed.

"*Shinha* locked inside, and us on the outside," Warrick said as he hobbled away with one arm around Sophia for support and the other arm around Genie, upon whom he was leaning rather heavily. "From what I can see of the refugees camping along the road, we look much like them, dirty, weary, some injured. No one will think to question us. We are safe for a little while."

They found Robin camped a short distance off the road, just beyond the last group of refugees from the city. He had a fire going and a pot of lentils cooking. Staked near the fire were four nondescript-looking horses, and Sophia recognized the pile of bundles that contained the men's possessions.

"How glad I am to see you," Robin exclaimed,

throwing his arms around Warrick. "But what's wrong with your leg?"

"Let me sit down and I'll explain." Warrick lowered himself to the ground, his injured leg held out stiffly in front of him.

"Before you do anything else, take off your boot," Sophia said. "We'll have to see how much damage has been done to your foot." She reached for the boot, but Warrick's hand clamped around her wrist, stopping her.

"Let Robin do it," he said.

"As you wish." She moved aside, trying to hide the hurt she felt at his rejection.

"Genie, if you will heat some water I will be most grateful," Warrick said. "I'd like to wash my face and hands, and I'm sure Sophia would like to wash, too. Then I'll brew some tea, and while we drink it we can tell each other what we've been doing since last we were together."

"I'll get the packet of tea leaves." Sophia picked up Warrick's sack of herbs and medicines. Again he stopped her.

"Leave it alone," he said. "Don't touch my sack."

Stung anew by Warrick's rejection of her aid, Sophia stood up and walked away so he wouldn't see the tears in her eyes. An instant later Genie was beside her, with an arm around her shoulders.

"Sophia, have you considered the possibility that Warrick is distressed because he had to be rescued by women?" Genie asked. "Surely by now you know him well enough to understand that he is the kind of man who believes he ought to be the protector."

"He did protect me," Sophia said. "He saved my life twice, once when he rescued me from the *shinha*, and again when that pile of stones tumbled down on top of us. It was only fair that I should help save him."

"Gafar might see it that way. I doubt if Warrick does," Genie responded with a faint smile tilting her lips.

"Do you know what is hidden in that sack of his?" Sophia asked.

"I have no idea. I suggest we return to the campfire, eat the evening meal that Robin has so kindly prepared for us, and give Warrick a chance to make the explanation he promised to provide."

"I thought he would treat me more kindly," Sophia whispered.

"Why? Because you have survived two perilous days together?" Genie paused, her eyes narrowing as she regarded Sophia more closely. "Or did you look for tenderness from him because you spent last night in each other's arms?"

"We didn't—Warrick didn't—I mean, he said I am still a—" Sophia ceased her halting description and covered her face with both hands.

"Yes," Genie said. "I should have known without question that Warrick could be trusted not to stray very far beyond the boundary of rigid honor. You need not tell me everything that happened between you. What is important is that, while he gave you pleasure, he did not satisfy his own desire, so that to his very natural weariness after your adventures together, after being pinned to the ground by a large stone and his annoyance at being saved by women, we must now add sheer masculine frustration to the mix. No wonder he's in a bad mood!"

"So am I in a bad mood," Sophia muttered. "Warrick has the most annoying habit of making decisions and setting plans in motion without discussing them with me first."

"And you think that's unusual? How little you know of men," Genie said with a teasing smile.

"Warrick's lack of concern for my wishes or opinions proves that he does not care about me," Sophia said.

"Everything that Warrick has done since the night we left Baghdad, including the restraint you say he exercised last night, reveals to me that he does respect and care about you," Genie stated firmly. "Sophia, are you planning to spend the entire evening standing here in an open field? Aren't you hungry? Or curious about the mysterious contents of Warrick's sack?"

"Am I an unpleasant and selfish person?" Sophia asked suddenly.

"You are more than a little stubborn, but not half so difficult now as you were when we first met," Genie responded, laughing.

"I will follow your good advice, Genie. I'm glad you are my friend." Sophia put out her hand and Genie took it in a warm clasp. "I am so hungry that I will devour that stew Robin has cooked. But I swear to you, Genie, when this journey is over, I will never eat lentils again!"

"Genie noticed the man watching Mosud's inn," Robin said, recounting his activities during the absence of Warrick and Sophia, "so she slipped into the inn without being seen and gathered up our belongings. Then we took the horses we had bought and our newly purchased supply of food, and left Tabriz late yesterday. We camped here, near enough to the caravan road to see you if you were traveling along it, just as you ordered me to do in case we were separated."

"We were both very worried about you," Genie added, "and rightly so, judging by the story you have told us. I must say that except for the brief period when the earth shook, Robin and I had a boring time in comparison.

"Now, Warrick," Genie went on, "I cannot bear my curiosity another moment. What have you hidden away in your sack?"

The four of them were sitting around the campfire. The evening meal had been eaten and Warrick's injured leg had been examined. Both he and Genie had pronounced it unbroken, thanks to the padding of his trousers and boot. But his calf was badly bruised and the leg was swollen from knee to foot. As a result Warrick lounged on a mattress and pillows that Genie had provided by magic. Two more thick pillows kept his leg elevated, and Genie had wrapped the leg from knee to toe in a cloth soaked in water that she kept icy cold.

The rest of them had bedrolls and warm blankets, but there was to be no tent that night. Warrick had refused Genie's offer to conjure a tent, saying they ought to avoid looking different from the other groups of people who had fled Tabriz.

Genie had also provided a new sack for Warrick with a sturdy strap long enough to fit over his shoulder and a slightly used appearance. Warrick was transferring the packets of herbs and jars of prepared medicines to the new sack. He picked up an irregularly shaped object that was wrapped in linen and held it up so Sophia could see it.

"Your father gave this into my keeping just before he died," Warrick said to Sophia. "It represents

John's promise to me that I will see my friend Hua Te again, for I have sworn to keep it safe and place it into Hua Te's hands when next we meet."

"What is it?" Sophia asked. She leaned forward eagerly to watch Warrick unwrap the object.

First Warrick pulled from the folds of linen a glittering ring of gold that was heavily encrusted with jewels. Shades of blue and green twinkled in the firelight. Warrick set the ring down and Sophia saw that it was a stand made to hold the second piece that he drew from the linen.

"A crystal ball," said Genie, her eyes wide. "A crystal without flaw. How rare; how beautiful."

"I have never seen either of these objects before," Sophia said.

"Your father kept both of them hidden in a secret niche." Warrick set the ball into its stand. "He was afraid the sultan would seize them after his death."

"The sultan knows about these?" Sophia waved a hand toward the ball and its stand, but she wasn't looking at them any longer. She was looking at Warrick and thinking about the meaning of the valuable objects.

"Your father believed that the sultan suspected he owned them, and that the sultan coveted them," Warrick said.

"Now I understand why the *shinha* are after us," Sophia exclaimed. "It's not me the sultan desires; it's this crystal ball. With my father dead, the sultan believes that I, John's only child, will know where these pieces are hidden."

"You are probably right," Warrick said.

"I am fascinated to learn that, after all the years my father served as his astrologer, the sultan knew nothing about the way the mind of John of Cornwall worked. Foolish sultan; he misjudged his servant's cleverness," Sophia said bitterly. "Of course my father thought of a way to keep his beloved artifact out of the sultan's hands, and I am sure it mattered not at all to him if he destroyed his daughter's life, so long as these pieces were preserved."

She snatched at the crystal ball, wanting to smash it against the nearest rock. Warrick caught her hand, stopping her before her fingers could make contact with the crystal. She stared at him, so angry and hurt that she was almost unware of the tears flowing down her cheeks.

"Robin," said Genie, "let us take a walk." She tugged at his sleeve and without a word Robin unfolded his long legs and followed her into the darkness.

"Warrick," Sophia asked him through choking tears, "do you know how much such an object costs? Did my father say how he acquired it? Was it a gift, or did he buy it?"

"I don't know," Warrick said. "I cannot answer your questions."

"I had to beg him for money to run his household," Sophia said. "I wore clothing that I sewed from the cheapest fabrics, and I convinced myself that I didn't like silks or bright colors, because they are more expensive. I told myself I didn't need any luxuries, that I was above frivolous nonsense. I chose the least expensive foods and seldom cooked meat. I prided myself on how little of my father's money I spent. And all the time he was secretly hoarding that—that priceless obscenity!"

Warrick did not speak. He just wove his fingers through hers as if to let her know he understood the pain she was feeling. His silent sympathy calmed her as no words could have done.

"It's not the ball and stand in themselves," she said in a voice less fraught with bitter emotion, "or even the way my father made me live as if we were poor when, obviously, we were not. It's what those objects represent. When I look at them I can no longer deny that my father did not love me. Ever since I was old enough to think about the way he treated me, I told myself it was because Father was so absentminded, and so deeply involved with his work, that he never took a moment to express any affection for me. But the truth is, he didn't have any affection to express. The truth is that I have had more genuine affection from my traveling companions since leaving Baghdad than I ever received from my father."

"Sophia, I am sorry."

"Don't be. It's time I faced the truth that I've known in my heart for years and never had the courage to admit. But Warrick, you should have told me about this." She waved her hand at the crystal ball again. "I had a right to know about it, and about the danger it posed to all of us. Wrap it up. Put it away. I never want to see it again."

Without a word Warrick rewrapped the ball and its stand and stuffed both into his new sack. Then he held out his arms.

"Come here, Sophia. I'd go to you, were I not under Genie's orders to keep my leg on these pillows."

She told herself she ought to walk away. He had been dishonest with her by not telling her about the crystal ball. But he had also saved her life, and kept her safe through every danger they had faced.

She went to him and stretched out beside him on the mattress, laying her head on his shoulder and giving herself up to the sweet pleasure of Warrick's strong arms around her and his lips on her brow.

"Weep, if you want," he said.

"I have no tears left and I'm surprised to say there is little anger left, either. Baghdad seems so far away, so long ago, as if it were another life."

"You are among friends here," he said, just before his mouth took hers.

She wanted to tell him that she regarded him as much more than a friend. She ached to say she loved him. But she had acquired a small portion of wisdom during her travels, and so she kept quiet and kissed him back.

"I do dislike to disturb you," Robin said, stepping into the firelight with Genie at his side. "However, we need to decide what we are going to do when daylight arrives."

"I can ride," Warrick responded, releasing Sophia from his embrace and sitting up with no sign of embarrassment. "Walking for more than a few steps will present a problem over the next few days, but not riding a horse."

"What about your headache?" Sophia asked.

"It's much better. I expect it to be completely gone by morning," Warrick said with a look of gratitude for her concern. "Robin can help me to mount, and we will ride for Erzurum at dawn."

"I do wish you would learn to discuss various possibilities with me before you make a decision," Sophia snapped at him.

"In this case there is nothing to discuss," Warrick said, grinning at her sudden display of spirit.

"I think there is," she argued. "Genie has warned of bandits lurking in the hills. We will need the protection of a caravan."

"After the earthquake there will be no caravans leaving Tabriz for several days," Warrick said. "I would far rather risk meeting a few bandits along the way than remain where we are and have to deal with the *shinha* again. They are preoccupied for now, but it won't be long before they resume the search for us, and for you in particular, Sophia."

"I have a map," Genie announced. She held out a ragged piece of parchment. "It shows the route from Tabriz to Erzurum, and on from there to Trebizond."

"How convenient," said Warrick, accepting the map from her.

"Sophia," Genie said, "I know you would like to discuss our next actions at some length, but I must tell you that I agree with Warrick. I have an uneasy feeling about Tabriz. I'm not sure why; perhaps it's because of the *shinha*, or perhaps there will be another earthquake. I only know I want to be away from here as soon as possible."

"How far will the *shinha* pursue us for the sake of that cursed crystal ball?" Sophia asked.

"Not beyond Erzurum, surely," Robin said. "The farther we are from Baghdad, the safer we will be. I agree with Warrick and Genie."

"Is the map accurate?" Sophia asked, looking at the piece of parchment that Warrick was studying.

"I believe so," he said. His eyes met hers. "What say you, Sophia? Shall we go next to Erzurum?"

She smiled at him; she couldn't stop herself. At that instant it mattered little to her that he had made up his mind in advance. Before their friends he was asking her for her opinion, and she could not recall him ever doing that. Warrick cared enough to ask her, and the caring warmed her heart.

"Yes," she said, still smiling, "Erzurum it is. At first light, Warrick."

"Agreed," he said, and grinned back at her.

It was not an easy journey. They skirted the northern end of Lake Urmia and headed into the mountains of Armenia. Warrick pushed them hard, for summer was waning and the nights were growing cold in the wild heights. They kept to themselves, staying away from caravansaries for fear of the *shinha*, and they counted themselves fortunate to meet no bandits. Each day they rode for as many hours as their horses could carry them and at night they slept in a tent that Genie conjured, which she kept as warm as possible, given the chill winds.

At each step of the way Sophia was more and more aware of Warrick, of his fortitude under harsh circumstances, and of her growing love for him. He did not appear to notice and did not approach her. She told herself it was because he needed all of his strength to guide them safely to Erzurum despite his injured leg.

There was a spare, desolate grandeur to the rugged land through which they were traveling. More than once Sophia wanted to pause and look more closely at a view, but Warrick allowed only one short respite for sightseeing. They rode out of the first range of mountains onto a high plain. The narrow road ran straight across the plain, its only deviation a curve around the base of the tallest mountain Sophia had ever seen.

"Mount Ararat," Warrick said, and pulled his horse to a stop. He sat gazing at the immensely high, snowcapped peak on which, according to legend, Noah's Ark had come to rest at the end of the great flood.

"There cannot be a mountain taller or wider in all the world," Sophia whispered in awestruck wonder.

A small, fortified church with a few outbuildings sat beside the road. The two elderly priests who lived there spoke an Armenian dialect and knew only a few words of Greek and no Latin at all, but they cheerfully drew water from their well so humans and horses could drink. Warrick gave them a handful of coins and the priests waved the travelers on their way with repeated blessings, which were unmistakable in any language.

Then it was into the mountains again and, finally, days later, they reached the walled city of Erzurum. They did not stay long. Warrick learned of a caravan leaving for Trebizond the next day, and so they set off once more. The weather grew warmer as they approached the seacoast, and it rained frequently, which made the rocky trail through the mountains slippery.

"I feel as if I have been traveling for years," Sophia complained, wiping rainwater off her face.

"Be glad it's not snow," Robin told her.

Through the Pontic Mountains they rode, and then down to Trebizond, built on a narrow strip of land along the Euxine Sea. The air was warm and moist, drenched with the fragrances of forest and garden, and containing also the pungent odors of a crowded city. The rain continued, and dense fog hung over the sea.

Sophia did not care about the weather. Warrick had declared that they were most definitely far beyond the reach of the sultan and the *shinha*. They were safe, and they were going to enjoy a well-deserved rest while they waited for a ship to take them on to Byzantium. As long as there was heavy rain and fog, few ships would leave the port. Even the ever-resourceful Venetian traders preferred to wait for fairer skies and a stiff breeze.

There was so little space between the sea and the mountains that most of the streets of Trebizond were steeply inclined and the most sharply angled streets featured steps. Sophia discovered an advantage to the precipitous streets when Warrick rented three adjoining rooms in a small inn. The room Sophia shared with Genie boasted a balcony from which she could see into the sodden garden below and over the wet rooftops to the misty harbor.

"When the sun comes out we will have a fine view of the harbor and the sea," Sophia said. She lowered her gaze to the lush greenery, which was balm to her eyes after rocky mountains and barren plateaus. "How pretty it is."

"If the sun ever comes out, we will be leaving long before the garden dries enough for you to walk in it," Genie responded. "Sophia, you and I have neglected ourselves since we left Baghdad. It is time for long, hot baths and perfumes and silken robes. We don't have to hide anymore. We are free."

"Am I?" Sophia said. "Knowing how little my father cared for me, am I still bound to honor his wishes and go to Byzantium?"

"Warrick will insist upon taking you there," Genie said, "because he promised to do so. After you have met your mother's family, only you can decide what you ought to do next. Perhaps they will be kind people and you will want to live with them."

"I'll be very surprised if that happens," Sophia said. She did not reveal her secret hope that after they reached Byzantium, Warrick would decide his duty had been discharged and would say that he wanted her to remain with him. She was afraid that what she wanted was impossible. As a result she dreaded her arrival in Byzantium so much that she could not think about it. She resolved to think only of the moment and of the respite in Trebizond.

She gave herself up to Genie's ministrations, allowing Genie to see to her bath, to pluck her eyebrows and trim her hair and buff the nails of her hands and feet to a smooth shine. When Sophia and Genie joined the men for the evening meal, Sophia was gowned in sapphire blue silk and the golden hoops in her ears were set with sapphires. The scent of hyacinth wafted about her when she moved. Genie wore a brilliant orange silk bodice and trousers patterned in gold, and all of her gold necklaces, earrings, bracelets, and rings were set with rubies.

It was obvious that the men had visited the local bathhouse, or else Genie had worked her magic on their behalf. In his russet silk tunic Warrick was to Sophia's eyes the handsomest man in the world. His leg was taking longer than it should to heal because he had not been able to keep it raised while he was riding. As a result he walked with a slight limp, which he insisted would soon disappear.

Warrick had ordered food sent to the third room of their suite, which they were using as a sitting room. They feasted on roasted chicken with artichokes, a salad of greens with olive oil, and thick, crusty bread. There was also a tray of fresh, ripe melons and peaches, and a plate of honey-drenched pastries sprinkled with ground pistachio nuts.

"Not a lentil to be seen," Sophia said, sinking her teeth into a plump chicken leg. "And no dried fruit either. How wonderful."

"There's Greek wine, too," Warrick said, pouring a cup for her. "Drink it slowly. You aren't used to it."

"How long do we have to enjoy this city of culinary delights?" Genie asked. She was sitting on a low divan and she stretched against the cushions like a contented cat. The jewels of her necklaces winked in the candlelight.

"We'll be here three or four days, perhaps more," Warrick said. "Robin and I are to meet one of the Venetian traders at his house later this evening. His name is Marco and he says by then he will have a clearer idea of when he can leave for Byzantium. His ship is a stout vessel, with plenty of room for passengers, so unless he is greatly delayed we will sail with him."

"You never mentioned this to me," Sophia objected.

"Only because of the uncertainty involved," Warrick said.

"I will go with Robin to see this Marco so you may rest your leg, Warrick," Genie said, leaping to her feet. "When we return I will report every detail to you, Sophia, so you won't have to worry about secrets being kept from you. Come on, Robin." She took his hand.

"Genie, you cannot go into the streets dressed like that," Robin declared.

"Why not? I think it's a lovely costume. Oh, very well." Genie released Robin's hand and spun around. "Will this do?" A dark brown cloak covered her bright silk trousers and the midriff-revealing top, with the hood of the cloak hiding her red hair.

"I prefer not to take a female with me," Robin said, frowning. "Warrick ought to go. You are still much too bewitching, Genie. Your presence at Marco's house will surely lead to trouble."

"Do you really think so? Well then, what about this costume?" Genie turned around again and when she faced Robin she appeared to be a trim young man wearing dark green tunic and hose. A short cape was draped around her shoulders to hide her bosom, and her hair was caught up into a green cap with a long feather. She sent a cocky grin in Robin's direction. "You may call me Jean."

"Take her with you, Robin," Warrick said with a chuckle at Genie's sudden transformation. "She will make certain no one cheats you, and I would rather sit with my leg on a pillow than walk any distance."

"No one ever cheats me, and well you know it," Robin said. Then he looked at Genie. "Come on, lad, and step to it. I don't wait for lagging boys."

"Does your leg really hurt so badly?" Sophia asked Warrick after Robin and Genie were gone.

"No, but I thought Robin would like an hour or two alone with Genie before they see Marco."

"I see." Sophia paused, hoping Warrick would add that he also wanted time alone with her.

Warrick did not speak; he acted. Rising from the table he caught her face between his hands and looked deep into her eyes. The power of his smoky gaze made her dizzy. Sophia put her hands on his shoulders, her fingers digging into the russet silk.

"What am I to do with you?" he murmured.

"You could begin by kissing me," she suggested.

"I could. And then what?"

322

"You could hold me as you once did, and touch me until I am again transported to the stars."

"If I do I'll die of wanting you." His mouth became a grim line.

"You don't understand," she cried. "Warrick, I want you, too. I want to please you." She fell silent when his thumb rubbed across her lips, stilling the eager words.

"It's you who don't understand," he said. "My pleasure would dishonor you—and myself."

"Not if I want it, too."

"I made a promise to your father."

"A man who did not love me. He cannot have loved me, or he would not have sent me to a family that treated my mother so shamefully."

"Nevertheless he did want you to go to your mother's family to live, and I will not break my promise."

"A meaningless promise. Why are you laughing at me?"

"Have you never heard about the Greek love of arguing?" he asked. "I suppose that's why we quarrel so much. You cannot help yourself; it's in your blood."

Before she could argue further, he kissed her. It began as a quick, light caress of his mouth on hers, a touch obviously meant to stop her protests. For a man trying to maintain his self-control with a woman who wanted him, it was the wrong thing to do.

Sophia's hands slid up from his shoulders to encircle his neck. She moved closer and leaned into him. And she opened her mouth, as Warrick had taught her to do. When he attempted to pull away, she let her tongue touch his. After a moment of tense hesitation on his part, he responded to the intimate caress.

Sophia was cast into a fiery emotional furnace. Warrick's hands moved down her spine to catch her hips and pull her closer until the heat and the hardness of him seared the flesh of her lower body as if she were wearing no clothing at all. His hot, moist tongue burned across hers, the kiss demanding that she surrender everything to him. She was more than willing. So tight was his embrace that her breasts were crushed against his broad chest, and the friction of silk gown against sensitive skin was almost unbearable. She could feel the tightness of her nipples and she ached to be closer still to him. She wanted his hands on her breasts, and his mouth, too.

He gave up her lips to kiss her throat, his mouth scorching downward along the neckline of her gown. She wound her fingers into his hair, directing him to her breasts, and she exulted in the moist sensation of his tongue stroking across the thin silk until he reached one hard tip and lingered there. His hands on her hips tightened still more and Sophia moved against his masculine hardness.

She was shaking with the strength of her desire before Warrick scooped her up in his arms and carried her into the room she shared with Genie. Gently he placed her on the bed. He stood looking down at her, his eyes dark with eager passion. She was so certain he intended to join her on the bed that she began to fumble with the fastenings at the front of her gown.

He went to the door and she assumed he was going to lock it so they would not be interrupted. She did not doubt for a moment that he desired her as eagerly as she wanted him. And she could not believe what he was doing when he stepped through the door, leaving her alone.

Warrick locked Sophia's bedroom door on the outside, then stood in the middle of the sitting room, his fists clenched, fighting the passionate longing that threatened to undo all of his good intentions. He dared not answer Sophia's confused cry to him to come back and tell her what was wrong.

She ought to know what was wrong, for she had invited him to kiss her and thus she had begun the interlude. And yet she remained remarkably innocent, as her surprised reactions to what he did to her proved. He was far more experienced and knew what he was doing. Sophia had no inkling how overwhelming, how consuming, sexual passion could be.

Shame flooded over him and he cursed himself for what he had just done to her. If only his sense of honor were weaker, he could unlock her door and go to her and do all that he wanted. He could make her exquisite body his and give her the sweet pleasure she craved. It would ruin her, and break her heart when she realized how he had used her.

He could not do that to Sophia. Quite apart from the promise he had made to her father, he was concerned for her future. Sophia deserved the love and happiness her selfish parent had denied her, and Warrick hoped she would find it with her relatives in Byzantium. He had to believe that she would be happy there.

Her confusion had turned to anger. Sophia was

banging on the bedroom door, demanding that he let her out. Leaving that task to Genie, Warrick went into his own room and quietly closed the door.

Chapter Nineteen

The humiliation of being rejected by Warrick was too great for Sophia to face him, so she kept to her room the next day, emerging only when Genie reported that Warrick and Robin had gone off together for further discussions with Marco.

The day was bright and clear, with the last drops of moisture sparkling in the sunshine. The sea beyond the harbor was a dark, glittering purple, and the sky above Trebizond was unmarred by any cloud. Sophia stood on the balcony gazing into the lush greenery below, her eyes blurred by tears, thinking that the storm of injured pride, thwarted love, and aching desire raging within her heart was a sad contrast to the calm weather.

She did not know enough about men to understand why Warrick had rejected her, and she could not bring herself to ask for Genie's opinion. To add to Sophia's distress, she was angry with Genie, whose reaction to Sophia's greatly abbreviated account of the previous evening was laughter.

"I should not have left you alone with him," Genie said, and gave way to a fresh bout of giggles. "You must admit that Warrick does employ original ways to keep you safe."

"I don't want to be safe," Sophia said, and turned her back on Genie.

As the day warmed the breeze increased. In late afternooon Robin appeared in the garden, where Sophia and Genie were walking, Sophia in cool silence, Genie making occasional cheerful comments to which Sophia did not deign to reply. She feared that, if she tried to speak, she would burst into tears and not be able to stop weeping. She did have a slight shred of pride left, and she was going to hang on to it by not revealing her disappointment at Warrick's lack of affection for her.

Upon seeing Robin, Genie favored him with a bright smile. Sophia glared at him.

"We are to sail in two hours," Robin announced. "I am here to settle our bill with the innkeeper and escort you to the ship."

"Two hours?" Sophia gasped. "Why so quickly? Please don't tell me the *shinha* are still pursuing us."

"Not at all," Robin said with a laugh. "Marco the Venetian trader is leaving for Byzantium as soon as his men finish loading his ship. Marco wants to take advantage of the good weather to reach Byzantium well ahead of the other ships that have been confined to port during the last storm. He has a full cargo of silk, dyes, and spices, and he hopes to get the highest prices and make a large profit."

"I'm glad we don't have a lot of baggage to pack,"

Genie said. "See to paying the innkeeper, Robin, while Sophia and I gather our belongings. We will be ready to go by the time you reach our rooms."

Robin left them and Sophia transferred her glare from him to Genie.

"Must I remind you who is the jinni and who is the mistress?" Sophia said. "You have no right to give orders in my name."

"Whenever you speak to me as unkindly as you did on the first day we met, I can be certain that you are unhappy," Genie responded. "Your emotions at this moment are a mixture of fear about your future in Byzantium and hurt at the way Warrick has dealt with you."

"Do not presume to tell me how I feel," Sophia snapped.

"You must face reality," Genie said. "Warrick is going to conduct you to Byzantium even if he has to throw you over his shoulder and carry you to Marco's ship. If you fight him on this, you will only make him angry with you."

"I know you are right," Sophia said, unable to maintain her anger against Genie, who did care about her, even if Warrick did not. "Warrick won't allow me to remain in Trebizond, so there is nothing for me to do but go aboard the ship." She did not add that, for her pride's sake, she would act as if she did not care where she was going.

Two hours later, Sophia, Genie, and Robin were greeted on the dock by a wiry, middle-aged man with flashing dark eyes and a head of thick, dark curls that were heavily touched with silver.

"I am Marco Faledro, merchant, owner and captain of this fine ship, and I am at your service, ladies," he said in perfect, though heavily accented

Greek. "Please call me Marco, and allow me to welcome you aboard my ship."

"I thought women were not welcome on shipboard," Genie said, accepting Marco's hand to help her onto the gangplank.

"Some foolish, superstitious men do believe women will bring bad luck," Marco said with a broad smile. "However I do not subscribe to such base allegations against your lovely sex."

"What you mean is that Warrick has paid you well to take us as passengers," Sophia grumbled.

"Not only are you beautiful," Marco responded, "you are also most astute. I am in business to make money. Why should I refuse a generous offer when one is made to me?" Still smiling, he assisted Sophia onto the gangplank.

Warrick was awaiting her on the deck. With Robin and Marco following her up the narrow gangplank, Sophia had no choice but to grasp Warrick's hand and let him help her along the last few steps and onto the ship.

"Good evening, Sophia." Warrick's eyes were warm, his lips curved into a smile.

Sophia refused to respond to his greeting. It was all she could do to keep from pummeling his chest with her fists and screaming out her anger and hurt at him. To divert herself from Warrick until she had regained her composure, she made herself look away from him and at her surroundings. She knew nothing about ships; still, the one Warrick and Robin had selected for their passage to Byzantium seemed entirely too small. She wasn't sure she ought to trust Robin's claim that it was a sturdy ship, for once the lines were cast off and they were under way, the timbers began to creak and groan with every sea swell they crested, and the sails made strange noises, too.

Sophia and Genie were given a tiny cabin with two narrow beds built against the cabin walls. There was no other furniture. A single porthole provided light. The cramped quarters forced them to spend most of their time on deck. Fortunately the sea remained calm, and before long Sophia was able to walk easily on a surface that was in constant motion.

Marco did not sail directly across the Euxine Sea to Byzantium. Instead he stayed near the coast, which was largely unhabited. They dropped anchor only once, at Sinope, an ancient city ruined by war and fire. A stone citadel stood guard over a cluster of small houses and a fleet of fishing ships in the harbor.

"We will take fresh water aboard," Marco told the women, "but we won't be here long enough for you to go ashore. There is nothing to see anyway, and no suitable accommodations for ladies."

"During this journey I have seen worse places," Sophia said, "and slept in some of them, too."

"Am I correct that this is Byzantine territory?" Genie asked Marco.

"It is," he replied, "which is why it's a regular stop on the route to and from Trebizond. By treaty with the Byzantines, Venetian merchants have special privileges at settlements along this coast, including free entrance and exit for their goods. That is how we left Trebizond so easily, without having to deal with customs officials or to declare every item in our cargo and each passenger traveling aboard the ship. Ladies, I must ask you to excuse me now. I have business ashore."

"So that's why Warrick chose a Venetian ship," Genie murmured, watching Marco climb down a rope ladder to the boat that was going ashore for water. "No one asked any questions of us at Trebizond, and we will probably have easy access to the port at Byzantium, too."

"I wish the Byzantines would deny us entrance," Sophia said. Warrick was standing by the rail just a short distance away. She longed to go to him, ached to feel his comforting arms around her. She could not. Her pride prevented her, and Warrick had made a point of keeping his distance since they had left Trebizond. Sophia wished she could believe Genie's claim that Warrick was simply trying to behave honorably.

With the water casks filled and loaded, they sailed from Sinope late in the day, rounding the peninsula on which the little town sat and heading due west into a glorious sunset and a warm, moonlit evening.

Sophia was alone on deck, Genie having gone below for a few minutes. A short distance away from her Warrick and Robin were leaning on the rail and talking in low voices. Sophia decided the time was right to approach Warrick. She could no longer bear his continued coolness and she was tired of being stubborn. If Warrick could not love her, then let them be friends. As she drew nearer to the two men, she overheard Robin's words.

"I grow weary of Genie's constant refusals," Robin said. "She is driving me mad. I cannot tell whether she cares for me or not. I want to get away from her before I do something foolish that will make her hate me."

"I understand," Warrick said. "I am close to madness myself."

"Have you forgotten Hua Te?" Robin asked.

"Of course not." Warrick took a deep breath. "I have thought of him frequently during these days of confinement aboard ship. Here there are no imminent dangers to occupy my mind. Consideration of where Hua Te has gone has been one way to divert myself from subjects on which I ought not to dwell."

"What have you decided? You know I am with you, wherever you choose to go."

"I do know that, and I thank you for your loyalty. No man ever had a truer friend." Warrick fell silent for a moment, then said, "After I turn Sophia over to her family, I want to take ship again, to return to Trebizond and find there a caravan that is heading along the silk route to Cathay. It's where Hua Te planned to go, so I hope we will find some trace of him along the way. If not, we will continue our search when we reach Cathay."

"Good," said Robin, striking his fist on the railing. "It's what I want to do, too. The farther we are from Byzantium, and from Genie and Sophia, the happier both of us will be."

"Go, then," Sophia cried, coming up behind them. "Go away and never see me again. I don't care and I'm sure Genie doesn't care either."

"You have always known we will part company after we reach Byzantium," Robin said to her. "What can it matter to you where Warrick and I go after you are delivered to your relatives?"

"Delivered?" Sophia exclaimed. "Do you mean like a bundle of silk from Cathay, or a rolled-up carpet from Persia? Or perhaps a crate of figs or dates? Am I no more than an inconvenient cargo?"

"Sophia, don't." Warrick caught her, pulled her into his arms, and held her there, where she wanted to be. "I never meant to hurt you."

"I know you don't care about me." With his arms holding her close, she could almost believe that he did care. It was so right for her to be in Warrick's arms, with her face pressed against his chest and his cheek on her hair. Why couldn't he love her as she loved him?

"We both have duties to fulfill," he said, his lips brushing her forehead. "You to obey your father's last wishes, and I to find my lost friend. Our journey together has been a deviation from my true path. I beg you, Sophia, do not continue to tempt me with your misplaced affection. You only make it harder for me to do what I must."

With that he left her, and when he took his arms away, he also took away any remaining hope that he might choose to keep her with him.

Sophia was not disposed to like Byzantium. She saw no beauty in the many domed churches or the broad parks. In her opinion the bazaar, the fine houses of the nobles, even the royal palace, suffered in comparison to similar sights in Baghdad.

Marco's ship was moored on the eastern side of the harbor, the famed Golden Horn, in a location reserved for Venetian traders. At Marco's invitation, the four travelers joined him in the boat in which he was rowed to the quay across the harbor to transact business. After parting from Marco, they walked through the city to the neighborhood that John of Cornwall had described to Warrick.

Sophia's heart sank lower with every step she took. Still, she kept her head high and she told herself that she gave every outward appearance of being a Byzantine noblewoman. Genie had insisted on providing a gown for her that was made of pale blue brocaded silk cut in the stiff, long-sleeved Byzantine style. Her hair was braided, the braids wrapped tightly around her head and covered with a sheer silk scarf. Genie had dressed herself as a servant, and Warrick and Robin were in matching russet tunics and hose, posing as Sophia's guards.

"I detest this gown," she grumbled. "The skirt is so tight and stiff that I am forced to take small steps. I am used to moving more freely."

"This," Warrick told her, "is the way in which Byzantine noblewomen go about the city on the rare occasions when they leave their homes. They never go alone. Always they are properly dressed and accompanied by servants and guards. It will be best if you present yourself to your relatives as a noblewoman equal in status to them; it will make acceptance easier."

She wanted to cry out that she didn't care what her mother's family thought of her, but she knew Warrick was right. Her initial appearance would make a difference in whether or not they accepted her, and in how they later treated her. The remainder of her life depended on what happened in the next few hours.

Having reached a neighborhood of large houses, they paused at a corner so Warrick could look down a narrow cross street that was lined with tall buildings. While his companions waited, Warrick began to count the houses.

"According to the directions your father gave

me," Warrick said to Sophia, "your family's house is the third one on the right."

It was one of the largest houses on the street, a cream-colored stone building, and it looked deserted. All of the shutters were closed over the windows and two armed guards stood before the front door.

"The family must be out of town," Sophia said. "Or perhaps they've moved away and we will never find them."

"Robin," Warrick ordered, "take Sophia and Genie back around the corner, where they can't be seen. The three of you stay there while I speak to the guards."

"Why should we do that?" Sophia asked.

"Sophia, I am not going to discuss this with you here in the street," Warrick said. "Please, just do as I say, and don't say or do anything that will cause those guards to notice us."

His voice was little louder than a whisper, but it conveyed such urgency that Sophia did not argue. She did as he wanted, letting Robin escort her around the corner, where she could not see what was happening to Warrick. He was gone for what seemed to her a very long time. When he rejoined them, his face was grave. He said nothing at first, just took Sophia's arm and started walking away from the side street and the neighborhood.

"Why are we leaving?" Sophia demanded. She tried to wrench her arm out of Warrick's grasp. He did not let her go. "Answer me," she cried. "What happened back there?"

"At every step along the way since leaving Baghdad, you have insisted that you want nothing to do with your mother's family," Warrick said. "I tell you now, Sophia, if you raise your voice or continue to protest and thus attract attention to yourself, the chances are very good that you will spend the rest of your life in the same manner as your female relatives. From what I have just learned, I assure you, you will not like it! In the name of heaven, keep quiet and walk with me as if you were the noble-woman you appear to be."

He had seen her safely through enough dangers that she trusted him in a difficult situation. From the way he was acting she thought they were in a difficult situation right now, so once again she did as he ordered. With Genie in a servant's position a step or two behind her and Warrick and Robin on either side as guards, Sophia retraced her steps to the more crowded, commercial section of the city. Warrick looked back several times, as if he expected someone to follow them.

As soon as Sophia noticed that Warrick had relaxed, she began to question him. "Where are we going?"

"Back to Marco's ship," Warrick responded shortly.

"Why? What has happened?"

"The ship is the only place that I can think of in this entire city where you will be safe," Warrick said. "The Venetians have a treaty with the Byzantines that grants them special privileges, remember? I'll be very much surprised if anyone knows you are in the city, but all the same I want to see you in a place where the authorities won't be able to find you."

"You haven't told me much," she said. "You haven't begun to answer all of my questions."

"I'll explain my reasons for what I am doing once

we are on the ship," he told her. "Be patient until then."

When they reached the harbor they found Marco's rowers still on the quay, awaiting their captain's return. It took half an hour for Warrick to convince the men to row his party across the harbor to Marco's ship. Agreement was reached only after Warrick and Robin consented to take the oars in place of two of the rowers, who were delegated to remain on the quay to explain the situation to Marco, should he return and want transportation to his ship before the rest of his men were back at the quay. This was in addition to a cash payment to all of the rowers, with another payment to be made to Marco later.

"Marco will understand and will not punish us if we make a profit for him as well as for ourselves," said one of the rowers to Warrick.

"It's settled, then," Warrick said. He removed from his shoulder the bag of herbs and medicines in which the crystal ball was packed, and gave it to Sophia to hold. They all piled into the boat and Warrick and Robin took the oars assigned to them. The men made short work of the trip across the harbor, and as soon as they drew up next to the dock where Marco's ship was berthed, the four passengers climbed out of the boat and Marco's men at once began the return journey.

"They've taken the last of our money," Robin said. He rubbed his blistered palms. "Not to mention taking the skin off my hands."

"We have all the medicine we'll need for our hands, right in here," Warrick said, taking his sack from Sophia.

He led the way up the gangplank and onto the

ship, where he hailed with jovial assurance the first sailor he met.

"I will be using my cabin for a few extra hours," Warrick said.

"I thought the four of you were gone," the sailor said, looking uncertain.

"As you have seen, your fellow crew members rowed us here," Warrick said, "and we will be meeting with Marco as soon as he arrives, when we will pay him for the half day's use of the cabin, and for the boat trip across the harbor."

"Pay him after you have used something that belongs to him?" the sailor said. "That doesn't sound like the Captain Marco I know. He always insists on payment in advance."

"These are special circumstances," Warrick responded. "There's no one using my cabin, is there?"

"Well, no," the sailor admitted, adding, "I'm not sure I should allow you to stay on board without express permission from the captain."

"There will be an extra payment for you after I've settled with Marco," Warrick promised.

"Go on, then," said the sailor, and stepped aside to let them go below.

"They all want money," Sophia complained as she went down the ladder to the lower deck.

"They are merchants," Warrick responded with a laugh. "What do you expect them to do, give you everything you want at no cost?"

Sophia had not previously been in the cabin Warrick and Robin had been using. It was only half as large as her own cabin, and the two beds were stacked one above the other. When Sophia sat on the lower bed she had to be careful that her head didn't bump against the upper one. Genie sat beside her, hunched over as Sophia was, to keep from hitting her head. Robin stood by the door and from time to time he opened it a crack to be sure no one was listening to their conversation.

Warrick was next to the porthole, where the light shone upon his handsome, chiseled features. He had shaved and trimmed his hair that morning in anticipation of meeting Sophia's relatives, and the tunic and hose Genie had provided were exactly the right shade of russet brown to complement his dark hair and smoky eyes. Sophia's heart ached at the sight of him, for she feared they would be permanently separated by the end of the day.

"You will want to know what I learned from the guards at your family's house," Warrick said to her.

"We are all curious," Genie said, and put her hand on top of both of Sophia's hands, which were clasped together in her lap. She pressed Sophia's fingers in a comforting way. "Warrick, why did you hurry us away from there and speak as if Sophia is in danger? Surely no one in Byzantium knows she is here."

"I hope that's true. According to the guards the authorities have been alerted that she will be arriving soon," Warrick said.

"How can anyone here know that?" Sophia cried.

"I can guess," said Robin. He leaned against the cabin door with his arms folded. "Either John sent a message before he died, or Daoud wrote ahead to let the family know that John's possessions were on the way, in case they arrived here before we did."

"I'm not sure which it was," Warrick said. "I only know that the guards posted at the house are expecting Sophia. Fortunately I identified myself to the guards as a scholar newly arrived from England, who had been asked by an elderly friend to call on Sophia's uncle if ever I reached Byzantium during my travels. I was so honestly astonished to hear the story they told me that I think they believed me when I said I have never met any member of the family and claimed that, as a newly arrived foreigner, I know nothing of Byzantine politics."

"Warrick," Sophia said, "why are those guards at the house? Why are they waiting for me to appear?"

"I am sorry to tell you this, but your uncle and your male cousins were involved in political machinations that the emperor interpreted as treasonous. Two weeks ago the entire family was arrested, the women as well as the men."

"Then they are all in prison?" Sophia asked.

"All of the male members of the family were publicly executed a few days ago," Warrick said.

"Dear heaven." Sophia looked down at her clasped hands, at Genie's soft hand atop hers, and then she raised her eyes to Warrick's face. "I held no tender feelings for any of them, because of the way they treated my mother. Still, they were of my blood, and they must have suffered greatly after they were arrested. I am sorry for their terrible deaths."

"What has happened to the women of the family?" Genie asked.

"The ladies and the female children have been confined to strict convents for the rest of their lives," Warrick said. "Separate convents, so they will have no opportunity to conspire together. I dared not ask the guards for more information, lest they become suspicious of me. I tried to appear no more than a curious foreigner who could scarcely credit what he was being told."

"What will happen to Sophia if her presence in Byzantium is discovered?" Genie asked.

"I don't know those people!" Sophia exclaimed. "I have never met any of them and I have nothing to do with their schemes, treasonous or otherwise."

"The authorities won't see it that way," Warrick said. "You are of the same blood as the condemned men, as you admitted a few moments ago, and blood ties run deep here. It is not unheard of in Byzantine history for a female relative of a convicted traitor to marry a man who is willing to carry out blood vengeance against those who ruined her family and, having wreaked full retribution, then to reclaim the family's former rank and fortune. As I recall, one or two emperors have been made that way. Since you are the only member of your family still at large, the authorities will consider you a danger to the state."

"We must take Sophia away from Byzantium," Genie said to Warrick.

"I begin to think there is no safe place for me," Sophia said. "Perhaps I ought to volunteer to enter a convent."

"I know you too well to believe you will be happy in strict confinement," Warrick said. "You have grown used to greater freedom than most women ever know."

"We cannot take a woman with us to Cathay," said Robin from his position by the door.

"Your promise to my father is accomplished with honor," Sophia said to Warrick. "You have delivered me to Byzantium. It is not your fault that you cannot make direct delivery to my family. You are free to leave me. Genie and I will decide for ourselves where we want to go next." It was difficult to keep her voice steady, but she did it. She wasn't going to let Warrick know that Robin's words were breaking her heart.

"I have a better idea," Warrick said. He opened his sack and drew out of it the crystal ball. "Let us try what we see in here." He held the crystal sphere up on his fingertips, so the light coming through the porthole struck it, making the clear crystal glow. A faint smile touched his lips.

"Look into the crystal ball? You will have a severe headache afterward," Sophia warned him.

"Perhaps not." Warrick's eyes were warm when they met hers. "Your safety is worth a headache, Sophia. Will you join me?"

She rose from the bed and took the single step that brought her to his side.

"What shall I do?" she asked.

"Look deep into the crystal," he said. "Empty your mind of all thoughts. If there is a message to be found in the ball, it will come without effort on your part or mine."

She did as he told her, and looked into the center of the crystal, which was like a drop of pure water balanced on Warrick's fingertips. The spherical shape distorted both the light and the images of the cabin that were reflected in the smooth surface of the crystal. Sophia cleared her mind as Warrick had instructed, and tried to think of nothing at all.

Far inside the crystal a wisp of fog unfurled itself and began to spread outward. Slowly a shape emerged from the fog, a formidable stone castle with square towers rising above its walls. Then the castle dissolved and a man in a blue robe appeared. No sooner had Sophia recognized the man's black hair, high cheekbones, and dark, almond-shaped eyes than the crystal cleared, returning to its former pristine state.

"That was Hua Te," Sophia said.

"Yes." Warrick continued to stare into the crystal as if he saw something there that Sophia could not see.

"Does your head hurt?" Sophia asked, aware of a faint discomfort at her own temples.

"Not badly," Warrick said. "It will pass. How very odd." His gaze was still on the crystal ball.

"What's odd?" Robin asked.

"We are not going to Cathay," Warrick told him. "We are going home to England. I am surprised, yet it seems exactly the right thing to do."

"We don't have any money left," Robin reminded him.

"Yes, we have." Warrick gave the crystal ball to Sophia to hold while he pulled his ever-present knife from its sheath at his belt. Reaching into his sack, he took the jewel-encrusted golden stand from its protective linen and began to dig at one of the jewels with the point of the knife. "We have more money than we can ever use. I am sure Hua Te will not object when he learns what I have done." The stone he was working at popped out of its setting. A large, flawless emerald dropped into Warrick's hand.

"You can't offer that to Marco," Robin objected. "He will want to know where you got it, and he'll probably suspect that we have more stones."

"Quite right." Warrick passed the emerald to Robin. "That's why I am sending you and Genie to find a jeweler and sell the stone. You won't have to go across the harbor again to do it. There's so much trade going on right here in Galata that you ought to have no trouble finding a jeweler or a goldsmith who is willing to buy such a stone with few questions asked." With a smile for Sophia, Warrick took the crystal ball from her and replaced it and the stand in his sack.

"What will you do while we are gone?" Genie asked.

"Sophia and I will plan our wedding," Warrick answered.

"What?" Sophia's first impulse was to flee from him. In the small cabin there was no place for her to go, and Robin's tall, muscular form was blocking the door. "Warrick, have you gone mad? I cannot marry you."

"You cannot do anything else. Should the authorities find and question you, your marriage to me will demonstrate that you have no interest in pursuing vengeance for the sake of your relatives. I am not Greek, I am about to make my permanent departure from Byzantium, and you are going with me."

"After Robin and I sell the emerald," said Genie, "we will locate a priest who is willing to write out a marriage contract and bless the union in return for a handsome donation to his church. You will want it done quickly, I suppose?"

"As soon as possible," Warrick said.

"Warrick, are you sure about this?" Robin asked his friend.

"You know I am," Warrick said.

"Robin, do stop frowning and move away from the door," Genie ordered. "We have a lot to accomplish and, if I comprehend Warrick's intentions correctly, not much time before we leave Byzantium." She took Robin by the elbow and led him out of the cabin.

"I refuse to marry you," Sophia told Warrick when they were alone.

"I apologize for not discussing our nuptials with you before announcing them," Warrick said. "I assumed that you would understand how pressed we are for time. You will be safer if we are wed before the authorities locate you. Then I may justifiably claim my intention of taking you to England with me."

"I won't marry you!"

"You are far too intelligent to be so difficult about this, Sophia. I don't understand your objection."

"You don't care about me," she cried. "I am a burden to you, an obligation to fulfill. You imagine you are still bound to protect me because of the promise you made to my father. Well, I hereby free you from that promise."

"I freed myself from my oath as soon as I made it," he said.

"You did not! It's the only reason why you traveled so far with me. You have done what you swore to do. You may leave me now. I know you want to go."

"Your father forced me to give him my promise, in return for information about Hua Te," Warrick explained patiently. "The information he provided eased my conscience, but it was of little practical use. Aside from that, Sophia, has no one ever told you that a promise sworn under duress is no oath at all?"

"If your promise meant nothing, then why did you bring me here from Baghdad?" she demanded.

"Why have you repeatedly protected me from danger?"

"Because I saw and heard how little John loved you. I thought you deserved better, and I hoped your mother's family would love and care for you."

"So you undertook our long journey out of pity? I don't want your pity, Warrick!"

"Not pity," he said. "Sympathy. It's a different thing from pity. I also spent my youth with a parent who did not love me, and I know the empty spot the lack of love left in my heart. It was easy enough for me to see a similar emptiness in you. It's why you are sometimes difficult; you are trying to protect yourself from further hurt.

"Sophia, I do care for you," he said softly. "I couldn't have endured our long journey together if I did not. Nor would I have restrained myself as I did."

"Restrained yourself from beating me?"

"From making passionate love to you when I had no right to make you mine, nothing to offer you in return for taking your virtue. Now you are without family or home, and I can offer you both. In England I have both a loving family and a manor house that my father is holding until I return. All that I have will be yours."

His hands came to rest on her shoulders, drawing her closer, but Sophia stubbornly refused to look directly at him.

"If you truly care," she said, "why did you order me to marry you?"

"Is that what I did?" His lips skimmed along her cheek. "I thought it was a timely and logical suggestion."

"It sounded like a command to me. And, as you

have just said, vows made under duress are no vows at all."

"Then I will have your free consent." He released her shoulders and stepped back. With one hand he caught her chin, tipping her face upward and forcing her to look into his warm, smoky eyes. "Will you marry me, Sophia?"

When she stared at him in mute confusion, unable to respond for the emotions churning inside her, he laughed softly and kissed her once, quickly and lightly.

"What, no argument?" he teased. "No demand for further discussion?"

"Are you certain it's what you want?" she asked.

"Completely certain. It's you or no one, Sophia. I have never asked another woman to marry me, and I seriously doubt I'll ever find the courage to do it again."

"In that case, I will marry you, Warrick."

He hadn't said he loved her. She believed he was continuing his habit of protecting her and keeping her safe from all danger. Based on her past experiences with him, she did think he wanted her. That would have to be enough.

Chapter Twenty

The church to which Robin conducted Sophia and Warrick for their wedding presented a glaring contrast to the other churches Sophia had noticed in Byzantium. The building was in a state of serious disrepair. The door hung on rusty hinges, the paintings of saints on the plastered stone walls were peeling from dampness, and the air inside the church smelled of mildew and old incense. The robes worn by the elderly priest were as fragile in appearance as the wearer.

"I can do nothing to repair his vestments without revealing my magical abilities," Genie whispered to Warrick. "If I do that he will throw us out, crying anathema and heresy."

"Could you find no better church?" Warrick asked, looking about in unconcealed disapproval of what he beheld.

"There is no more appropriate church," Genie answered him. Leading Warrick and Sophia to the old man who stood near the altar, Genie said, "This good priest is Father Andros, a distant relative of the men who were recently arrested and executed. Like the rest of Sophia's family, Father Andros has lived for several years under the emperor's displeasure."

"John II Comnenus will not cast a priest into prison without overwhelming evidence," Father Andros said to Sophia. "Instead, after he withdrew his favor my parishioners fled to other churches, so that I and my little church are left impoverished, as you see.

"Cousin Sophia," the priest continued, "your good serving woman has explained how you came to Byzantium from a distant city seeking your relatives, and how your protector during your journey has decided your continued safety lies in marriage to him and a quick departure from the emperor's domains. As your only remaining male relative, I am more than willing to help you, so that some member of our family will survive outside a convent. The marriage contract is prepared as Genie directed. It requires only your signatures."

"Thank you, Father," Sophia murmured. "And bless you, Genie, for finding my cousin, so I will not be without family at my wedding."

"Indeed, you have done well, Genie," Warrick said. "Father Andros, allow me to make a contribution in memory of Sophia's mother, whom I knew as a sweet and gentle-hearted lady."

"Thank you, my son." Father Andros stared at the pile of coins Warrick placed into his hands. "With this I can have the paintings restored and purchase a new set of vestments. Perhaps when my former parishioners see that I am not completely bereft of support, some of them will return.

"Now," said Father Andros, "let me read the contract without further delay, for I think you young people are eager to be on your way to a safer place, and I will not keep you when remaining here may bring you to harm."

They all took their places before the altar and Father Andros read aloud the contract, which he had written in both Greek and Latin. The document was simple enough: Warrick bestowed all of his worldly goods on Sophia. Since she came to him with no possessions except her clothing and a few personal items, she had nothing to give in return. She regretted the lack, but there was nothing to be done about it. Warrick seemed to understand the emotions surging within her. He took her hand and smiled at her while her aged cousin blessed their union.

The newlyweds paused only long enough to drink a cup of wine with Father Andros before they bid him farewell. Sophia embraced him, kissing him on both cheeks. She noticed moisture in his eyes and turned away quickly, before she could begin to weep.

They were back at Marco's ship by midafternoon. There they discovered Marco waiting for them, newly arrived from the city on the other side of the harbor and eager for answers to all the questions raised by the reappearance of passengers whom he had sped on their way that morning and had not expected ever to see again. He listened with undisguised amusement to Warrick's request that the four of them continue as passengers. When Warrick was finished, Marco named an exaggerated

fare to carry them from Byzantium to Venice, the
final stop of his long voyage.

"That is much more than you charged to carry us
from Trebizond to Byzantium," Warrick said.

"It's the end of the season," Marco responded.
"Winter is coming, when many ships remain in port
because of foul weather. You will not easily find
another captain who is sailing westward."

"We'll take our chances," said Robin.

"Then again," Marco drawled, looking from Warrick to Robin to the women and letting his specu-
lative gaze rest on Sophia, "there is the matter of
certain gossip I heard in the city today. I won't repeat it; I never carry gossip, and who knows better
than a Venetian that there are spies everywhere?
However, I plan to leave Byzantium before the end
of the day. Am I correct in assuming that you are
also eager to be gone from here and are therefore
willing to pay whatever fare I ask?"

"You are little better than a pirate," Robin told
him.

"Far from it. I am a businessman who must take
full advantage of every opportunity that comes my
way," Marco responded with an injured air. "If I do
not make a profit from my voyages, my wife and
children in Venice will starve. Well, do we have a
bargain?"

"We have," Warrick said, cutting off Robin's further protests.

"Payment in advance," Marco said, holding out
his hand. "You may have your same cabins back."

"Are you saying that you don't have any other
passengers?" Warrick asked. "If that is the case, I'll
take a third cabin for Sophia and me to share. We
were married today."

"Is that so?" Marco's dark eyes gleamed. "You will want more spacious and comfortable accommodations for your new bride. For an additional fee I'll let you use the captain's cabin, and I will take the third passenger's cabin."

"Agreed. Will you show my wife and her friend to the cabin?" Warrick gave Sophia a quick look that warned her not to object to what he said. "I will join you later, my dear. For now I want to speak with Robin."

"No doubt you will be making more plans without including me," Sophia muttered under her breath. She sent a dark glare in Warrick's direction. He did not see; he and Robin had their heads together.

"This way, lovely ladies." Marco ushered them below deck.

"Warrick is only being considerate and granting you a little time to yourself before your marriage night begins," Genie whispered to Sophia as they followed Marco through a short, dark passage.

The captain's cabin was in the stern of the ship, and it boasted a row of square windows that let in considerable light. At one side of the cabin was a real bed that was bolted down so it could not shift around during a storm. The cabin also contained a narrow table and a bench, both fastened to the floor on the other side of the room from the bed. After Marco's two chests of clothing were removed, there was space enough between the bed and table for Sophia and Genie to move around with ease.

"I don't like the looks of these linens," Genie said when she and Sophia were alone in the cabin, "and I am sure the mattress is infested with unspeakable vermin." She waved her hand in an elegant gesture and mattress, linens, and soiled quilt all disappeared. Another wave of Genie's hand and the bed was fitted with a thick mattress and heavy linen sheets. There were at least a dozen pillows in various sizes and shapes, all of them covered in pale gold silk, and a plump quilt covered in matching silk.

"That's much better," Genie said with an air of satisfaction. "I'll see to a nice meal for you and Warrick this evening and, if you want, a hot, scented bath beforehand. I know just the thing for your night robe, too. Warrick will lose his head when he sees you in it."

"I suppose it's possible that he will, for a little while," Sophia said with a sigh. "I do think he wants me. But he doesn't love me."

"Successful marriages have been made on less than physical attraction," Genie said.

"You are more fortunate than I. Robin does love you."

"Never!" Genie cried. "Sophia, don't say that."

"He told me so," Sophia said, eagerly seizing on a subject that did not include discussion of what she and Warrick would do in the silk-covered bed. She began to chatter nervously, revealing her conversation with Robin. "It was while we were still riding through the mountains with Gafar. Robin asked me if I knew what your feeings toward him were, and he said he loved you. And then, aboard ship between Trebizond and here, I overheard him telling Warrick that your constant rejection was driving him mad."

"I have to reject him," Genie said. "I cannot love him. I must not."

"Whyever not?" Sophia asked. "You have said

something like that before, but never explained just what you mean. Why can't you love Robin? Are the jinn incapable of love?"

"To love a human means doom to a jinni. Besides, I am here as your servant and friend, not to dally with handsome young men. Turn your thoughts to your new husband and do not think of me."

"I am thinking about you, and talking about Robin's affection for you, because I'm afraid," Sophia whispered. "When I am with Warrick, when he puts his hands on me, I ache for him to do everything that a lover can do. But still, I am afraid. Back in Baghdad, my old nurse Hanna loved to tell stories about the unkind ways in which men treat women when they are in private together."

"Warrick will not be unkind to you," Genie said. "Of that I am certain. I suspect that what you are feeling is not real fear, but nervousness caused by lack of experience. Are you sure that you know what will happen between you when you and Warrick lie together? I am talking about the facts, not Hanna's sour warnings."

"My mother did explain some of it to me when I was twelve years old," Sophia said. "But then she died, and there was no one else I could ask, except for Hanna. Genie, can you tell me what it will be like?"

"I don't know from personal experience," Genie said. "However, my observations of the behavior of lovers during several of my previous Callings leads me to believe that when the woman is willing and the man is patient and kind, lovemaking is pleasant for both of them."

"Pleasant doesn't begin to describe what I felt

when Warrick touched me that night we were together." Sophia's cheeks began to burn at the memory. "He made me feel as if I had touched the stars."

"I am sure that you will feel the same way again tonight," Genie said.

"Listen." Sophia held up a hand, silencing Genie. Through the open windows came shouted orders and the sounds of ropes being released. The deck beneath her feet moved slightly. "We are leaving Byzantium. We are at sea again."

"Do you want to go above?" Genie asked.

"No. If I do, someone on shore may see me and make Marco heave to so I can be taken off the ship."

"That cannot happen," Genie said. "No one in Byzantium except for Father Andros knows you have been there, and that dear old man won't betray you."

"I know that, Genie. It's time for me to stop being afraid. I have overcome so many fears since leaving Baghdad. I was afraid of heights, I feared large animals, I had no idea how to make friends, and I believed that all men were as unreliable as my father.

"I do have one fear left." Sophia swallowed past the lump that was lodged in her throat. "It's the greatest fear of all. I am afraid that Warrick will never love me."

"I cannot help you there," Genie said. "That is beyond my magical ability. Love is a matter between you and your husband. What I can do is prepare you for this night, so Warrick will know how beautiful his bride is. First I suggest a hot, scented bath, full of bubbles."

"Genie, you always advise a hot bath," Sophia exclaimed, laughing in spite of her growing disquiet over the night to come. She desperately wanted Warrick to be pleased with her, but she was too inexperienced in lovemaking to know exactly what he would require for his pleasure.

"A bath is the very best way to relax," Genie said. "Just leave everything to me."

An hour later Sophia stood below the open windows at the rear of the cabin, watching as Genie put the final touches on her arrangements. A fine white cloth covered the narrow table, on which a silver platter displayed lamb kabobs. Along with the lamb there was a bowl of rice with herbs. A second silver platter was heaped with luscious ripe apricots, bunches of purple grapes, and richly scented melons. There was even a silver pitcher brimming with red wine and a pair of matching silver goblets. Blue and white hyacinth blossoms were strewn among the dishes, and their fragrance lingered in the cabin air after Sophia's bath.

Then there were the candles: tall, thin candles in a triple-branched candelabra in the center of the table; short, stubby candles set in a row along the window ledge; taller, thicker candles lined up on the bench behind the table. Genie was using a taper to light all of them.

Outside the windows a velvet blue dusk was falling. Inside, the cabin was filled with golden candle glow, and the salty tang of sea air mingled pleasantly with the scents of hyacinth and candle wax.

"Where are we to sit?" Sophia asked, regarding the lighted candles on the bench.

"On the bed, of course. It's the only place," said Genie with a conspiratorial grin. "Now let me look at you." She touched Sophia's hair, straightening a curl that was still damp.

"I feel naked," Sophia said.

"Nonsense. That ancient Greek style suits you very well."

The robe Genie had provided was of sheer, pleated linen in a pale shade of blue. It was no more than a tube of fabric caught at each of Sophia's shoulders with a small gold brooch, so that her throat and arms were bare. A gold cord cinched her waist, with the fabric loosely bloused over the cord. Her feet were bare.

"It's perfect." Genie stepped back, admiring her creation. "You look lovely. I wish you joy of your husband, Sophia." She started for the door.

"Wait," Sophia cried, giving way to sudden panic. "Please don't go."

"I cannot stay. You know that." The door opened and closed and Genie was gone.

Sophia stood alone in the candlelight, every nerve on edge, more than a little apprehensive of what was to come, and yet eager at the same time.

She did not have long to wait. Warrick came into the cabin wearing the familiar russet silk caftan that she had seen on many evenings during their journey.

"Genie has outdone herself," Warrick said, looking around the cabin. He laughed softly. "She does delight in exaggerated luxury. I am surprised that you aren't wearing rings on every finger, twenty bracelets on each arm, and sixteen necklaces."

"She did offer," Sophia said wryly. "I refused. I wanted you to find me as I am, with no decoration."

"You need none." He took the hands she was nervously clenching together and kissed them. "Are you hungry for the marvelous feast Genie has prepared?" he asked, sparing only a glance for the table before looking back at Sophia.

"I am sure I couldn't eat a thing," she said. "But if you are hungry, then we will dine."

"Sophia," he said softly, "you are not obliged to cater to my every whim."

"But you are my—my husband." She could hardly get the word out. It sounded strange on her lips. "It is my duty to please you."

"That is the first time I have ever heard you speak of duty," he said.

"It is not! I was always a dutiful daughter, and I was prepared to obey my father's last wish and spend the rest of my life in Byzantium—Warrick, stop laughing at me!"

"Ah, Sophia, how can I help laughing?" His hands held her face with a gentle firmness. "Will you believe me when I say that I am glad you are here with me, and not in Byzantium with your mother's family?"

"You are?" She stared at him, seeing warmth and humor and compassion in his handsome face. But not love. Warrick did not love her.

"If you had remained in Byzantium I could not do this," he said, and put his mouth on hers.

His hands were at her waist, unknotting the golden cord that bound her robe, letting it drop away. Sophia sighed and nestled closer when the cord was gone. Warrick's arms wrapped around her. She put her arms about his waist and clung to him, aware as never before of his tightly leashed strength, of the self-control he exerted with such ease. She opened her lips to his plunging tongue and gave herself up to the growing heat inside her body. Each time Warrick embraced her, he created the same heat. On this night there was no need for her to fight the encroaching warmth.

Still, she was so unsure of him that when he lifted her in his arms and laid her on the bed, she half expected him to leave her alone, as he had done once before, in Trebizond. This time he did not go away. He bent over her, his fingers working at the brooches on her shoulders, unfastening them so he could draw the top of her robe down to reveal her breasts.

"No, Warrick," she cried, instinctively trying to cover her exposed flesh. He pulled her hands away and gazed upon the lushly rounded breasts that quivered with every gasping breath she drew.

"Don't fear me, Sophia. We've done this before. I've kissed you here," he said, lowering his mouth to one nipple. She cried out in mingled alarm and delight. After a moment or two she ceased all protest against what he was doing. Warrick moved on to her other breast. "I have kissed you here, too," he whispered.

Sophia's fists were knotted into the linen bedcovers, holding tight under the onslaught of Warrick's hot, moist lips and tongue. She moved restlessly, shifting her legs. Warrick pushed on the pale blue robe, sliding it lower, until her waist and abdomen were uncovered, and then her thighs. The silk of his caftan brushed against her skin with every caress he bestowed on her. And where his hands roved, his mouth soon followed. Sophia whimpered with the pleasure of his touch.

He found the place between her thighs and his questing fingers stroked her there. Liquid fire shot through Sophia, searing her heart and making her yearn for more than Warrick had given her the last time he had caressed her so intimately.

His caftan was gone. She did not know exactly when he had removed it; she knew only that now it was Warrick's flesh and not smooth silk against her skin. There was hair on the strong, straight legs that tangled with hers, and when he held her close the hair on his chest rubbed against her nipples, already sensitized by his earlier attentions, and made them stand up hard and aching all over again.

She felt him move between her thighs and became aware of something large and hard and very hot pressing where his fingers had been, but his mouth was on hers in a wild, demanding kiss, so she could not ask him what he was doing, or argue about the suddenly increased pressure that threatened to rend her in two. There was no time to protest, and Sophia suddenly discovered that she really did not want to argue or complain. All she wanted was for Warrick to come closer, and closer still. Her body received him with only a slight twinge of discomfort and he slid into her in a warm, sensual rush. He stayed there deep inside her without moving, and she could feel him trembling.

"Sophia." He took his mouth from hers and raised his head to look into her eyes. His gaze was smoky with passion, his face set in hard lines of self-control.

"Don't stop," she whispered.

"Give it a moment, till the pain is less." He spoke through gritted teeth.

"There is no pain. I am stretched until my body can stretch no more, but it is a wonderful thing and not painful." She moved her hips, experimenting.

"Don't," he ground out, "or I won't answer for what I do."

"What will you do?" she asked, and moved again, more certainly this time, seeking the pleasure she had discovered once before in his arms. What she found was a new and different sensation, for this time Warrick was buried inside her, a hard, masculine presence penetrating to the depths of her femininity.

She realized that she could not stop moving, that what was occurring between herself and Warrick was beyond her control. Beyond his control, too, for he gave a great cry and began to plunge into her over and over again, timing himself perfectly to meet her upsurging body, until the passion building between them carried them to a new place, where Warrick plucked every star from the sky and gave them all to her, burning star by burning star, and the skies went dark and soft, and Sophia sank into his arms knowing that he would forever keep her safe.

But he did not love her. He had not said he did, not even at the height of his passion. She could no longer doubt that he cared for her, that he would honor and protect her, with his life if need be.

He owned her heart, her soul, and her body, and she loved him as she had never before loved anyone, man or woman. But he did not love her.

Chapter Twenty-one

"Depending on the winds, it will take two months or more for us to reach Venice," Marco said to Warrick. "You will be too late to accompany the last shipment of the summer season through the Alps. Therefore you must winter in Venice."

The two of them were standing on the deck of Marco's ship, their eyes trained on a distant bank of clouds that obscured the line where sky and sea met. Thanks to the special treatment enjoyed by Venetian traders, they had sailed through the Bosporus and into the Middle Sea without being stopped, and Warrick was certain that Sophia was well beyond the threat of harm from the Byzantines.

"I am eager to reach England," Warrick said.

"I trust not so eager that you would endanger your life, or the lives of your wife and friends, when you have so recently escaped from danger," Marco responded. "No one can cross the Alps in winter.

Nor will ships venture beyond the Pillars of Hercules and into the Atlantic storms. You must wait until spring.

"A man with a pretty new wife ought not to complain about spending the cold months in peaceful domesticity," Marco said with his eyes on the figure in a blue cloak making her way across the deck. He excused himself and went to tend to ship's business, passing Sophia with a smile and a few pleasant words.

"Will there be a storm?" Sophia asked, joining Warrick at the rail. She frowned at the clouds ahead.

"Marco says no, but the wind has dropped, so we may be a day or two late in reaching port."

"I won't mind a longer voyage. Will you?"

She turned an innocent face to him. Warrick reached out to catch a loose curl and twine it around his finger. He heard Sophia's quick little breath and caught a whiff of her hyacinth perfume. His body tightened in response to her nearness. He thought of the bed they shared and of Sophia's eyes dark with passion, thought of her eager cries and her fingers digging into his shoulders.

"Where is Genie?" he asked.

"She and Robin are talking to the cook about providing tastier meals for passengers and crew," she answered with a laugh. Her eyes met his for a heartbeat or two. "Warrick? What is it?"

"Come below," he said, an unmistakable urgency in his voice.

"Now? But it's midday."

"What of it? I want you, Sophia." His firm hand on her shoulder directed her toward the hatchway and the unlit hall, then into the cabin they shared.

"Secure the door," he ordered, his back to her while he unbuckled his belt and stripped off his tunic. When he faced her again she was backed against the closed door, fists clenched at her sides. She had not removed her cloak.

"You think you can command me to satisfy you whenever you wish," she said, her eyes flashing dangerously.

"I know I can. It's my right as your husband."

"It's not fair."

"No?" He could not stop himself from smiling at her aggrieved expression. Her mouth was so tempting, and he knew how easily the anger in her eyes could be converted into smoldering desire. "Are you claiming that when our encounters are finished, you remain unsatisfied?"

"Of course not." She transferred her gaze from his face to his bare chest. Her moist, pink tongue came out to wet her lips.

Warrick had learned the havoc that same tongue could work on his senses. A tremor coursed through his frame at the memory of the previous night. He caught the clasp of her cloak in both hands and tore the two pieces of metal apart.

"If I satisfy you when we come together, then what is your objection?" he murmured. He stepped closer until he was pressing Sophia against the cabin door.

"Always you decide when we should couple," she said.

"Couple?" He frowned, disliking the blunt word. "I'd prefer a kinder term. If I leave it to you, how long will I have to wait until you approach me?" With the cloak gone and her throat bare, he began to nibble at her fragrant skin, from earlobe to the neckline of her dress, savoring the piquant taste of her. Sophia tasted like no other woman, sweet and tangy and tart, all at the same time.

"That isn't the point." Her clenched fists pummeled his bare back a few times before her fingers spread over his skin, caressing and then kneading the hard muscles of his shoulders.

"What is the point?" he asked. She was too short for him to get as close to her as he wanted by pushing her harder against the door. He caught her firm, rounded buttocks in his hands and lifted her off her feet, to the exact height where he wanted her. "Isn't this the point?"

"You don't care."

"I cared enough to marry you."

"It was just a way for you to keep me safe one last time," she cried. She began struggling against him, fingernails raking his back, legs flailing so that her lower body rubbed on his in a way that further inflamed his senses. It apparently inflamed her, too, for she wound her legs around him to bring herself closer still.

"Do you call this safety?" he said with a growl. Lurching away from the door he tossed her onto the bed. She fell so that her skirts flipped up over her legs, revealing her shapely calves and rounded knees, and just a glimpse of soft white thighs.

Warrick's original intention had been to remove her clothes slowly, to kiss and coax her into a languid state of desire, but the sight of Sophia's thighs set his pulse racing. She glared at him and bared her teeth, and her fierceness sent a gust of fiery passion into his loins.

"You drove me mad with wanting you all the way from Baghdad to Byzantium," he said, tearing off his trousers. He caught her wrists, holding them above her head with one hand and thus preventing her from pulling her skirts below her knees. With his free hand he raised her gown higher, baring her to the waist. "And still you drive me to madness, arguing, complaining, protesting every decision I make."

"Because you don't include me," she said.

He pushed his thigh between her legs and put his hand down to touch her. She cried out and raised herself against his fingers, inviting further exploration. She was so hot and moist, so eager that he could wait no longer. He surged into her, driving deep as he could, wanting to possess all of her restless, passionate spirit.

Sophia screamed in excitement and convulsed around him. The rhythmic contractions of her body sent Warrick over the edge of sanity into a sudden, blinding state of ecstasy in which he knew only that, contrary to what he had planned, it was she who possessed him.

"You didn't even kiss me," she said later, when he lay with his head on her still-covered bosom.

"I'll kiss you now."

When he raised his head she stopped him with her fingers against his lips.

"You do satisfy me," she said. "Always you take care to be certain that I find pleasure, too. Here in bed with you I have no complaint, nor any reason to argue with you. It's when we leave our bed that you begin to disregard me."

She did not say she loved him. She refused to give him so much power over her until after he had said he loved her. If he ever did.

He kissed the fingers resting on his lips, and then he kissed her mouth.

"This hasty bedding was not what I planned when I brought you here," he said. "Seeing you on deck, I was minded to spend a leisurely hour or two exploring every part of you. But you have a maddening way of sparking both irritation and violent desire in me."

"There isn't much of me that you haven't explored already," she said. "And as for rousing your ire, all I did was comment on your unpleasant habit of ordering me about."

He rose from the bed so swiftly that she knew she had annoyed him. She watched him as he clothed his magnificent naked form, and she felt a stab of heat in the core of her being. Even though he did not know she loved him, still Warrick held such power over her that it frightened her and made her say unpleasant things to him, made her begin quarrels when she didn't want to fight with him. All she really wanted was for him to love her.

Meanwhile, he wanted only to possess her in bed, and to be the primary mover in their marriage. Fully clothed again, Warrick bent and kissed her inner thigh. He pulled her skirt down until she was decently covered, and then he left her.

Venice in winter was cold and damp; it even snowed a few times. They rented the top floor of a house belonging to Marco, for which he charged them an exorbitant fee. Warrick pried a second jewel out of the crystal ball's golden stand and sold it for enough money to see them through the winter.

Sophia did not remember much about those

months. On the third day after their arrival in Venice she fell ill with a high fever and a headache so severe it made her eyes water.

"It's swamp fever," Marco said when he heard the symptoms. "It's very common. I know of a good physician."

"Bring him to me," Warrick ordered. "I will allow him to examine Sophia, and I'll listen to what he suggests, but I will make my own decision about how she is to be treated."

The physician concurred with Marco's diagnosis of swamp fever. He proposed to bleed Sophia every day for four days, to administer emetics, and to feed her a medicine concocted of ingredients so disgusting that both Warrick and Genie vehemently refused the man's prescription. The physician left with his dignity gravely insulted and did not call again.

Warrick sent Genie and Robin out to buy the herbs he needed. He alone prepared Sophia's medicines, using all of the knowledge Hua Te had imparted to him during years of study. Together Warrick and Genie sponged Sophia with cold water when she was feverish. Together they piled quilts on her during the hours when she shivered with sudden chills. At night Warrick lay beside her, hoping to infuse her with some of his body heat and wishing he could give her his strength.

Genie made nourishing broths and coaxed Sophia to swallow them a spoonful at a time, and it was Genie who daily provided fresh linens and a clean nightgown for Sophia. Genie held Sophia's hand when she was gripped by terrible abdominal pains that even Warrick's strongest medicines could not ease. She did her best to comfort Warrick when the reason for the pains became obvious and Sophia lay insensible of the fragile new life her ailing body had rejected.

Genie tended to the practical needs of their little household and encouraged Robin to insist that Warrick seek his bed for a few hours each day lest he, too, fall ill.

Sophia was sick for more than a month and when she began to mend she lay listlessly in bed, too weak to think of getting up.

"Warrick saved your life," Genie told her. She sat on Sophia's bed and curled her legs up under her. Gone were the brilliant silks and the multiple necklaces. Genie was clad in a simple dark woolen dress and her hair was neatly braided and covered with a white linen scarf.

"Where is he?" Sophia asked in a voice that was little stronger than a whisper.

"I talked Robin into taking Warrick out for a stroll," Genie said. "That man has been in constant attendance on you."

"What of Robin?" Sophia asked, to turn the subject. She felt so debilitated that if she began to speak of Warrick, she was sure she would begin to cry.

"Robin is well."

"You sound hesitant. Does Robin still profess eternal affection for you?"

"Don't say that, please." Genie turned her head to look out the window, but not before Sophia noticed a suspicious moisture in her eyes.

"I didn't know a jinni could weep. You do love him."

"I cannot," Genie cried. She swung around to look directly at Sophia. "If I admit to love for a human man, and then in love I allow that man to embrace me, I will lose all of my magical powers and I will never again be permitted to return to the Land of the Jinn. I will become no more than a human."

"Would that be so dreadful a fate if you can love and be loved for the rest of your life?" Sophia asked. "If I held magical powers I would gladly give them up for Warrick, if only he loved me," she added sadly.

"A jinni's life is very long," Genie said. "Human life is so brief in comparison. Only love makes the shortness of human lives bearable."

"You do love him," Sophia whispered.

"I cannot say it!" Genie cried. "I dare not speak the words aloud, for speaking them will make it so, and I will lose my powers."

"Do you really prefer a long and lonely life, Genie?"

"How can you think that Warrick does not love you when he has spent weeks sitting by your bedside day and night, and has seldom left, not even to eat or see to his own needs?" Genie asked.

"Because he has not said aloud the words that will make it so," Sophia answered. She took Genie's hand in hers and was surprised to see how thin and pale her own fingers were, and to notice how weak was her grasp.

"I have been thinking," she said. "When we reach England, after Warrick is reunited with his family, I am going to continue on to Cornwall to search for my father's relatives. Perhaps they will take me in and let me live with them."

"That's the fever talking," Genie exclaimed. "How can you bear to think of leaving the man you love?"

"Ask rather how I can bear to continue to live with him when he does not love me."

"Sometimes humans can be remarkably stupid," Genie said.

"You are welcome to go to Cornwall with me. Perhaps someone there will know the spell that will free you from your human form."

Genie released Sophia's hand and went to stand at the window with her back to the room. She was silent for so long that Sophia almost drifted into sleep.

"I will think about it," Genie said at last.

They left Venice with the year's first shipment of goods sent across the alpine passes into northern Europe. A third stone from the bejeweled stand went to pay their way. Sophia was still not fully recovered and she was grateful that the heavily loaded packhorses could not travel very fast.

Warrick had not returned to her bed. Sophia longed for him to hold her, but with sleeping space at a premium at stops along their way through the mountains, she and Genie roomed together with two other women who were making the trip, while Warrick and Robin joined the men in one large sleeping room.

"It's just as well," Warrick said on an evening when she felt well enough to complain about the arrangement. He had just assisted her from her horse at the tiny guest house they were to use that night. "You need to rest as much as possible, and I don't want to get you with child again so soon. After we are out of the mountains and travel is not so difficult, then we can share a room."

"With child?" she cried, stunned by his words. "What do you mean, *again?*"

"There was a child." He spoke with obvious reluctance. "It was apparently conceived shortly after our marriage. You miscarried it during the worst day of your fever. It's part of the reason why you were ill for so long."

"You never told me!"

"I didn't want to upset you."

"You have upset me more by keeping something so important from me. This is too much, Warrick. Too much by far! How could you be so callous, so unthinking? Surely you know me well enough by now to understand that I would want to know about a child—our child." Her voice broke on the thought of Warrick's child growing inside of her and lost before she knew of its presence. "Once again you have made a decision without considering my feelings."

He reached for her and she thought he wanted to hold her, to calm her anger by his physical closeness. Sophia did not want to be calmed. She ran away from him, stumbling along the high mountain track until her legs gave out and she sank down onto a flat rock. Below her spread an alpine valley in verdant spring colors. Pale, delicate flowers blossomed at her feet. Sophia saw none of the springtime beauty. Her eyes were too full of tears and her heart was too empty.

"I am sorry," said Genie, coming up from behind and perching on the rock beside her.

"You should have told me when he did not," Sophia cried.

"You are entirely in the right. Warrick or I should have told you before we left Venice, so that you could grieve, as he did. On the day it happened he wept for the loss of your child as you are doing now."

"And then he hid the news from me."

"To protect you," Genie said.

"I am sick of being protected!" Sophia shouted. "Why can't he understand that?" She buried her face in her hands and wept so hard that she did not hear Genie leave or Warrick sit down in Genie's place.

"Sophia." Warrick touched her hair, then took his hand away. "Why can't you understand that I protect you because I love you?"

She lifted her wet face to regard him from eyes still swimming with tears. In her desolate, lonely heart a faint glimmer of hope began to shine. Even so, being Sophia, she was compelled to test and question what he was trying to tell her.

"You have never said you love me before. I am not sure I believe you."

"Nonetheless, it is true. My desire to keep you safe is proof of my love. At the moment my protection is all I have to offer you. I think I have known that I love you since the night in Baghdad when you conquered your fear of heights and trusted me enough to put your hand in mine and step from one rooftop to the next."

"You knew I was afraid?" She was so surprised that her tears stopped.

"Of course I knew," he said. "Do you think I am a blind dolt?"

"Sometimes that is exactly what I think. I do not want you to protect me by keeping from me facts that I ought to know. I want you to prove your love for me by sharing the whole of your life with me, the bad as well as the good.

"I am stronger than you think, Warrick. I can bear any sorrow, any hardship, so long as we face it together. But I cannot continue to live for another day as your wife if you continue to exclude me when there is a decision to be made, or if you keep important news from me. You should have told me about the child. If you had you would not have mourned alone."

"I did mourn, for your loss and mine." The smoky eyes that met Sophia's gaze were moist. "The reasons I gave you for our hasty marriage were true enough, but none of them was the most important reason. I wanted to marry you because I could not endure the thought of leaving you in Byzantium, of being separated from you. I married you because I love you with all of my heart and soul."

"You do?"

"I love you," he repeated, speaking with a firmness that left no doubt.

"I did not know," she said. "I never guessed. On our wedding day I thought you were just ordering me around as you always do and making yet another decision without consulting me. I must have been blind until this moment."

"How were you to recognize love when you've had so little experience of it?" He touched her damp cheek, then slid his hand around to the nape of her neck and drew her head down to his shoulder. "Let us begin again, Sophia. As you have trusted me with your life, trust me now with your heart. I swear I will not disappoint you."

"I cannot easily give up the habit of arguing," she

murmured, and felt his broad chest rumble with repressed laughter.

"Say it," he commanded. "Look into my eyes and say the words I have waited so long to hear."

He released her and she sat up very straight on the rock, with the alpine peaks around her soaring as high as her sudden, sweet hopes, as loftily as the new happiness filling her heart.

"I love you," she said.

"I love you, Sophia. I always will."

"And in the future you will tell me everything," she concluded.

"As much as possible." He was grinning at her.

Sensing reservation in his words, Sophia opened her mouth to protest. Warrick's finger on her lips prevented her from speaking. And when he removed his finger, his mouth on hers made her forget the argument she had intended to make.

Chapter Twenty-two

In midsummer of the Year of Our Lord 1139, four weary travelers presented themselves at the gate of Wroxley Castle in Lincolnshire, England. They were admitted at once. Scarcely had they ridden through the gatehouse and into the outer bailey before a tall, stocky man raced down the steps from the castle walls and grasped the reins of Robin's horse.

"Hello, Oliver." Robin greeted his stepfather as if he had seen the man only yesterday.

"Is it really you, returned safe and whole? Come down from that horse, my boy, and let me embrace you. Ah, how happy your mother will be to see you."

"Sophia," Warrick said, helping her to dismount, "this exuberant person is my father's seneschal, and a true and honest man."

"Warrick, welcome home." Oliver shook hands with his master's son. "I have sent a man to tell your father and Lady Mirielle that you are here. Let the squires take your horses and I'll conduct you to the keep." Oliver gestured to two boys who were lingering by the stable door to watch the joyful scene.

Sophia looked around at the space enclosed by the high stone walls and shivered a bit at the dampness and the shadows. Warrick had described the castle to her, so she knew what to expect as Oliver conducted them across the outer bailey, which was a man's province with its smithy and stables and the kennels, to a stout inner gatehouse and thence to the inner bailey, where the more domestic activities were conducted. There was a large herb garden to one side, fenced in with a wooden palisade, and a smaller lady's garden where roses and white lilies bloomed.

Then they were hurrying up a steep flight of steps, through a narrow door to an entry hall, and finally Oliver brought them through a wide double doorway to the great hall. The midday meal had just ended and the lord and lady of the castle were still in their chairs on the dais.

Sophia's heart began to beat hard. She knew how much Warrick loved his father and stepmother, and how unhappy he was at the prospect of revealing to them the loss of their old friend, Hua Te. Sophia no longer believed that Hua Te's disappearance had been caused by any fault of Warrick's, but her own experiences with an angry and resentful parent made her fearful of the reactions of Warrick's family.

Gavin, the baron of Wroxley, rose and stepped away from the table. He was as tall as Warrick, and a bit wider at the shoulders. His brown hair was lightly touched with silver at his temples, and the fine lines radiating from his eyes made him look as if he smiled often. He was smiling now, opening his arms to his son.

"Father," Warrick said, embracing him, "I have much to tell you, and not all of it will please you."

"Whatever it is can wait until later," Gavin said. "First eat if you are hungry, then bathe and rest. We can talk this evening. You and Robin will entertain the folk of Wroxley with tales of your adventures during the years since we have seen you. Robin, welcome home." Gavin embraced the young man almost as warmly as he had greeted Warrick.

"Father," Warrick said, drawing Sophia to his side, "this is my wife."

For just an instant Gavin appeared startled. Then he put his arms around Sophia and kissed her on either cheek.

The lady on the dais had been giving orders to a pair of servants. Having dismissed them, she stepped forward to join her husband and the guests. Lady Mirielle was slender and graceful. Her black hair was smooth as a bird's wing under a gold circlet with the round, red stone set at its center, and her exquisite face was untouched by time.

As Mirielle hugged Warrick tightly, a shorter lady in a brown dress rushed into the hall and flung herself at Robin.

"From the reddish brown color of her hair, I believe that will be his mother, the lady Donada," Genie whispered in Sophia's ear. "Robin has sung her praises to me all the way from Venice. She was a widow for most of his childhood, until she married Sir Oliver."

Having greeted her stepson, Lady Mirielle gave her full attention to Sophia. Her clear silver-gray eyes were direct and piercing, and Sophia felt as if Mirielle knew her soul before she smiled in approval.

"I am so glad that Warrick has found the woman who is right for him," Mirielle said.

"It took him long enough to admit it," Sophia responded, and laughed with Mirielle. Then Sophia sobered, for she wasn't certain what reaction the next introduction would elicit. "This lady with me is my cousin Genie, from Mosul."

A slight frown touched Mirielle's lovely face. "Look at me, girl," she said in a steely tone that allowed no disobedience. Genie's glittering emerald eyes met Mirielle's silvery ones.

Sophia held her breath. She knew that Mirielle held magical powers and she feared a clash between sorceress and jinni. She almost fainted from relief when Mirielle put out her hand to Genie.

"I see," Mirielle said, as if a silent question had been asked and answered between herself and Genie. "You are welcome here."

"Thank you, my lady," Genie murmured. To Sophia's amazement, Genie sank into a deep curtsy before Mirielle.

"I have ordered guest chambers prepared for you," Mirielle said, "and hot water for baths. All that we have here at Wroxley is yours. We won't delay the welcoming feast; we will hold it this very evening."

The guest room assigned to Warrick and Sophia boasted a large, curtained bed that took up most of the space. There were narrow slits for windows, and the thick stone walls held a damp chill, which Genie quickly banished using her magical art.

"Lady Mirielle is a fine chatelaine," Genie said,

prowling around the room, poking into every corner and commenting on what she found. "Not a speck of dust anywhere, fresh linens on the bed, dried lavender and rosemary strewn on the floor. There is nothing more for me to do here. I'll come back later and see to your clothes for tonight." She left just as the servants finished filling a large wooden tub with hot water.

Warrick bolted the door, ensuring their privacy. He paced toward Sophia with a light in his eyes that she could not decipher.

"Will you bathe first or shall I?" he asked. "Or shall we bathe together?"

"Warrick," she said, putting her hands on his shoulders to stop his forward progress. "Tell me the truth."

"What truth?"

"I can sense the unhappiness in you. Why is that, when you so clearly love your father and stepmother?"

"I have two half brothers and a half sister, all of whom are fostering elsewhere," he said. "I'll have to wait to meet them. And my sister Emma is married and living in Wales."

"The absence of your brothers and sisters isn't what's disturbing you. Now is the time to keep your promise, Warrick. Speak your thoughts to me."

"I think you know already what disturbs me," he said. "This evening I will have to tell my father and Mirielle that Hua Te has been missing for more than a year. I fear the parents I love will blame me, and there is nothing I can say in my own defense."

"I will speak in your defense."

"Sophia, my heart. My only love." He gathered her close.

"Do not give up hope of finding Hua Te," she said. "Remember, the vision you and I saw in the crystal ball suggested the answers you seek will be found here at Wroxley."

"How I love you," he murmured. The moment his lips touched hers the ever-present passion between them flared into demanding urgency.

"Let me bathe you first, while the water is still hot." She struggled out of his arms.

"I do not think I can wait," he complained. "It has been weeks since I made love to you."

"It has been five nights," she said, laughing at him, "and only because your English inns are so inadequate that the four of us were forced to room together, and because we were given separate cells in the abbey guest houses where we stayed after crossing the Narrow Sea from France. I want a hot bath, and to wash my hair, and I want a clean husband." She began to remove her clothes.

"Demanding wench," he teased, watching the gradual appearance of her alluringly rounded shape as cloak and gown and underdress fell to the floor.

"You knew what sort of woman I am when you married me," she told him. "Take off your clothes, Warrick."

"Now there's an invitation I cannot resist." He tore off his garments and was naked before Sophia had finished with her shoes and stockings. His aroused state was so obvious that she stared and ran her tongue over lips suddenly gone dry.

"Oh, dear," she said. "Perhaps I ought to call Genie back to chill the bathwater."

"Perhaps you ought to join me in the tub instead." He stepped into the water and sat down, leaning against the coarse sheet that had been laid over the wooden tub as a way to avoid splinters.

The tub was a good size, but it was not big enough to hide all of Warrick beneath the water it contained. Sophia could see his chest and his knees, and the other part of him that stood up straight and proud.

"Come, Sophia," he said, extending a hand. "Join me."

The sight of his rigid manhood sent a surge of warmth through her. They had been eager lovers since the day of their reconciliation on that alpine mountainside. Sophia was incapable of denying Warrick, or herself. She accepted his hand, but not without a token protest.

"There isn't much room in there."

"You may sit on my lap." He tugged on her hand.

"What a dangerous idea." She stepped into the tub and knelt over him, leaning back against his raised knees.

"You will have to come forward to kiss me," he said.

She did, and felt his hardness rubbing against her. She could not stop herself; she took him in her hands.

"Gently," Warrick cautioned. "You are dealing with a starving man."

"I am surrounded by a sea monster," she cried, for his wet arms were encircling her. He laughed and crushed her to him and kissed her until the breath was drawn out of her. He grasped her hips, lifted her, and sat her down so hard on top of himself that she screamed in delight, and then moaned her pleasure, which came upon her almost instantly, in a whirl of churning water and splashing arms and legs, with Warrick's mouth on hers again and again, and his heat far inside her, filling her, sealing their love forever.

"The water is cold," she said later, when her head was tucked into the place between his throat and his shoulder, when his hand was softly caressing her breast and she could feel him still inside her. Warrick never withdrew from her immediately. He always stayed with her for a gentler form of loving after their first wild desire was spent. It was a sweet intimacy that she cherished, but at the moment she was growing cold. "Shall I call Genie to warm our bath again?"

"I can tolerate cold water, if it means our privacy will not be disturbed."

He washed her, soaping all of her including her hair, and rinsed her with the pitcher of cool water left near the tub for that purpose. In return Sophia bathed him, all of him, and by the time she was finished and Warrick lifted her dripping out of the tub, he was ready to love her again.

He laid her on the bed and aroused her with lingering kisses from her toes to her hair. When Sophia was aching and sighing he took her with tenderness and care, making her shiver in delight.

"I love you," he whispered. "Wild and hot and furious, or sweet and slow like this, I love you, Sophia. I will never stop loving you."

"Warrick," she cried as the shimmering warmth began to disrupt her ability to think, "how can you do this to me in so many different ways?"

"I'm a magician," he said, and laughed softly, and gave her what she most desired.

*　　*　　*

Warrick's mood was far more somber during the evening meal in the great hall. He ate little of the feast that Mirielle had ordered, and drank only a few sips of Gavin's best wine.

"It takes no magical skill to know that you are sorely troubled," Gavin said to him. "I want to hear what has happened during your travels to make you so unhappy. Has it aught to do with Hua Te? You have not mentioned my old friend. Why is that? Is he dead?"

Sophia was sitting between father and son, and she could feel the tension emanating from Warrick as if it were a living thing. She was sure Gavin could feel it, too. Certainly Mirielle did. She was sitting on Gavin's other side and she leaned forward to look across her husband to Sophia, as if she expected to discover answers in her daughter-in-law's face.

"I came home to Wroxley knowing that I must confess everything," Warrick said to Gavin. "When I have finished, you may tell me that Wroxley is no longer my home. You may decide to take from me even the manor house you have been holding in trust for me during the years of my absence."

"I do not think you will do that," Sophia said to Gavin. Defiantly she looked into his eyes. "But if you do, my lord baron, I will not leave Warrick, though he be homeless and penniless. No power on earth can separate me from him, and if I, with my unhappy and loveless past, can learn to love your son so completely, then he cannot be a wicked man, nor a bad magician."

"I never imagined he was either," Gavin said to her. "I thank you for the love you bear my son. Now, Warrick, you can postpone the accounting no longer. Speak at once, and I will listen without interruption."

"Of the journey that Hua Te, Robin, and I made to Baghdad, I will tell you later, if you still wish to hear of it," Warrick said. "Before anything else, I must answer your questions about Hua Te, and that account begins when we had all been living in Baghdad for some years. We were there to study the Arabic sciences—astronomy, astrology, mathematics, and magic."

Warrick paused as if considering what it was best to say next. Into the silence came the sound of hurrying footsteps, and a man-at-arms burst into the great hall, followed by two figures in dark, dusty cloaks with the hoods drawn up to conceal the faces beneath.

"My lord Gavin," the man-at-arms cried, "here are two more guests who insist they must see you immediately. They claim to be friends of the four who arrived earlier today, so I brought them here at once."

"Warrick," Gavin said to his son, "you did not tell me there are more members to your party."

"That is because Warrick did not know we were so close behind him." One of the cloaked figures stepped forward, a hand going to his dark hood. "I presume we have reached him before he could confess to murdering me." The hood was pushed back to reveal a high-cheeked face, with dark, almond-shaped eyes and black hair cropped close to his head.

"Oh!" Recognizing the man standing before the high table, Sophia gasped, one hand going to her mouth. Warrick sat motionless beside her, apparently as dumbfounded as she was.

"Hua Te!" Gavin rose from the table to hasten off the dais and embrace his oldest and dearest friend. "I just asked Warrick where you are. What is this about murder?"

"Knowing Warrick's sensitive conscience, I believe he feared he had killed me while working a magical spell that was new to him," Hua Te answered. "As soon as I returned to Baghdad and learned from my former servant, Daoud, what had happened there and why Warrick and Robin had taken Sophia and left the city, I set out to follow them."

"Where did you go when you disappeared?" Warrick was not content to walk around the high table as his father had done. He leaped over it, landing beside Hua Te.

"What happened was not of your doing," Hua Te responded. "Do you recall the transparent blue egg that I picked up moments before I vanished?"

"Yes," Warrick said. "It disappeared when you did."

"It was a magical device that transported me to another time and place," Hua Te explained. "I will recount the details of my adventure to you later. For now let it be enough that I have returned in excellent health, bringing with me a treasure beyond all earthly value.

"This lady," Hua Te said, turning to the person with him, "is the other half of my soul, my predestined mate. This is Imilca."

Slender fingers tipped with pale pink nails worked at the clasp of the dark cloak. Then cloak and hood fell away, drifting onto the floor, and Hua Te's lady stood smiling at them.

Her red-gold hair grew into a thousand tiny curls

that clustered about her face and fell loosely down her back. Her eyes were a soft shade of gray, her features delicately carved. The gown she wore was made of pale blue wool, simple in style, and her jewelry, a gold necklace with matching earrings and a single ring, was wrought in an exotic design.

"What beautiful jewelry," said Genie, moving to stand behind the chair where Sophia still sat. "And what a great magician is Hua Te. He moves surrounded by the purest white magic. I can see that his lady is worthy of him.

"Now Warrick is relieved of his guilt," Genie continued, crouching beside Sophia. "He is free at last to love and be happy with no shadow to mar his joy."

"Genie, are you thinking that Hua Te will know the spell to return you to the Land of the Jinn?" Sophia asked. "Do you believe your duty to me is discharged and now you are free to go home?"

"Home," Genie repeated with a sigh. "It is possible that Hua Te does know the spell."

"I don't want you to go," Sophia whispered. "I know it's selfish of me to want to keep you with me when you are eager to be gone but, Genie, you are the best and truest friend I have ever had, and the finest teacher. You have been to me what Hua Te was to Warrick—a wise and kind influence on an angry and ill-informed young person."

"Thank you, mistress," said Genie with unusual gravity.

"I can never repay you for all you have done for me," Sophia said. "I can only send you away with my thanks, and tell you that I love you as if you really were my dear cousin from Mosul."

"I'm not going yet," Genie said. "Warrick is beck-

oning. He wants you to join him, and I expect Hua
Te wants to introduce you to his lady. And I do believe Lady Mirielle could use some help from me
with matters domestic."

A short time later Hua Te and Imilca were seated
at the high table and the feast began anew, far more
joyfully this time. During the meal Warrick, Robin,
and Hua Te took turns recounting their adventures
along the way from Wroxley Castle to Baghdad.
Then Warrick and Robin took over the story to tell
of the return journey. The night was far gone before
the inhabitants of Wroxley sought their beds.

In the morning Sophia was violently ill. Genie
came to her while Warrick was still holding his
wife's head over a basin, and Mirielle was not far
behind.

"Find your father and stay with him until I call
you," Mirielle ordered Warrick.

"She was so ill when we were in Venice that I
despaired for her life," Warrick said. "It's Hua Te
she needs."

"Don't disturb him; he's still sleeping," Mirielle
said, and shut the door in Warrick's worried face.

"Let me look at you," Mirielle said to Sophia. She
laid her cool hand on Sophia's forehead, inspected
Sophia's tongue, and made her lie down so she
could poke at her abdomen.

"Just as I thought," Mirielle said. "You may sit up
now."

"I have been sick only twice in all my life," Sophia
said. "In Venice, when I nearly died, and now today.
Is it a recurrence of the fever I suffered in Venice?"

"You aren't sick." Mirielle was smiling and so was
Genie. "I can give you some powdered ginger in hot
water to settle your stomach, or an herbal prepa-

ration, but even without any medicine you will soon feel better. I will give you something to take tomorrow morning before the sickness returns."

"What's wrong with me?" Sophia demanded.

"Nothing is wrong," Mirielle answered. "You are with child."

"It cannot be," Sophia cried. "I miscarried in Venice."

"I can only assume that you and Warrick have made love since then," Mirielle replied. "Most likely six or seven weeks ago."

"Many times," Sophia admitted.

"Don't be embarrassed." Mirielle patted Sophia's shoulder. "It's a happy thing. Warrick will be delighted."

Mirielle offered advice on what Sophia ought to eat and warned her to get plenty of rest, then left to tend to her duties. Genie regarded Sophia soberly.

"I do hope this means you will give up your foolish plan of traveling to Cornwall to seek your father's family," Genie said.

"I may decide to make inquiries later." Sophia placed one hand over her still-flat abdomen. "For the present, my duty is to keep Warrick's child safe, and I do confess that I have no inclination to leave my husband now that he has said he loves me."

"I am glad to hear it." Genie paused, then said, "You cannot expect complete honesty from Warrick if you do not give honesty in return. Don't wait too long before you tell him about the child."

"I won't," Sophia promised. "Tonight, when we are alone, I'll tell him."

* * *

At Gavin's request, his six guests met with him and Mirielle in the lord's chamber after the midday meal. There, in private, Hua Te described his adventures from the moment when he disappeared in Baghdad until his return.

"I trust all of you not to reveal what I have said," Hua Te warned. "I doubt if any but you few will believe me, but it's best not to alarm anyone needlessly. There is no danger now, nor for centuries to come."

"We will keep your secret," Gavin promised, and all of the others in his chamber agreed never again to speak of the subject.

"Warrick," Gavin said, turning to another matter, "you and Sophia are welcome to live at Wroxley for as long as you like. However the time has come to hand over to you the land I have been holding in trust while you were away."

"I'll take it gladly," Warrick said, "and live there with Sophia, and ask Robin to join me there as my seneschal." He lifted the worn sack he had brought to his father's room.

"Hua Te, I was commanded by John of Cornwall to give this to you when next I saw you. I suspect that he knew where I would find you." Warrick unwrapped first the jeweled stand and then the crystal ball and set them together on a small table. "A few gems are missing from the stand. We converted them to coins to pay our way home to Wroxley."

"I cannot object to the use you made of them," said Hua Te. "However I cannot keep these objects. As I understand the story, all of John's other possessions, which were meant to be Sophia's inheritance, were confiscated by the sultan's men somewhere between Baghdad and Byzantium. The ball and stand ought by right to go to Sophia. They are all she has left to remind her of her father."

"I don't want them," Sophia said quickly. "I have a few pieces of my mother's jewelry to remind me of the happiest years of my childhood, while she was still alive. I need nothing more. Warrick, I give the ball and its stand to you, as my dowry. Do whatever you want with them."

"Do you mean to tell me I carried those cursed objects all the way to England from Baghdad, and now no one wants them?" Warrick exclaimed.

"They are not cursed if they helped you to come home again," Mirielle said.

"They are yours," Warrick told her. "In the name of heaven, Mirielle, take them. I know you will put them to good use."

"Yes," Sophia agreed. "Keep them, Mirielle."

"Thank you." Mirielle took the crystal ball in her left hand, holding it up to the light. "It really is a lovely thing, and absolutely perfect. I have a much smaller ball that has an imperfection. I shall treasure this one because two dear relatives gave it to me."

"I think that concludes our business," Gavin said.

"Not quite." Robin faced Genie. "We have in this chamber three practitioners of magic, Hua Te, Warrick, and Lady Mirielle. Genie, if you wish to return to your home, one of these three, or all of them together, will know of a way to release you from your human form.

"I love you, Genie," Robin said, taking her hand. "I will never love another woman. In this life only you hold my heart. But if you cannot love me, if you feel you cannot stay in this time and place, then

I will help you to leave, for I want your happiness more than my own."

"By the spell that called me into human existence, Sophia is my mistress," Genie said. "She must release me before I can make the decision to leave."

Sophia caught her breath. She wanted to beg Genie to stay. For Genie's sake she could not. She had to be as generous with her love for Genie as Robin was with his.

"I don't know the correct words," she said.

"Say, 'I release you,' " Genie instructed.

"Dear friend of my heart, I release you," Sophia told her. "Do what will make you happy."

"Hua Te," Genie said, looking into his eyes, "do you know how to return me to the Land of the Jinn?"

"I do," Hua Te said. "Only ask and I will speak the words. But say your farewells first, for in the moment when I give voice to the spell, you will be gone from here."

Genie looked from Hua Te to Sophia, to Warrick, and on to Mirielle and Gavin and Imilca. Her gaze settled on Robin.

"How very strange humans are," Genie said. "You cling to each other in the name of love, yet out of love you will let a loved one freely depart."

"That's what love is," Robin said, "a longing to hold the loved one close, coupled with a willingness to let her go for her own sake."

Genie stared at him, her eyes wide. "The jinn know nothing of love," she said. Another long moment passed before she spoke again. "Robin, several times you have asked me to marry you."

"I meant it every time," Robin said. "I love you."

"Will you kiss me?" Genie asked.

Robin opened his arms and Genie went into them. She was trembling, yet she did not hesitate. She put her arms around Robin's neck and lifted her face, and when he kissed her, she kissed him back. Robin's arms tightened about her.

"Oh!" Mirielle staggered, a hand to her forehead. "Oh, it hurts so much!" She sank into Gavin's big chair. Gavin knelt before her, concern filling his handsome face.

"My head!" Warrick raised both hands to his temples, pressing hard as if he had just worked a magical spell and was suffering for it. Sophia put her arms around his waist and let him lean on her.

Hua Te groaned and his head fell forward. He slumped until Imilca caught him and pulled him upright again.

And in Robin's arms Genie shrieked with sudden pain, just before she went limp.

"She's fainted!" Robin cried. He scooped Genie off her feet to lay her on Gavin's bed. "Genie, speak to me!" He began to rub her hands.

"Robin?" Genie opened her eyes.

"I'm here. What happened just now?"

"I love you," Genie said. "At last I can say I love you. How my heart aches. How strange it is to be a human. And how wonderful."

"Genie, what are you saying?" Robin exclaimed.

Genie was smiling at him through tears and stroking his face with trembling fingers, so it was Hua Te who answered Robin's question.

"Genie is saying that she is no longer a jinni. She has chosen to give up her magical abilities for your sake. She will never again see the Land of the Jinn."

"Genie?" Robin lifted her into his arms.

"No," she said. "I am not Genie anymore. I must take a new name. Sophia, help me. I am weak and afraid." She held out one shaking hand.

Seeing that Warrick had recovered, Sophia left him to go to her friend's side. She clasped the hand extended to her and sat on the bed across from Robin.

"Dear cousin from Mosul," Sophia said, laughing and crying at the same time, "dear Jeanne."

"Jeanne it is. Genie no more." Jeanne sniffed. "How easily humans cry. I must learn to control these unruly emotions."

"I hope you never regret the sacrifice you have made for me," Robin said to her.

"I expect I will regret it from time to time," Jeanne responded with her old, saucy grin. "But so long as you love me, I'll find that adequate recompense. And if you agree to become Warrick's seneschal, we will all four of us still be together. Now, Robin, I will need wedding clothes. I understand your mother is an expert seamstress. Do you think she'll be willing to teach me to sew?"

"I am sure of it," Robin said. "She will be in the great hall supervising the servants who are preparing the evening meal. We can ask her after we tell her the wonderful news that we are going to be married."

"Which reminds me that I am hungry," said Gavin. He looked at his guests with a knowing smile. "If you have all finished working magic for this day, may we go and eat?" He held out his arm to Mirielle. She, quite recovered from her brief headache, placed her hand on his wrist and allowed him to lead her out of the room.

Robin picked Jeanne off the bed and stood her

Flora Speer

on her feet. With an arm around her waist, he took her to the door. Hua Te and Imilca followed them.

"Jeanne made the right decision, you know," Sophia said to Warrick. "The greatest magic of all is love."

"I do know," Warrick said, pausing to kiss her as they followed their friends toward the great hall. "I've known it since the first time my lips touched yours."

AUTHOR'S NOTE

For readers who are curious about Hua Te's adventures during his absence, they are recounted in full detail in my time-travel romance *Love Once and Forever,* which will be published by Love Spell. In this story of Laura Morrison, a twentieth-century woman who is transported into a far-distant past, Hua Te proves to be a true friend to both hero and heroine and his subtle, sensitive wooing of Imilca reveals a long-repressed romantic side to his character.

Heart's Magic

Flora Speer

Bestselling author of *ROSE RED*

In the year 1122, Mirielle senses change is coming to Wroxley Castle. Then, from out of the fog, two strangers ride into Lincolnshire. Mirielle believes the first man to be honest. But the second, Giles, is hiding something–even as he stirs her heart and awakens her deepest desires. And as Mirielle seeks the truth about her mysterious guest, she uncovers the castle's secrets and learns she must stop a treachery which threatens all she holds dear. Only then can she be in the arms of her only love, the man who has awakened her own heart's magic.

___52204-7 $5.99 US/$6.99 CAN